Matt H... ...security and the police force in Cumbria. He is a 4th ... blackbelt and coach in Ju-Jitsu. He lives in Cumbria ... his wife and son.

...se for Matt Hilton and NO GOING BACK:

...tt Hilton delivers a thrill a minute. Awesome!'

Chris Ryan

...pace rattles along with the intensity of a disgruntled ...snake ... A fantastic tale of "derring do" ... The ... is Lycra tight and there is more atmosphere than ...ous novels. The Arizona desert is so well drawn it ...st becomes a character itself.'

www.crimesquad.com

...rp and hard hitting ... Matt doesn't allow himself ...et complacent, but continually delves deeper into ... psyche of Joe ... Fast-paced, action-filled and ...pletely addictive, Matt shows his continuing ...urity as a writer with an exhilarating ride that still ...intains humour and wit.'

www.shotsmagazine.co.uk

...cious, witty and noir, Hilton is a sparkling new talent.'

Peter James

Also by Matt Hilton

MATT HILTON

No Going Back

HODDER

First published in Great Britain in 2012 by Hodder & Stoughton
An Hachette UK company

First published in paperback in 2012

1

A CIP catalogue record for this title is available from the British Library

ISBN 978 1 444 71271 1 (B format)
ISBN 978 1 444 71270 4 (A format)

Typeset in Plantin Light by Hewer Text UK Ltd, Edinburgh
Printed and bound by Clays Ltd, St Ives plc

Hodder & Stoughton policy is to use papers that are natural, renewable
and recyclable products and made from wood grown in sustainable
forests. The logging and manufacturing processes are expected to
conform to the environmental regulations of the country of origin.

Hodder & Stoughton Ltd
338 Euston Road
London NW1 3BH

www.hodder.co.uk

This one is for my son,
Jordon

... there was about him a suggestion
of lurking ferocity, as though the
wild still lingered in him and the
wolf in him merely slept.

Jack London

Pain lays not its touch upon a corpse.

Aeschylus

I

Jay couldn't believe it.

She thought she'd seen the last of them. But they were back and by the way they pushed their pick-up over the humps in the road they intended catching her. Should have shut my mouth, forgotten about the gas and got the hell outta there, she told herself. She shouldn't have got involved. But she'd always had a nose for trouble, and a mouth big enough to sink her right in the middle of it. At first the patched old Dodge had been a pale blur dancing in the heat haze, but now she could make out the blocky shape and could see it was missing a mirror on the right wing. It was them all right.

'Why didn't I just keep my fat mouth shut?'

'That's what I've often wondered.'

Jay glanced over at Nicole. Sweet little Nicole with the size-zero frame and timidity to match was perspiring and it had nothing to do with the desert heat. Normally she had a neat Louise Brooks bob, but right now the dark strands were being whipped around by the wind blasting through the open window. Under any other circumstances it would have been a good look.

'Why are they following us?'

'They probably didn't have enough fun back there at the gas station,' Jay said. 'Don't worry, Nic. I'll get us out of this.'

'You're sure about that?'

'Yeah. We just have to show them we aren't afraid of them.'

'That's just the thing, Jay. I am.'

'I won't let anything happen. I promise.'

Nicole was a year older than Jay, but you wouldn't think it. The energy of their pairing wrongly matched them as siblings, and strangers always assumed that Jay was the elder sister. It was the way she looked out for Nicole, as if her petite friend would snap under any strain. It came from being what her grandma called an old soul in a young body. More likely, Jay thought, it came from her given name. Joan was a name for someone of her grandma's vintage, not a twenty-two year old. When meeting people for the first time, Jay Walker only ever introduced herself by her initial and surname, which earned her a raised eyebrow or two. 'I like to live dangerously,' she'd say with a wink. Now, watching that pick-up truck growing in her mirrors, she thought her words had caught up with her. Her next thought: what name would be written on her gravestone?

Jay had only wanted a comfort break. The litre of spring water she'd downed in the last hour had made a stop a matter of urgency, and though they had enough gas for another hundred miles or so, it had made sense to fill the tank before entering the desert. Kill two birds with one stone: that was the idea.

When she angled her father's SUV up the dirt ramp and between the pumps at Peachy's gas station, there was already another vehicle filling up and she had to wait. Squeezing her thighs together, dancing in the seat, she knew she couldn't last.

'She's all yours, Nic. I gotta go.' She shut off the engine and slipped out on to wind-marbled concrete. She tossed the keys to her friend. 'Fill her up, OK? I'll pay on the way out.'

As she approached the teller's shack, she glanced over at the old Dodge and the man feeding gas into its greedy tank. The man was tall, gaunt, with sun-dried skin and the cowboy duds to match. He'd taken off a battered straw hat and placed it on the cab while he drew on a hand-rolled cigarette. Even from there, Jay saw that the whites of his eyes looked jaundiced, almost as yellow as his nicotine-stained fingertips. He saw her, tipped an imaginary hat with his thumb. Jay smiled, but quickly averted her gaze. His gap-toothed grin wasn't friendly.

She looked for a separate bathroom, but the teller's booth looked like the only structure on the site. The restroom had to be inside. At the front, two glass doors smudged with thousands of fingerprints were wedged open, racks of spoiling fruit and yellowing newspapers standing sentry. Inside was a dim little space, with a cooler offering drinks and snacks on one side and racks with cans of oil, maps and postcards, and turquoise trinkets on the other. The teller was an old Native

American man in trousers and braces over a checked shirt. Standing on the customer side of the counter was a man with wide shoulders and long straw-coloured hair. The man was in the middle of showing the teller something when Jay bustled inside. She caught the teller's eyes, knew immediately that what the stranger was showing him wasn't nice.

That was when she'd first opened her big mouth.

'Hi,' was all she said but it was enough to ruin everything.

The teller flicked a cautionary glance at her.

The man with straw for hair turned and regarded her with a look to spoil milk. His mouth drooped open at one corner, and Jay saw he was chewing on a Chupa Chups lollipop. As he appraised her, taking in her athletic figure, her short cropped auburn hair, and lingering on the swell of her breasts, his expression changed. Now it felt like it was Jay who was spoiling from the bilious suggestion in his gaze.

'Well, hey!'

Jay was no fool. She knew that she'd walked into something best avoided, but she had reached a point of desperation. She gave the man a tight-lipped smile, but aimed her words at the teller. 'Excuse me, sir? May I use your bathroom?'

The old man waited a fraction too long to respond. His reply sounded forced. 'Out of order, ma'am, I'm sorry.'

Jay glanced at the door next to the counter. There was no sign on it, nothing to hint that the toilet was broken. But she got the man's words, his subtle warning that she should leave now. She glanced outside to see that the pick-up truck had moved forward and Nic was now taking a turn at the pump. The older cowboy was leaning on the wing of his truck, toying with the space where a mirror had been broken off, but his gaze was fixed on her friend. His gaze was as lascivious as that of the younger man.

Get out, get out now, her mind screamed. Yet she was caught in a dilemma. How could she leave without first paying for the gas? She knew that the teller wouldn't demand remuneration, but the young man would immediately say – or worse do – something about it.

'How much do I owe you?' She pulled cash from her jeans pocket.

The teller squinted at a display. 'Twenty dollars should do it, ma'am.'

Jay leaned past the young man, extending two tens. The teller reached out for them, his fingers trembling. Then a palm slammed the notes down on the counter, and the young man snapped, 'The hell is this? Don't I get the same discount?'

At his intervention both Jay and the teller had reared back, and the young man stepped into the gap between them. He grabbed Jay, snaring her wrist in his rough palm.

'Get your hands off me!'

The young man leaned close, saliva bubbling around the stick of the lollipop. She could smell his sickly-sweet breath as he exhaled. 'Now this just ain't right. There's one price for me, another for a pretty city girl?'

The teller quickly dipped his hand into a drawer, came out with a clutch of dollars. 'Here, take them. Take them all back.'

'So now my money's not good enough? I'm goddamn offended by that!'

Jay tried to twist out of the man's grasp, but his fingers were like steel coils. 'Get off me or I'll call the police.'

'The po-lice, huh? Well that would be a damn fine idea . . . seeing as I've found myself a couple thieves working in cahoots here.'

'Thieves? Are you mad?' Jay snatched her hand loose this time, but the young man wasn't finished. He grabbed her by the front of her jacket and pulled her tight, thrusting her against the counter with his hips. Her kidneys were forced against the wood, but she'd lost the urge to urinate.

The teller pulled more dollars out from under the counter. 'Look, son, just take it all, OK? We don't want any trouble. Just take the cash and be on your way.'

The young man crunched, then spat out the stick of his lollipop. He'd sucked it down to the paper. 'Are you sayin' I'm a goddamn thief now? Shee-it! I was offended before, but now I'm pissed.'

'Please,' Jay said. 'Before this gets out of hand, let me go.'

'Things got outta hand a long time ago, missy,' the man said against her neck. Jay squirmed, but he jammed her with his hips again as he dug into his shirt pocket. 'You see this girl here?'

The man waved a sheet of paper under Jay's nose. It

was a Xeroxed photograph with a name under it. It was far too close for her to focus on. The man reversed it and waved it in front of the old man. 'I'm looking for her. Either one of you seen her?'

'I already told you, son. No I ain't seen her.'

'So you said, but I know now you're a goddamn liar! Like you lied about the bathroom being broke, like you lied about the price of the gas! Makes me wonder if you've got Helena tucked up back there in that goddamn booth of yours. I've a mind to—'

'You've a mind to apologise to these good people is what you've got.'

The pressure went off Jay and she spun away from the young man, placing her back to the cooler. The perspiration on her skin felt like ice, but she didn't move, just stared wide-eyed at the older cowboy as he stood in the doorway. He'd placed the straw hat back on his head, and it was sitting at the raffish angle adopted by the good guy in Western movies. Jay doubted there was anything good about the cowboy, though. His reason for intervening wasn't well intentioned, but because there were too many witnesses. On the forecourt another vehicle had arrived: a station wagon with a young couple and three children inside. Nicole was also standing by the SUV, her hands at her throat as she watched the drama.

The blond man said, 'Why, heck! If you ain't right.' He quickly moved away from Jay, raising his hands. He still held the Xerox and Jay saw a smudged image of a young woman on it. Beneath her name was printed the fateful word: MISSING.

The cowboy came inside. 'My buddy is hurting, folks. His woman has gone and run off someplace. You can imagine how upset he is, I'm sure? Now let's all just calm down, shall we, and get about our own business?'

Jay opened her mouth to object, but the teller jerked his head at her, another warning to get out. For all she joked about enjoying walking on the wild side, Jay had experienced enough of it for one day. She hurried for the door. Before she could escape, the cowboy lifted his arm and blocked her way. 'It's finished with, right? There'll be no making complaints to the po-lice?'

That was when her big mouth got the better of her and said, 'I'm not surprised that his woman ran away. Your *buddy* is an animal.'

The cowboy showed her his gap-toothed grin, revealing stumps of rotting teeth. 'Yup. You got that right. He probably should be in a cage, but I'm not gonna let that happen.' He leaned in close. 'You get me, miss?'

'I get you,' Jay said, as she ducked under his arm and scurried back to the SUV.

'What was all that about?' Nic asked, her face drained of colour.

'Just get in, Nic. We have to get out of here.'

Jay glanced over at the pick-up truck. The sunlight was making a prism of the windscreen, causing rainbows to bounce back at her. She thought she saw another figure seated in the cab, but couldn't be sure. Forget about it, she told herself. Two maniacs are enough for anyone to contend with.

They scrambled inside the SUV, and Nic tossed over

the keys. Jay jammed them into the ignition and roared out on to the highway. As dust rose in a cloud behind them, she could have sworn a figure alighted from the pick-up and moved towards the family's station wagon. Then she could no longer see anything for the trail dirt.

'What happened?'

Glancing across at Nicole, Jay guessed her face was as pale as her friend's. 'Just a couple of crazy men,' she said. 'If I ever see them again, it will be way too soon.'

Her words, said in hope, would come back to haunt Jay tenfold.

2

I'm a firm believer in employing economy of motion, and that extends to the day job as much as anything else in life. I'd set off from my home near to Mexico Beach on the Gulf Coast to meet Jameson Walker, but I had a couple of hours to kill. My route took me past Tyndall Air Force Base, and over water on the Parkway, before reaching Panama City, where Walker's flight was scheduled to land. Off and on for the past fortnight I'd been engaged on a job in the neighbouring town of Callaway, and it was only a minor diversion to go there and tie up the loose ends.

I had my military pension, as well as funds from the sale of my house in the UK and other savings and investments I'd set in place over the past eighteen years, but I still needed a wage. I'd signed on as a partner in my friend Rink's private investigations business, albeit I didn't see myself as much of a detective. The work I tended to take on was where a person's guilt wasn't necessarily the issue, but how they could be made to pay for their transgression was. Sometimes, by the nature of their crimes, the law couldn't touch them. That was where I came in.

Maria Purefoy worked hard at a major chain store. It was thankless work, with long hours and a minimum wage. It was difficult for her to raise her four boys after their daddy ran off and left them to fend for themselves. Her eldest son, Brian, sixteen, had fallen in with a group of youths who believed that the only life was one spent on a skateboard. They hadn't anticipated that the older boys would force them into using their wheels to *run errands* for them. Brian Purefoy had been arrested for dealing cocaine, then got himself a criminal record, a fine neither he nor his mother could afford, and threats demanding allegiance from the older gang. Maria was worried that her son was being forced down a slippery slope, and wanted things stopped.

I wouldn't normally involve myself in a job like that – sadly they were ten a penny these days – but Maria had reported that her boy was terrified of saying no. A week before, one of his friends had been the victim of a hit and run accident where he'd ended up with two broken legs and a perforated spleen. The friend had recently told the gang where to shove their drugs. It wasn't in me to stand idle while kids were being hurt.

Like Maria, the local cops had a thankless task on their plate. With witnesses too afraid to come forward they had no way of bringing the offenders to justice; their hands were tied. I was sure they knew why I was around and were steering a wide berth. Still, they could only allow me so much leeway before the press got hold of the story and started screaming about a crazy vigilante stalking their town. I couldn't go in all guns blazing, but, as long as nobody died, the cops kept out of my way.

I'd already pulled two of the older skater guys; showed them the error of their ways. Still, their leader, a twenty-three-year-old punk named Joey Dorsey, had the balls to front things out. Dorsey could have made it big on the boarding scene, not that he was in Tony Hawk's league, but he'd allowed his wilder urges to get a hold of his good sense, and had gone off-track. Now he fancied himself as the local king of anarchy and lived up to the image. The trouble with following his ethos is that there's always someone else tougher, more brutal, and prepared to bend the rules that much further. I decided that, seeing as I was passing, I might as well go and teach Joey that valuable lesson.

When I arrived at his house, I had to smile. Like many who embraced the notion of anarchy, Dorsey came from a privileged background. Basically he was a spoiled brat who'd had everything he'd desired, but was so greedy he wanted more. His house, or more correctly that of his parents, was on a huge plot of land on Callaway Point overlooking the still waters of a lagoon. It was a sprawling mansion with five bedrooms, three bathrooms, and a separate three-door garage to accommodate the family Jags and Mercs. A private road ran up to a turning circle outside the house, and I was glad to find a number of vehicles sitting out in the Floridian heat. If I was going to show Dorsey up for what he was, it was better that the message rang loud and clear.

Parking my Audi alongside a black SUV with tinted

windows, I exited on to hard-packed sand. I stretched, releasing the kinks from my muscles, then made for a paved walkway that led between the house and garage. There was a babble of raucous laughter, punctuated by enough four-letter words to keep an ignoramus happy, the clink of bottles, and the splashing of bodies plunging into deep water. Smoke wafted on the breeze: a potpourri of barbecue sauce and marijuana.

It must have been a business meeting, because thankfully there was no sign of Dorsey's parents, and there were none of the young girls who occasionally hung with the gang, just the eight youths who were terrorising their younger skating buddies into dealing dope for them. The two guys I'd already had a word with were there: I recognised them by the bruises around their eyes. Another three were splashing in a large swimming pool, one more lounging on an inflatable bed at the side of it, toking on a joint. A tall, skinny guy with blond dreadlocks was turning burgers on a barbecue. Dorsey lorded it over the scene like the king of the castle, his throne a striped deckchair.

Everyone fell silent as I appeared on the paved area next to the pool.

'The SUV back there,' I said by way of introduction. 'Whose is it?'

'Who the fuck are you, dude?' Dorsey scrambled up from the deckchair, and stood breathing hard, his hands fisted by his sides. He was wearing board shorts and a TAP OUT T-shirt that moulded to his muscles.

Ignoring him, I repeated, 'Whose is it?'

On my way in I'd noted the dent in the front fender of the SUV; it approximated to the height of a kid squatting on a skateboard.

'Who wants to know?' Dorsey said.

'I'm not making myself clear enough?'

One of the guys with a bruised face moved close to Dorsey, whispering and jabbing his hand my way.

'You're the asshole who thinks he's gonna shut me down?' Dorsey sneered as he looked me up and down. He didn't look too impressed, but that was good because it meant he'd underestimate me.

'I'm Joe Hunter,' I said, 'and, yeah, I'm shutting you down.'

'You're fucking kidding me! You walk in here like King Shit and think that's going to frighten *me*? Big mistake, asshole.'

There were a couple of empty beer bottles lying on the floor by my feet. I flicked one of them into the pool with the toe of my boot. The bottle made a splash, and all eyes turned to it. Distraction move only: before they could return their gaze to me, I slipped my hand under the tail of my jacket and pulled out my SIG Sauer P226. A murmur of fear spread through the group, but Dorsey wasn't having it. He stepped forward aggressively, raising a finger to point at me. 'You ain't gonna do a goddamn thing with that!' Turning to his buddies, he said, 'He hasn't got the balls to shoot anyone. He's just trying to scare us.'

'You're right about one thing,' I said, as I circled the pool. One of the youths scrambled out of my way, and I stood over the one lying on the inflatable bed. 'I am here to scare you. But you're wrong if you don't think I'll shoot.'

The youth on the bed let out a high-pitched shriek, flicked away his joint and tried to scramble off, but he wasn't as fast as a bullet.

The SIG cracked.

The youth rolled over and splashed into the water, and all around me the others leaped for cover.

Over the sounds of their bleating cries came the hiss of the deflating bed.

The youth from the bed erupted out of the pool gasping, blinking chlorinated water from his eyes. Frantically he checked for blood frothing around him.

'Relax,' I told him. 'I didn't shoot you.'

Trying to live up to the size of his ego, Dorsey laughed. It was forced and everyone there knew it. 'I fucking told you he wouldn't.'

'Want to try me again?' I stalked forward; in his haste to get away the dreadlocked guy bumped the barbecue, knocking hot coals on the floor. He danced as the cinders invaded his sandals, then launched himself into the water with a howl.

Now the only ones on dry ground were Dorsey and his two lieutenants – the ones I'd already slapped around. 'One of you owns the SUV. Which is it?'

The three of them shared glances, and I could tell from the youth on my left that the vehicle was his. Without taking my eyes off Dorsey, I lifted my SIG and aimed it at the guilty youth. 'So it's his? But who was driving?'

'Not me, man!' Suddenly Dorsey had lost all pretence at being a tough guy. Now he was just an overgrown, spoiled baby with tears on his face.

I looked at the youth I held under my gun. 'You knocked that boy off his skateboard.'

The youth's face folded in on itself. 'I didn't mean to run him down, man! We were just trying to frighten him . . . we didn't mean to put him in hospital!'

'The thing is, you did. And someone should pay for that.'

'Not me, man! It was Dorsey who told me to do it!'

'I know.' I turned the gun on their leader.

Dorsey hands were still up, but they were no longer threatening. 'Jesus, dude! C'mon . . .'

'Only one way I can see to put this right.'

Urine splattered down Dorsey's legs. 'Don't do this, please. *Don't shoot me!*'

'OK,' I said, and lowered the gun. 'But there's still a price to pay. Are you familiar with the concept of an eye for an eye?'

Before he could register my meaning I swivelled and snapped a kick into his knee. The joint went sideways and I heard the click of rupturing tendons. Dorsey hit the deck squealing.

'Get up tough guy,' I said.

'*You broke my leg!*'

'At least I didn't shoot you. Don't worry arsehole, you'll heal, but riding your board will never be the same again.' I indicated his friends with the barrel of my gun. 'Help him up.'

The two punks dragged their moaning leader off the floor, but as soon as he could support himself on his good leg they quickly retreated. Dorsey stood trembling, his good leg partly buckling, the piss pooling around his feet. 'You still owe that kid another leg, and a spleen.'

'Jesus,' Dorsey wailed. 'You're not gonna . . .'

'No, so you can stop crying like a baby. But you are going to pay. You'll go to the police and tell them what happened.'

'I can't do that!'

'OK. The alternative is I leave you the same way as that boy in hospital.' I lined my boot up so that it was trained on his one good knee. He moaned as another trickle of urine darkened his shorts.

After that he was receptive to my deal, and agreed to hand himself and his buddies in to the police.

'I'll be listening out,' I warned. 'You don't do as we've agreed, I'm going to come back and next time I won't be shooting inflatable beds.'

I returned to my car while Dorsey searched for a towel. No way was he going to hospital in soiled shorts.

Back in my Audi, I made for the airport. I wasn't proud of terrifying Dorsey and his friends. They were just young punks. On reflection, the hit-and-run accident was just a stupid idea that went wrong, but at least this way Dorsey and his crew had learned that they were heading in the wrong direction, and they wouldn't be trailing anyone else along with them. Brian Purefoy would be safe from them now, his friend's medical bills would be covered by the culprits' insurance, and there'd be less cocaine on the streets of Callaway. Weighed and bagged, not a bad couple hours of work. Plus I was on time for my meeting with Jameson Walker and the money he was offering for a job more to my liking.

3

Jameson Walker's tipple of choice was whiskey. It made me chuckle, considering his name was that of two popular brands from back home. He probably wouldn't have known that, though, and I noticed that his drink was poured from a bottle bearing an American label.

He was a big man with sloping shoulders and a square head topped with salt and pepper curls. He looked like he'd been a jock in his earlier days, but had allowed his physique to slip in his late forties. His chest swooped out into a large gut pinched in at the waist by a thick belt with a silver buckle. His voluminous shirt was decorated with small horseshoes, blue jeans and cowboy boots. He'd shrugged out of a jacket and string tie and looked like he was struggling with the heat. He used a napkin to mop his jowls. I found the interior of the bar cool, but I'd been acclimatised to the subtropics by then.

He sipped at his drink and placed it down on the napkin. He peered at me from under bushy brows, watching as I downed a mouthful of Corona directly from the bottle. There was a slice of lemon wedged in the neck, allegedly – I'd read somewhere – to keep the insects away, but I just enjoyed the bitter tang on my tongue. Walker waited until I placed my beer down.

'Are you a family man, Hunter?'

His attention was on my hands. They were tanned by the Florida sun, but there was the occasional patch that wouldn't colour; white scar tissue on my knuckles and on the back of my right hand where I'd taken the slice of a knife. I noticed that his gaze lingered over my left hand, in particular my ring finger.

'You're not thinking of asking me on a date, are you?'

Jameson smiled at the quip, but there was little humour in his expression.

'I've been married twenty-eight years,' he said. 'In all of those years my wife and I were only blessed with one child. After Joan was born, well, my wife had some problems . . .'

I got the gist. 'My wife couldn't bear children either,' I said.

'So you are married?'

'Was.' It was uncomfortable talking about my divorce because, frankly, I felt the breakdown of my marriage was my greatest failure. However I knew where Walker was leading the conversation, and didn't see the harm in reassuring him: family meant everything to me too. 'Diane and I were together over fourteen years. If it was up to me, we'd still be married.'

'Another man?' As soon as he asked the question I could tell he was uncomfortable about it. 'I'm sorry. That's none of my business.'

'She's remarried since, but at the time there was no

one else. It was me . . . let's just say I committed myself to my job too much for Diane's liking.'

Walker scratched his curls, then reached for the whiskey. He downed it, looked for the waitress and called her over. 'Want another drink?'

Tilting the three-quarters-full bottle, I said, 'I'm good.'

'You wouldn't like something a little stronger?'

'Not while on a job,' I told him. 'But you go ahead. Looks like you might need it.'

'I'm just thirsty,' he said with a wink. 'This damned heat! How do you stand it?'

I'd been in much hotter places and situations, but I only offered a shrug. 'You get used to it.'

Walker ordered another drink and the waitress wandered away to the bar.

Walker watched her go. She was a good-looking woman, slim with long legs accentuated by a short black skirt, but Walker wasn't thinking like that. I guessed she reminded him of someone.

'Your daughter still hasn't been in touch?'

He toyed with the rim of his empty glass, tilted it as though checking there was nothing left. 'I'm getting real worried now.'

'How long has it been?' I'd already read the email that Rink received, so I knew that Joan Walker and her friend Nicole Challinor had last called home from a motel in New Mexico three days earlier. But it did no harm to check.

'There's been no word since Monday evening. It's now Thursday morning. Jay should've been in California by now.' He drained his glass of a drip of whiskey that had grown in the bottom, then looked for the waitress. She was on her way back with a fresh tumbler perched on a silver tray. Walker placed a few dollars on the tray and transferred the full glass to his lips. 'Maybe you could bring me another?' he asked. When the waitress returned to the bar, he carried on. 'The obvious things have gone through my mind. Jay's a free spirit and not one to check in with her mom and pop every two minutes, but she knew that we were worried about her and Nicole taking this road trip and promised to call every night. Even if their cellphones aren't working she'd find a landline to use, or she'd email me. I've even been on her Facebook page and she hasn't updated it since Monday. Jay's a fanatic for recording her trips and usually writes daily updates. But nothing has been added at her blog either.'

Mulling that over, I decided that Walker had a good point. Even if his daughter hadn't found it necessary to check in with her parents, she'd hardly have resisted the temptation of her blog and social networking sites; these days it was like people had to share their innermost thoughts with strangers across the world.

'Have you checked her cellphone?'

'Called her, you mean? Of course I've tried.'

'No. What I meant was, is it still switched on? Can you leave a voice message?'

'No, there was just an automated message saying the calls couldn't be connected.' Walker downed another mouthful of liquor. 'It's the same with Nicole's phone.'

'Have you contacted their service providers and checked for their location?'

'You can do that?'

'I'm not sure how, to be honest, not without jumping through bureaucratic hoops first, but I know someone who can check for us. Didn't the police suggest it?'

'The cops aren't taking me seriously. They more or less told me that it's none of my business. Jay is an adult and it's up to her whether she chooses to get in touch or not. Yes, Hunter, she may be an adult, but she's still my baby girl.'

Three days wasn't exactly an eternity. Many people had gone missing for much longer and hadn't suffered for it. Maybe the young women were just cutting the apron strings and letting themselves fly for a while. That didn't mean I couldn't sympathise with their parents: if either girl was my child, I'd be as frantic as Walker.

'I'll need you to tell me the places they planned on visiting, plus the hotels they've already stayed at. Also, if you can get me their credit card or bank account numbers, I can check if they're still using their cards.'

Walker reached for his jacket and pulled out a large envelope from an inside pocket. 'I already thought about that. I brought photographs of both the girls, plus a route planner that I found stored on Jay's computer. It's marked with places of interest, as well as prospective hotels along the way.'

'That's very helpful,' I said, 'but there's always the chance they veered off course and have taken a different route. Hopefully they're just distracted by all the new things they've discovered and haven't got round to calling yet.'

Walker believed that as much as I did, but the least I could do was offer him some hope.

'There's something else in there . . .'

At first I thought he was referring to the down payment on his fee, but, when I looked into the envelope, I found a couple sheets of folded paper alongside the photos and map.

'It's maybe nothing,' Walker said, and downed the remainder of his whiskey. 'In fact, I damn well hope it's got nothing to do with Jay and Nicole.'

The waitress came back with Walker's third drink while I was busy smoothing out the papers, but this time he wasn't concerned with the liquor. He was too busy watching me for a reaction.

The papers carried printouts from a couple of news websites, all reporting on the same story dated two days earlier. At a gas station in Arizona an apparent robbery had gone terribly wrong, with the elderly teller shot dead. Tragically a young family had arrived at the scene while the robbery was underway, and whoever was responsible had shot all four dead in an attempt at silencing any witnesses. To cover up the crime further, those responsible had set fire to the gas pumps and an explosion had ripped the scene apart. Reading the story, and absorbing the senselessness of the violence and the sheer overkill of it, made me sick to the core. But I didn't know why Walker thought this news snippet important.

Walker touched the pages with a thick finger. 'Jay called from a Best Western hotel in Gallup, New Mexico, east of that gas station the night before this happened.

They would have stayed the night, had breakfast and then hit the road. I've a horrible feeling that the girls might have been nearby when the robbery happened.'

Walker left the suggestion hanging in the air. It was only supposition, but what if he was right? If the robbers had gone to such lengths to silence the witnesses at the gas station, what would they have done to Jay and Nicole if they'd also been there?

'I don't think you have to worry about that. The police will be hunting for the people responsible, and I'm pretty sure that if Jay or Nicole had been harmed you'd know it by now.'

'I hope you're right, Hunter.'

'I'm sure,' I said as I folded the papers and slipped them back in the envelope. 'In your email you mentioned that the girls were travelling in your vehicle. Well, if anything had happened I'm certain that the cops would've come across it by now. It doesn't look like the robbers were interested in taking cars with them, because they just burned those at the gas station.'

'I suppose that's true. But I'm still worried.'

'You've every right, but please try not to be. Go home to your wife and I'll be in touch.'

'So you are going to help?'

'I've got your cell number and email address. I'll call you, OK?'

'You're not going to start straight away?'

I tapped the envelope on the table top. 'I already started. I'll call you when I'm in Arizona.'

4

A flight took me to Gallup Municipal Airport, only a stone's throw from the Best Western hotel where Jay and Nicole spent Monday night. Ever since I'd heard the Nat King Cole song, or more likely the rock 'n' roll version by Chuck Berry, I'd fancied taking a trip on the historic Route 66. I just hadn't thought that it'd be under these circumstances. I decided to pick up the trail at the girls' last known location. For all I knew they'd hooked up with some guys in town and were still in Gallup. Maybe they hadn't phoned home because they were having the kind of fun you didn't share with your parents.

I hired a car, a blocky, navy-blue GMC Yukon 4×4, and threw the bags I'd brought with me in the back seat, before heading for the Best Western. I considered renting a room but decided against it, and only stayed long enough to show photos of the girls to the desk staff. A helpful young guy remembered Jay and Nicole and brought their booking up on a computer. It showed that they'd stayed only one night, checked out at ten on Tuesday morning, and paid their bill in full. The guy said he'd chatted with them and that both girls had been excited about their impending trip into the Painted

Desert later that day. I thanked the guy, tossed him a few dollars off the roll handed to me earlier by Jameson Walker, and asked him where there was a good place to eat. He directed me back along the highway to a diner making the most of its Route 66 association. There was a huge sign outside so Technicolor-vivid it reminded me of the graphics from an old Warner Brothers' cartoon, but it appeared that burritos and tacos were the only items on the menu. I continued until I found another diner advertising eggs and ham and suchlike. A waiter led me to a table at the window, and I had a great view over the highway to a huge railroad depot where dozens of freight carriages were parked on the sidings. Red dust billowed on the breeze. Some of it had adhered to the glass, giving everything a pinkish hue. I ordered a special from the menu, plus a large coffee. It was approaching evening, but it would be hours before the sun went down over the desert, so I'd time for a few calls, for filling my stomach, and for making it over the border into Arizona before nightfall.

While I forked down scrambled eggs and rashers of bacon, I used my cell to call Rink.

Jared Rington's more than a friend to me; he's like a brother. Sometimes he even acts like he's my mother. 'Where the freakin' hell are you, goddamnit?' Then again, my mum, Anita, wouldn't use language like that.

'Gallup, New Mexico.'

'What the hell are you doing there?'

'I'm on that missing person case that came in, the Walker job. I told McTeer to let you know I'd pick it up.'

'I didn't go back to the office today.'

'So it's your fault you're not up to speed.'

Rink was the owner of Rington Investigations, based in Tampa, but when I'd signed on it was as an invisible partner. Although I didn't have to answer to him for my actions, there was rarely a thing that we kept from each other. We had both been in the same Special Forces unit, had fought side by side, saved each others' lives on a number of occasions, so there was little that we didn't know about each other. Rink knew how impulsive I was; he wasn't that surprised that I'd jumped straight into a job. He just liked to be a mother hen; like I'd get myself in hot water if he wasn't holding my hand. Trouble was, he was usually right.

'The Walker job? I thought you were helping out with Maria Purefoy's problem?'

I explained how I'd fixed that one on my way to the meeting at Panama City. 'So it was one of those "for the love of" jobs?'

'Rink, the Purefoys could scarcely put food on the table, let alone pay for my services. I told Maria it was on the house.'

'Jesus! Tell me this one isn't a pro bono case you've taken on, brother.'

'I've already done my charity work for the month,' I reassured him. 'Walker's paying top whack. Don't worry, Rink, he's rich enough to afford it.'

Unlike Maria Purefoy, Jameson Walker was incredibly wealthy. He owned a chain of steakhouses ranging all the way down the Eastern seaboard from Maine to

North Carolina. He was rumoured to be edging billion-aire status.

'You don't think this is about his money, Hunter? Kidnap for ransom?'

'Nah, it's too random. Why would kidnappers wait until his daughter was halfway across the States before lifting her? Plus, there's been no contact, no demand for cash. Truth is, Rink, I'm not that concerned yet. Jay – that's the name his daughter Joan goes by – has been planning this trip for over a year. She and her best friend, Nicole, don't get out from under the eyes of their parents that often. I get the impression that Jameson's the protective type and this is the first opportunity the girls have had to enjoy a little freedom.'

'You're talking about guys?'

It was an old chestnut of our trade. Half the missing people we searched for ended up being found in some-one's arms – or bed. But then there was my brother John. I'd actually ended up coming to the States in search of him, and we'd assumed something similar had happened. We couldn't have been more wrong. John was on the lam after stealing property belonging to a gangster, pursued by gunmen. That was before he'd fallen into the sights of a demented serial killer and the real trouble started.

'There doesn't seem to have been anything funny going on here in Gallup. I spoke with a young guy at their hotel who told me they were heading off to Arizona and they were alone.'

'When was that?'

'Tuesday morning.'

'A lot could've happened between then and now. How'd you know the guy hadn't been in their room with them?'

'From the forlorn look on his face when I flashed him their pictures,' I laughed.

'So what's your plan, buddy?'

'Something happened a couple hours away from here. I don't think the girls were involved, but it won't do any harm to talk with the local cops.'

'What kinda somethin'?'

'A gas station robbery where a few people were killed. It probably had nothing to do with them, but I want to check things out.'

'And you couldn't have done that from the office?'

'I fancied a drive,' I said.

'It's a good job I've got McTeer and Velasquez to pick up your load,' Rink grumbled. 'I'm taking a couple days out myself, brother.'

'Going to visit the good lady vet?'

'Yup. My boosters are due a top-up.'

'Well, tell Rene hello from me, and enjoy yourself.'

'How am I gonna do that with you charging around unchaperoned?'

'Don't worry about me. I'm a big boy. And this thing with the girls . . . well, what exactly could go wrong?'

'I wish you hadn't asked that.'

'Go, Rink. Get yourself up to Rene's and have a good time, and don't worry about me.'

'Yeah, right.'

'Stop being an old lady.'

I hung up while he was still swearing at me, and watched a waitress approaching with a fresh jug of coffee. I'd been trying to cut down on caffeine lately. Allegedly I drank far too much of the stuff. Maybe it was the caffeine buzz that turned me into a lit fuse. No, my impulsive nature went deeper than that. I could feel a bubbling in my guts that had nothing to do with stimulants, and everything to do with the thrill of the hunt. I held out my empty mug. 'Top me up, please.'

5

My flight from Florida to New Mexico came with a small drawback. In the past I'd managed to take my gun on to flights with me. On a number of occasions I'd used fake air marshal documents and on the others I'd been given special dispensation by the government, but neither was the case this time. Grabbing the first available flight, I hadn't had the time to organise anything. I was licensed to carry a firearm in Florida, but that didn't extend beyond the state line, so I had to lock my SIG in the trunk of my Audi when parking it at Panama City. I hadn't even brought a knife along with me. I felt naked without them.

I had to rectify that situation, because, despite what I'd said to Jameson Walker and to Rink, I had the horrible feeling that I might need a weapon before I was finished. On occasion our mutual friend, Harvey Lucas, had supplied both Rink and me with weaponry, as Harvey had a network of contacts throughout the States, but they tended to be specialist firearms. Knives were easy to come by, but I'd have felt much better getting my hands on a gun.

There wasn't much call for hunting supplies in that

corner of Gallup, but I found a pawn shop where I picked up a sturdy lock-knife with a five-inch blade. Folded, it fit neatly into my jeans pocket. The shop also had guns, but the owner was adamant that he'd have to fill in the obligatory paperwork and I'd get the gun I wanted after a few days. That didn't work for me, so I left with only the knife.

I headed out on Route 66, making steady progress for Arizona. By then the sun was setting and I drove towards a horizon that was on fire, while behind me it was inky black. There was no moon out, but the stars were vivid sparks in the heavens. As I drove, the rail tracks paralleled the road for a while and I had a freight train keeping me company. The clatter of the wheels had a lulling effect. I found a radio station playing old-school country, and, though it wasn't to my particular taste, I allowed Patsy Cline and Hank Williams to drown out the railroad sounds. Mesas and cliffs built around me, monoliths of red stone that glowed like old blood under my headlights. Somewhere along the way I crossed the state border and pushed on through Lupton and a proliferation of signs indicating I was now in Navajo country. There was even a sprawling trading post set against a cliff-side pocked with caverns and cave art depicted in stark turquoise lit with spotlights. I considered pulling over, to see the sights as Jay and Nicole would have, but decided against it and continued to the junction with state highway 77 where I angled north for the Painted Desert.

A couple of miles into the desert there was a truck

stop and I pulled in. It didn't look the kind of place where the girls would have felt safe; they would likely have continued up towards Indian Wells looking for somewhere more appealing. But it suited me fine. I wasn't intimidated by the big rigs or the rough men that drove them; in fact, the rougher they were the better for me.

Inside the diner, I showed the photos of the girls to some of the staff, but I knew I was wasting my time. These were the night shift, and if by chance the girls had been through here, a different bunch of workers would've been on duty then.

An elderly Navajo guy I found leaning on a broom in the washroom said, 'Good luck, man, but you're wasting your breath round here. People like me, well, we keep our noses outta other people's business.'

'Even if that means not helping someone?'

'Some people just can't be helped.'

At my bemused expression, he led me back out of the foyer and indicated a noticeboard tacked to a post. On it were upward of ten curling Missing Persons posters. Barring one which depicted a middle-aged white man, all the others were of females ranging from thirteen up to sixty-three years of age.

'We get lotsa those things turnin' up,' the old man said, tapping the board with his broom. 'Not so sure any of them missin' folks get found, though.' He glanced at the ground, ran the bristles of the brush through the dirt. 'Not alive anyways.'

Thanking the old man for his candour, I went back

inside and ordered coffee and a supper of cold meat and cheese. Sitting at a corner table, picking at the food, I thought about the old man's words. In a country as immense as the US, tens of thousands of people went missing every year. I didn't know the statistics, but there had to be a fraction of them that were never found again. Talking fractions kind of minimised the seriousness, because when you converted it to percentages then you suddenly had a very real figure. If one in ten never turned up again, then the number truly became shocking. People would disappear for many reasons, many of them innocent enough, but then there were the horrifying realities of kidnap, murder and abduction. How many of those who disappeared under those circumstances ever returned home to their loved ones?

I still entertained the notion that Jay and Nicole were simply enjoying their freedom and soon enough Jameson Walker would inform me he'd received word from them, but that could prove to be wishful thinking. No, on seeing those weathered posters, it had sunk an icy talon into my guts, focusing my mind on the urgency of finding them. The police speak about the forty-eight-hour rule: if a person who's been abducted isn't found before that time elapses, then tracking them down becomes very difficult indeed. Truth was, I'd already gone beyond forty-eight hours and was rapidly approaching the next marker. It was often believed that if abductees hadn't turned up within seventy-two hours, then you could expect only to find a corpse.

Sitting there, eating and swilling down coffee, I felt

guilty. But I wasn't wasting time, I was watching, waiting for the correct moment to move. A good mix of people came into the restaurant, truckers, road workers, business people, the occasional family, but none of them were giving off the vibe I was seeking. I ordered more coffee and waited.

My second coffee had become a muddy pool in the bottom of my mug by the time I saw some likely contenders stride in. There were three of them, two men and one woman, all of them high. The two men were rednecks, while the woman looked like she might have a little Navajo blood running through her veins, though I could have been wrong. She didn't look like one of the noble savages of myth; she was pie-faced, with spindly limbs, and she tottered on red high heels. What made me think she might be of Native American ancestry was the dusky cast of her skin and the proud hawk-like nose. Nothing else about her was proud, in fact she looked like a skank. So for that matter did her male friends.

They sat in a booth, demanding the waitress who couldn't get away from them fast enough. The noise of their raucous laughter was harsh and aggressive, and I noticed that some of those customers nearest to them moved away or left the establishment altogether. I ordered a fresh coffee. Then I waited a bit more.

Some time later, the woman got up and headed for the washroom. I let her go. The two rednecks paid their bill as noisily as they did everything else and went outside. I placed dollars on my table and followed them. As I left, I caught a glimpse of the old Navajo guy with the broom. He was just finishing a cigarette which he doused under his boot heel before flicking it into a dustpan with his brush. He looked once at me, then over at the two rednecks making their way across the parking lot to a souped-up first generation Camaro that was older than I was. He shook his head slowly as he mouthed something to me. 'Good luck,' I believe he said. Then, true to his word, he paid me no further heed and went off to find somewhere else to sneak a cigarette.

One of the rednecks, a tall, skinny man with short cropped dark hair and moustache, leaned on the hood of the Camaro while his shorter friend decided to relieve himself against the kerb. Across the lot, a couple of truckers moved for their big rigs and one of them hooted at the pissing guy. The redneck hollered wordlessly, then wagged his penis at the men. All three laughed loudly. Scumbags, the lot of them. I moved towards the Camaro, casting an approving eye over it as it glistened redly under sodium lamps.

The man leaning on the hood watched me approach. He wasn't concerned. I was a lone man, my attention definitely on the car, and it was probably something he was used to.

'Is that a nineteen sixty-seven first gen?' I asked.

'Sixty-eight, buddy,' he corrected me, like I was about a million years out.

'Wow,' I said, leaning down to inspect the front grille, 'you don't see too many of these beauties these days. Not in this condition. Did you renovate it yourself?'

'It belongs to my bro,' he said, with a tip of his head to the stockier man. The other was just zipping up as he walked over. I grinned at him.

'Man, I'd shake your hand,' I said, nodding down at his fly, 'but not yet, eh?'

'What do you drive, buddy?' The tall one asked, as he plucked an insect from his moustache and flicked it away.

'Nothing as beautiful as a first gen.' I jerked a thumb across the lot to where my GMC was parked. While I did so, I checked that their lady friend was still inside the building. Yes, she was a skank, but that didn't mean I'd changed my opinion of the way women should be treated. I didn't want her around if things turned awkward – a real possibility if I'd misread these men. Moving around the Camaro, I peered inside, not inter-ested in it, but in what extras I might see. 'I think we're guys of a like mind. We have the same kind of *tastes*?'

The men shared a glance, then studied me keenly. They were probably deciding if they'd heard right and were trying to make me as a cop. My English accent would throw them off that line faster than anything.

'You buying?' the first man asked.

'Depends on what you're selling.'

'Just grass, man.'

I shook my head. 'I'm not talking drugs.'

A quizzical look shot between them.

'I've a little problem to deal with, but I don't have the tools for the job.' I was being purposefully vague, hoping that they would offer the conclusion. If they were just low-end potheads, they were no good to me and I'd walk away.

'What kind of problem?' The stocky one had jammed his hands into the pockets of his jeans. No way was he carrying, and the manner in which he'd just compromised himself meant he was no immediate danger. Not a good sign, considering.

'Personal problem.' I just stood looking at them.

The taller man sucked his teeth, before jerking his head for me to follow him. To his friend he said, 'Pop the trunk.'

The boot was full of junk, a toolbox, a blanket, and a spare tyre. The tall man dug around inside the toolbox, lifting out wrenches and hammers and placing them on the rolled blanket. From under the tools he pulled a bundle of rags, and even though there was a musty odour in general, I recognised the more familiar scent of gun oil. Taking a look over his shoulder, he checked that no one was spying on us. His action was the mark of an amateur, but it didn't matter now. He unfurled the edges of the cloth and disclosed what lay within. It wasn't a semi-auto handgun, the likes of which I usually carried, but a six-shot revolver, and a box of ammo stained dark with lubricant. It was a workhorse weapon, a Smith and Wesson, chambered for both .38 Special and .357 cartridges, and as good a gun as I could hope for. I leaned past the man and lifted the gun out of the rags, worked the cylinder, checked the piece over. 'Is it clean?'

'It hasn't been used in a stick-up, if that's what you're gettin' at?'

'The serial number's been filed off.'

'Didn't say it never would be.' The guy gave me a shit-eating grin, playing the tough guy. He wasn't the real deal. I considered taking the gun and the ammunition off him. I'd be doing a service, probably to him. During one of his highs he might shoot himself in the foot. But I was no thief. I peeled three hundred dollars off Jameson Walker's roll. 'That's all I'm willing to pay. But that includes the shells.'

'Three hundred? Damn, I'd throw the bitch in as well for that price.'

Recalling their girlfriend's pie-dish face, her spindly legs and tottering gait, I declined politely. But that was the deal done. I wasn't going to shake on it; they were drug-dealing arseholes, not the type I'd normally give the time of day. I took the gun, wrapped it in the cloth, stuffed the box of ammunition into my jacket pocket and then headed for the GMC.

Now that I'd prepared myself, the hunt was on. It was time to go find Jay and Nicole. Maybe I wouldn't need the gun. But that was unlikely.

6

Some time later I came to the gas station mentioned in the news articles Jameson Walker had provided. Coming upon it in the dark, it looked different from the images on the printed sheets. It was no less stark, and if anything even more terrible in real life. The shack that had served as the teller's booth-cum-convenience store had collapsed down on itself. Fire crews had sifted through the wreckage while recovering the corpse of the teller and much of the building now lay in mangled heaps about the original foundations. The fuel pumps had been taken by the explosion that ripped through the site, as had an awning erected to offer shade to customers as they filled up their gas tanks. The vehicles belonging to the teller and the family who were also murdered had been lifted and taken away for further forensic study. If it wasn't for the signage at the side of the highway, you'd be hard put to guess Peachy's gas station had ever been there.

Crime scene tape fluttered on the desert breeze, like bunting after a celebration but as a more sinister reminder to the world. Here people had died: senseless slaughter. Standing there among the damp ashes, I could picture the wraiths of the murder victims standing beyond the ring of yellow tape, staring back at me with sunken eyes. They were probably wondering why I was there. This wasn't my battle; sadly I couldn't help them. I could not exact retribution from their killers.

Or could I?

Perhaps I was mistaken and what had occurred here did have something to do with the missing women. I had an odd feeling that tickled the back of my brain, something I'd come to recognise over the years. Cops call it a *hunch*. The army I belonged to called it rapid intuitive experience or RIE. Then again, maybe it was simply wishful thinking. I was once cautioned that I couldn't save everyone. That was infinitely apparent; a good number of people I cared for had been killed despite my best efforts. But, if the people who'd died here had done so under the guns of those responsible for taking Jay and Nicole, at least I could try to avenge them.

I heard the car coming along the road, then its tyres juddering on the rumble strip as it took the ramp to the gas station. When a Navajo County police cruiser pulled up alongside my GMC, I can't say I was particularly surprised.

I just stood there, looking at the devastation, and waited for the officer to approach me. He was a young man, thick about the shoulders and neck, his dress shirt straining around his overdeveloped biceps. He'd doffed his Smokey Bear hat while in the car but, as he approached me warily, he jammed it over his crew-cut

as a sign of officialdom. Then he laid his hand on the
butt of his sidearm.

'Excuse me, sir?' His teeth were very white, offset by
his permanent tan, and vivid against the night. 'Can I
ask what business you have out here?'

The cop had most likely been briefed to spin by the
gas station regularly. It wasn't uncommon for looters
to go to a scene of destruction, or ghoulish souvenir
hunters either. Family members of those murdered
sometimes had to see where their loved ones had died,
as a form of closure. And then, sometimes, the perpetrators of a crime also liked to return and view the
aftermath of their work. By the way he studied me
from head to toe he was determining which bracket I
fitted into.

'I'm just taking a look, Officer,' I said.

He waved at the fluttering crime scene tape. 'You see
that, sir? It means *keep out*. You shouldn't have come
back here.'

'It was broken when I arrived.'

'That doesn't make any difference, sir. It still says
"Do Not Cross", and it's an offence to do so.'

I paid his last comment no mind. Instead, I slowly
reached for my jacket pocket, letting him see exactly
where I was reaching. His fingers hovered over his service pistol, but I was posing no threat. I pulled out a
folding wallet and opened it for him. 'I'm a private
investigator. I'm looking for two women who might or
might not have been through here.'

The cop accepted my wallet, and studied it. It couldn't

have been easy in the darkness, but there was enough of a glow from his cruiser's headlights to see the heading on the licence inside. 'You're a long way from home,' he concluded. He didn't clarify if he meant Florida, or if he was referring to my English accent. I didn't take him up on it.

'I was employed by the father of one of the women. He was sure that his daughter and her friend would have passed this way around the time the gas station was robbed.'

The cop moved closer to me, and he appeared to be checking my belt line. 'Are you carrying?'

'No.'

'You mind if I check?'

'Go ahead,' I said, holding my arms out. 'I've a folding knife in my back pocket, but that's all you'll find.'

I was glad that I'd left the revolver purchased from the potheads in my GMC. I hadn't tried the weapon out yet, and wouldn't trust it to work proficiently until I'd stripped, cleaned and test-fired it.

'You're licensed to carry, aren't you, sir?'

'Only in Florida, Officer.'

He offered a slight smile – the son of a bitch had been testing me. He neglected to continue his search and nodded me over to his cruiser. 'You understand I'm going to have to run a check on you, sir? If you'd just walk over this way so we can get a bit of light, it'll make things much easier for the two of us.'

Maybe if he got the full details, then he'd try to be a hero and take me in. That would've been unfortunate, because I'd no desire to spend a few days behind bars until things could be cleared up. Luckily I had friends in high places and much of the activity I'd been involved in on US soil had been sealed. The cop used the radio in his cruiser, and when he got back out he was frowning, snapping my wallet against his thigh. 'Your details check out.'

'I'm a good guy,' I said, offering him a smile.

'That's debatable.' He started to hand back my wallet, but as I went to take it he held on. 'I think it's best you get on your way, sir. Don't be coming back here, OK?'

'I have no reason to. I've seen what I wanted to see.'

'I've had to move on a few lookie-loos,' he said, and finally let go of my wallet, which I placed in my jacket pocket. 'I don't expect to tell *anyone* twice.'

I pulled out the photos of Jay and Nicole. 'Have you moved these two on?'

He gave the photos a cursory inspection, shook his head. 'I think I'd have remembered if I'd seen them. Good-looking girls. You said they're missing, but there's been nothing logged about them back at the station.'

'This girl here.' I tapped the picture of Jay. 'Her father reported her missing but was given the brush-off by someone on the other end of the phone.'

The cop made a sound of disgust in the back of his throat, and thumbed back the brim of his hat. 'Typical,' he said. 'Like everywhere else, we're short-staffed. Most of our resources have been thrown into finding the perpetrators of this crime. Whoever he spoke to will have had orders to prioritise incoming calls. If those ladies hadn't been gone more than forty-eight hours, then I doubt their details were even noted.'

'It's almost three days now,' I said. 'How's about I have her father call again?'

'I'd advise it, sir. In the meantime, I'll keep my eyes open while I'm on patrol.'

'Appreciate it, Officer.' I gave him the number of my cellphone, as well as a description of the vehicle they were travelling in. 'If you see anything, could you give me a call?'

'Sure.' He paused. 'But it makes no difference, sir, you'd best get yourself outta here.'

I took a look at his badge. 'Consider it done, Officer Lewin. But first . . . you mind if I ask you another question or two?'

'Who's the cop here?'

'Who's the investigator?' I countered.

He grunted out a laugh, but started walking towards my car. 'Ask away, I don't guarantee to answer.'

'I'm not after state secrets. Do you get many missing persons reports here?'

'No more than anywhere else, I guess. Sometimes tourists get lost out in the desert, but we usually find them within a couple hours.'

'I called at a truck stop a few miles back. There seemed to be quite a few missing person posters.'

'If you'd read the details you'd have seen most of them were from outta state. People driving through slap the posters up on an off-chance, that's all.'

'So, you don't have a problem with people going missing?'

Lewin eyeballed me. There was a muscle jumping on

the side of his jaw. 'If you're suggesting we have some-one abducting people, then the answer's no. We have no more problems here than anywhere else, just like I said. There's only . . .'

'Only?'

'. . . only one outstanding issue that I'm aware of. Helena Blackstock. She's still on our books. It's been four months since she disappeared.'

'She's from around here?'

'Up nearer to Indian Wells.' Lewin stopped, realising he'd just overstepped the mark. A woman missing four months had no bearing on the disappearance I was investigating, and was therefore none of my business. We'd reached my GMC and he gave it a cursory once-over. Then he held out his hand, directing me inside. 'I think we'll leave things at that, sir.'

'Hunter,' I reminded him. 'That's my name. For when you call me.'

'If I call you. I can't guarantee I'll come across the women.' With that he walked away, snatching off his hat and dashing sweat from the inner rim.

Inside my GMC, I watched him get in his cruiser, but he wasn't going to leave before I did. I started the car, and drove down the off-ramp, before turning, not for Indian Wells, but back the way I'd come. I didn't know much about Indian Wells, other than it was an historic site of some sort, but was only a collection of home-steads. I needed a much larger conurbation, so set out to find Holbrook, which was further along Route 66 than I'd made it earlier.

My route took me via the same truck stop I'd visited before. I pulled into the car park. There was no sign of the Camaro, for which I was glad. I walked over to the noticeboard and studied again the various missing person posters. Officer Lewin hadn't been spinning me a PR line; all of the posters did depict people missing from various parts of Arizona and beyond. All except for Helena Blackstock. The old *spider sense* was tingling, and for what reason I'd no idea but I plucked the poster off the board and stuffed it in my pocket alongside the photos of Jay and Nicole.

'I don't think taking that's a good idea.'

I turned to the quiet voice and found the old Navajo cleaner leaning on his brush. I hadn't heard his approach.

'Why's that?'

'Her husband won't be a happy man. He comes in here every other day to check there's still a poster up. Doesn't take too kindly to when he has to post up a new one.'

'I intend to speak to her husband. Have you any idea where I can find him?'

The old man laughed, swept grooves in the dirt by his feet. 'Some detective you're turning out to be. Didn't you see the phone number on the poster before you tore it down? Why don't you give him a call and ask him yourself?'

The thought had already gone through my mind, but I'd discarded it. My reason for returning to Holbrook had been to find an internet connection where I could check out the background story surrounding Helena's disappearance. From there, I intended to search for an address I could snoop out prior to contacting her husband. But I had to admit the old guy had a point: why not just make a call and cut to the chase?

'I'm about as good a detective as you are a cleaner, I guess. That brush doesn't see too much action, does it?'

The old guy found that amusing and showed me a gap-toothed grin. 'Why, this old thing?' He lifted the brush and shook dust from the head. 'I just carry it with me. Makes me look busy if nuthin' else.'

That was something I'd learned while in the army. Always walk fast, carry something with you, and try to look like you're on an important errand; otherwise you could bet your arse you would be soon enough.

Nearby a huge rig started with a roar and a belch of smoke and began rumbling out of the lot, heading for points north. 'Actually . . . you sound like a man who knows his stuff.' I tapped the poster in my jacket. 'And I think I'll take your advice.'

The old man slipped a hand-rolled cigarette from his shirt pocket, lit it with a match. He dumped the dead stick on the floor at his feet. Winked at me and said, 'What do I know about anything?'

Then he moved off, brushing the matchstick ahead of him.

I watched him go, puffs of smoke marking his progress to wherever his next hidey-hole was located. The old guy had found a way of getting by, and good luck to him. I was wrong about him though; he was better at his job than I was a detective, because I didn't seem to be getting far with my own task. I thought about telephoning Helena Blackstock's husband there and then, but any link she had to those I was seeking was very tenuous. Instead, I elected to phone McTeer and Velasquez and check on what they'd been able to glean regarding the women's movements.

Out here it was 'mountain time' and late evening, but back in Tampa it had to be approaching midnight. Nevertheless I was confident that one of Rink's associates would be on the end of a phone. I got Velasquez.

'We've searched on both girls' credit cards, and on their bank accounts. Nothing, Joe. McTeer has been checking Joan's Facebook and Blogger sites, but again there's been no activity. As you know, the last time their accounts were accessed was on Tuesday morning at Gallup, but since then, nada!'

'You have it set up to alert you if there's a hit?'

'Yeah. We could patch it through to your cell if you'd like? Then you're getting the message the same time as we do.'

'Yes, do that for me, please. Anything on their phones?'

'No,' Velasquez said, 'but Jameson Walker was in touch. Still nothing from his end. He asked when you were going to call him with an update.'

'I'll call him soon,' I promised. 'Set that alert thing up to this cell, but if you find out anything else ring me immediately, OK?'

'Will do, Joe.'

I thanked him then rang off. I decided to head south towards the junction with Route 66 where I could strike westward for Holbrook, which was only a few miles along the way. I should book a room somewhere, get some sleep and start fresh again in the morning. Before sleeping, I'd have to call Jameson Walker with a report, and I guessed he wouldn't be too impressed by how little progress I'd made in finding his daughter. Plus, it would do no harm to call Helena's husband and have him agree to meet me.

Setting off, I glanced over at the cloth bundle. Inside it something else demanded my attention. I considered pulling up by the highway, marching into the desert and taking a couple trial shots, and that briefest of distractions was almost my undoing.

A pick-up truck roaring up the on-ramp almost sideswiped me, and I had to swerve out of the way to avoid a collision. The truck missed my GMC by inches, and if not for the fact it was already gone, the truck would have lost its wing mirror. As it was, the driver yelled abuse at me, but then kept speeding on into the parking lot.

I got a snapshot of the man driving the truck, and as I was wont to do, I filed the image away for later. Should I ever come across the gaunt cowboy again I'd teach him a lesson on how to be a courteous driver.

I laughed off the thought. What were the chances of coming across him again in a country with a population of hundreds of millions?

7

Jameson Walker expected more than a call to say I hadn't found his daughter yet, but once I'd clued him in on the searches that McTeer and Velasquez were also conducting he settled down a bit. I told him to get some sleep and assured him I'd telephone him again the following morning. 'Sleep? There's little chance of that,' he said. I knew how he felt.

I took a room at a Holiday Inn at Holbrook, my window giving me a great view of the endless mountain desert. It reminded me of when I'd chased the serial killer, Tubal Cain, to his Mojave hideaway in an ill-fated attempt at saving my little brother's life. Before I'd arrived, Cain had already stripped the flesh from John's back and had begun whittling away at his ribs. I stopped Cain but it hadn't been enough to save John. My brother had died within three days; no one could have survived his injuries. I closed the blinds.

I'd purchased a sandwich and carry-out coffee from a nearby 7-Eleven, and made the most of both while studying the photographs of Jay and Nicole. I'd placed the missing person poster alongside them on the bed. It hadn't struck me before but Nicole Challinor and

Helena Blackstock were not unalike. They were both of a similar age, with tiny features apart from large, dark eyes. Both women wore their jet-black hair in bobs, though Nicole's salon-styled cut was more refined. Helena appeared to have taken a pair of scissors to hers, trimming the hair at a point level with her jaw, probably out of a need for an easily maintained style. Nicole, I knew, was the kind who frequented the boutiques of Madison and Park Avenues in New York City, while Helena was a country girl. There wasn't much call for a $400 hairdo when living in a trailer park. A telephone directory in a drawer in my room only had one listing for Blackstock, and had given me an address up near to Indian Wells, with the same number as on the poster. Her husband was called Scott.

Nicole and Helena's likeness must be purely coincidental. I gave up on that line of thought, and switched my attention to Jay Walker. Cute name. Cute face. Her picture showed a young woman who looked as if she could handle herself. Not necessarily physically, but in an argument. Her mouth was turned up at one corner, and her eyes were focused on the lens, as if she was challenging the photographer. Without ever having met her, I took a shine to Jay. I found a self-assured woman attractive. My ex-wife Diane had known what she wanted, as had Kate Piers, a woman I'd fallen for before she was brutally snatched away from me by an assassin's bullet. In the last few months I'd been seeing Kate's sister, Imogen Ballard, after she'd proven that she too was tough and dependable. Some would find the women

I'm attracted to an anomaly: after all, I was in the business of protecting those incapable of doing it for themselves.

'Where are you, Jay?'

I wasn't hoping for divine inspiration or a psychic moment or anything, the question had just come unbidden to my lips.

Looking into those vibrant eyes, I refused to believe that she was dead. There was too much life there to have been extinguished so easily. Of course, that was fanciful thinking at best, because it didn't matter if she'd the determination of an Olympic athlete, she couldn't outrun a bullet. If Jay and Nicole had been near that gas station when the robbers struck, then I didn't hold out much hope of finding either of them alive. Whoever had killed the teller and the family had been both callous and meticulous. They intended covering their tracks and that would have included silencing all witnesses to their crime. If they'd murdered the women, the desert out there was immense; they could have concealed their corpses in any one of a million locations. The thing that wouldn't be hidden so easily was the SUV the women were driving, and probably my best chance of finding Jay and Nicole was to concentrate on finding it. I hoped that Officer Lewin would come through on that.

My gaze skimmed back to Nicole's and Helena's photos.

Their likeness was troubling me and I didn't know why.

Glancing at my watch, I saw that it was late, but not

too late to call Helena's husband. I used the phone in the room, hitting '9' for an outside line, before carefully tapping in the number printed on the poster.

The phone rang and rang, and I was on the verge of hanging up when the receiver was finally lifted.

'You know what time it is?'

'I do, Mr Blackstock. It's near midnight, but I think you're going to want to hear what I've got to say.'

'Who is this?'

'My name's Joe Hunter, I'm a private investigator—'

The phone was slammed down. I looked at the receiver, before carefully tapping in the number again.

This time the phone only rang once before Blackstock snatched up his handset. 'Goddamnit! I'm sick of you parasites pimping for business. Why don't you leave me alone and go chase after adulterers like you usually do?'

'I'm not soliciting work,' I said. 'I'm engaged by another client whose daughter has gone missing along with a friend. I thought you'd talk to me about Helena's disappearance.'

'Other people's business is no concern of mine. I've enough to contend with. Now, if you don't mind, fuck off and leave me alone!'

Throwing caution to the wind, I said, 'Helena is a dead ringer for one of the girls I'm looking for. I think there might be a connection.'

'What do you mean a dead ringer?' His words were challenging, as if I'd suggested that his wife was no longer unique and by that I was besmirching her memory.

'I mean that Helena and Nicole look similar.'

'What? Someone out there is taking women with a particular look?'

'I could be totally off-track, Scott, but there could be a connection.' I waited for him to absorb that. He was breathing harshly through his nose, short sharp blasts into the mouthpiece, still angry at my intrusion. 'Then again, maybe not, but it's an angle I want to investigate. It could be beneficial to the two of us to speak.'

'How's it going to benefit me? My wife's probably dead.'

'Your wife's only missing,' I corrected. 'And you believe she's still alive, otherwise you wouldn't keep replacing the posters.'

'You've been checking up on me? Stick to your own case, asshole.'

'I'm only asking for half an hour of your time. What harm could it do? I can come up to your place.'

'No.'

'Why not?'

'I'm not interested, that's why. Don't come near my house and don't call again.'

Scott Blackstock slammed down the phone.

'Arsehole,' I growled.

The axiom that someone who protests too loudly usually has something to hide rang true. I looked again at the address of the trailer park that I'd scribbled on the back of the poster, and then left the room, thinking I could pick up a map of the local area at the 7-Eleven. I wanted a refill on my coffee, anyway. The caffeine hit would make it difficult to sleep, but I doubted my mind would settle enough for that. I was buzzing, wanting to get going. Scott Blackstock was as good a starting point as any, and, whether he liked it or not, he was going to be paid a visit.

I walked through Holbrook, my boot heels making soft 'chucking' sounds on the pavement. It was cooler now, but some of the stored-up sunlight made the side-walk reluctant to release the rubber of my soles. Traffic was light, and there weren't that many pedestrians either. Nevertheless, the 7-Eleven beckoned me forward with welcoming lights. I took it that the sign above the door didn't mean too much, and as long as there were customers the doors would stay open. Outside the store were newspaper boxes where you could feed coins in a slot and take a newspaper without having to go inside to pay. I wouldn't normally bother to grab a paper, but something caught my eye. Though it was the best part of three days since the terrible incident at the gas station, it was still making news.

I paid for a paper and lifted it under the shop's neon signs. The front page showed an image of a young girl called Ellie Mansfield and at first glance you would expect the girl to be one of the victims found dead at the scene. But though she was expected to have been amongst those found slaughtered in the station wagon, she wasn't there. There should have been five corpses, but I recalled the original news releases only mentioned four. Ellie was a friend of the Corbin family, who had gone along as company for thirteen-year-old Tracey Corbin. It had taken this long for the police to identify the family, and for the horrifying news to leak back to

Ellie's parents who'd only this afternoon reported that their daughter had taken the road trip with the Corbins.

Perhaps I was jumping to conclusions, but there was only one thing I could come up with. The robbers had taken the girl.

That meant they could also have taken Jay and Nicole, particularly Nicole, because Ellie Mansfield too was petite with dark eyes and dark bobbed hair.

The earlier fluke of Helena Blackstock and Nicole Challinor being similar-looking may have been just that, but with Ellie added to the mix it went way beyond coincidence.

Someone out there was taking females of a particular physical type. That was bad enough, but it also begged another question. Jay Walker didn't look like any of them, so what had happened to her? Had she been discarded like a worthless piece of trash?

8

At first light I was on my way, skirting Indian Wells and heading for the trailer park where Scott Blackstock lived. Up this far into Navajo County Scott would be in the minority, because approaching ninety-five per cent of the population were of Native American descent. I was assuming a lot: I hadn't seen the man, had only talked with him on the phone, but during our short discourse he had come across as poor white trash and an arsehole to boot. Then again, what gave me the right to judge him? He was simply a man whose wife had gone missing, presumed dead, so how should he be expected to greet a stranger stirring things up again?

The trailer park was on a low plateau, static caravans set around a circular compound formed of a shoulder-high breeze-block wall. Within the compound was a collection of squat buildings with tin roofs, which I guessed housed washing machines and dryers and suchlike. The caravans were huge compared to those I was familiar with back home in the UK, some of them silver bullet-shaped affairs, others square and ugly with lean-tos and porches tacked on. There was little in the way of grass or flowers or anything that would offer any beauty, and dust devils whirled across the dirt roads. Cars and trucks with a coating of trail dust were parked outside each trailer.

As I drove in, I looked at the mailboxes on poles jammed in the grit to determine which Scott's trailer was. There was no one up and about yet, other than a couple of skinny dogs rooting in the spillage from a trash can. They stopped and watched my approach, but soon went back to tussling over a choice morsel. I continued towards the far end of the park and finally found the caravan I was seeking.

Parked outside was a battered pick-up truck, alongside a newer jeep. A small lot at the front had once held a flower garden of sorts, but it appeared that Scott wasn't into watering and weeding. Maybe the garden had been Helena's way of making the place look more appealing, and now she was no longer around it had been left to return to its natural state.

I parked the GMC alongside the jeep, but didn't immediately get out. Scott's trailer was one of the older square type, with a porch and decking, and an annex had been tacked on at the far left corner making it an L-shaped structure. There were no tyres on the hubs, and it didn't look like the caravan had moved in many a year, nor would it for many more to come. The windows were covered by Venetian blinds, one of them hanging askew. Through the gap, I could see a face peering back at me. Then it was gone, and I got out the GMC and kept my hands by my sides.

The door of the trailer slammed open and Scott

Blackstock stamped on to the porch, his face twisted with rage. I had been correct in my assumption: he was no Native American. He was tall, with blond hair and green eyes, a spray of freckles across the bridge of his crooked nose. He had a shotgun broken over his left elbow and was in the process of feeding cartridges into both barrels.

'You're the fuck-shit that called me last night,' he said, snapping shut the gun and lifting it my way. 'What do they call you again? Hunter? Well, I'm telling you, get off my goddamn property or I'm gonna be doing myself some hunting. You've ten seconds and then I'm gonna give you two loadsa buckshot in the ass.'

I didn't move, apart from to lift my empty hands higher. 'Take it easy, Scott. I'm not here for trouble.'

'Shame,' he crowed. ''Cos if you ain't outta here in ten seconds like I said, trouble's coming your way.' He leaned back towards the trailer door. 'Boys, you want to come on out here?'

There was a rumble from within the caravan, and two more rednecks joined Scott on the decking. One was taller than Scott, an older man, while the second was short and stocky, bearded and with a prodigious gut poking out from the hem of his off-white shirt. The fat one had a liquor bottle in his hand, half empty; but perhaps that was just the pessimist in me. It looked like Scott had been keeping an all-night vigil, awaiting my arrival, and had called in his buddies just in case I did show up.

This could still end up reasonably, but I didn't think

so. The older guy was holding a baseball bat, whacking it into the leathery mitt of his palm. By the look of him, he was lining my head up for a swing. He didn't worry me: I moved right up to the edge of the decking so that he couldn't swing at me without first connecting with the uprights holding together the lean-to porch. The stocky one chugged another mouthful of whiskey. Scott made a big deal of pulling back the hammers on the antiquated shotgun.

'I think if you let me explain myself, you'll want to listen to what I have to say.' I stood looking at him.

Scott glanced once at each of his friends. He'd promised them some fun, I guessed. 'I'm starting to count now. Ten. Nine. Eight . . .'

'Quit the melodramatics, Scott,' I said. 'We both know you're not going to shoot.'

'You don't think so?' Scott raised the stock to his shoulder.

I pulled out the S&W and aimed it at him. 'No. You're not.'

Scott licked his lips.

'Neither are you, dick,' said the fat guy. He took a cumbersome step down off the deck and stood in front of my gun. His grip had shifted on his bottle so that he now held it by the neck. 'Now get the hell outta here before I kick your ass all the way back—'

Before he finished his threat I slapped the butt of my gun against his temple. The man dropped as though pole-axed, his knees folding under him so that he went down on his backside. Slowly he toppled sideways and

I toed the bottle away, to avoid it ending up jammed in his open mouth.

'Hey!' The older guy came at me then. True to form he couldn't get a good crack at me and had to weave past Scott to gain space. By the time he made room it was too late. I shot a sidekick into his front leg, straightening his knee, and as he jerked against the pain I snatched the bat out of his hand and threw it away. A slap of the gun butt to his head sent him down so he was lying across his fat buddy.

'Are we all done now?' I asked Scott.

He had taken a couple of steps back, the gun forgotten in his hands. Just as I thought, the weapon was all bluff. If he'd intended using a gun, he wouldn't have brought the two so-called hard-asses in on the action.

'Jesus, man, you knocked them out!'

'I don't care for people who make threats to me.' I allowed my words to hang in the air and Scott finally figured them out.

'I wasn't really going to shoot.' He slowly placed the shotgun down by the door to the trailer. 'Even if I wanted. It doesn't fire, and hasn't done for years.'

Maybe he thought I wouldn't notice that the barrels were plugged when he pointed them at my face. Things like that don't go unnoticed by someone who's been on both ends of guns for the past twenty years or so. I shoved my S&W away. 'Come here, Scott.'

'What are you planning to do?'

'Don't you think we'd best get your friends inside if

we're going to talk? It wouldn't do to leave them lying here, not with those starving dogs around.'

Scott actually looked to where the mangy hounds were rooting through the garbage, as though they were a threat to the unconscious men. Then he came and helped me haul the older guy into the trailer. It was surprisingly spacious inside, and nothing like the caravans I'd holidayed in as a lad in North Wales. We laid him out on a bunk, made sure he was breathing, then went to wrestle the fat one inside as well. It wasn't an easy task.

I was sweating by the time I sat down next to a counter in the kitchen area. 'Could have saved us all a load of bother if you'd agreed to talk in the first place.'

Scott sat next to me, but his eyes were on the two sleeping beauties. 'The boys ain't gonna be happy when they wake up.'

'The *boys* should thank me for not shooting them in the face,' I said. 'Good job I'm one of the good guys, eh?'

Scott glanced once more at his friends, then turned and rested his forearms on the counter. He clasped his hands. 'What exactly was it you wanted to know?'

'The circumstances behind Helena's disappearance,' I said.

'You're a detective, surely you've read all about it?'

I didn't mention that I'd only learned about Helena last night, or that at the time I'd called him I'd been clutching at straws. 'There's a difference between what's reported in the papers and what really happened.'

'You think I had something to do with her going missing?'

'No, Scott. If that was the case we wouldn't be having this friendly chat.'

His gaze flicked back to his friends and I noticed his fingers entwine to stop them shaking. Good. I'd finally gained his full cooperation. I dropped the tough guy act, pulling from my pocket the various pieces I'd put together. I placed the photos of Jay and Nicole down, then the poster with Helena on it. Finally, I unfolded the clipping I'd taken from the newspaper last night and laid out Ellie Mansfield's image beside the rest.

'You notice anything about those pictures?'

Unfolding his hands, Scott touched the one of his wife, then his fingers did a slow dance over both Nicole and Ellie's faces. 'They look like they could be sisters,' he admitted.

'Not sisters,' I corrected, 'but the same woman at different ages.'

To prove my point, I lined them up: Ellie, Nicole and then Helena.

He pursed his lips, studied them again. 'Yeah,' he breathed quietly.

Then his gaze went to Jay Walker. He said, 'I can see what conclusion you're drawing from the disappearance of the others, but what about her?'

The term *collateral damage* went through my mind, but instead I said, 'Wrong place, wrong time. I think she was taken because she just happened to be with Nicole.'

'Who is the kid?'

'Did you hear about the robbery-homicide a few days ago?'

'The one at Peachy's gas station? Yeah, but I thought everyone there died.'

'So did everyone else. But then Ellie's family came forward and said Ellie was accompanying the Corbin family. It looks like the girl was snatched by whoever murdered them.'

'Jeez . . .' Scott's hands folded again, and there were tears in his eyes. I figured that with Nicole and now Ellie going missing it meant that Helena could have been used and discarded by her abductor, and I believed that Scott had come to the same conclusion.

I felt bad for forcing the idea on him, but the more I thought about it, the more weight it held.

'Are you taking this idea to the cops?'

'No,' I admitted. 'Not yet. It's only a theory and I could be way off-track. The truth is I don't know if any of it's connected. That's why I need to hear about how Helena disappeared.'

Scott surprised me by clicking his fingers. 'Like that,' he said. 'One minute she was there, next she was gone.'

Our conversation, or perhaps the intrusion of the loud click, caused the stocky guy to stir. He groaned and placed a hand on his head, his blunt fingers measuring the egg on the side of his skull. He swore, but that was to be expected.

'Gimme a minute, huh?' Scott got up and went to his friend. 'OK, Burt, take it easy. I had this guy all wrong.'

'Son of a bitch got me with a sneaky punch . . .' said

Burt, struggling up to a seated position. 'I see him again I'll show him I'm not one to be fucked with.'

Then he noticed me sitting there and shut up. He looked at Scott, his eyes wide, then rolled his head to take in their other buddy who was still out for the count.

'Rob's fine. He'll be OK when he's slept it off,' Scott said.

'What the hell happened?'

'Like I said, I had this guy all wrong. He's not another parasite who's after money.'

At Scott's words I took a look around the trailer. Judging by the poor state of repair, the cheap TV and accoutrements, there wasn't much in the way of cash in the Blackstock household. To think that some private dicks had tried to play on his grief and worm cash out of him made me feel a little sick.

Scott passed a mug of cold coffee to his pal. 'When you're done with that, check on Rob, OK? Me and Hunter are still talking business and don't want him going off on one when he wakes up.'

When Scott returned to the counter and sat down, I prompted him. 'You said that Helena just disappeared?'

'Yeah, she was walking into Indian Wells to fetch some groceries. She never made it there. When she didn't get back, I drove in and had a look around but no one had seen her.'

'You drove in, but Helena walked?'

'She couldn't drive and I was sleeping off a hangover. The boys had been over and we'd been playing poker. You know how it is, man.'

'Had you argued?'

'First thing the cops asked. No. We didn't argue. We were good together. Son of a bitch! You know what the cops suggested . . . that I was no good and Helena had finally seen the light and had upped and left me while she had the chance.'

'They don't seem to take missing persons reports very seriously,' I said.

'Same with your girls, is it? The cops just brushed it off?'

'At first, but I spoke with a cop last night. Officer Lewin. He seemed OK.'

Burt, listening from his end of the trailer, chose then to intrude. 'Lewin? He's an asshole like all the other cops. He ran me in on a driving under the influence charge.'

'Were you drunk?' I asked.

'Yeah, but . . .'

I didn't say anything more and he finally got the message.

He lifted both palms. 'Ignore me. I'm not here, OK?'

Just about then the other man, Rob, began to come round, and Burt helped coax him back to lucidity with a whispered warning not to try my patience again. Rob seemed content to sit cradling his head in his palms.

'So . . . there was no reason you can think of for Helena to leave you? You were good together. No other guy? No other girl with you?'

Scott shook his head sadly. 'People take a look at us, see poor white trash, and think we go round humping anything that moves. It wasn't like that with me and Helena. We loved each other. I still love her.'

'I had to ask,' I said. 'But it's behind us now. Next obvious question . . . did you and Helena have any enemies?'

'None to speak of.'

'What about anyone giving Helena the eye? You know the type I'm talking about. She wouldn't have to reciprocate for them to show an interest.'

'I occasionally caught some of them Injun boys giving her the glad eye, but that was about it. They wouldn't have done anything about it, they knew better than to mess around with me.'

Yeah, the back-up his *boys* offered made him a real force to be reckoned with, I thought sourly. Like they were going to put off anyone determined to catch Helena's attention.

'Anything out of the ordinary happen before or after Helena disappeared?'

'What, like a ransom demand? No, nothing.'

I was floundering a little, not quite sure where to go with the questioning. I'm not much of a detective and right then I could have done with Rink or Harvey along: someone who knew how to conduct a real interview. It struck me again that I was tugging at a few loose threads – probably unconnected – and trusting too much in the coincidence that three of the missing four girls looked alike. But then again, coincidences do happen, and they often interlink to become synchronicity. And synchronicity can affect the eventual outcome of incidents in the real world. From his bunk, Rob muttered something. Scott and I looked his way, and he stood up and ambled towards us, hanging on to the trailer wall for support. 'You're forgetting about the Logans, Scott. Why not tell him about those crazy Logan boys?'

'The Logans?' I echoed. 'Yeah, Scott, why don't you tell me about them?'

He did.

Before he was even halfway through his story I was itching to get on my way.

The Logans – those *crazy* Logans – were definitely due a visit, and, judging by their local legend, I was pleased that I hadn't wasted any bullets on Rob or Burt.

9

Jay woke up in a strange place. Stranger than even the two places she'd awakened in the past two mornings. For the briefest of time she'd no memory of how she'd got to this new place and she lay there, attempting to make sense of her surroundings. Above her was a ceiling so close that should she reach out with her fingertips, she would scrape her nails on the corrugated tin sheets. Spider webs clung to the grooves, old and dusty, and here and there corrosion had nipped at the edges of old nail holes to widen the gaps. Through the holes she could discern the pale blue of a sun-bleached sky. To both sides of her were walls made of timber that smelled faintly of creosote, and if she could see that far in the dim light she was sure that a similar wall would enclose the far end.

The heat was stifling.

She could barely breathe.

Panic struck and she tried to throw her hands out, to push up on the tin sheets, but a rope had been tied to each wrist and passed beneath her lower back. She struggled in vain to pull free, but all that she gained was chafed skin and less oxygen. Her heart hammered in her chest and she realised that she had to concentrate, to stop herself from hyperventilating, or she would pass out again and then she would be no use to anyone.

That random thought brought everything flooding back to her, all of the memories crashing down on her like an avalanche. She decided the crushing feeling in her chest was the weight of all she'd endured until she understood that she was still straining against the rope and it was actually the pulling of her overtaxed muscle fibres.

Finally she sank down, making an effort now to subdue her frantic breathing, to calm herself. But it wasn't easy.

She recalled the incident at the gas station all those days ago, and the subsequent chase by the mad men in the pick-up truck.

'Why didn't I just keep my fat mouth shut, Nic?'

Her words came back to her, and not for the first time either, because never had a sentiment proved more exact. It was wholly unjust that she'd been so right then whereas her next statement had turned out so wildly wrong: 'I won't let anything happen. I promise.'

The second she'd seen the pick-up truck materialise from the heat haze she'd known they were both in big trouble. Nicole had known it as well, but had placed her faith in Jay to get them out of it. The problem was her promise had been empty: she'd no idea how she was going to stop the men from catching them.

As the truck had speeded up, Jay told Nicole, 'Call nine-one-one, Nic. Tell the police what's happening and to get here as quickly as possible.'

Nicole tried, but with no luck. 'I can't get a signal, Jay. We're out in the desert... there's no network coverage!'

'Keep trying,' Jay said. Beside her, Nicole bounced in the seat, her frustration at her cellphone manifesting itself upon her features so that she looked like she was about to implode.

'It's no use!'

The pick-up loomed in the rear-view mirror, growing exponentially so that all Jay could see was the front grille of the large truck. Momentarily Jay thought they were going to be pushed off the road and in reflex she jammed down hard on the gas pedal, winning them a few seconds' respite as their car surged forward.

'Oh God, oh God,' Nicole cried like it was a litany.

'Strap in tight, Nic,' Jay yelled. 'I think things are going to get worse.'

'Why are they chasing us? What have we done to them?'

'They don't need a reason. They're just crazy!'

As though to prove the point, the driver of the pick-up pulled alongside them, driving parallel in the opposite lane, and it was a good job that the road was otherwise deserted or they'd risk a head-on collision. From the passenger window leaned the young man with the straw-like hair. He was slamming his palms on the outside of his door and yelling obscenities. Jay yelled back, but that only caused the young man to lean out further and reach for her, as if intent on tugging her out of the window. Although it was practically impossible for him to do so, Jay reacted by swerving away, and her offside wheels went off the road and into the soft sand of the shoulder. The SUV was sturdy enough to power through the grit, but it was still enough to cause the steering wheel to judder and almost rip out of Jay's hands. Beside her, Nicole screamed in terror.

'Call the police, Nicole!'

'I'm trying but it's still no good!'

Jay yanked on the wheel, sending the SUV back on to the carriageway and again the pick-up truck hastened towards them. It was so close that Jay could have reached out and touched the hole where a wing mirror was once fixed.

She snatched a glance at Straw Hair and wished she hadn't. He had pulled out a gun and was aiming the shining steel barrel directly at her face.

'Pull over, bitch, or I'll ventilate your goddamn head!'

In response, all that Jay could think to do was scrunch her head down into her shoulders and keep on going as fast as possible.

The pick-up continued to parallel them, easily matching them for speed. Jay wished that a huge rig would come from the other direction and smash the crazy men off the road, but she could see way across the desert and nothing moved except their racing vehicles.

'Last chance, bitch. Now stop the goddamn car!'

The boom of the gun was so close that Jay expected to be dead in the next instant. She even pictured the hot bullet taking out the side of her face and spraying blood and brain matter all over Nicole. When she tore her gaze from the road ahead, she saw that the man was already lowering the gun so that the next shot wouldn't be fired into the sky.

'OK! OK! Take it easy. I'm pulling over.'

From beside her Nicole's voice was plaintive. 'You can't stop, Jay. They'll kill us.'

'They're only trying to frighten us. They'll just do what they have to do, then leave us alone once they've had their fun.'

'Jay, for God's sake, don't stop! You know what kind of fun those beasts are after . . .'

'What else can I do? If I don't stop they're definitely going to kill us, Nic.'

And that was how she'd ended up here, in this coffin-sized structure, covered over with a tin sheet which she now recalled had been wedged over her and then chained down.

Before this, there had come two horrendous days that she could hardly bear to contemplate. Except the memories kept on coming, little snippets of terror and humiliation that stacked up in her mind, threatening to topple her into an abyss of endless torture.

Forced to stop, Jay had foolishly wound up the windows and locked the doors of the SUV while Nicole continued her fruitless task of attempting to call the police. Straw Hair smashed the window nearest Jay with the butt of his pistol and jammed the barrel under her ear. 'Get outta the goddamn car.'

Jay was dragged on to the road and thrown down on

her knees. Straw Hair straddled her back, holding her between his legs as he shouted to the older cowboy.

'Quit your hollerin',' the cowboy yelled back. 'I've got her.'

Straw Hair gripped the back of Jay's head and she felt the cool steel of his gun alongside her jaw. Something inside forbade her to fear her own fate: she was too busy worrying about Nicole.

In the next instant her friend was forced to the ground beside her, the cowboy pushing her belly down on the dusty road. Nicole looked across at Jay, her eyes bottomless holes of despair.

'I'll get us out of this . . .'

'You won't do a goddamn thing, little miss,' Straw Hair growled. The clicking of the hammer going back on his gun was super-amplified in Jay's senses.

There was a crack and a flash, followed by interminable blackness, and this time Jay really did think she was dead.

When she woke up that first time, it was in the back of her father's SUV. Straw Hair was driving, following the pick-up truck along a dirt trail. Beyond the windows, huge weather-worn mesas dominated the sky, but Jay barely noticed them. Crouching over her was a third man, who reminded her of the gargoyles that decorated the rooflines of Gothic cathedrals. He was broad and squat, with greasy black hair slicked back from a bulbous forehead. His pig-like eyes were small beads of light enfolded in puffy eyelids, and his mouth was a slack gash that showed yellow teeth as he grinned down at her. She hadn't been mistaken back at the gas station. She recalled seeing a bent shape slipping from the pick-up and approaching the family in the station wagon. Looking at him, you could be forgiven for concluding that the man was of low intelligence, but Jay didn't think that was the case. The way in which he stared down at her, the inner turnings of his mind were painted clearly on his features, and Jay knew that of the three crazy men, this one should be feared most.

'You're awake? Brent must have hit you hard with his gun . . . you've been out for more than an hour.' The man wasn't showing any remorse, merely stating a fact.

Jay now knew that Straw Hair – or Brent – had knocked her out and didn't have to feel the large lump on her skull for confirmation. All that she was concerned about was the whereabouts of her friend, because Nicole wasn't in the SUV with them.

'Where's my friend?'

'Hush now,' the gargoyle said. 'You don't have to worry about her. She's with Carson.'

Carson must be the name of the older cowboy. 'What is he doing to her?'

'Why, giving her a lift, of course. What do you expect? Now don't you worry, he's treating her like a princess.' The man smiled, reminding Jay of a toad. 'And don't you worry about yourself, miss. A princess needs her handmaiden to be treated with the same amount of respect.'

'Why are you doing this?' Jay croaked. 'Where are you taking us?'

'We have to take you back to where the princesses belong.'

Princesses? Jay looked through the gap between the front seats and could see a leg, too thin and dainty even to be Nicole's. The man leaning over her made it difficult to see further, but for a second he jiggled to one side and Jay craned forward. In the passenger seat a small figure turned its face towards hers. A teenage girl blinked back at her in a mix of shock and dismay. The girl couldn't speak. She'd been gagged by gaffer tape wound round her head, but she conveyed the bleakness of their situation through her horrified stare.

Now, lying bound in this sheet metal and timber coffin, Jay recalled the young girl's look. She had been seeking help from Jay, and Jay had returned a look of her own that spoke a silent promise. The only thing was, until now, there had not been a damn thing she could do to help. Plus, the prospects of anything changing in the future were scant.

Yet she must try.

Nicole and the girl were relying on her.

Jay screamed . . . but that was about all she could do.

10

In hindsight, I should have gone to the police, perhaps asked them to check things out, but I'm not the most patient of types. Not when the buzz of adrenalin kicks in and I have the scent of a trail. My impulsive nature took hold of me and I drove out into the desert, taking with me a four-litre jug of water, my newly purchased gun and lock-knife and very little else that would keep me alive in the wilderness. I had brought my belongings from the hotel: a change of clothes, as well as the paperwork I'd come armed with, but that was it. In my defence, I was only following a lead that might turn out to be nothing, and thought that within a few hours I'd be back at Scott Blackstock's trailer reporting a dead end. I didn't know how woefully misinformed that assumption would turn out to be.

Prompted by his buddy, Rob, Scott had told me about the run-in he'd had with the family who owned a homestead out in the desert, and how one of the Logan men had shown an unhealthy fascination with Helena, and had gone as far as pawing his wife's hair before Scott had intervened. They'd been drinking in a bar that was frequented primarily by a local Native American contingent, but Scott and Helena were regulars and had been accepted into the community. The Logans were a different story: when they entered the dimly lit bar room, the promise of unrestrained violence in the air became palpable. The Logans made no secret of their dislike for their Navajo and Hopi neighbours, and made it plain with their unchecked insults and racial slurs. Some of the local men might have stood up to them, but they knew it was a pointless exercise, and one that would bring them further trouble. They took the Logans' belligerence, kept their heads down and hoped they'd pick on someone else.

That was when, uninvited, they had joined Scott and Helena at their table.

'Guys,' Scott had tried, 'you mind? Me and my wife are trying to have a little privacy here.'

'We don't mind,' their elected spokesman said. All three Logans sat down, the spokesman, Carson, slapping a bottle of bourbon on the table top. 'You go ahead with what you were doing and pretend we aren't here.'

Scott and Helena shared a grimace. 'C'mon, guys. Give us a break will ya?'

'We ain't sitting with any of those savages.' Carson tipped his head at the other customers with a sneer. 'Besides, these are the best seats in the house.'

'They sure are.' Brent Logan leered at Helena, admiring the swell of her breasts beneath her white blouse in open disregard of Scott.

Scott glanced at Helena and could see the flicker of uncertainty in her eyes. He couldn't allow Brent to be so brazen without appearing a coward, but he'd heard rumours about these bad asses and didn't want the kind of trouble they could bring. 'C'mon, guys? We're only having a quiet drink, winding down. There's plenty other places to sit.'

'Relax.' Carson splashed bourbon into glasses, shoved one across the table to Scott, and took up one of his own. 'Have a drink with us, man.'

Helena bumped Scott's thigh under the table. Scott got the message: she wanted to leave before things got out of hand. Scott was in agreement but couldn't see how he could do that without drawing the ire of the Logan boys.

Helena offered a plausible get-out. 'You're driving, Scott. You've had enough to drink already. We can't afford for you to lose your licence.'

Scott pushed the glass of bourbon back towards Carson. 'She's right. The cops have been after me long enough . . . don't want to give them a reason to run me in.'

Carson shoved the glass back again. 'One more won't hurt.'

Brent's eyes had fixed on Helena's face since straying up from her chest. His pupils dilated as he watched the play of light on her dark hair. He reached up with trembling fingers and pinched a bunch of his coarse blond mane. Scott's gaze flicked from him to Carson, then across at the third Logan. The stocky, dark-complexioned man merely returned the look, a faint smile playing about his thick lips.

'OK,' Scott relented, as he picked up the glass of bourbon. 'But just this one, OK?'

He downed the bourbon in one long gulp then stood up and reached a hand for Helena's. 'C'mon, babe, we'd best git going.'

'Sit down.'

Scott looked at Carson, but it wasn't he who had spoken. It was the dark one.

'I gotta go, buddy,' Scott said.

Carson slammed his empty glass on the table top. 'Samuel told you to sit down.'

Scott shook his head. 'Look, guys, I don't want no trouble, but me and Helena are leaving.' He pulled his wife up beside him, but Brent mirrored the action and stood directly in front of her. He was still teasing the strands of his thick hair. Brent mouthed her name, mimicking Scott: 'He-lena.'

'We just bought you a drink,' Carson said. 'It's only fair you do the same for us.'

'Fine.' Scott dug in his jeans pocket and pulled out a wad of dollars. He dropped them in front of the man. 'Get yourselves a drink on me.'

Samuel Logan reached for the small stack of bills, and scrunched them in his fist. He tossed them at Scott and they bounced off his chest and on to the floor. Scott stiffened. Helena's hand in his had also tightened up. 'C'mon, Helena, we're leaving.'

Brent stepped in front of Helena, while Samuel also came to his feet, blocking the other route around the table. Up close Samuel's face was a criss-cross of old scars like white threads in his sun-parched skin. His hands were lumpy, as though his fingers and knuckles had been broken many times and had failed to set properly.

'Oh, c'mon,' Scott said. In the bar room the buzz of conversation had dropped to a hush. All around them was a static charge, like ozone building in the atmosphere before a lightning storm. Some customers left hurriedly.

'You think you're too good to drink with us?' Carson asked as he refilled glasses.

'No, I don't. But like Helena said, I've already had too much and have to drive back to Indian Wells.' He looked at Brent, just as the young man let go of his hair and reached for Helena's. He pushed his fingers deep under her bobbed cut and cupped the back of her head. He pulled her towards him. Helena let out a gasp, at the same time as Scott grabbed Brent's wrist. 'Hey! Git your hands off my wife!'

Without warning Samuel lunged forward and slammed his curled fist into Scott's solar plexus.

The air whooshed out of Scott and he folded, his grip falling from Brent's wrist to the pain in his gut. Carson reached up and snagged a handful of his hair and pulled him across the table. With his other hand he splashed the glass of bourbon in Scott's eyes. Scott yowled word-lessly and tried to wipe the stinging liquor from his face. Distantly he could hear Helena shouting, and he knew that Brent was still holding her hair in his fist.

Carson forced Scott's right cheek against the table, using the leverage on his hair to hold him there. Scott struggled, but he'd no purchase with his feet to force himself backwards, and he felt Samuel's hammer-like fist jab him in his right kidney. Something silver flashed in his vision, and when he blinked some of the liquor from his eyes he saw that Carson had laid a revolver on the table alongside his face. There was a hubbub in the bar now as people fled for the exits. 'You really want to mess with us, boy?' Carson asked.

Before he could answer, Samuel pressed a cheek to the table so he could meet Scott's gaze. 'Do it. Say yes. I will make you hurt *everywhere.*'

'Jesus, God!' Scott's cry was because of the knuckle Samuel rotated into a nerve cluster on the side of his jaw. Scott had never experienced localised pain like it before. Words failed him, the noise coming from his mouth became an animal-like howl of agony.

Suddenly Samuel stopped pressing, and the grip on his hair was loosened: Scott reared back, his face flushed with anger and shame, and not a little fear. Carson slid the gun into his shirt front. When Scott searched for Helena he saw her a few feet away, and Brent taking a step back. Samuel had sat down again.

Two state troopers had entered the bar.

They stood silhouetted in the doorway. One of them had his hand on the butt of his sidearm.

'There a problem in here?' the trooper called.

Scott glanced at Helena again, giving a subtle shake of his head. Her face was pinched with fear, and a clump of hair stood out from the side of her skull from where Brent had held her. She smoothed it back quickly.

'No problem, Officer,' said the bar manager coming out from wherever he'd been hiding since the Logans entered. 'None at all.'

The state troopers strode further inside. They were no fools, and they surveyed the small group arranged around the table, eyes slipping from one to the next. But they also knew that they were on to a loser if they expected anyone here to come clean about what had just happened. These kinds of bars, these kinds of people, they knew to keep their mouths shut and their problems to themselves.

'See that things stay that way,' said the trooper with his hand on his gun.

The other, reading the probable cause of the situation, pointed at Scott and Helena. 'You two . . . I think it's best that you get yourselves home.'

Scott saw the opportunity and snatched it. He took Helena by her elbow, whispering a warning to stay quiet, and led her towards the exit. Brent stood aside for them, allowing them to move past him, but he held Scott's gaze. 'You're a pussy, Scott,' he whispered. 'And you don't deserve such a fine-looking woman as Helena. She'd be far better off with me.'

Those were the words that told me the Logans were likely suspects in Helena's subsequent disappearing act, little more than a fortnight after the incident in the bar. Scott had related the details to the police who were tasked with investigating her disappearance. However, the cops hadn't placed much credence in Scott's abduction theory. In fairness, they'd visited the Logans and made a cursory inspection of their property but had found nothing untoward. The family had all offered alibis that they backed up for one another. On their own, those alibis didn't hold water, but they'd also got corroboration from a third party. Their friend, Doug Stodghill, a mechanic from Holbrook, swore that the Logans had all been at his auto shop working on their pick-up truck at the time Helena had walked into Indian Wells. The police suspected that Stodghill was lying, either on the Logans' behalf or under threat, but with little else to go on, and no proof of a crime, their line of inquiry fell flat.

I wondered if, since the robbery and shooting at Peachy's gas station, the Logans had entered the frame of inquiry and if I was perhaps stepping on the toes of the local law enforcement community by driving out to their homestead. If that was the case, then tough; because I wasn't going to give up on Jay, Nicole and now Ellie Mansfield so easily, the way that the cops had on Helena Blackstock.

11

The heat had grown stifling, so much so that Jay's clothing was soaked through and chafing her skin. She was very thirsty, her mouth sticky with foamy saliva that worked to seal her lips shut. The ropes that bound her wrists were shrinking, or her hands were swelling, and causing intense pain. Jay imagined that the circulation had been cut off completely and soon her flesh would necrotise and drop off her bones. She had not realised it earlier but her ankles were also bound together, though only loosely so that she could walk if needs be, but would be unable to run. Not that there was much chance of either in this box.

She kicked up with her feet. At the far end of her tomb-like prison the tin sheets buckled slightly, but that was all. A chain had been fastened over the roof and held it in place. Testing the tin sheets with a shoulder, she'd found that they were chained down in two further places: no way could she force her way out without leverage. The sturdy wooden sides had resisted her attempts to kick the planks loose, and now that she thought about it, she believed they had been buried below the surface of the desert to strengthen them. The roof was level with the ground outside, but at least it hadn't been covered by sand. Light spilled inside through the old nail holes, like thin lasers that she feared might burn her exposed flesh.

She had no conception of time. She did not know how long it had been since she was placed in this coffin and left to stew in her own juices; she did not know if her captors were ever going to release her. Only the fact that they hadn't fully concealed her prison gave her some hope.

But if they were coming back for her, that gave her a new sense of urgency. If she was ever going to escape and bring help for Nicole and the girl, then she needed to do something quick.

Earlier she'd screamed and pleaded, then demanded that she be released; now she held her peace, because she did not want to face the men again. Fancifully she'd thought of them as characters from *The Wizard of Oz*, but twisted into evil caricatures. The brainless idiot with the yellow hair could only be the Straw Man. The cold and heartless cowboy, he was the Tin Man. The third one, squat and ugly, was the Wizard himself. He was a sham, a fake, but worse than that: something evil and demented lurked beyond the curtain he hid behind. What did that leave her: the Cowardly Lion? She joked about living dangerously, but up until now she hadn't shown that she was prepared to do so. She needed to get a grip, she realised, grow some balls as her dad would say, and get them all out of here.

Lying on her back, bound as she was, she could achieve nothing. But that was only an excuse.

She looked at one of the pinpricks of light, and then twisted on to her side so that she could probe the hole in the tin with a fingertip. Her fingers were almost numb, but she could feel a burr of sharp metal. It was corroded and brittle but would it be enough?

Jay rocked sideways, then allowed herself to roll over on to her belly. The position severely limited any hope of offering resistance if her captors returned for her, but there was nothing else for it. With the pressure off her ropes she was able to manipulate her arms and she drew in some of the slack until it was bunched next to her right fist. She began rubbing the rope against the metal burr, taking it easy, though desperate to move faster, so that she didn't break it off. Perspiration flooded from her hair, streamed down her face and invaded her eyes. She squeezed her lids tight, because there was no need of vision at that moment.

While she laboured, struggling for each breath, she recalled what happened after she was brought to this place in the desert, though the memories boiled through her mind in an incoherent jumble. She had to concentrate before she could bring them into order.

The teenaged girl was carried from Jay's dad's SUV by the young man with blond hair, Brent. She remembered his name with a stab of revulsion. She was led by the gargoyle, both her wrists enclosed in one big hand. While she was pushed towards a decrepit wooden shack, she squirmed round, looking for Nicole. Her friend was unconscious and lying over the lanky cowboy's shoulder as he strode from the pick-up towards an equally decrepit house half-concealed beyond a zephyr of dusty air. 'Nicole!'

Her captor's spare hand clamped hard over her mouth, muffling her next yell as he rasped in her ear. 'Make another sound and I assure you it will be a scream of pain.'

Jay peered about frantically, wondering why his warning had been so explicit. Was it because they were in earshot of a neighbouring property? She doubted that very much. All she could see beyond the ill-kept homestead were wind-scoured mountains and strangely shaped rock formations. To think the beauty of the desert was what had brought her and Nicole out here in the first place. Now all it denoted was a barren hell-scape. As though the man had read her mind, he said, 'There's no one within twenty miles of here. I just don't like people shouting round me. Screams I'm fine with.'

He forced her to the shack and through the door. Inside was even shabbier than the disintegrating boards outside. It was dark, although strips of light punched through chinks in the walls allowing a strobe-like perusal of the interior. It smelled dry and musty, underlain by the bitter tang of corroding metal. Old tools and implements hung from the wall at the far end and a large wooden bench dominated the centre of the space. Rusting chains hung from worm-holed beams, from which dangled dusty cobwebs. Another chain lay in a loose coil on the floor, attached to one of the sturdy bench legs, large steel bolts fixing it to the wood. At one end was a half-moon of thick leather, hinged where it met the chain link. Jay's vision fixed on it and she began to shake her head furiously.

Her captor spun her, slapping her hard across the face with a hand that was as hard as steel, and she almost blacked out. While she slumped at the knees, the man danced round her and hauled the chain off the floor. Jay felt the two horns of leather clasp round her throat, forming a tight collar. Before she could pull free, the man snapped some kind of hasp shut and secured it with a padlock.

When he stood back from her Jay wilted, going all the way down to the floor as her hands came to the collar. Within the leather she could feel iron: no way on earth could she pull it free.

'I need to go and help with your friends, Nicole and Ellie. Be good, do as you're told, and maybe I'll bring you food and water. The choice is yours.'

With that ominous warning, the man had walked out without a look back. Jay knew why: he had no immediate interest in her. But was he as engrossed with Nicole and Ellie as his two crazy friends? She thought not. His gaze fell on them with a different hunger.

The night had been long in coming.

Jay tested her bonds but they were solid. She thought about demolishing the bench, but it resisted her efforts. The chain was old but strong. She couldn't reach any of the tools on the wall. Finally she'd fallen asleep on the warped floorboards as insects and rodents scuttled among the filth.

A scream woke her.

'Nicole!' she'd yelled in response, because her friend's howl had been tinged with terror. 'Nicole? *Nicole?*'

There was no reply and all went quiet again.

Panting she'd crouched on the floor, pulling futilely on the chain where it was bolted to the bench. She rubbed the skin raw on her palms. But she kept on tugging.

What in God's name was happening in the house? She didn't want to imagine the scene but she couldn't help it: Nicole writhing in agony beneath the beasts as they tore off her clothing and invaded her most private places.

When she heard Ellie scream she vomited on the floor. 'No . . . no . . . no . . .'

She'd wept.

She woke up without any awareness of having slept. Daylight poked tremulous fingers through the chinks in her prison walls. In darkness she'd been spared much of her prison's appearance, and now she would have preferred for night to fall again. In this weird half-light she was reminded of a haunted house, and every shifting shadow, every creak of wood or shuffling animal became a demonic creature coming to drag her down to hell.

A plate with some scraps of meat and beans sat on the floor next to her. A spoon had been thrust into the food. There was a chipped jar containing water. A bucket so she could go to the toilet. She resisted them all, until thirst won out and she gulped down the tepid water. It was only after downing the water that she realised that, at some point in the night, one of the monsters had come to her. She'd lain there oblivious while he'd stood over her. The thought made her skin crawl.

She again fought her chain, with less success than before. Her palms became a mass of weeping blisters. She wept too.

She must have slept again because the next thing she knew the gargoyle was back. He grabbed at her hands, inspected them with an angry expression. He struck her in the face again. 'You are an ungrateful bitch. I tried to make you as comfortable as possible, and this is how you've repaid me?'

'Please. Why are you doing this to us? You have to let us go.'

He struck her again, using his curled fist to jab her under the ribs. Jay collapsed on the floor, her arms wrapped around the scalding white heat in her body. Never in her life had she been hurt in such a way. But it was only the start. His fingers dug under her ribs again, probing at the point where her liver nestled, and if she thought that the punch was awful she had to think again. Not that she could string a coherent sentence together, and managed only a groan of agony that had her lips buzzing.

Next the man moved to her neck. She tried to pull away but there was no strength in her. He unlocked the leather collar from her throat, but it was no relief, because in the next instant he'd spanned her neck and sunk his fingertips into the nerves under her ears. Pain jabbed to the tip of her jaw and she drooped in his grip. The man adjusted his hand and now his fingers dug into her carotid arteries. Thankfully she did not experience pain this time, only the billowing black wings of a vulture fluttering through her mind.

When next she opened her eyes she was lying in the wooden coffin set in the desert floor and all three men were standing over her. Each held aloft a tin sheet and a chain. They were talking amongst themselves but she couldn't make out their words. Someone was wailing and at first she thought it was Nicole or the girl.

'Shut up!'

Blinking up at the trio of ogres standing over her, she realised the command had been snapped at her. She was the source of the wailing. She shut up, tried to lift her arms to plead with them but found her wrists had been bound beneath the small of her back. She tried to sit up.

Brent leaned into the box and forced her down with a boot heel.

'Do not move, goddamnit!'

Jay opened her mouth to beg, but knew that these pitiless monsters would only punish her for it.

'We can't trust you to stay put in the shack,' the cowboy said, adjusting his hat with the swipe of his wrist. The chain dangling from his fist rattled like a viper's warning. 'So we're moving you here. Now, if you prove yourself, then perhaps we'll let you out. But—'

The gargoyle interjected, 'Try to escape and I'll do worse to you than you've already suffered.'

Carson – that was the cowboy's name she recalled – chuckled at his friend's bluntness. 'By God, Samuel! Say it like it is, why don't ya?'

'She's got to learn to behave,' he said as though talking about a naughty schoolgirl.

The tin sheets had been piled on top, sealing her in, and Jay lay in stunned silence as the chains locked her in position. Her mind was in a state of close-down. Shock, she realised.

Only when the faint strains of screaming filtered into her prison did she vocalise her terror, but this time on behalf of her friend and young Ellie.

Perhaps it was her screaming that overtaxed her, because she'd drifted then into Stygian darkness and had known nothing until waking, disoriented and bewildered, this morning.

Now, with those memories pulsing in her skull with each beat of her heart, she rubbed the rope on the shard of tin, growing ever more furious at her own ineptitude as for the third time she heard the screams of terror drifting on the desert wind.

12

I found the landscape stunning and surreal at the same time. A breeze was cutting across the valley from the north-east, causing a blanket of umber sand to obscure much of the first hundred feet or so at the bases of the mountains. From the low vantage of my GMC their crowns seemed to grow from the billowing dust, huge edifices sculpted by the elements. They had to be ancient ranges, now stripped of their outer shells that lay in a jumble of boulders at their feet displaying their immortal hearts. Strata laid down during different epochs banded the cliffs in myriad colours and textures the likes of which an artist could never conceive. Further to the north was what the Navajo had termed the Painted Desert: if this little-known area was anything to judge by, then that Mecca for tourists must have been truly remarkable.

Scott Blackstock had given me directions to the Logan homestead, but had also said that he'd never been there so couldn't describe its layout. Apparently there was only one road in and out, but I detected dozens of minor trails leading through the hills, in older times probably traversed on horseback or foot. I suppose he was referring to an actual highway, because other than the compressed dirt I currently drove over there were no maintained roads. I was off the beaten track: a term that held significance here.

Since leaving the highway, I'd travelled the best part of twenty miles and knew that soon enough I'd have to abandon my vehicle. Not that I couldn't drive all the way in, but I didn't want to announce my arrival to the Logans. If indeed they had anything to do with the disappearance of the women, I wanted to discover that without them being aware of my presence. If there was nothing untoward then I'd leave them be. They sounded like arseholes, the type I normally went up against, but I couldn't indulge myself while the women were still missing.

Two miles out from their ranch, I drove the GMC into a steep gulley that was hidden from view to anyone on the road below. I left the keys in the ignition. I wasn't thinking about a quick getaway at the time, just being pragmatic. Should I never return to the vehicle, at least someone else might get some use out of it.

Taking a bearing off the sun, I headed due west, choosing to move steadily instead of jogging in. The water was a heavy weight in a rucksack on my back, but I'd secreted my weapons about my person. Within seconds I was lathered in perspiration, and glad that I'd driven here without the aid of the GMCs' air-con, because I was at least part-way acclimatised to the oppressive heat. Stepping out of a chilled vehicle into this temperature I'd have possibly keeled over in a dead faint. It wasn't quite Death Valley but near enough.

The going was easy on the road, but soon I veered off and entered the twisting canyons between the towering columns of rock. They weren't the labyrinth I had assumed, and I could regularly view the sun so kept on track. Here, though, the ground was littered with boulders and drifts of red dirt stripped from the mountainsides and I had to be more careful. Twisting an ankle didn't concern me, but making a noise did. Out here in the still desert, a falling rock would sound like a gunshot and alert anyone within a mile of my presence. Shaded by an overhang of rock, I chugged down an eighth of my water. It came nowhere near replenishing what had already soaked through my clothing and then evaporated into the overheated air. While there, I took out the Smith and Wesson revolver and checked it and each of the .357 shells thoroughly, for any grit or dirt that could cause it to misfire. Everything was in good order, but I was conscious that the firepower was limited. My usual guns, either a SIG Sauer P226 or 228, were automatics and could – depending on the magazine – lay down up to seventeen rounds without the need to reload. When I'd purchased this old-time gun from the rednecks at the truck stop it hadn't occurred to me to check for a rapid loader. I was going to have to feed each bullet into the six chambers manually every time I depleted the ammo.

Hell, it was as though I was preparing for a war. There were only three Logans, and two bullets aimed at the right places were enough for any man. Of course, the opportunities for perfect shooting were few and

far between in a real conflict, so maybe I'd need to
reload many times before they were finished. Then
again, that was assuming that the Logan family had
anything to do with the missing women. With luck
there wouldn't be any shooting, but I couldn't deny the
old Boy Scout in me.

I chugged down another eighth of the water, and
then took a leak against the rock overhang. I wasn't
marking territory, just detoxifying. When the container
was back in the rucksack on my shoulder, I set off again.
Passing beyond the ravines, I came on to a wide boul-
der-strewn plain dotted with mesquite and ironwood
shrubs. Scott Blackstock had told me to watch out for a
huge mushroom-shaped mountain that marked the
head of the trail before entering the Logan property.
There was a likely contender about half a mile ahead,
though through the dust I could only make out the
upper cap that shimmered through the haze like an
alien Mother Ship. Using it as a landmark, I followed
the northern edge of the plain, staying close to the
ragged mesas in case I had to go to ground in a hurry.
When I was parallel to the giant mushroom I turned
south, using the towering boulders as cover. The land
was parched, but judging by the way the mountains had
been weathered and the proliferation of boulders depos-
ited on the plain, I guessed that in some dim prehistoric
time flood waters had regularly teemed through here.

The sun was a milky disc in the heavens, high cirrus
giving it an indistinct appearance, but none of its heat
was diminished. Having lived in the subtropics of Florida

for the past couple of years I'd earned a decent tan, but it was no defence out in the desert. My exposed skin prickled, and the constant trickling of perspiration down the small of my back caused me to move my gun from my usual carrying position to the front of my jeans.

More water went into my gut; it didn't surprise me how much I'd consumed already. I'd fought in deserts before and knew that it was a constant necessity to replace lost fluids. What was sometimes neglected was the need to also replenish essential nutrients and salts, and I hadn't given that much thought before setting off. Already I could detect the first buzz of a headache behind my ears; as a result of dehydration it could progress to migraine proportions. Not that I foresaw a problem, because I'd no intention of wandering round in a furnace all day. I set off again, intent on reconnoitring the area, to determine if my hunch was right and then decide how I was going to play things after that.

The military are planners. Before a mission is launched every detail is analysed to the nth degree. It is then conducted with strict purpose with each problematic facet taken into account beforehand. Yet missions often fail due to the intrusion of a previously unidentified snag, usually the enemy responding in an unpredictable way. For that reason I wasn't a firm believer in forward planning: I'm not talking about going into a hazardous situation with my eyes closed, but with the knowledge that if something could go wrong it probably would. I was often in conflict with my commanders, but it was my arse, and often those of my friends, that were on the line, so I preferred to prepare for the unexpected by entering a mission firmly in the red zone. Expect to kill or be killed: that was the ethos I subscribed to. Therefore I only had one objective in mind: if the Logan family were holding the women, I would go in and rescue them whatever it took.

Mushroom Mountain loomed overhead as I approached the pass on to the Logan property. Up close it reminded me more of a petrified thick-trunked oak, only a hundred times as large. The road actually passed to the south of the mountain, but I took the path under the northern bulge. It abutted another lower line of rock that made a ridge in the desert floor. I considered clambering up to the ridgeline as it would offer me a better vantage point for viewing the homestead in the valley beyond, but didn't trust the ridge to extend as far as I needed it to. More than likely it would be split into fissures and separate rock formations as the fold petered out on to the Logans' land. I stayed close to the wall of stone instead and made steady progress. My assumption proved correct when in little under a hundred yards I saw that the ridge broke up into a series of rocks jutting from the orange sand like teeth in a crone's jawbone. The Logan land didn't benefit from fencing or any other boundary except from the rock formations that offered a natural crescent around them. The mountain range bordered a huge dust bowl many miles across and disappeared into the far heat haze. I wondered who had originally built their home there, and how they managed to exist in such an inhospitable place. There was no grass for grazing, certainly no crops, so how they had made a living seemed a mystery. In this modern era, the Logans would have other opportunities for revenue, but their forebears?

The answer presented itself soon enough. The ranch-style buildings were clustered on the northern shore of a shallow watering hole. From the desert floor bubbled an underground spring, a remnant of the time when this place was lush and vibrant, which must have offered life to people traversing the desert. Water was probably worth its weight in gold during the pioneering days. Whoever had lucked upon this spot and laid claim to it would have charged other travellers and their beasts to drink. Maybe they had also raised crops along the shoreline, but not now, because these days it was the home of tangled patches of prickly pear. The Logans didn't have to grow their own food when their pick-up truck could take them to civilisation in no time. They weren't farmers and neither were they the type interested in manual labour. At least, judging by the state of the buildings they had no interest in maintaining their property. Even their truck, a lifeline way out here, was scabrous and missing parts.

The pick-up should have been the least of my concerns, but I found my gaze straying to it again. It looked familiar, although I couldn't at first place where I'd seen the damn thing. Then it came back to me, how I'd been leaving the truck stop last night and was almost sideswiped by a pick-up missing a wing mirror. The jackass who was driving it had levelled a hail of foul language my way. I was certain that it was the same vehicle, and thought that even if they had nothing to do with Jay and the others' disappearance then maybe I'd be having words with the Logans after all. It was a ridiculous thought, but it was there, and it helped get my blood up.

What was the driver's purpose for visiting the truck stop?

There were many mundane possibilities but I wondered if he'd been there to check up on the local gossip, to determine if his family was being mentioned in connection with the murderous hold-up at Peachy's gas station only a few miles distant, or the subsequent disappearance of the three girls. Whatever his purpose was, it made me wonder again if there was such a thing as coincidence or if some unknown power was at work conniving to bring us into conflict. Maybe it wasn't chance that three missing females bore such similarities, or that a random visit to a truck stop in the middle of nowhere led me to make that link, not to mention placing one of the possible culprits in my sights at much the same time. Then again, it could all prove a pile of crap if my recce turned up nothing untoward.

The Logan family.

At first I'd assumed that they were brothers, but Scott had put me right. Carson was the elder, and father to Brent. The other, Samuel, was a cousin. Once there had been a couple of women living at the homestead: Brent's mother Arlene, and also Carla, Samuel's younger sister, but I was glad to hear that neither woman was there now. Arlene had passed away from throat cancer fifteen years back, while it was believed that Carla had headed for the West Coast and a new life just over a year ago. That, at least, was the story told to anyone who asked about the young woman. No one had heard from her since, but then most people tried to stay out of the Logans' business and didn't raise the subject very often.

It's shameful, I know, but there have been times in my life when I've hurt women. Not out of choice, but during the wild firefights I'd been involved in during my military days there had to have been some women injured if not killed. I wasn't proud of the fact, and had never intentionally targeted a woman or, God forbid, a child, and for that reason I was happy that neither Arlene nor Carla could fall into my sights if things did come unstuck with their menfolk.

From my position I could see a ramshackle dwelling of sun-bleached boards and shingles, and beyond it further barn-like structures in equal disrepair. There was a stockade at the back, empty of animals, and then a mound of junk and debris comprised mainly of deteriorating mechanical implements, empty plastic sacks and steel drums. An ancient wagon rested up on blocks, but now it was little more than a disintegrating feature of the landscape. The Dodge pick-up was drawn up at the front of the house, telling me that at least one of the Logans was at home, but there was no movement or sound to give them away.

Crouching behind a boulder that reminded me of a lion's head, albeit ten times the size, I downed some more water. Then, with half of it now gone, I replaced the container in my rucksack, but propped it in the shade in the lee of the rock. I'd made myself a promise earlier that I wasn't going to spend all day in this furnace but if I just stayed put and watched for an obvious sign that my suspicions about the family were true I could be in for a long vigil. For all I knew they were sleeping through the hottest part of the day, and I wasn't prepared to wait them out. Before setting off, I made another inspection of my weapon. Having already loaded my pockets with spare ammo, I was good to go.

That wasn't exactly true. I should let someone know where I was, because with the exception of Scott and his buddies, no one did, and I didn't trust them to race to my rescue if anything bad happened. I took out my cellphone, intent on dropping Rink a text message, but true to form there was no signal. At least I tried. I pocketed the phone again.

I was on my own but it wasn't the first time. Having Rink or Harvey at my back would have been a bonus if indeed this was a hot zone, but I hadn't confirmed that yet. I slipped out of concealment, and staying low and utilising the natural hiding places that the landscape offered, I headed for the homestead and into another desperate chapter of my life.

13

Long before the rope gave way, the sharp burr of tin plate blunted, caught in the strands and snapped off. Frustrated, Jay screamed into the ground, but would only allow an almost silent exclamation by pinching the sound in her throat. Though she rocked back and forth, straining against her ropes, she could not snap them. It was a pointless waste of energy, as was the way of anger. Better that she concentrate on finding some other protrusion to snag the rope on. It was a difficult search to undertake, bound the way she was, but by twisting and contorting and throwing one scapula almost out of joint, she discovered the protruding head of a bolt where the planks had been bolted together. No sharp point, but the threads were abrasive against her thumb. She had to lie on her side, hook the rope over the bolt then hurl all her weight towards the head of the grave. Not once, but over and over again. Jay set to a rhythm, jack-knifing open and closed, pulling at the strands of the rope with each jerk of her body. It was tortuous, but she felt a sense of impending success and set to the task with new fervour. If her captors suddenly threw back the lid of the coffin they'd probably think she was having a fit.

Exhaustion beat her.

Jay collapsed on her chest, sucking in air that felt as thick as oil. Pain flooded her arms and shoulders, burning like fire as her muscles cramped. She sobbed as she writhed against the agony.

This was hell.

Yet compared with the terror and humiliation and God knows what else Nicole and the girl were enduring it was nothing.

Ignoring the pain and the rebellion fronted by her cramping muscles, she went at the bolt again, ripping harder and harder. When she halted this time, gasping and sweating bucketfuls, she could feel that the rope had frayed and was almost eaten through. With a surge of energy she yanked her hands wider and felt the rope weaken. There was no sudden loosening, but she could feel each strand pulling free. She uttered a wordless groan, snatched at the free lengths of rope and applied concentrated effort on one point. Her arms sprang apart, the knuckles of one hand tearing as they struck the old bolt, but she didn't care. She was free!

Actually, she wasn't: her legs were still bound and she was chained inside the coffin-like structure, but that meant little now. At least she had hands to work with. First she untied the lengths still wrapped round her wrists. The surge of blood returning to her fingertips stung like crazy, but was also welcome. She twisted round on to her back again and fanned her hands over her chest, promoting circulation. If the structure had indeed been the size of a coffin she'd have been finished, but there was room to manoeuvre now that she had more mobility. She could pull her ankles towards her backside and it was only the task of a minute to undo the ropes there. With that done she took a moment to steady herself, because the trickiest phase of her escape plan still remained. As she lay, sucking in air, she understood that she didn't have time for this. She was putting off the real task.

Escaping through the tin sheets and the chains that held them in place wasn't the difficult part; it was doing so without alerting her captors to what she was up to. She had no idea how close they were to her prison, and any untoward noise might bring them running. She could just lie there, wait for them to open up the grave and then leap out at them like a vampire. Only that idea was just ridiculous. She had no way of fighting the men, and all she'd achieve would be a quick death. No, better to escape from the grave before they returned, make her way to civilisation and bring the police back. That idea died swiftly as well. Even if she was able to get away and to make it across the desert, her escape would be discovered before she could return with help. The men would murder Nicole and Ellie, then disappear. No, somehow, some way, she had to get out of her prison, release the girls and get them all to safety. To do so successfully would be a gigantic task for anybody, but both Nicole and the girl were relying on her, and Jay would rather die than not try.

She tested the tin sheets.

Although the chains held them in place when met

with direct pressure, Jay found that they were ineffective when sliding one sheet under the other. Thank God the corrugations ran vertically because if they'd gone horizontally then she'd have never moved them. She found she could gently move the sheet closest to her head until she'd made a space a little larger than a mailbox slot. Gratefully she sucked in fresh air, hot and stifling but still better than the stale atmosphere she'd been inhaling since God knew when. She listened, dreading a shout of anger as one of the men charged over to take hold of her, but the shout didn't come. Curling her fingers over the top edge of the tin sheet she pushed it further towards her feet.

When she'd cleared enough space she wriggled out the hole, peeping out like a groundhog alert to danger from above. She had been prone for so long that the blood rush made her woozy and her vision blackened at its edges. She clung to the tin sheets to avoid slipping back inside the coffin again. If she was to pass out then she doubted she'd get another chance at saving her friends. Fighting the rush, she pushed free with her shoulders, then grabbed at the orange earth to help claw her way out. All the while she listened for a shout of alarm.

Finally on her hands and knees she rearranged the tin sheets, closing the gap she'd made. The first her captors would know of her escape would be when they unlocked the chains, threw back the sheets and found only empty space. She'd love to see their faces. Then again, she'd rather never see any of them again.

Her limbs felt cramped and sore and it took her a

few steps before she fell into a rhythm that didn't threaten to pitch her on to her face. After all that time in near darkness the sudden intrusion of sunlight felt like needles piercing her retinas. She staggered away from her prison, heading for the only form of cover she could detect nearby. It was a mound of junk, master of which was an old lorry that had all but rotted away. Reaching the truck she moved round the rear of the cab so she could use the empty windows to peer back the way she'd come. Leaning against the corroded metal, the heat from it almost scorching her palms, she searched for any sign of movement between her and the cluster of wooden shacks. Nothing was apparent, but then she began to wonder about the men; Samuel in particular. Was this some new torture that he'd devised? Was he watching her from behind his stained curtain, allowing her the illusion of freedom before snatching it away from her once more? She wouldn't put it past the sadistic piece of crap to take pleasure from something like that.

Her gaze wandered from the ranch to the nearby pool of water. What she'd do for a mouthful of that was best not mentioned, but she knew she'd be chancing her luck to get there and back before she was spotted. Just the sight of the pool reminded her of how thirsty she was, and she wished now she'd kept her eyes on the ranch instead. It was such a temptation she could barely deny herself. She crouched, hands folded across her stomach, lids squeezed tightly as she pushed aside her own needs. An argument raged inside her; if she wanted to release Nicole and Ellie then she'd need all her strength and wits about her, and without water she had neither. But if she chanced sneaking to the watering hole and was seen then her plan was finished. She slowly opened her eyes; her mind was made up.

She needed water.

Stumbling around through dehydration she was no good to anyone. It was one thing growing balls as her dad said, but quite another doing anything with them when she was bone dry. If she could make it to the pool, quench her thirst, then she'd be in a much better position to help her friends. It was funny how she was now thinking of both Nicole and Ellie as friends; she didn't know the younger girl from Adam, had merely spent time as a captive alongside her during the trip back here, but already they shared a common bond that transcended that. Somewhere along the line Ellie had grown as important in her mind as her best friend was, and Jay would do anything to free them. After she quenched her thirst.

It had been eerily quiet for hours now. Not since last night when the sound of screaming had filtered into her prison had she heard proof that her friends were still alive. What if they were already dead? What if they'd been moved elsewhere? She didn't think that was the case because at no time had she heard the engine of the pick-up growl to life, or the commands of the men as they ushered her friends on to the flat-bed. She was certain that any of those sounds would have roused her from her sleep, exhausted as she'd been.

No, they were still inside one of those buildings, and most probably asleep if the men had left them alone. Perhaps they were tethered as she'd been her first night, and gagged so they wouldn't disturb their captors' rest. The bastards would want to be on top form for more partying tonight.

She needed water, but more than that she needed a weapon. There was no way she could match even Brent, let alone the cowboy or Samuel, in a physical confrontation. She didn't fancy her chances without a gun. Not that she knew the first thing about firearms, but surely they were easy enough to handle. She'd watched plenty of movies and was pretty sure she could figure out how to pull back a hammer and then squeeze a trigger. Could she kill, though? Before she'd have said no, have screamed no, but now it was different. After what those three had done to her and her friends she'd gladly exterminate the lot of them.

But all that lay around her was disintegrating paper, plastic drums and empty tin cans. Forget the weapon, go for the water. Maybe down by the watering hole she'd find a stone just the right size to fit in her palm.

Gathering herself, she leaned out past the front of the truck. It was a three-hundred-yard dash to the pool and ordinarily she could cover that distance in no time. However, here and now, stealth was her best option. Not that she was prepared to belly-crawl the entire way, but she had to stay low, moving from one piece of junk to the next. She lined up a mound of broken machinery about fifty yards away, decided that was an achievable first leg.

She rose up, ready to push herself hard, and that was when something detached itself from the rubbish pile behind her. She was only aware of movement, a sudden rush as the air was compressed between them, and then hands clamped on to her, one round her waist, the other shutting off the cry of denial she let loose.

Samuel, she realised. The sadistic bastard had been watching and waiting all along.

When she was dragged backwards, forced down on to the sand, she wasn't thinking about her own selfish needs any more, but how she'd failed her friends: how would any of them be saved now?

14

In this heat the body could lose approximately a litre of fluid per hour without you ever realising it, the perspiration evaporating from the skin and misting from your clothing. Without replenishment you'd be dead within twenty-four hours. I wasn't worried about me, but about the woman I saw poking her head out from under a stack of old corrugated sheeting. I'd no idea where she'd come from, maybe an old root cellar, or somewhere that stores were kept out of the sun, but it must have been hot in there going by the beetroot colouring of her face. From the furtive way she glanced around, she was fearful of detection, and unsure where to go next. I considered making a noise, to attract her attention, but that would only frighten her, maybe set her off screaming which would cause untold trouble. I kept quiet and watched as she clawed her way out from under the tin sheets, then carefully arranged them to conceal the fact she'd escaped via that route. Momentarily I wondered if it was the entrance to a passage that led back to one of the buildings, but gave the thought no further time to brew when the woman made a jerky run for the old flatbed truck near the rubbish tip. My mind went back to the necessity for water and I wasn't surprised to see her staring intently at the watering hole a few hundred yards distant. She was going to make a try for it, and if she did so she'd be spotted by the Logans, because what she didn't know and I'd only just noticed was that one of them was sitting in a rocking chair on the porch of the house. He'd been sitting so still that he'd blended in with the weathered boards, and if not for the fact he'd shifted to reach down and lift a jug to his lips, I might not have seen the man in the straw Stetson hat.

The woman was now squatting down, her hands pushing hard at her stomach. Experiencing cramps, I decided, from being confined for so long without nourishment. Even with her face twisted in agony, I recognised Jay Walker. She didn't look like she had in the photograph her father supplied to me. She was gaunt and pale, her dark auburn hair slightly longer in style, but now matted to her skull with a mixture of grime and perspiration. An ugly bruise marked her right cheek and her lips, swollen at one corner, looked dry and cracked. Red, angry bands ringed both wrists; it was obvious that she'd recently been bound there.

One thing I was sure of, she hadn't come here for a good time with the Logan boys: not of her free will. Jay had been snatched and held prisoner, and the likelihood was they were also holding Nicole, Ellie and maybe even Helena Blackstock. If that was so then it meant that the purpose of this mission remained the same as it always had been: go in, find the women, and get them all out safely. But, as I'd also known from the beginning, any plan was prone to collapsing in an instant. If Jay tried for the watering hole, the man on the porch would spot her and I'd have to kill the prick. I didn't mind that so much; the way I saw things, anyone who'd take the women like that deserved putting down. Only if I killed him it would alert his family to my presence and I dreaded to think what they'd do to their other hostages before I could get them out too.

It left me with no other course of action. I had to stop Jay from doing anything foolish, in silence and without attracting unwanted attention. I had to move silently and without alerting either of the possible witnesses: Jay might try to run, and the man would definitely raise the alarm. Luckily I had the pile of debris as cover and keeping low I made it all the way to the old truck without catching anyone's attention. With only seconds to spare I'd got there while Jay was still fighting the urge to quench her thirst. As she came up from her crouch, searching the area for a route to the water, I moved closer. I watched her rock back on her heels, readying herself, then just at the last moment I lunged forward and grabbed her round the waist to stop her rising. She was terrified, expecting the worst, and in all probability would have screamed if I hadn't clamped my hand across her mouth and pulled her backwards. I couldn't afford for her to thrash and kick out, for fear she hit the truck and the noise brought the Logans running. I turned her, so that she went down on her belly in the dirt, and stretched my weight over her to hold her in place. 'Take it easy, Jay, I'm not going to hurt you.'

My reassurance went unheeded. She fought me at first, thinking no doubt that I was one of the Logan men. In her mind I was one of the beasts who'd abducted her, and it would take a little longer for the truth to sink in. I rode out her thrashing, my hand clamped firmly over her mouth while I continued to whisper.

'Jay, it's OK. I'm not here to hurt you. I'm here to help you.'

When that still didn't work, I decided on a different tack.

'Do they have the other girls? What about Nicole? Ellie? Helena?'

Before I'd said the last two names there was a reaction. On hearing her friend's name she stopped struggling, almost as if she deflated and sank into the sand. I didn't trust her to react logically, and kept my hand firmly in place. 'I'm not one of the men who have hurt you. My name is Joe Hunter. I'm here to help you . . . nod if you understand.'

Jay nodded weakly.

'Good,' I went on. 'Your father sent me.'

I felt her shiver and realised that she was possibly assailed by mistrust. She'd suffered at the hands of brutal men, and now she'd been grabbed and forced face down in the dirt by another. I could be lying to her for all she knew. Maybe I was another of the Logan clan brought in to torment her further.

'Your father is Jameson Walker,' I told her. 'He owns a chain of fast food restaurants and is a big guy who dresses like someone from the Wild West. He has a fondness for whiskey and, Jay, your father loves you very much.' Jay sobbed. She convulsed against my palm, and mucus spattered from her nostrils. I relieved some of the pressure on her mouth, but still wasn't ready to release her. 'I have no way of proving any of this to you right now, but I can do it if necessary. I have papers he gave to me. If I was going to hurt you, I would have done so already. Do you understand? Nod, Jay. Nod if you understand me.'

She nodded.

'Do you trust me?'

Again there was a movement of her head.

'Good. I'm going to take my hand away and let you go, but you have to promise to be quiet. One of the Logans is less than two hundred yards away and will hear if you say anything. Will you keep quiet?'

My last question had been pointless, because already I had relaxed my hold and slipped my fingers from her lips. I felt her breath on my hand as she said, 'Yes.'

My weight had been holding her flat, but even as I eased away from her I could feel that she wasn't yet ready to move. She lay there, breathing shallowly as she tried to make sense of what had occurred. If anything she flattened further into the ground as relief flooded through her. Touching her gently on one shoulder I came back to my feet, but stayed in a crouch to peer over the rim of the flat-bed. From this angle I couldn't see the man in the Stetson, but I was sure he was still there on the porch.

Moving close to Jay, I indicated that she should speak very quietly. 'How many men are here?'

'I've seen three,' Jay said, and I was happy to hear there was only a trace of fear in her voice. 'They're brutes, every last one of them.'

'They're all here now?'

'Yes.' Jay then frowned, shook her head. 'I'm not sure. They locked me in that hole yesterday and I haven't seen them since.'

'There's one of them on the porch,' I began. 'He's wearing a straw hat.'

'That's the Tin Man.'

At my bemused expression, Jay gave a disparaging snort that was anything but laughter. She rolled up from the floor, on to one knee. 'That's how I think of him, the heartless pig! He's called Carson.'

'So the other two are Brent and Samuel?'

'Yes, they're the Straw Man and the Wizard.'

I understood her earlier nickname for Carson Logan then, but didn't comment on it. I was weighing up if I could get to Carson without giving myself away. If I could take him out quietly, then perhaps I could burst inside the house and drop the other two before they could hurt their captives. Ordinarily I'd have tried for it, but what if I failed and it was me who got killed? Where would that leave Jay and the others?

'Come on, we're leaving.'

Jay looked at me like I was an enemy. 'No way.'

'Come on, stay low and only move when I say so.'

'I'm not leaving without Nicole and Ellie.'

'They're both inside, Nicole Challinor and Ellie Mansfield?'

'I don't know the girl's full name,' Jay croaked. It was almost as if the admission was a miserable failing on her part.

'She looks a little like Nicole, almost as if she could be her younger sister?'

Maybe that hadn't struck Jay before, but the realisation was plain to see on her face now. 'Yes, she does look like Nicole. My God, I hadn't given that any thought. Is that why those monsters have taken them? What do they want with them?'

My best guess was for sexual gratification. Yet there had to be something deeper than that involved. Jay Walker was a beautiful woman, and if the Logans only wanted to rape their captives then she'd have been used like the others. I pictured Helena Blackstock and how much she looked like Nicole and Ellie. It was pretty obvious now that the Logans had been responsible for her abduction, and that they'd targeted her and their subsequent hostages due to a specific look. And that led me to the other woman who'd disappeared off the face of the earth: Samuel's sister, Carla. I wondered what she looked like, and if her sudden disappearance had anything to do with the subsequent snatching of the other women. Men directed by an unhealthy sex drive were bad enough, but I didn't like to think of where my mind was leading me: along a dirty path heading directly to a deep cesspit.

'I don't know,' I said.

Jay placed a hand on my knee. 'What did you say your name was?'

'Joe Hunter.'

'Are you a policeman?'

'No. I'm just someone your dad hired to find you.'

'A private detective?'

'Sort of. It's not important. Now come on, I have to get you out of here.' I knew from her questions she was trying to work on my sense of duty. I'd no shortcomings in that department, but I wasn't about to be swayed. 'Don't worry, Jay. I'm going to get Nicole and Ellie free. But I can't do that while you're out here. I can't leave you alone in case I don't make it.'

'I can help you—'

'You can barely see straight from dehydration. I'm taking you out of here and getting you something to drink.' I raised a hand to allay any further argument. Then, to add validity to mine, I cupped her face between my palms and stared into her eyes. 'Listen, Jay! Every second we waste here is a second closer to those bastards discovering your escape. Do you know what they'll do to the others if they think you've got away? Now, here's what we'll do. We're going to where I have water waiting for us. Then I'm taking you back to my car. Can you drive? Yes, of course you can, you were using your father's SUV. You will drive to the nearest place to call the police and get them here as soon as possible. I'll come back here. I promise I won't leave the girls to those monsters.'

Finally sense soaked into her parched synapses and she nodded gently in my hands. 'OK, OK, you're right, Joe.'

'Right. Let's go then, and stay low and only move when I tell you.'

Helping her to stand, I could detect her weakness, but, giving her her due, she steeled herself and moved quickly at my side to the far end of the junk pile. There we could stand a little straighter and I took hold of her hands and looked at her. 'Everything's going to work out fine, Jay. I know what I'm doing so you can trust me, OK.'

I've heard it said that pride comes before a fall. The fact that I was only offering reassurance to a trauma-tised young woman didn't matter, because the proverb rang true.

There was the metallic bang of tin sheets being thrown aside at much the same time as a shout of anger rang clear through the desert air.

15

Carson Logan was approximately midway between the house and the hole in which Jay had been held. He scanned back and forth, his gaze on the house, then on his cousin who still threw aside tin sheets even though it had to be obvious that the woman was no longer inside. From the cover of the junk pile I watched them both. The older man tilted his hat back on his head with a sweep of his thumb, as he hollered something akin to an animal's howl. The third member of the family appeared on the stoop, his hair sticking out in wild tufts, and I guessed he'd just been roused from a nap.

I glanced at Jay crouching beside me, her arms wrapped round her body, and saw that she was full of fear and loathing for the men, or rather for what they might now do. I regretted my earlier warning that the Logans would kill her friends if they discovered she'd escaped, and saw that she was now considering sacrificing herself to keep Nicole and Ellie alive.

'Don't move,' I said, more a command than a caution.

'If I go back they'll punish me, but at least they'll spare Nicole.'

'No,' I said. 'I won't let you do that.'

'I have to. You said it yourself, they'd kill them if they thought I'd escaped and could bring back the police.'

The revolver was in my hand and I thumbed back the hammer. 'Things were different then. If it looks like they're thinking along those lines I'll take the chance of killing them first.'

Jay's eyes widened as they fixed on the gun. 'Shoot them! Shoot them now!'

I was tempted. Maybe I'd even get Samuel and Carson, but the younger man, Brent, was out of my line of fire, not to mention too far away. If I ran out, started killing his kin, he'd barricade himself inside the shack and use his hostages as human shields.

'No, they only think that you've given them the slip. They don't know I'm here. I want to keep things that way for the time being. They're not going to kill Nicole and Ellie immediately; they'll try tracking you first. They think you've escaped on foot, so they'll expect to run you down in no time. Now come on, my first plan still stands . . . we just have to get back to the ravines over there without them seeing us.'

'I don't want to leave. If anything happens to Nicole . . .'

'The longer we wait here, the less time they have, now come on.'

Before she could argue further, I grabbed her elbow and led her quickly towards a stand of weirdly shaped rocks that reminded me of a huddle of gamblers over a roulette wheel. Pushing Jay before me, I glanced back to make sure we'd gone unseen.

'Brent, goddamnit boy, get yoursel' back in there and make sure them others don't get ideas about runnin' away!'

Carson, having yelled the command, strode towards his cousin. Samuel, a stocky man with shoulders that looked too wide for his height, had his hands bunched in his greasy black hair. His face was livid, and he was ranting about something but his accent was so thick that I barely caught a word. I took it that he was describing what he was going to do to Jay when he caught up with her. Well, he'd be disappointed if I had anything to do with it.

Carson grabbed Samuel by his shoulders, and it looked like he shook some sense into his volatile cousin. Again their slurred vernacular escaped me, but I didn't need to understand their speech when their body language spoke volumes. They were gearing up to give chase. Both men rushed towards the battered old pick-up and clambered inside. My greatest hope was that they'd head directly towards the pass near to the mush-room-shaped mountain. If they did that then I would have chanced returning for their other captives. I didn't doubt that I could take Brent without him being aware of my presence until it was too late. Sadly, that eventual-ity didn't offer itself, because the men swung the truck towards the watering hole, expecting to find Jay there. I could have still made it to the house without them seeing me, but I doubted I could get the girls free and lead them back here before we were spotted. I grabbed Jay and headed in the opposite direction, moving from boulder to boulder, and, where there wasn't enough highline cover, I made her get down on her knees and crawl. All the while I kept one eye on the circling truck.

Samuel had climbed out of the cab and on to the flat-bed. He clung to the truck while leaning out over the sand, and there was no mistaking what he was doing: he was looking for tracks in the softer ground. Time was still on our side, because their search radius hadn't expanded as far as the junk pile yet, but it was only a matter of time. They'd see the tracks we'd made as I propelled Jay towards the huddle of rocks and would easily pick up our trail from there. I studied the topography ahead. There was an ancient gully, through which water had once snaked, and I directed Jay towards it. Once inside, we could stand upright. I urged her into a jog, aiming for the nearby hills. Sweat spilled from the two of us, dotting the ground, but I was less worried about leaving a trail than how long Jay could maintain her speed before collapsing under the strain. I could have traversed the gully to the cover of the high ground in a few minutes, but Jay was already staggering and almost sinking to her knees with every other step. Enough was enough, I thought, as I pulled her to a halt.

'I'm so thirsty,' she moaned.

'Just hang in there girl,' I said. Then, before she could resist, I grabbed her by both wrists, stooped low and pulled her across my shoulders. She wasn't a tiny woman, in fact ordinarily she would be described as voluptuous, but neither was she a heavyweight. I carried her in the classic fireman's lift, galloping along at a quicker pace than she could have kept up. It took me back to my former life, and how I'd carried a number of my comrades-in-arms from battlefields throughout the world. Sadly most of them hadn't survived their injuries; I hoped that the same wouldn't hold true for Jay Walker.

We'd gained the best part of a half-mile when a shout rang across the desert, followed by the roar of an engine as the truck kicked up dust. Samuel had found our trail. From our position I couldn't see them, and could only hope that they'd waste more time searching the first boulders we'd hidden ourselves among before discovering that we'd fled east. Unfortunately it didn't sound like that because the roaring of the truck was getting closer. It was likely that they'd recognised the gully as our escape route and weren't wasting time searching every step of the way but cutting off our route out of the valley.

I hoped that Jay had fallen unconscious and was spared the panic that she might be recaptured, but as I ran I could hear a corresponding sob with each step. Fuck this, I decided, there was no way that I was going to let any harm come to this poor woman. If the Logans did cut off our escape route then they'd be sorely disappointed when they found not a defenceless woman but an armed man as mean as a shithouse rat.

The Logans were calling to each other, Samuel the most vociferous as he guided Carson along the brink of the gully. Luckily for us it didn't run in a straight line, but twisted and turned with the contours of the desert, and we stayed beyond their line of sight. I spurred on: speed was still our greatest ally. Suddenly, looming over the edge of the gully I saw a tall crag and knew that we'd made it to where the ridgeline broke up as it entered the desert in a series of jagged teeth. As I slowed, looking for a way to clamber up the gully's bank and into the rocks, the engine sounds drifted away. Thinking that Jay might already have made it this far, they must have decided to head directly for the pass under the overhang of the mushroom rock. Well, that suited me just fine.

Placing Jay back on her feet, I dashed sweat from my eyes. Salt was on my lips, and my shirt was soaked through with a mixture of both our bodily fluids. Jay looked like she'd been through a wringer. She looked back at me with a dazed expression, her eyes barely focussing. 'How are you doing, Jay? Are you still with me?'

She held out a palm and braced it against my shoulder, smacking lips that would crack into oozing sores if she should attempt a smile. With her other hand she attempted to straighten her twisted clothing. Her expression said, *That was a little undignified!*

'It's OK, don't try to speak. We haven't far to go now, and you can drink your fill. The only thing is I can't carry you any further, you're going to have to walk.'

'I . . . I can do that.'

'Good girl,' I said, and there was nothing patronising about it.

I had my right hand full with my gun, so I offered her

my left, gently tugging her up the embankment behind me. Cresting the rim of the gully, I looked towards the opening of the pass but couldn't see the truck now. A cloud of disturbed dust hung in the air obscuring much of the space below the overhang. Any second now, I thought, and the truck would burst through it and race towards us.

'Up there.' I indicated the narrow trail I'd followed into the valley and Jay set off. Having made it this far, the thought of escape and the subsequent release of Nicole and Ellie spurred her on with more determination than before. Her footing was steadier, and she managed a jog so that she was a few steps ahead of me all the way. She looked the type who was ordinarily health-conscious, someone who'd work out regularly, and on a good day might well have been solid competition in a race through the desert. Then and there, I knew, only the adrenalin was pushing her on.

I admired her. I hadn't heard her complain once about her predicament; all of her energy was concentrated on saving her friend, a trait I found very attractive. She was cut from the same cloth as I and those I called friends were. My interest had nothing to do with her good looks, or her lithe athleticism that was only partly blunted by fatigue, but neither had they passed me by. She reminded me a little of my girlfriend, Imogen, though almost half her age. Shit, throw that thought away, it made me sound too much like the Logans. Nevertheless, if I'd found myself following her in less desperate circumstances, my gaze would have fallen upon her in a different fashion. I was watching her for any sign that her strength was going to give out, or that she was about to stumble and fall. It was bad enough moving her quickly and silently without an injury to contend with.

We followed the trail, swerving among boulders, and I was searching now for landmarks as often as I was for our enemies. I almost missed the lion-head rock, coming on it from a different angle. Approaching it via this direction it was just another formless hunk of weathered stone, and, if a chance look back over my shoulder had come a few seconds later, I might have missed it as we padded on by.

'Jay,' I called softly. 'Here.'

She stumbled to a halt, both hands on her thighs as she caught her breath.

My rucksack was undisturbed and I drew out the container of water. Unscrewing the lid, I heard Jay scrabbling through the dirt as she came down on her knees and held out her hands gratefully.

'Take it real easy. Just sip the water, slow and steady or you'll make yourself sick.' That was like placing an unaccompanied child in a sweet shop and telling them not to touch. She grabbed the container greedily and began chugging down mouthfuls at a time. Her eyes rolled up at me, as though she expected me to snatch the water away any second. I let her get a good litre inside her before gently pushing the container away. 'Slow down, Jay, or there'll be none left.'

'God, do you know what that tastes like?'

Like warm plastic, I assumed, as I took the container from her.

'Delicious.' Jay's gaze never left the bottle as I raised it to my parched mouth.

'Yeah,' I agreed as I let the water trickle between my lips. I held on to a mouthful, slowly swilling it round my gums and the roof of my mouth before allowing gravity to do its job and take the water down into my stomach. I shoved the cap back on, but Jay's desire couldn't be ignored. I handed her the bottle. 'Make sure you save some for later.'

She must have been as parched as the desert that surrounded us, but she didn't go over the top. She only took another couple of long gulps before replacing the cap and putting down the bottle on her folded knees. Dribbles had made rivulets in the dust on her chin, but had almost moistened her lips and they looked a little plumper than before. A sparkle of life had reignited in her eyes.

From my rucksack I withdrew the photos given me by her father. I showed her the news clipping reporting the murders at the gas station, followed by the one that named Ellie Mansfield as having been snatched during the robbery. She only studied the photos for a second before nodding her head. 'Yes, that's the girl,' she confirmed. Her lids drooped, and a tear trembled on her lashes. 'Those monsters murdered that poor old man and the family in the station wagon. Dear God, I didn't want to believe that, but it's true. Yet they spared Ellie and Nicole, they wanted them for something else.'

'Did they, uh, touch you?'

'Not like that, they were happier beating me, especially the ugly one, Samuel.' Jay placed her head in her palms. 'But I heard Nicole and Ellie screaming. Oh, my God, no . . .'

It was an uncomfortable discussion, and not one I wanted to dwell on. Placing a consoling hand on her shoulder, I asked, 'What about this woman? Have you seen her?'

Jay lifted her face to look at the missing person poster and the fading image of Helena Blackstock. She shook her head sadly. 'No. I'm sorry.'

'Her name is Helena, maybe you heard the Logans mention her?'

'No. But I think they probably did take her as well. I mean, look at her. If Ellie could be Nicole's little sister, then Helena could be her twin.'

'Yeah,' I agreed, but didn't mention the theory that had been growing in my mind like a cancer.

Last time I'd been at the same place my phone hadn't been able to find a signal; the same proved true again. I handed the phone to Jay. 'Keep that safe. Once you're on the road, try to get through to the police and then direct them back here. You might also want to—' I was about to say phone her dad, and tell him she was safe, but that wasn't a good idea yet. Not until I'd freed Nicole and Ellie. I didn't want Jameson Walker contacting their families with false hopes. Instead, I ended my thought with, 'phone my friend, Jared Rington, and tell him what's happening. You'll find his number on there under "Rink". He'll help you.'

'Then you *are* going back?'

'Yes, but not yet. We still have to get you to my Yukon and out of this damn desert.'

'Where is your car?'

'A short run from here. Are you up to it?'

She took a generous gulp of water and handed the bottle back to me. 'I'm good to go,' she said, which made me smile. That was one of Rink's favourite sayings, so maybe my friend was already helping us on a strange metaphysical level. Taking one pull on the water, I returned it to her.

'Take that with you, you'll want more before we get to the car.' I paused. 'Speaking of cars, your father's SUV? You were driving it when the Logans snatched you, but it wasn't found on the highway.'

'No. They brought it back here to their ranch with me and Ellie inside.'

'So where is it now?'

Jay looked confused, the significance of the vehicle's location lost on her.

'It doesn't matter. Come on, let's get going. Through there, between those rocks, we can't go via the trail or they might come across us.' I urged her towards the broken ridgeline and a way through to the labyrinthine route I'd come in by.

As she set off, I bent down to stuff the papers back into my rucksack. My attention was only off her for a few seconds, but it was enough to change everything. As I straightened, something had detached itself from a boulder at the trail head and lunged at her.

It was short, squat and ugly, shaped not unlike a hairless ape, and possibly as powerful. It looked like it was capable of ripping her limb from limb within seconds, or twisting her head from her shoulders with one snap of its thick forearms.

My gun came up in one swift movement, but I didn't have a shot.

Samuel Logan had reclaimed his prize and I couldn't see a safe way of taking it away from him.

16

'I don't know who the hell you are, but you're gonna put down that pistol or I'll break the bitch's neck.'

'Let her go,' I countered. 'That's the only way you'll live through this.'

Samuel Logan grinned at me over Jay's shoulder, showing teeth that gleamed against his dusky features. He understood the dynamics of the situation clearly enough. If he did hurt Jay, then he'd have no leverage over me and in the next instant I'd blast his skull clean off. Yet I couldn't make a move on him without him going through with his threat. It was stalemate. Thankfully he hadn't come armed with a gun of his own or it would have forced both our hands. What he did have in his spare hand was a walkie-talkie radio, and it was likely that he'd already called Carson and told him to get here as quickly as possible. This added urgency to how I planned on reacting: basically I didn't know if Samuel had informed his cousin of my presence or not, and how that would affect my sneaking back to the ranch to free Nicole and Ellie. Best-case scenario was that Samuel had been dropped to continue his search on foot while Carson intended cutting off

Jay's escape route and had driven beyond the radio's range.

My options tumbled through my mind, each vying for prominence, but this mental overload made me pause. Not a good situation to be in, and it allowed Samuel to pull Jay backwards towards a jumble of rocks. I advanced, looking for a shot, but the man was wise enough to keep her firmly between us. Jay was staring back at me, her mouth an open chasm of shock.

'This is pointless,' I called. 'It's over now, Samuel. Let the woman go and maybe you'll live to see the end of the day.'

'How'd you know my name?' he asked. 'You a fuckin' cop? I don't think so. Or the place would be teeming by now.'

'The police are on the way. That's why you need to let her go, before things get out of hand.'

'The cops ain't coming,' he laughed. I wondered why he was so sure, and his explanation only went so far to enlighten me. 'No one's coming, buddy. Out here there's no cellphone that can get a signal. The way I see things, you're on your own, and it's you who won't live to the end of the day. And neither will this bitch if you don't stop waving that pistol at me.'

'The others are still alive, right? The women you took? That's a good thing, but if you harm her,' I nodded at Jay, 'everything changes. You and your cousins will do time, there's no denying that, but if you kill her, it'll be for ever.'

'Nope, if I kill her then you're likely to shoot me. I'll be dead and won't see a jail cell, but then I don't care about that one way or another. See, all you want is to save this bitch, while I've no hesitation about twisting the head off her scrawny neck. So I reckon you've more to lose than I have. You're the one who's gonna put down his gun, get down on his knees and put his hands on his head.' To emphasise his directions he gripped Jay's chin in his thick fingers. He squeezed and Jay yowled in agony as her skin round his fingertips blanched.

I'd heard and seen enough.

I was loath to shoot, because I'd no idea where Carson was, and recalling his run-in with Scott Blackstock, it was a sure bet that he was carrying. If I fired, he'd hear the shot and come at speed. I didn't fear the man or his weapon, but I didn't want Jay injured in the crossfire. I lowered the S&W.

'Not good enough,' Samuel said. 'Throw it over here.'

'No.' As if I was going to hand over my gun so that he could shoot me? 'Release the woman and walk away. I won't kill you. So long as you and your cousins let the other women go, then I'll even allow you to get in your truck and drive away. I'm not one bit interested in any of you, or if you go to prison or not, I'm only interested in the women getting out of this unharmed.'

Samuel smiled at my words, and that was good, because I wanted him to think I was weakening. There was no way in God's creation that I'd allow any of the punks to walk away from this, but while he saw a chance, and was mulling over his options, then there was still a way to save Jay. I caught her terrified gaze and offered a wink, which I followed with a dip of my chin.

Comprehension registered in her features, and I only hoped she'd wait for the exact moment to act.

Samuel shook his head, the grin never leaving his face. 'Like I said, I'm not afraid of going to jail. I'm not afraid of dying either, so there's no deal you can strike that's gonna make me let her go, other than what I already said.'

'I'm not getting down on my knees for no one,' I said. The gun I placed on the ground between my feet. 'Now let her go.'

Samuel took another step back, hauling Jay along with him. He glanced through a gap between the boulders, no doubt seeking Carson. Jay was still watching me, and as Samuel's gaze flicked away, I nodded. There was still the problem of Carson hearing the gunfire, so I left the gun exactly where it was, lunging towards Samuel even as Jay brought up the container of water and rammed the thick plastic base into her captor's chin. There was little more than a litre of water in the bottle now, but whipped round at speed it was enough to add extra weight behind the smack of the bottle against his jaw. He let out a shout of surprise, his natural reaction to pull back, eyes screwed tight. At the same time, Jay twisted out of his grip and threw herself to the ground. Twenty feet had separated us, but I covered that in less than two seconds, launching myself through the air at Samuel before he'd recovered. As his eyes came open my fist was only inches from his nose, and no way could he avoid the blow. The impact rocketed up my arm all the way to my shoulder, but it had to have hurt him more. Not that it showed.

My lunge took me against him, and we both continued among the boulders. Samuel was off balance, and
by virtue of the fact that I'd grabbed hold of his shirt
with my free hand, so was I. He went down on his back,
his head caroming off a rock, and I landed on top of
him. He uttered a wordless grunt, but that was the only
sign of discomfort. I hit him again, pulping his nose and
mashing his lips against his teeth. Luckily I had landed
with both my feet flat on the ground either side of his
body, so I didn't continue to tumble over him. I drew
back my fist to strike him again.

Most others would have been stunned, maybe out of
the fight altogether, but Samuel Logan was made of
sterner stuff, or maybe his brutal mind refused to feel
pain the way gentler souls did. He spat a mouthful of
blood-laced saliva in my face, even as he reached for my
throat with one hand and my cocked elbow with the
other. His action forced me to draw my throat out of his
clutch, but it also served to make me miss my next punch.
Samuel came up, trying to get his hips beneath him. His
arms swiped at mine, and this time he did get a grip on
my elbow. His fingers dug for the ulnar nerve and a
tingling pain shot the length of my forearm into my ring
and pinky fingers. He also nipped at the radial nerve,
intending to immobilise my arm, but we were beyond
pain compliance techniques. Caught cold, or already
beaten down, I'd have groaned in agony at the assault on
my nervous system, but I was too fired up to be slowed
by it now. I wrenched my arm free, then aimed an elbow
into his face that knocked him sprawling under me.

He was a child of this desert. His heart was as barren of pity as the wasteland, and his flesh was forged of the same rock as its landscape. Or that was how it felt fighting him. Counting being whacked with the water container, he'd now taken four heavy shots directly to his face, but it wasn't slowing him down. I contemplated going for the knife in my back pocket, but the thought was too fleeting to act upon, because he was already coming back at me, more furious now than before. He bellowed like a wild thing, bucked beneath me and I was sent flying off him. My left shoulder slammed the rocks, and I rebounded on to the trail. Smaller stones dug painfully into my knees as I scrambled up and turned to meet him.

'Gonna make you sorry for that!' he snapped as he came to his feet. I was only sorry I didn't kill him when I first had the opportunity. 'Go for it!' I launched myself at him, throwing a knee into his chest. He rocked on his heels, but then came back swinging.

His punches were well aimed, and flashes of black edged my vision.

Samuel kicked at my gut, and I folded round his foot. The blow hadn't landed cleanly, and I used the ruse to get in close. My headbutt cracked directly into his already smashed nose. Samuel grunted, but only at being caught out. I rammed my forehead into his face again, until he snapped out of it and almost took my throat out with a knife-hand slash. I danced back, then immediately launched in at him with a kick to his balls.

Shockingly, Samuel took the blow and wrapped me

in his arms. A taller man's ears would have been an open target for both my palms, but he was shorter than I and his head was jammed against my chest. I punched him in the skull, but couldn't get the leverage for a full-on knockout blow. Samuel hauled me off my feet, spun me like a pro-wrestler and slammed me down on a boulder and almost separated my spine for me. He knew how to fight.

Once I had fought a giant of a man, and he'd manhandled me in a similar fashion, but on that occasion his sheer size had also been his weakness and I'd been able to kill the fucker using speed and mobility. But Samuel wasn't hindered by size, and he was canny enough to keep his vulnerable targets well hidden while he pounded me with one hand. With my back bent tortuously over the boulder I wasn't in the best position to fight back. His right hand drummed my ribs in a staccato beat, each exhalation of pain I emitted giving him encouragement to hit me again. At the edges of my vision danced blackness that had nothing at all to do with dehydration, and in reaction I struck back.

When caught in a life or death struggle it isn't easy to control your bodily reactions: instinct takes over and both physical and psychological switches are thrown in order to help you survive. When your vision tunnels to a pinpoint, your hearing becomes a dulled hush, and your scrotum shrivels tight, you can forget about applying intricate combat manoeuvres. The only thing you're capable of is the most gross of motor functions, those that include holding on and clubbing arm movements.

It's why so many fights that start on the feet end on the floor with both combatants doing little more than gripping each other. So, Samuel wasn't aiming to dig into nerve clusters now, he was only intent on smashing me to a pulp. I admit it: I was in the same place, and it was now a matter of who was going to land the most telling blow. For a second or two, my money was on Samuel Logan.

I was enshrouded in the red haze of battle, where only my enemy existed. I'd forgotten about saving the women, I'd forgotten about Jay and Carson or whoever might be bearing witness to our fight, I'd forgotten about the knife in my pocket, I'd forgotten about the heat and the rocks, and the entire world. Now all that mattered was someone was trying to kill me, and all I wanted to do was kill him first.

Even the crack of a revolver wasn't enough to sway my mind; it was one more bang that rattled inside my ear canals along with all the others. Only when the gun barked a second time and Jay screamed real close in our ears did we struggle apart. I grabbed at Samuel, but he slipped beyond my fingers, and I ended up colliding with yet another boulder and almost finishing what Samuel had started. I didn't exactly see stars, because the void I looked on for the briefest of moments was pitch-black. I yanked back from the brink of unconsciousness, blinking rapidly to clear my vision and gulping in air to my straining body. By the time my head was clear enough to make sense of what was going on, Jay was already past me and pursuing Samuel through the maze of boulders.

'No, Jay!' I stumbled after her. 'Get back here!'

She came to a halt, panting, the gun held in both hands shaking in time with her body. Samuel disappeared among the rocks. His escape was both a blessing and a curse: thank God both Jay and I had survived, and bollocks that Samuel had got away. For a second I considered snatching the gun from Jay and chasing him down, but good sense wriggled its way into my pounding skull. 'Give me the gun, Jay.'

She did so, her face a picture of confusion. 'I couldn't do it,' she moaned. 'Even after everything he did to me, to Nicole and Ellie, I couldn't shoot him in the back.'

I was glad that she hadn't. 'That makes you a better person than you'll ever understand,' I said. The truth was, even though he was trying his hardest to pierce my insides with my ribs, I wouldn't have condoned shooting him in the spine. Not because it was a cowardly thing to do, but I wanted that bastard to die looking me in the eyes. Except, if I said that to her, Jay would wonder what kind of man she was relying on to save her and her friends' lives, and perhaps decide she'd merely traded one kind of monster for another.

Also, the fact that she'd used the gun went unsaid. I wasn't ungrateful that she'd possibly saved my arse, but if I'd wanted Carson or Brent to hear gunfire I'd have just shot Samuel at the start.

I opened the chamber, fed a couple of fresh shells from my pocket into the cylinder and snapped it closed. 'Fetch the water, then let's get going. Time's against us now.'

While Jay went to gather up the water container, I pulled myself together. At least that's what it felt like: after the hammering I'd taken my joints felt like those of a marionette, only held to my torso by loose strings. Pretty soon though the tightening would begin, and if I didn't get moving, I'd seize up, and Jay would have to find a new nickname for Carson Logan because I'd be moving like the Tin Man in need of lubrication.

'Think we can use this?'

Jay approached me holding out the radio that Samuel must have dropped during the fight.

I didn't see that it was much use to us, for it was even less effective than my cellphone currently was for calling the police. However, one thing was instantly apparent: Samuel had no way of contacting Carson and bringing him back to this spot. He'd have to return to the pass to flag him down as he responded to the gunshots – supposing he'd heard them – and by then we could have moved a considerable distance.

Taking it from her, all I could hear was static. I thumbed down the volume and jammed it into my shirt pocket so I'd hear any transmission, but wouldn't give our position away. We'd won a slight reprieve, but the chances now of getting Jay to the Yukon and safely away, and then returning to release the others before the Logans got back to the ranch, were growing very slim.

'Excellent,' I said, feeling anything but. 'Now let's get moving.'

17

Jay considered this man who'd come from out of nowhere to act as her protector. He said that he'd come at her father's behest, but had not related how he'd ended up at the Logan ranch so, in keeping with her earlier analogy, she fancied that a tornado had plucked him from wherever it was he hailed from and dropped him at the ranch just in time, like the house that flattened the Wicked Witch. Pity she didn't have a pair of ruby slippers whose heels she could click and take them all safely home.

He was English, but didn't talk with any definite regional inflection she could make out. It was more a cosmopolitan accent, or one that had been shaped through some kind of institutionalisation: the military she assumed, from the skills he'd exhibited. Occasionally he slipped into a US vernacular that sounded a little odd to her ear, and she wondered how long he'd been living here in the States. He stood under six feet, but only by a shade, and had the tight build of an athlete, broad-shouldered and slim-hipped; however there was nothing that would make him stand out in a crowd. Not until you looked into his features and noted a stoic calm that could be mistaken for an uncaring attitude. His outer shell was a lie, she knew. If he only cared for his own well-being, he'd have shot Samuel when he had the opportunity, and the rest be damned. He hadn't, he'd forfeited his own safety for hers and for her friends', and chosen to risk everything in hand-to-hand combat with the brutish man. That was where he also stood out; she'd never seen anything like the way he'd gone at Samuel outside the frame of an action movie, or believed that after the beating he'd endured anyone could still operate without complaint. Jeez, if Samuel had been punching her as hard as that, she'd have been hospitalised, or dead. Yet Joe Hunter was up and jogging, moving with a grace she'd never seen in any man. When she was at Penn State she'd been surrounded by football players and boys from the wrestling team, tough, fit and aggressive guys, but she doubted any of them could have stood for more than a few seconds against Hunter. There was something about him, like a smouldering fuse you couldn't detect until you looked deeply into his eyes. They had the same intensity she'd once seen in a caged wolf, a beast tamed only so far that could return to its intrinsic savage state at the flip of a coin. She thought she should fear such a man, yet she didn't. She was only thankful that he was on her side.

She wished to know more about him, though this was neither the time nor the place. All that was important was that he was there and prepared to do everything to see her to safety, coupled with his promise that he'd return for Nicole. She knew he could be trusted to do everything possible to save her best friend. His was a selfless attitude: she didn't doubt that her father had paid handsomely for his services, but she suspected that Joe Hunter wasn't motivated by money. His reward was his opportunity to help others. She wondered what would feed such altruism in a man, or if indeed she was even on the right track. Perhaps his need to help others was his way of atonement, making up for some perceived sin from his past. Or maybe she was totally off base and he was simply someone who, as she often joked about herself, liked to live on the wild side. Perhaps he required the adrenalin rush guaranteed during a conflict with the Logans and it was his way of unleashing his ferocious side without having to turn it on to those closest to him.

That was a sobering thought. She couldn't picture him turning on his loved ones, quite the opposite in fact; he was the type who'd die for them first. She imagined that hc was loyal to a fault. His friends would be very important to him, the reason he'd asked that she telephone his friend, Jared Rington, at her first opportunity. Something about that name sounded familiar, his nickname more so, and she was certain she'd heard her father mention it in passing. Perhaps her dad knew these men from the days when he was in the army. She didn't know much about her dad's military past, only that he'd served his term as a chef to the guys who did all the fighting. She wondered now if that tale was true, because you didn't get to know the likes of Joe Hunter dishing up chicken and fries.

Joe was running a few yards ahead of her, his attention on the rocks around them, but regularly straying back to ensure that she was keeping up. On occasion he'd held out a hand to help her over the most rugged obstacle, but had quickly released her again, not because the gesture was too familiar but because he was trained not to compromise his weapons. What must it be like being in a constant state of readiness like that? Jay believed that she would burn out within days and couldn't fathom how Joe had attained the age he had. Not that he was old, but he had to be in his late thirties, though his stamina belied that somewhat.

Hunter had come to a halt, and was staring out from between two large rocks. Their run had brought them towards a massive structure that reminded her of a petrified mushroom, with a wide umbrella-shaped overhang. Hunter seemed to be listening, his head scanning back and forth like a radar dish. He nodded silently to himself, then beckoned her forward.

'That's the trail down there, the one they'd have to use with their truck. We can't afford to be out in the open so we're going to continue up this way. Once we're beyond the trailhead it's only a short run to my car.' He paused. 'You still OK? You can make it?'

'I don't need carrying any more if that's what you're asking?'

A smile turned up the corner of his mouth, the first she'd seen from him, and it softened his features in a way that she liked. He had eyes the colour of the desert sky, but they were changeable, sometimes shifting through light brown and green, though that could have been down to reflections.

'Come, then.'

'Hold on,' Jay said, passing him the container of water. 'Have another drink while I sort myself out.'

Her shoes were full of sand and larger pebbles, making walking painful. She removed each in turn, and shook them out. Hunter took a small pull on the water, but handed it back. 'You'll need that before you're done. I'll get plenty later at the watering hole.'

That was a sign of confidence. Or maybe he was only trying to allay her fears that he might fail. She glanced down at the revolver in his hand, and knew he'd deal with the Logans differently next time. He wouldn't be as restrained when he didn't have her well-being to worry about. She only hoped that her friends would be more important to him than his personal agenda.

'When my dad hired you, he did ask that you find Nicole as well?'

'I'm here for all of you,' he said. 'Nicole, Ellie *and* you.'

'You mentioned that other woman earlier, Helena Blackstock.'

Hunter's head dipped, and for the first time since his fight with Samuel Logan he looked weary. 'I'm afraid I might be too late to help her.'

In the next instant Hunter straightened, and the wolf was back in his gaze. Jay had the feeling that he spared her his next words because of her earlier inability to shoot Samuel in cold blood. Nonetheless she could guess what he was thinking: he was too late to save Helena, but he would avenge her.

18

From somewhere to the south-west of our position came the thrum of an engine and it sounded like Carson had extended his search around the far side of Mushroom Mountain. I doubted that he'd hooked up with Samuel yet, because the truck sounded the best part of a mile away. I couldn't be certain, because the canyons had strange acoustics, and for all I knew the pick-up was nearby, but the sound had been carried and brought back to my ears via a different route. Thumbing the volume on the radio, I listened. I thought that I'd heard a short query come over the air earlier, but it could have been static. Now I longed to hear the bastard call out for his cousin, because it would mean both men were still separated and Carson would have no idea of my involvement. While they were apart, it gave me a window of opportunity to get Jay out of the way and return for the others. If I could return to the cabin before them, then I could drop Brent and lead the others somewhere safe. I could have my time with Samuel and his older kinsman on another occasion.

We had made it beyond the pass, the mushroom shape now well behind us. The breeze still stirred the sand, and the enveloping cloud helped to conceal us. My only misgiving was that it also offered cover to Samuel. We'd hear the truck coming and be able to hide, but for all I knew the ugly troll I'd battled earlier could have picked up our trail again. If he ambushed us, it wouldn't matter if he was armed with a gun or not, because there were plenty of rocks lying around he could brain me with. If that happened, then Jay would be defenceless.

I pulled her to a halt, digging my hand into my back pocket.

'What is it? What's wrong?' she asked.

'Nothing. I just want you to take this.' I handed her the folding knife and she looked at it like it was an extra-terrestrial artefact that had fallen out of the sky. 'It's a knife,' I explained.

'I know what it is,' she said, with a roll of her eyes. 'What do you expect me to do with it?'

'Just keep hold of it, OK.'

'I could have used this a few hours ago when I was trying to get out of that box.'

She told me about being confined in a sunken box, how she'd been bound at her ankles and wrists and how much effort it had been to cut free of her ropes. Jay had proven resourceful, unlike her predecessor who I suspected had gone into a similar box. That made me more determined than ever that the Logans would pay for all the misery they'd inflicted on their hostages. It wasn't something I was about to share with a girl who found the thought of stabbing someone abhorrent.

'Yeah, it would have been useful. Never mind, you have it now and it might come in handy.'

Jay couldn't use the gun on Samuel, but it had been different then. He was engaged in a fist fight with me, and in her eyes that didn't qualify for a cold-blooded execution. At the time her own life wasn't in peril; I only hoped that if she was threatened in the future she'd have the fortitude to do the right thing. It would be best if she never had to use the blade, but supposing things went to hell then at least she'd have a chance.

Jay secreted the knife away, pushing it deep in a trouser pocket. I'd have preferred that she held on to it, but at least she hadn't dropped it like it was a hot brick.

Leading her again, I followed the route into the labyrinth of gullies, my gun held close to my side. With each step she took, the water sloshed back and forth in the container, a reminder of how little there was left. It would have to be enough. I'd no intention of being stuck out here in the heat for much longer.

It was disturbing to think about what must have happened to Helena Blackstock. I didn't doubt that the Logans had snatched her, and used her for whatever abominable purpose they'd taken the subsequent women for, and it hurt that I'd come too late to help her. Something about the sequence of events told me that the Logans had been seeking a replacement for her when they'd happened across Nicole and Ellie at the gas station. To my mind that meant one of two things: the Logans had killed her, or Helena had managed to escape their clutches. The problem with the latter scenario was that if she was still alive, then surely she'd have shown up somewhere by now. I wondered if, like Jay, she'd managed to get free, but had chosen the wrong route through the desert. Without water, she'd have perished in no time. By now the sun and the wildlife would have been busy, and I didn't want to picture the poor woman as a rack of bleached bones out there in one of those canyons. Then again, perhaps it was better than the alternative, that she'd remained in the hands of those sickos to endure further humiliation and pain; at least she would have died a free person. More than ever, I was determined that Jay, Nicole and Ellie wouldn't face a similar fate. If it meant my own death, then so be it.

The Yukon was where I'd left it, and I was glad to find the keys were still in the ignition, meaning that it had gone undiscovered. It was a huge vehicle, but I didn't doubt that Jay could handle it, having driven her father's SUV the length of Route 66 to here. I started it up, reversing it out of the S-bend gully so she'd have a good start. Clambering out, I left the engine purring. We couldn't dawdle, because even if Carson didn't hear the engine over the top of his own, then Samuel might and come running. He could run for me now, I didn't care, in fact I relished the idea, but not until Jay was clear.

'Do you want this back now?' Jay held out my knife.

Call me a pessimist, but I wasn't ready to let her go unarmed. 'No, keep hold of it. Think of it as a lucky charm.'

Tears were in her eyes as she tilted her head up to me. 'I think I already found one of those. Thanks for everything, Joe.'

Before I could stop her she threw her arms round my waist and hugged me tight. I gave her a brief hug back, but it was a little too early for her thanks. She could give me a proper cuddle when I got back with both the other girls in tow.

Extricating myself from her arms, I took the container of water and splashed some of it in my mouth. It went as far as swilling down the grit that had embedded itself round my gums, but that was all. The rest I handed back to Jay. 'You know your way out of here? Just keep the sun over your right shoulder and it'll take you back to State Highway seventy-seven. When you hit it, try the phone, you should get a signal there. Don't go north to Indian Wells, head south for Holbrook because that's the direction the cops will likely come from. When you find the first truck stop, pull in and wait for them. You'll be safe there, OK?'

'Yes, I remember that place. We passed it on the way towards the Painted Desert on Tuesday. God, what day is today? I've no idea how long those animals have been holding us.'

'It's Friday,' I said.

'Four days? It felt like for ever . . .'

I touched the side of her cheek, my palm cupping her jaw. 'It's over with now. You don't have to be frightened any more.'

She blinked tears from her lashes, and her gaze was forthright. 'Not for myself, I don't.'

'I'll get them out. Trust me.'

'I do. I really do.'

'OK, get going then.' I turned her towards the Yukon, and gently pressed her inside. She slung the water container on the passenger seat, then looked back at me. Her mouth opened to say something, but I anticipated her. 'Don't come back here with the cops. Just tell them where the girls are being held and who's responsible. Tell them that I've gone to get them free. I don't want to be confused with those arseholes and have a well-meaning cop put a bullet in my brain. And remember, as soon as you've spoken to the cops, ring my friend and tell him where I'm at.'

Jay shifted into drive as I closed her door. I scanned the desert for movement but could neither hear nor see any sign of the Logan pick-up. Flat-handed, I banged the door. 'Go, and don't stop for anything.'

The Yukon spat gravel at me as Jay gave it a tad too much throttle. The thick tyres chewed at the desert, found traction and then surged forward. I watched it go until it was enveloped by the sifting dust clouds. Finally, I thought, as I allowed my body to fold slightly. I massaged my ribs, but it did little to alleviate the pain I'd suffered since Samuel hammered me. At least one of my ribs felt like it had cracked, and the flesh around it was puffy with bruising. If only Jay had suspected how much pain I was in, then maybe she wouldn't have trusted me to get her friends out alive. She would have quite rightly argued that we should both leave and allow the police to handle the rescue. Ordinarily I might have gone along with her, but I wanted my time with the Logans before the police could arrive. Jail wasn't good enough for those sick bastards.

'OK, suck it up, Joe,' I commanded.

I straightened, feeling the pull of tissue in my side, but ignored it. I'd had worse injuries before, some of them life-threatening. Then I began to jog. By the time the mushroom mountain came into view I was up to full pace and the agony in my body had been pushed to the dim recess where all my other troubles were shelved.

I felt fine, and ready for the Logans.

I'd have felt better if Samuel had appeared out of the dust before me, but he didn't. That was OK, I was happy to leave him to last. Carson and Brent weren't going to be personal kills, but Samuel was a different matter. The father and son were just for starters. Samuel Logan: he would provide the icing on the cake.

19

'You'd better not be dead, goddamnit! Now answer me, Sammy.'

I had made it back to the junk pile unhindered. Now, peering across at the ranch, I was tempted to take out the radio and reply to Carson Logan as he grew more frantic by the second. For the last few minutes he'd been calling out regularly, and his tone had gone from one of slight concern to one of anger. That was good, because he wouldn't be thinking straight. His cousin's silence was helping to both demoralise and confuse his own search.

I could hear the pick-up truck out there in the desert but couldn't see it. There was too much dust in the air as the afternoon began to slip towards evening and the wind started to kick up again. The acoustics were still hit and miss and occasionally I couldn't pinpoint the direction of the truck, but it was still behind me. Since he'd disappeared among the ravines I'd had no sign of Samuel. Part of me hoped a rattler had bitten him, or he'd fallen and smashed his skull on a rock, while another part looked forward to a rematch. My only worry was that he'd actually returned to the house and was now inside, preparing to move the girls as soon as the older cousin returned. I had to plan for two men at the house, which could cause me major problems if they each held one of the girls when I entered. Not to mention that both Samuel and Brent had assuredly armed themselves by now. Best-case scenario would be if Samuel was still out there trying to pick up my and Jay's trail and Brent was still oblivious to the danger. I wouldn't know how things would play out while crouching there listening to Carson's rant over the radio, and the longer I waited, the greater their chances of returning before I got moving. I resisted the amateurish temptation to taunt him, knowing that would only bring him back here at speed.

Before moving on the ranch, I gave the gun a cursory inspection and found everything in order. Jay had test-fired it for me, so I knew that it was a reliable piece. I positioned fresh shells in my pockets for easy access. Then I advanced, moving in a crouch for the outbuildings. Even if Samuel had made it back, there was nothing like the present for a rapid assault on the ranch while even he would think that Jay and I were still running in the opposite direction.

Earlier, Carson had commanded his son to guard the others, waving him back inside off the porch, so it was a good bet that both girls were inside the house. The outbuildings didn't require checking for hostages, but I still wanted to scope them out. The first was a barn that hadn't seen livestock in a generation, but what I found was very troubling. A huge table that weighed more than I did – perhaps more than I would with my big friend Rink on my shoulders – dominated the centre of the space. Trailing from one leg was a length of rusty chain with a robust dog collar on the end. The food bowl, spoon and bucket left untouched beside it told me that the chain hadn't held a mutt.

Moving on I checked out another shed, this one a three-sided structure, with a tin roof and a large board jammed at the front to act as a door. Through a gap between the planks I found what I was expecting, and that was even more troubling than the barn where women had been leashed. Frowning, I headed for the house, thinking now that just maybe there was more to this than I'd originally suspected. I hoped I was wrong, but it was imperative that I act and get Nicole and Ellie the hell away.

From across the wide basin I heard the pick-up return through the pass. At this distance I couldn't see it, but Carson was talking on the radio again. 'I'm going back to where I dropped you off, Sammy. If you can hear me, git your ass back there and I'll pick you up. I think we'd better git a move on and prepare for some unwelcome company.'

The cowboy was beginning to think straight, but little did he know he'd just offered me a huge advantage. He'd no idea that Jay had escaped in a vehicle, and would be returning with the police, though not immediately. He thought the woman was on foot, and if she could make it across the desert safely it would still be many hours before she could raise help. He was going to waste valuable time waiting for Samuel to rendez-vous with him, by which point I planned on being in and out again. If and when he came back to the house it would be with the intention of mounting some kind of damage limitation, more probably to plan a getaway, and he wouldn't expect an armed man to be waiting for him. As long as he didn't hook up with his cousin he'd remain ignorant of my presence until it was too late.

Ifs and whens: not something you could rely on.

I ran across the yard, heading for the back of the house where there was a door but no windows. Plan A was to crash through the door and shoot any man inside. Plan B was more sensible. I couldn't count on the fact that Brent hadn't prepared for such an assault and had placed the girls in front of him, so I had to check what to expect before going in. It didn't rain here that often, and the caulking between the boards had been neglected for the last few years, so I found plenty of places to peer into the house. What I first looked upon was an untidy bedroom with two sets of bunks piled with dingy blankets and stained pillows. Soiled underwear lay piled in one corner, alongside dusty boots and a denim jacket on a peg. A crooked picture frame hung from a nail, but over time the painting had slipped and it now hung askew showing empty space between it and the frame at the top left corner. So the Logans weren't art lovers. I moved on to the door itself, careful not to set my feet too hard on the wooden stoop. I couldn't see through the door, but from within filtered the low buzz of voices in muted conversation. I couldn't discern the individual voices, so wasn't positive that it was the girls whispering together or if in fact Samuel had returned and was making plans with his cousin.

Continuing to the right, I again found a chink in the wall, and this time could make out a kitchen, replete with a pot sink and hand pump faucet. Dirty dishes were stacked on a draining board, but only enough to have been used during one meal. I could just make out the corner of a stove, and to the other side a table and chairs, and directly across from me a window overlooking the front porch. There was no movement, and the voices were quieter here. If things didn't change in the next minute, that would place Brent and the girls at the front left corner of the house.

Returning to the door, I tried the handle. Bingo! The door swung open. I controlled it, teasing it an inch at a time so that it didn't make a noise and alert anyone to my presence. Opening inward, left to right, it compromised my gun hand somewhat, so I had to stand well to the left jamb while opening the door. I continued pushing as the gap widened, making sure that no one was hiding behind the door by pressing it all the way against the wall it abutted at the hinges. The wind was still blowing and a gust chose then to dance its way inside. I could only hope that Brent wasn't perceptive enough to notice the change in pressure and correlate it to an invasion of the house. In case he did, I moved quickly after the breeze, bringing up my gun.

To form the bunk room, an interior wall had been erected opposite a similar one that partitioned off the kitchen, so I moved through a short hallway. The air inside was rank: the stench of spoiled food, spilled alcohol, and unwashed bodies blended together. I breathed through my mouth. A threadbare rug softened my footfalls. Over my own movements I heard a thump, followed by the shifting of a body on floorboards. A voice snapped, 'How many times have I to tell you to shut the hell up? If I have to come over there I'll bust both your heads.'

Something else followed Brent's warning that I hadn't expected. There was a high-pitched squeak followed by a rising and falling wail, then a buzz. Brent was trying to get a CB radio working, and didn't seem to be having much joy. Perhaps he was trying to patch into what his father and Samuel were saying over their walkie-talkies, which boded well for me because it meant Samuel hadn't returned yet. Also, his warning revealed that both girls were in the same room as him.

I chose to step directly into the living space, my gun twisting towards the static shriek emitted by the CB radio.

What I saw made ice flood my veins and I'd no second thoughts about shooting Brent Logan.

Both girls were there, Nicole and Ellie, sitting side by side like conjoined twins in the corner of the room, a rope fixed between their ankles so they'd have to walk in unison. Otherwise they were as naked as babies, and that's what infuriated me the most. It was a probability that their bodies had been violated, a sick enough thought, but the Logans had gone further than that and sought to humiliate them by constantly parading their nudity.

There was an ounce of me that wanted answers, primarily why the Logans had done this, but the rest of my being screamed for vengeance for these girls, and also the ones I'd been too late to save. If Brent hadn't already started to rise at my sudden appearance I would have ordered him to stand, because before he died I wanted to shoot off his balls.

As it was, the young man came up with startling speed and made a grab for something propped next to the CB base station. It was the stock of a sawn-off shotgun. Hanging from his mouth was the white paper stick of a lollipop. In the dim light it was a flag to the business end of my gun. I aimed and fired, the gun bucking in recoil.

The remains of Brent's lollipop flew across the room and landed at the feet of the girls, who both flinched back, emitting squeals of horror. Not so much at the sight of the lollipop as at the chunk of lip that adhered to it.

Brent fell over backwards, upsetting the chair he'd been sitting in, and crashing against a low couch with sunken cushions. He wasn't dead and was trying to scream in protest, but it was difficult with half his lower jaw missing. I felt a savage sense of justice uncommon to me, knowing that he must be insane with agony, and tempered my next shot so that he continued to suffer a little longer. Normally I take no satisfaction in killing, but for what he'd forced these girls to endure, I gladly made an exception. I shot him square in the gut.

Coming from a Special Forces background, I preferred a lower calibre shell than the .357s I used here. When conducting hostage rescues the last thing you wanted was for your bullet to pass through the bad guy and kill their prisoner behind them. In the heat of the moment I'd forgotten about that, but Brent was well away from the girls, so the bullet just went into the cushions. As he rolled to the floor, I saw a huge open wound in his back. Nevertheless the man wasn't dead yet and he was still gripping the shotgun. No way could he bring it on me, but it was aimed at the girls. I couldn't take the chance he'd get off a shot so put him out of his misery far too soon for my liking. My bullet almost split his skull in two, leaving bloodied tendrils of his straw-like hair jutting out of the wound.

Hurrying over, I plucked the shotgun from his grasp. His finger was twisted through the trigger guard but pulled loose and allowed his arm to drop lifeless to the floor. I stood, looking around quickly to check that nobody had followed me into the room. The girls were horrified at my appearance, but there was also a note of hope in their gaze.

'I'm a friend. Don't be afraid, I'm here to help you.'

There was a knife on the table near to the CB radio. I retrieved it, having jammed the S&W into my belt. As I approached the two young women they flinched, grabbing at each other. I decided on a new tactic. 'I'm a friend of Jay Walker. I'm here to get you both free.'

Nicole Challinor was slight of build, but there was no denying she was all woman: on the contrary Ellie was still a child in my eyes and it made my skin crawl to view her nakedness. I felt dirty approaching them the way I did, but there was nothing for it. I crouched, then split the rope binding them together with one yank of the blade. It seemed that Jay's name did the trick of winning over Nicole, just as mentioning Jay's dad had for her. She stood up, unabashed by her state of undress, and reached back to help the younger girl off the floor. 'I told you everything would turn out fine,' she said to Ellie. Then, with Ellie held in her arms, Nicole said to me, 'Is she safe? Did Jay make it?'

'Yes,' I said. 'She's safe.'

'Where is she? The men discovered that she'd escaped from the hole and were chasing her.'

'She's safe,' I repeated, as I ducked and secreted the knife inside my boot. 'She's in my car and already on her way to the police.'

The expression that descended over Nicole's face took me by surprise. Her eyes welled with tears and she sobbed. Something in the look told me it wasn't entirely in relief.

20

The Yukon was a huge, very masculine beast of a vehicle, but Jay found that it handled the desert in a way her father's SUV would never have managed; the lighter model car would have been bouncing and skipping all over the place. It was a good job that the Yukon was so massive, because Jay often had to apply brute force to keep her heading in a straight line. Sand drifts and even some of the smaller rocks were no object and it blasted through with no problem. Twice her concentration was so distracted that she ploughed through mounds of grit and stone she'd have been better avoiding, but they didn't halt the Yukon. It suffered a few dints to the paintwork, that was all.

Jay had no idea how long she had been driving. Probably nowhere near as long as it felt. Her mind was working at hyper-speed as she tried to make sense of all that had happened, and all that still needed doing. Coupled with that, dozens of *what if?* scenarios concerning Joe Hunter, Nicole, Ellie and the Logan family were tumbling through her mind. Most of the developments she imagined ended with Joe and her friends dead, and it made her sick with anxiety. She should drive faster, but to do that could mean her mission ceasing abruptly when the Yukon met an obstruction even it couldn't handle and she ended up dead in the mangled wreckage. More prudent to take things steady, make it to the highway in one piece and then call the cops as Joe had commanded. She glanced over at his phone where she'd placed it on the passenger seat, but no signal registered. The red SOS icon that flashed in place of the signal strength bars was an ominous reminder of her situation.

She thought about her parents, as well as Nicole's. They must be frantic with worry by now and she had mixed feelings about their reunion. Though they'd be infinitely relieved that their daughter had returned home to them, Jay could expect huge recriminations. It was her idea to come on this damned trip, after all, she who'd promised that she would keep Nicole safe from harm. Well, she'd failed in that, hadn't she? Blame might go unsaid, but it would be there, in the looks she received and the loss of trust she'd have to work hard to regain. That was supposing they ever did have the reunion, because it wasn't a sure bet yet. No, she had to stop thinking like that. Joe Hunter *would* save Nicole and Ellie as she *would* bring back help.

Again she pictured what might be happening back there in the sun-parched desert. Was Joe Hunter even alive? She didn't doubt his abilities, but he was going up against three monsters who had no care for the sanctity of life. They thrived on hurting others and would have no compunction about murdering Hunter or the girls. What if their savagery proved too much for Hunter?

What would they do to him? What would they do to
Nicole and Ellie?

'Stop it!'

Her voice surprised her.

She had not meant to shout out loud. Since it was the
first time she'd said anything above a whisper in the last
few hours her voice sounded alien, the shout of a stranger.

The desperation was enough to clear her mind and
she understood how close to hysteria she'd come. She
hadn't even been aware of the tears smearing her face
and wobbling on her lashes. She batted them aside with
a grimy hand, before fixing both hands on the steering
wheel again. 'Stop it, stop it, stop it,' she said, much
calmer now. Worrying about hypothetical scenarios was
getting her nowhere, and certainly wasn't helping her
friends. Be strong, she commanded herself, and do what
you have to do.

Hunter had told her to keep the sun over her right
shoulder. She had mostly done so during her flight from
the desert. Occasionally the trail had disappeared under
drifting sand, or had followed the contours of the land
around some of the larger mesas, but she was happy
that she had not deviated from her heading. Soon she
should see the highway and a route south to Holbrook.

A check of Hunter's phone showed the SOS symbol
still displayed.

She was thirsty and the water was a temptation but
she ignored the container. It would be unwise to try
driving in this rough terrain while juggling the container
to her lips. Nor did she want to stop; while she was

moving she felt she was doing something positive and she wouldn't jeopardise that sense of worth for anything.

Regularly her gaze slipped from the road to her mirrors. She expected to see that damn pick-up truck materialise from the dust haze as it had when the Logans chased her from the gas station. Had Samuel made it back to a rendezvous with Carson, and were they even now chasing her down? She didn't think so, but it was always a possibility. One thing she knew for sure was that she wouldn't stop this time. If a gun was pointed at her head again then she'd rather chance a bullet than let them have their way with her.

She thought about how easily she'd given in that first time when she should have fought harder to get away. Had she done so then Nicole wouldn't have had to suffer the way she had, but what of Ellie? Jay was under no illusions; she'd have put the run-in with the Logans down to the crazy antics of some rednecks letting off steam, would have fled the desert and picked up the route west as they'd initially intended doing. She wouldn't have reported the incident to the police, having no desire to have to attend court hearings and face those crazies a second time. No one would have known that the Logans had the teenager. God, she didn't want to think about that. Maybe the torture she and Nicole had been put through was for a greater cause; perhaps a controlling force was ensuring that Ellie's suffering wasn't prolonged. No, she realised after a moment, no unseen hand was at work here, just a sequence of unfor-tunate events that had enmeshed her in the warped plans of a group of mad men. She'd had no power over these events, but things had changed in the shape of Joe Hunter. He was the only thing she could rely on now, not divine intervention, and by a strange quirk of fate he was now relying on her.

Power lines, strung from poles like serried ranks of soldiers, were the first indication that she was approaching the highway. The power grid led all the way from Holbrook towards Indian Wells, adjacent much of the time to Highway 77. Seeing the tall steel structures looming from the dust haze, she almost cried out in joy. It was way too soon for that, though, so she only gritted her teeth, fixed her hands on the wheel and headed directly for them. The phone's SOS symbol had been replaced by a single white cross. Still no signal; and it would only get worse as she drove closer to the pylons. Nevertheless, she believed that there'd be booster stations at several locations along the route where she could raise the alarm.

Within minutes she was under the power lines and seconds after that the Yukon found asphalt beneath its tyres and Jay swerved wildly on to the highway. She recalled the last time she was on a similar road and how she'd longed for a freightliner to be heading in the opposite direction; she was thankful that the road was deserted now. She floored the gas, shooting south, her concentration split between the road ahead and the phone which she'd now grabbed up and held against the wheel.

With only five miles until the truck stop, she finally found a signal.

21

It made sense to leave the ranch as soon as possible, but there were considerations to be taken care of first. Primarily the girls' nakedness: they would last no time out under the sun in such a state of undress. Not to mention that I felt self-conscious each time my gaze swept over them. To get them away safely I required their full trust, and I couldn't gain that by averting my eyes all the time. I asked Nicole about their clothing, but they had no idea where it was. Apparently they'd been stripped naked on their arrival and had remained that way since, with the Logans deriving great joy from their embarrassment. I pulled off my shirt and handed it to Ellie. Buttoned, it covered her and reached all the way to her knees. For Nicole I snatched the denim jacket in the bunk room off its hook, and found a pair of boxer shorts that were grimy but would have to do. There was no footwear fitting for the girls, so I had to fashion makeshift shoes from the stinking bedding which I tied on to their feet with lengths of string. Standing side by side, their fingers entwined, the girls looked like waifs from the poorest ghetto.

While engaged in making them decent, I kept one ear

cocked on the door, but it appeared that Carson and Samuel still hadn't found each other. The CB radio had been quiet for some time, as had the radio I'd taken from Samuel. The silence could be a harbinger of bad luck, I decided, because my first assumption could be wrong. The cousins could have rendezvoused and Samuel would have admitted that he'd lost his radio in the fight with me. Even now, they could be approaching on foot so as not to warn me of their arrival.

Ellie was sobbing softly, while Nicole's attention had barely strayed from my face. She had fully accepted me as a lifeline, indeed had grown dependent upon me for everything.

'Nicole,' I said. 'Find something to carry water in and fill it up. While you're at it, have a drink and make sure Ellie does too.'

She nodded, and led the girl towards the kitchen area. I checked the sawn-off liberated from Brent and found it to be an old-fashioned double-barrelled model chambered for twelve-gauge shot. There were two unused shells in it, and I discovered extra ammunition in a drawer in a rickety sideboard. I shoved a number of the shells into my pockets then went to the front window. Taking care not to offer a target, I only pulled the drapes aside by an inch and peered outside. This vantage offered me a view back across the wide plain towards the mushroom mountain, but there was no sign of the pick-up truck. That could mean anything: the Logans could be taking a different route back, or might even already be out there and beyond my line of sight.

When I turned from the window I found Nicole and Ellie staring up at me. Nicole's gaze was rapt on my face, whereas Ellie was studying a scar next to my heart, then drifting from it to the bullet wound in my shoulder and the tattoo next to it. I couldn't tell if she was troubled by the marks I carried as emblems of my trade, or if they gave her some kind of comfort. After weeping moments ago her face was now flat and without emotion; I worried that her mind had been irretrievably affected by the inhumanity she'd suffered these last few days. Damn it, the girl was going to bear witness to further horror before we were through, but there was nothing I could do about that.

To Nicole I said, 'Can you shoot a gun?'

'No,' she replied, her voice a thin whisper.

I handed her the shotgun. Firing it without any training would be enough to knock her on her backside, but that's not what I had in mind. 'Carry this for me, but be ready to hand it over when I need it.'

'OK.' She took the shotgun tentatively.

Jay Walker, for all her resistance to shooting Samuel when she'd had the opportunity, now seemed like a much stronger person than her friend. Then again, I'd no right making that assumption, because Jay had suffered differently. She had endured physical assault, and had been confined in a box, but that would be preferable to what I suspected Nicole had put up with. Maybe if she got a bead on the Logans she would blast them to hell without a second thought; though here I was probably imposing my sense of justice on hers.

Switching my attention to the girl, I touched her gently on the side of the face. She didn't as much as flinch. 'How are you doing, Ellie? Are you OK?'

'What's that tattoo for?'

Her question surprised me, and I glanced down at the ink on my shoulder. It was a reminder of my time with Arrowsake, the secretive Special Force I'd once been a member of and now longed to put behind me. They had owned me for far too long and to this day were still trying to exert their influence upon me. Back then I'd been an idealistic soldier, and had gladly gone to war for them, in denial that I was being used. I believed that my work was just, that I was making the world safe and free from tyranny and terrorism, when in fact the men I'd served were equally as despotic as those I killed. Once I'd worn the tattoo with pride, but now it was just an ugly reminder of my past, as horrible as the knife and bullet wounds in my chest.

'It's a reminder,' I said, 'so that I never go back.'

Ellie squinted, trying to make sense of the three intersecting arrows embossing a shield. Beneath the coat of arms was a weighing scale, both arms equally balanced, one side supporting an ellipse, the other a horizontal crescent. Symbolically it signified the balancing of good and evil – a halo and devil's horns – but I wondered about the validity of it now: perhaps, more pertinently, I'd come to understand that the balancing of right and wrong was a constant battle. Not that I suffered a moral conflict while looking down at the girl; I'd no qualms about taking the war to the Logans on her behalf.

My words were too cryptic to make sense to the girl, but she accepted them without question. Then she added her own doleful summation: 'I never want to come back here either.'

It was a good motivator.

We moved for the back door, but I halted them with a raised hand. 'Hold on a minute.' I looked at Nicole. 'Do you know where they put the keys to Jay's car?'

She shrugged. Things like car keys wouldn't have been important to her while she was being stripped and humiliated, but I hoped that she'd seen where they'd been hidden.

'Think, Nicole. Did you see any of the men hide them somewhere?'

She shook her head. 'I don't know. I'm sorry.'

'Ellie?'

The girl shook her head, then glanced back at Brent Logan. I knew what she was thinking, and guessed that it wasn't somewhere she'd like to look, but I wasn't as squeamish. I returned to the corpse and went through its pockets. Apart from a couple of Chupa Chups lollipops in his back pocket there was nothing. I didn't think that Ellie would appreciate them so left the sweets where they were. I looked around the living room. No keys. The kitchen and bunk room came up bare as well. At worst Samuel or Carson was holding the keys, but then again, for all I knew they could be in the SUV. When I'd spotted it in the lean-to shed outside, I hadn't been thinking of the car as a possible getaway vehicle. Its presence had meant something else to me then, and it did now. I wondered where Jay was and if I'd made a terrible mistake in sending her off alone.

If my suspicions were true, there was nothing I could do about it. Nicole and Ellie needed my help, and I had to prioritise.

The girls were each carrying a plastic bottle of water. Ellie held hers in her arms like a doll, while Nicole had jammed hers under her armpit so she could also carry the shotgun. I went quickly to the faucet and pumped the arm. The water tasted mildly salty, but it was better than nothing. Some of it dribbled down my chin, and I dashed it away with the wrist of my gun hand. I took another gulp, swilled it round and then spat the remainder into the sink. I was ready.

'Let's go, girls,' I said, as if I was about to take them on an exciting adventure. It was important to keep them motivated, and not have them dwelling on the alternative, that I was possibly leading them to an unmarked grave. 'Stay close to me at all times. Don't speak and stay low, OK.'

We made a ragtag group in our mismatched and generally ill-fitting clothing but that didn't mean a thing as long as it kept them safe. The overlarge clothing would help keep the sun off their bodies, even if I was condemning myself to a serious case of sunburn. I checked the way was clear, then guided the girls over to the lean-to and directed them to crouch in the shadows alongside its north-facing wall. 'I'll only be a few seconds,' I said. 'If you see or hear anything don't shout, just knock on the wall. I'll hear you.'

Checking all around, I backed up to the board covering the front of the shed and pulled it to one side. Jameson Walker's SUV was coated with trail dust, but otherwise it seemed as good as new. Moving quickly for the driver's door, I opened it and leaned inside. There were tiny cubes of broken window glass in the footwells. Luck wasn't with me. There were no keys in the ignition. I checked all the likely hiding places: behind the visor, under the seats, in the glove compartment, but my search didn't turn them up. Typical, I thought, because that would have been way too simple a get-out.

What I did find outweighed the disappointment that using the SUV for a getaway had proven a dead end. Both Jay and Nicole's belongings were still on the back seat, holdalls containing clothing. I searched through them, grabbing something more appropriate for the girls, as well as two pairs of sneakers. Since Nicole wasn't that much bigger than Ellie, I supposed there wouldn't be much difference in the size of their footwear. There was no time to change now, so I stuffed them into my rucksack, and returned to the girls.

'We can't use the car I'm afraid. We're going to have to walk out of here.'

They exchanged a glance, but neither looked perturbed by the prospect of having to traverse the desert. In fact they looked eager to get going, as if they wished to be anywhere but here, on foot or otherwise.

We used the trail I'd followed coming in, skirting the rubbish tip to the boulders where I held up a hand to stop them. The Logans' no show was troubling me, and caused me to rethink our options. It was one thing taking Jay in that direction when I'd a vehicle waiting for her, quite another to expect to guide the two girls all the way back to the highway on foot. Instead, I made them head to the west towards the sweeping range of hills. Not that I planned on walking them too far that way; all I was interested in was finding some place where I could hide the girls while I returned to the ranch. The only way I was going to prevent the Logans from pursuing us was to stop them dead in their tracks.

Dead, I decided, was a good choice of word.

22

Fortune shone on Jay in a totally unexpected fashion. The cellphone was proving wholly unpredictable, and when she'd tried to patch through to the local police the line had been so weak that she couldn't hear what the dispatcher was saying and suspected that her words were equally garbled. Frustrated, she'd pulled in by the side of the road, but when that had failed to make any difference she chanced calling Hunter's friend instead. She had no luck, but had the idea to write a text message instead. An old hand at SMS messaging, she filled a page with a brief description of what had occurred and a description of the Logan ranch's location in no time. She pressed the send button and it failed, but then set it to retry. The cell would automatically resend the message and she didn't have to concern herself with it while she drove nearer to Holbrook. Throwing the Yukon into drive, she was pulling back on to the highway when she saw a vehicle approaching. Her first fear was that it was the old pick-up truck, but in the next instant she yelped in joy as the gumball light rack on the roof of the vehicle became visible. She brought the Yukon to a halt and got out, running towards the police cruiser waving both arms over her head.

The police cruiser coasted to a stop a hundred yards from her position. Jay understood how crazy she must look and couldn't blame the officers for approaching her cautiously, but it didn't stop her. Both front doors opened and an officer exited each side of the vehicle, both resting their hands on the butts of their sidearms.

'Help me!' Jay yelled. 'Help me for God's sake!'

'Ma'am, stand still and place your hands on top of your head.'

Jay couldn't believe that they thought her a threat and continued towards them. The taller, younger of the two officers drew his sidearm. The other, a balding man whose gut shadowed his belt buckle, merely dug his thumbs into his gun belt. The two officers shared a measured glance. Then the younger repeated his command. 'Stand still. Place both hands on your head. I will come to you.'

Jay stumbled to a halt. Fifty yards still separated them. 'I need your help. My friend has been kidnapped.'

'Just take it easy, ma'am, and we'll have things sorted in no time.'

The younger officer continued to approach her, alert for any sudden movement. He also checked the desert on each side, and Jay wondered why the hell he'd do that. What did he think: that she had some friends hiding by the roadside ready to jump out on him? Who in their right mind was going to try to hijack a cop car? 'My friend and another girl have been kidnapped! You have to do something.'

'Everything's under control, ma'am, now take it easy.' The young cop turned to call back to his colleague, but kept one eye on Jay. 'You hear what she said, Sarge? Maybe you'd best call it in.'

'I'll try but you know how these power lines cause interference.' The older cop leaned back into the cruiser. Jay expected to hear his voice in stereo, coming from both the cruiser and the radio set clipped to the younger cop's shirt. She heard neither, and realised that the set in the car must work on a different frequency to that for the radio the cops carried. It didn't matter, some kind of action was being taken and that was all she cared about.

The young cop was now within ten feet of her and Jay saw a handsome, clean-cut face, a well-developed body. A badge pinned to his uniform shirt identified him as Officer Lewin. Jay opened her mouth to speak but the cop pre-empted her. 'Tell me your name, ma'am.'

'Jay,' she said. 'My name's Jay Walker.'

She saw the man's eyes narrow slightly at her name and again he glanced quickly at his partner. The older cop was still busy at the handset in the cruiser. Officer Lewin appraised her, taking in the bruising on her face, her dishevelled appearance, the dust adhering to her clothing, and believed her words. His gaze slid to the Yukon and it was as if he recognised it, though she couldn't imagine how. His next words made things clearer to Jay. 'The man who was driving the GMC, where is he?'

Jay turned to look at the vehicle as if it would help order her mind. 'He's called Joe Hunter. He helped me escape but has gone back to get the others out.'

'Joe Hunter.' Lewin nodded his head, confirming the name was the same one he had lodged in his memory. 'He's a private investigator from Florida?'

'Yes,' Jay said, eager to relate the rest of her tale. Her words came in a rush. 'They murdered those people at the gas station the other day. They kidnapped a girl called Ellie then came after me and my friend. They still have them: Nicole and Ellie. You have to do something *now*!'

Lewin moved closer, doing a visual check of her body a second time, and frowning. 'OK, slow down. You said your name is Jay?'

'Yes, Jay. It's actually Joan Walker, but I go by Jay.'

'OK, Jay. Tell me again: who committed murder, who took the other women?'

Jay threw a hand towards the desert. 'A family from out there. They're called Logan. Three of them.'

A dark cloud descended over Lewin's features. He looked back towards the cruiser and saw his partner staring back at them from behind the windshield. He lifted a hand to indicate that all was fine. When he turned back to Jay, his brow had knitted into a frown. 'You're sure it was the Logans?'

'They've held us prisoner for the last three days. Of course I'm sure. Carson, Brent and Samuel. They're monsters. They killed those people at the gas station and if you don't do something quickly they might kill the others.'

For a second time Lewin turned to regard the other cop. The older man slid out from the cruiser and stood with his thumb hooked in his belt. After a moment of reflection he began to walk towards them. Returning his attention to Jay, Lewin said, 'OK. The Logans.' He was thinking hard, and Jay sensed he wasn't figuring out a way to handle the situation, but his superior. He caught her looking and shot her a cautionary glance. 'Wait here,' he said.

He went to meet the sergeant halfway.

Jay stood watching as they conversed, but couldn't hear their voices. The sergeant scrubbed his palm over the back of his neck, a sign that he wasn't happy with what he was hearing. The older man snapped something guttural, then marched towards Jay. Looking abashed, Officer Lewin fell into step behind him. The sergeant looked angry with her and Jay couldn't guess why.

'What is this madness?' he demanded.

Madness?

'It's the truth. A family called Logan murdered those people at the gas station then kidnapped me and my friend. They also took a teenaged girl called Ellie Mansfield. I think they also took another woman. Helena Blackstock.'

Behind the sergeant, Officer Lewin slowly closed his eyes.

'Could you be confusing their names?'

Jay went from one foot to the other, restless, and eager to see action. 'Like I told your colleague, they're called Carson, Brent and Samuel Logan. Aren't you listening to me? They murdered those people and are going to do the same to my friends *if you don't get a move on*!'

The sergeant's hand went to the back of his neck once more. He shook his head, turning to appraise the younger cop. Lewin must have felt the sergeant's eyes on him because he slowly opened his own to meet his superior's stare. Jay felt a tremor pass through her: it was as if both men stood on different sides of the same fence, and she was unsure which way things would go with either. Jay saw the sweat on the sergeant's palm. Not all of it was from the palpable heat surrounding them. His hand slowly lowered to rest again on his belt, an inch or so from the snap holster holding his sidearm.

Jay knew instinctively that something was about to happen, but she was rooted to the spot, unable to make sense of the sudden note of challenge emanating from both men. Though she was baking in the desert heat, she fancied that a cold wind was blowing and she shivered. She heard their voices as if they came from inside a deep cave.

'You said you'd checked the Logans' place.'

'I did.'

'You can't have. Not if what she says is true.'

'I checked it. There was no one there.'

'You also said you checked their place when Helena Blackstock was taken. You put me off going out there myself.'

'I did check it, but I didn't have a warrant to search the entire ranch. She could have been anywhere, and anyway, their alibi checked out.'

'Their alibi wouldn't have held water if you hadn't also said you'd seen them in town. I think you lied about that, and I think you're lying about all the rest.'

'I'm not.'

'I think you're lying and covering for that damn family of yours.'

'They ain't my family.'

'They are. They're your blood. It's why you've always covered their asses.'

'You've no proof of that.'

Jay listened with a sense of dawning dread. She couldn't believe what she was witnessing here, or begin to understand the implications of what was being uncovered. She looked from one officer to the other, finally catching Officer Lewin's attention. He nodded at her, just once, short and sharp, to confirm her suspicions. Then he lifted his gun.

Jay flinched, but the gun was aimed at the sergeant.

'What the hell do you think you're playing at, boy?' The sergeant straightened his shoulders.

'You're an accessory to murder and kidnapping. I'm arresting you, Sergeant *Logan*.'

'This is ridiculous!' The sergeant twisted to look back at Jay and found her standing with both hands at her throat, a look of terror on her face. 'Don't believe him, ma'am. He's talking garbage.' He spun back to stab an accusatory finger at Lewin. 'In fact, why'd you even call me that? I'm not called Logan! It's you who's a goddamn Logan!'

Lewin shrugged his broad shoulders. Then he shot

the sergeant, the bullet knocking the man down on the pavement. The sergeant wasn't dead; his bullet-proof vest saved his life. The impact was enough to stun him, though, and he rolled over on his back and lay there a moment. Jay wanted to run, but the shock of what she had just witnessed held her in place. Oh, my God, she thought, oh, my God, this can't be happening. She saw the badge on the sergeant's chest: Sgt Espinoza. Then her gaze tilted up to the young cop, and she saw the family resemblance. He was a younger, fitter version, his hair cut short, his uniform neat, but he could be mistaken for a cleaned-up Brent Logan. Lewin sneered across at her as he moved alongside his sergeant. 'Don't know how I'm gonna sort this one out, Sarge, but I'm sure I'll find a way.'

Sergeant Espinoza craned round to stare up at Jay. His mouth was hanging open in dismay, not just at the realisation that the young man he'd patrolled with had turned out to be a monster, but that he'd failed in his calling. Protect and Serve: it wasn't something you could do lying on your back at the side of a road. 'Get outta here!' he croaked at her.

Jay wanted to run, but everything was moving in slow motion. Officer Lewin didn't seem so inhibited. 'Don't move, goddamnit, or the next bullet's yours.'

Espinoza grabbed at his gun, but he was partly lying on top of it and it wouldn't clear the holster. Lewin stamped on his elbow, pinning down his arm. Espinoza reached across with his free hand, trying to push Lewin away. Lewin shot him again. This time the vest couldn't protect him, because Lewin had aimed low. Espinoza screamed in agony, his left knee shattered.

'Did you call this in, Sarge?'

'Goddamn you!'

'That isn't helpful.'

'Yes, I called it in. You're finished!'

'Now who's the liar?'

'I used the set in the cruiser. Back-up's coming.'

'No one's coming. I had my radio on scan; you didn't get a line to the dispatcher because of the power lines.' Lewin moved the gun so it was pointing directly at Espinoza's face. 'Sorry things had to turn out this way, Sarge. I kinda liked you, but you know how it is. Blood is thicker than water.'

The crack of Lewin's gun startled Jay, but also set her in motion. She screeched out a cry as blood spattered next to her feet, and turned her jump of fright into a run for the Yukon.

'Stop!' Lewin's shout was almost as loud as the gunshot of a second before. 'I've just killed my fucking sergeant: don't think I'll go any easier on you!'

Jay didn't stop.

Earlier she'd thought that death would be preferable to being taken again by the Logans, but thinking it was one thing, quite another when a bullet could take out your heart in the next instant. She didn't want to die, and her body reacted without guidance, making her run faster than she'd ever done in her life. Behind her came the slap of Lewin's boots on the road.

She made it to the Yukon, and having left the door

open when first seeing the police cruiser she was inside
it within seconds. The engine was still purring. She
pushed it into drive and put her foot on the gas. But it
wasn't enough. Lewin was already there, reaching inside
and grappling her. The car shot forwards, knocking
Lewin aside, but she had no control of the wheel and
the Yukon went down off the road and into a dry ditch.
The collision with the opposite bank threw her foot off
the pedal and the Yukon's engine cut out at the same
time. Frantic, Jay looked around. Lewin was at the side
of the road, stunned, but already clambering back to his
feet. She twisted the keys in the ignition and relief
flooded her as the engine kicked to life with a low grumble. She gave it throttle, but even such a large vehicle
couldn't push its way perpendicular. She threw it into
reverse and tried again.

Lewin reached in and turned off the engine.

'I told you to stop, goddamnit.'

Jay didn't fight him this time; she lifted her arms to
show surrender. It was all she could do with the muzzle
of his pistol against her temple.

23

Once upon a time the Navajo must have lived all over this territory. I recalled passing the commercialised trading post the evening before while travelling over from New Mexico, and noting the ancient caves in the rock face beyond the stores. They had been decorated with vibrant turquoise pictograms, depicting hunting scenes. The cave that I found where Nicole and Ellie could shelter was nowhere near as dramatic, but even there I found signs of ancient occupation. The cave art here was merely scratches on the walls, and I couldn't really tell what the hands of men had formed and what were the results of weather or geological activity. Some of the pictures were easily identifiable: a spotted horse, a man, the sun, but the rest were nigh-on indecipherable. If I'd discovered the cave on another occasion I'd have been enthralled, but not while more pressing matters held my attention.

Natural steps allowed easy access to the cave, approximately fifty feet up the side of a rock face. It wasn't a single cave I'd found; that would have been too obvious a hiding place for the girls, but one of many in the pockmarked mountain. I wasn't sure about the indigenous life forms, or if the cave could be home to something dangerous. As far as I knew there were no mountain lions here and bears were confined to the northern states – I hoped. I checked it out first, just in case, before waving at the girls to join me inside.

'There could be snakes or scorpions, so be very careful where you sit,' I cautioned then.

They were too exhausted to care. I'd pushed them solidly for the last half-hour, setting a pace that had robbed them of their breath and slicked their bodies with sweat. They both sat down immediately, and Nicole's hands went to her feet to massage the chafed flesh under the tatters of blanket. While they groaned and busied themselves with their water bottles, I made my way to the mouth of the cave. From my high vantage I could see all the way back to the ranch. It looked like a cluster of bleached shoeboxes, the watering hole a shimmering ribbon alongside it. I didn't pay the ranch much heed but looked for the mushroom mountain at the head of the trail. At first I couldn't distinguish it from the rest of the hills because at this distance and elevation it had lost its distinctive shape. I traced a route from the ranch, to the huddled boulders, to the broken ridgeline and then, at the far end, found what I was looking for. Something glinted in the sunlight. It could only be the pick-up truck, I realised, because nothing else was moving out there. I couldn't make out the truck, but saw the plume of dust as it raced back towards where I'd fought with Samuel among the ravines.

It was only a matter of time.

I went back inside the cave and saw that Nicole had helped herself to the clothing I'd stuffed into my rucksack. She'd shrugged out of the denim jacket, and I caught her in a state of undress. Her face went beetroot as she covered herself with her arms.

'Sorry,' I said, showing her my back.

Her self-consciousness was a good sign. Earlier she had been so down-beaten that her nakedness hadn't been a consideration. She must have been operating on autopilot, the shock of what she'd been through dulling her senses. From behind me I heard her feet shuffle on the floor, followed by the rustle of clothing being hurriedly pulled on.

'It's OK, I'm decent now.'

Taking things easy, I approached the girls. Nicole was still standing, albeit on one leg while trying to pull a shoe on to her opposite foot. Ellie hadn't moved from where she'd collapsed in exhaustion, and she was now sitting cradling the bottle of water to her chest, her dark hair hanging in bangs over her features. My shirt had rucked up on her tiny frame and looked like a tent with her head poking out of the top.

'Is there something that Ellie can put on?' I asked.

Nicole delved in my rucksack and brought out a shirt and thick tights.

As Nicole reached for her, I held out my hand. 'Just give her a few minutes to get her breath back.' I nodded towards the entrance of the cave. 'Could I have a word, Nicole?'

The young woman must have understood what was

troubling me. She placed the clothes down next to Ellie, then gently ran her fingers over the girl's hair while whispering soothingly. Ellie nodded in reply but didn't as much as look my way. Nicole followed me to the exit where I indicated she should sit down out of view of the outside world. I sat next to her so that we could converse in whispers.

I didn't know where to start. Not that I was a stranger to victims of violence, inhumanity, rape, but this was somehow different. I felt a personal attachment to these girls I'd pledged to save, and broaching the subject felt like I was reinflicting the horror of their situation on them. Nicole must have sensed my reticence, so she said, 'They both raped me. Carson and Brent. More than once.'

'Oh God . . .'

'I'm all right. I've survived.' The way she said it, it was like she was repeating a mantra she'd clung to for the last few days. But I could tell it was not something she believed. I wanted to give her comfort, but physical contact might have been misconstrued. Instead I just sat there, offering a presence she could rely on. Though it wasn't enough, it was all I could think to do.

'What about Ellie?' My voice broke at the end. Jesus, it wasn't something I wanted to contemplate.

'They hit her, forced her to watch, but no, they didn't touch her like that.'

'Thank God.' I could have kicked myself for the insensitivity of my statement, but Nicole didn't appear to pick up on it. In fact, quite the opposite, judging by the way she looked at mc. Never throughout her ordeal, I believed, had Nicole wished it was someone else that the Logans assaulted. I could tell by the way she had comforted the girl that she felt protective.

'I wouldn't have let them.'

Her words were loaded, and I understood. She'd offered herself to the brutes to keep them away from Ellie. Allowing them to abuse her was a fair trade to ensure the girl was spared. Earlier I thought that, of the two of them, Jay Walker was the stronger, but now I suspected otherwise. There was more to strength than the obvious. I admired Nicole, but I also pitied her. A good person like her shouldn't have to suffer what she'd endured.

Checking that Ellie remained oblivious of our conversation, I said, 'I'm going back, Nicole.'

I expected her to argue, to plead for me to stay with them, but Nicole concurred with a nod. I wasn't the only one who could pick up on a hidden meaning. Nicole understood why I was going back, and knew what it signified if I did. Maybe she wasn't merely resigned to the idea but actually embraced it.

'I can't let them leave, otherwise they might disappear and they'd never be brought to justice,' I went on.

'Are you going to kill them?'

I didn't answer, but it wasn't difficult to figure out what my silence meant. The moment stretched out, though it wasn't uncomfortable. We were of like mind.

Finally, I said, 'If I don't come back it will be down to you, Nicole.'

Nicole hugged herself, the only sign that she feared such an eventuality.

'I'll leave you the shotgun. When it grows dark I want you to lead Ellie to the south. Don't go back near the ranch. Go that way.' I pointed across the desert towards a distant range of hills. From the maps I'd studied in my motel room in Holbrook, I recalled there was a small town just beyond those hills. 'There's a place called Dilkon. You'll find it, or you'll find a road. You'll be safe when you get there.'

'They could still come after us,' Nicole said.

'Not if I stop them.'

'When you stop them, you'll come back for us, won't you?'

'Yes, of course.'

'Then why are we having this conversation?'

'Just in case.'

'I don't want to think like that.' Nicole placed her palms over her face. For a second I thought she had started to weep, but when she lowered her hands her eyes were dry. She looked at me with a forthrightness that demanded the answer she sought. 'You have to stop them, Hunter. Not for me, not even for that girl in there, but for the other girls they'll do the same to in the future. It's too late for us now. Stop them for every other girl's sake.'

'I intend to.' I rose from the floor and offered her my hand, not to seal a bargain but to help her up. 'But if they get me first, then you have to do everything you can to take Ellie to safety.'

We were at an impasse but both glad of it. Nicole took my proffered palm in her delicate fingers. She stood elegantly, as if accepting my hand to dance, and I guided her over the uneven floor of the cave. Ellie still hadn't moved, other than to lift the bottle and cradle it against her cheek.

'Can you help her to dress?' I indicated my bare chest. 'I think I might need my shirt back, or I won't have to worry about the Logans: the sun will do their job for them.'

Earlier Nicole's mind had been in some other place, and as I'd noted, her nakedness hadn't been an issue. Not until a genuine possibility of salvation was on the cards had her natural instincts kicked in; now it was as if my semi-naked torso was a reminder of her previous situation and she blushed a second time. Or was it that? Her gaze had lingered for a few seconds while tracing the contours of my chest and shoulders. I wasn't averse to a beautiful woman eyeing me in approval but part of her embarrassment must have rubbed off on me, and I retreated quickly to the mouth of the cave.

I heard a low howl, but couldn't pinpoint its source, the reverberation effect of the cave making that impossible. It could have been the cry of an animal from somewhere back in the hills but I didn't think so: more likely it was Samuel's or Carson's voice carried on the breeze. All I could be certain of was that it came from some distance away. Behind me I could hear the girls conversing softly, followed shortly by the sounds of clothing being pulled on. For the sake of their privacy I busied myself with the S&W, checking it for dirt and finding it clean. Nevertheless, I kept checking until Nicole returned and handed me my shirt.

I slipped into it, feeling the prickle of sunburn on my flesh. I'd only been out in the direct sunlight for half an hour but it had done its work. I pulled my rucksack back in place, and then took Nicole to the opening to give her a crash course in handling the shotgun.

From this distance there was no way that we could be seen by anyone at the ranch, but I still wasn't happy about Samuel's no-show and wondered if he was nearby. The pick-up that had only been a glint in the sunlight earlier had now arrived back at the ranch. There was however, no sign of Carson, and I guessed that he'd already gone inside. I wondered how he'd feel when he found his son lying face down in the mess from his split skull. I waited for a shout of rage, but it didn't come. Perhaps Carson had cried out while I was busy putting on my shirt and I'd missed it, or that was the odd moan I thought I'd heard. Maybe he wasn't the type to scream, but had sunk down in silent grief, or, worse than that, was so cold and psychotic that his son's death had no effect on him. Those were the most dangerous of enemies. But then they weren't the only ones who could be cold, calculating killers.

Taking the shells from the gun, I encouraged Nicole to take a couple of dry shots. I told her to keep the stock snug in her shoulder and not to allow it any play otherwise it might knock her on her backside. I tried to imagine the target she formed in her mind's eye as she squeezed on the trigger. One thing I knew for sure was I didn't want to get on her wrong side, not when the steel edged into her irises and her jaw tightened like that.

'It's a sawn-off,' I pointed out. 'You don't have to be too specific about where you aim, but the range isn't that great.'

'Don't worry, Hunter. I won't shoot till I'm looking them dead in the eye.'

I smiled, but it was more of a grimace. Then again, so was the death's-head grin she returned.

24

The sky had turned to a milky haze on the far horizon, the distant hills purpling into evening, while behind me the sun was a fiery ball in the west. If you stood still, closed your eyes for a minute and opened them again, you'd see that the sun had dipped perceptibly. Not that I had the time or inclination for such games. Recalling other times I'd been in deserts, I knew that night fell rapidly and that darkness would soon be upon the land. The low visibility would help, but I reconsidered the instructions I'd given to Nicole. With luck she wouldn't take my words literally and set off for Dilkon the second the sun set, because it would take me longer than that to get into position, kill the Logans, and then return for her and Ellie. If my mission was successful, I didn't fancy having to track them across the desert afterwards. Forget about later, I told myself. Kill the Logans first: that was what I must concentrate on.

The rocks at the base of the escarpment offered plenty of cover as I made my way towards the ranch, but there was an open area of perhaps a quarter-mile where I'd be in the open. I trusted that, having returned to the ranch and found Brent dead and their hostages gone, Carson would be on high alert. He would recognise the killing shots as being from a handgun and correctly assume that someone else had freed the girls. Maybe that was why he hadn't screamed in rage: he was anticipating a second assault on the house and was even now preparing to defend himself. It could be that he was moving from window to window, trying to detect movement out here.

A set of desert cammo fatigues would have come in handy, but all I had was the clothes I stood up in. Thinking ahead, I'd left my rucksack with the girls at the cave in order to have a lower profile approaching the ranch, because there was only one way I could do it and that was on my belly. Taking a lesson from nature, my mission was to hunt the Logans the way a wild beast stalks its prey. My friend Rink is a master when it comes to insertion into enemy territory, and I'd learned a thing or two from him. Keeping low, moving very slowly, it's surprising how easily you can foil even the most alert sentry. Like a lion moving in on a herd of gazelle, you creep in as close as possible, then go for a dash at the final moment, and that's what I planned now.

Belly-crawling, the going was slow, but the floor of the desert undulated on occasion and offered places where I could gain on the ranch without fear of giving myself away. At those times I came up to my hands and knees and moved rapidly to where it flattened out and I was forced back down. I made it to within four hundred yards of the buildings without raising the alarm. I had three options from there and lifted my face to check each in turn. Moving directly for the house was out. If Carson was spying from behind the tattered blinds he couldn't fail to see me, even as the dusk spread like an ink stain across the land. The junk pile that I'd used when coming in from the north was the better route, but I was incredibly thirsty by then and thought that a trip down to the watering hole wouldn't go amiss. From this angle, the corner of the house blocked much of the view that way and down by the water I determined that there'd be enough of an embankment to conceal me while I drank. I set off: a body length at a time, then a pause while I listened for movement. I didn't want to twist my head to look around because my face would be detectable as a pale blur even through the shadows. Instead I kept my head down, concentrating on my peripheral vision, where even the slightest movement would be increased tenfold.

A stockade fence, where the dust had piled up against the lowest spar, offered easier passage, and I was able to move faster for the pool. Then I was on open ground and had to take it slow and easy again. It took me some time and by then night had fully dropped. The moon hadn't come up yet, but the stars were vivid sparks in the heavens. A soft glow seemed to emanate from the surrounding plain, but here and there lay pockets of shadow where the ground undulated. Using each feature of the land I made it to the watering hole and slithered down to its edge. Thankfully, I slaked my thirst: if I happened to be killed in the next few minutes, I didn't want to go to my grave parched. Not that it made much difference in the scheme of things, but I now had a bellyful of water, a comforting thought. It made me feel a little stronger, which helped dull the ache in my body from my earlier fight with Samuel.

I continued along the embankment so that I could come in towards the ranch from an unexpected angle. Out behind me was nothing but open desert and there'd be no way a launch would be anticipated from that direction. To keep my gun clean I'd carried it in my belt at the back with my shirt tucked around it. I drew it now and prepared myself for the last leg.

Continuing towards the house in the same fashion I got to within fifty yards of the right front corner. Here was the first of the outbuildings and I crouched against the back wall while I took a look around the corner. I was at an angle to the front of about forty-five degrees and couldn't see into any of the windows, but I could make out flickering light from within. The ranch was so off the beaten track that it wasn't served by the main grid and as I couldn't hear a generator running the light must have come from a lantern. Ignoring the house, I turned my attention to the Dodge pick-up.

The thought crossed my mind: take the truck, go and pick up the girls and get them the hell out of there. The Logans would be stuck out here, sitting ducks for when I sent the police back for them. But that wasn't going to happen. I was resolved to make them pay for what they'd done to their hostages. Watching the front of the house, I went to the pick-up and crouched down at the back wheel. From under the hem of my jeans I pulled the knife I'd earlier liberated from inside the house. It wasn't a fighting knife, the type I usually employed, but it was sharp enough for what I intended. I jammed the tip into the tyre, twisted the blade to widen the puncture then moved on to the next wheel. I made a full circuit of the truck, slashing each tyre, and though it wouldn't put the truck permanently out of commission it would definitely slow it down.

That done, I moved for the front of the house, my senses on high alert for anyone hiding in the darkness. I shoved away the knife and held my gun ready.

Kick the door in and go in blasting?

No, if Carson had readied himself for me I could be doing exactly as he hoped.

It was best that I take it easy.

I moved to the right of the front door, seeking a chink between the planks as I'd done during my first time here, all the while watching for the light from within to be disturbed by movement. There was nothing I could detect, possibly meaning that Carson was more disciplined than I'd given him credit for. I found a hole large enough to set an eye to, but thought better of it. Maybe Carson was waiting for me to do just that. It would be difficult for him to see me out here, but who knew what he was capable of?

I couldn't keep putting things off for ever: I needed to get a position on the man. Inhaling, I leaned forward.

To my right I heard the softest scuff of boots in dirt.

Son of a bitch! Carson wasn't inside the house. He'd made it look that way and had set me up with a trap. He'd been stalking me all along, I realised, waiting even as I disabled the vehicle before showing his hand. I couldn't think why he'd waited as long as this, maybe just to be sure of his shot. But now I'd presented myself as a target he was making a move.

I dropped to my knee, swinging my revolver towards the sound.

That's when I got my second surprise.

It wasn't Carson attacking out of the darkness. In fact the man lumbering in my direction wasn't even armed. And judging by the way he jerked, he hadn't seen me on the front stoop until now. He reacted the way many do when faced by the barrel of a gun: he launched himself sideways out of the line of fire.

I wanted my rematch so much I could taste it. I wanted to meet him fist to fist and pay him back for the hurt he'd put my body through. But I'm not an idiot. I fired.

My bullet hit him and Samuel Logan span with the impact, his arms flailing. He hit the ground and I lined up on him again. He had the sturdy body, the compact muscles, that one bullet might not be enough to finish. I would prefer a head or heart shot, but in the dark that wasn't easy. I fired again and saw him jolt as my bullet struck.

Coming up for a better shot at his prone body, I levelled the gun on him again.

Suddenly it felt like my cheek was on fire, and I heard the crack of a gun an instant afterwards. Splinters of wood made a cloud within the scope of my vision and forced me to turn away. Natural instinct took over and I threw myself down on my right side to avoid the next bullet that slashed through the wall and into the space I'd just vacated.

From inside the house Carson continued to fire, unloading half a clip of ammunition through the planks. All of his bullets went overhead but it could be seconds before he adjusted his trajectory and shot me like I'd just shot Samuel. I scrambled away, dabbing a hand to the bloody spot on my face. I couldn't stop to think about the wound, but was reassured not to find a huge hole where I'd been hit. Luckily his first bullet had missed and it was only the flying splinters from the wall that struck me. I'd been fortunate, but that could change with his next round.

While I was scrambling for my life I couldn't get off a clean shot, so conserved my bullets. My escape took me back towards the pick-up I'd disabled. Carson was yelling now, raining curses down on me for slaying his son. A window was shattered and the barrel of his gun poked out. Carson was firing indiscriminately and couldn't see me as I crouched alongside the pick-up. I aimed for his muzzle flash, then adjusted to the right where he was hiding behind the lintel. I returned fire.

A chunk of wood flew in the air and Carson let out a howl, but his muttered curses afterwards suggested I'd missed him. Thinking himself clever, he popped up at the opposite end of the window and unloaded four rounds at me. I'd been expecting the move and my gun was waiting for him. As his bullets whacked into the front grille of the Dodge, I leaned over the hood and loosed a single bullet. His yowl this time held a note of agony and there followed the solid thump of a body hitting the floor. No way was I going to lower my guard though, because until I knew otherwise I wouldn't presume that he was dead. I waited, enveloped in a cloud of cordite. I allowed my jaw to hang open, to cut down on the internal sounds of blood pulsing through my veins, and listened intently. Over to my extreme right wood creaked in the breeze but that was all.

It had been over so quickly that I was left a little dissatisfied. But the feeling could prove premature, because I still had to check that I'd dropped both Carson and Samuel permanently. Holding my position, I reloaded my gun, allowing the empty shells to fall by my feet. I didn't start spinning the cylinder or anything dramatic. Then I waited again. From my position I could no longer see where Samuel went down, but I was confident that I'd placed two bullets in his body and he wouldn't get up from them. I was more concerned that Carson was still alive. Until I was sure he was finished I couldn't relax my vigilance. I listened some more and the creaking noise fell silent as the breeze dropped. A hush stole over the desert.

After a minute or so I came out from my hiding place and walked cautiously towards the front of the house. The gun was ready should Carson suddenly jump up and try to kill me. Ten feet out, I stopped and listened once more. Some night creature called in the distance, its voice like that of a mournful spirit. I took another couple of steps, eased up on to the porch. There were holes in the walls the size of clenched fists and one of them gave me a view inside without having to lean in through the shattered window. The lantern light spilled across the boards and touched the sole of a boot. It didn't move. Taking things real easy, I took a better look around the edge of the window frame and was greeted by a satisfying sight. No, Carson wasn't dead yet, but a hole in his throat pumped blood with each heartbeat. He didn't have much time left in this world, but enough that he'd see the face of his nemesis. Shifting to the door, I pressed down on the handle and then nudged it open, following its swing as I stepped into the living quarters. Brent had been moved from where I killed him, and was now laid out on the couch with a blanket over his face, but I paid him little notice. Holding the gun steady, I advanced on his father who was propped against the back wall. The older man struggled to lift his head and meet my gaze. He'd lost copious amounts of blood already, but he still spat a mouthful on the toe of my boot. I didn't flinch, didn't give him the satisfaction.

Although his gun was lying on the floor at his side, it didn't look like he'd the strength to pick it up. Keeping aim on him I dipped and lifted it away: just in case I was wrong.

'You're the bastard who killed my boy.'

His voice was paper thin, but still challenging. His eyes were rheumy, but that was probably their natural state. He fixed them on me.

'Yes,' I said. 'I killed your son *and* I killed your cousin Samuel. Now there's only you left. But I don't think that'll be for much longer.'

'Who the fuck are you?'

It was only fair that he learned the name of his executioner. 'Joe Hunter.'

'Never heard of you.'

'You wouldn't have.'

'What's any of this got to do with you?'

'Call me a concerned citizen.'

Carson gave a disparaging laugh, but all that did was help pump further blood down his chest. He gave up trying to staunch the flow and his hands slipped into his lap. 'You came out here because of those bitches . . .'

'I came for the girls,' I corrected him.

'Fuck, I knew we'd overstepped the mark taking so many in one go. I did warn Brent that we were being too . . . ambitious.' He laughed again, but it was hollow. 'Was a time when he'd have listened, too, but there's no telling him lately.'

'You're trying to blame all of this on your son. Even when you're dying? Make no mistake, I'm not going to save you, so you may as well come clean. Confession's supposed to be good for the soul.'

Carson shrugged, and now his hands flopped by his sides. The signs were all there; he was leaving this world very soon. His eyelids slipped shut. I gave his boot a nudge. 'What happened to Helena Blackstock?'

He didn't even bother to look at me. 'Gone.'

'She's dead?'

'Gone,' he repeated, and that was all. The next sound was the rattle of air between his lips. The crotch of his jeans darkened as he voided his bladder.

Chewing a lip, I stared down at the corpse. I had hoped

to see him dead, and was happy that he'd paid dearly for his crimes against the women. But, having started questioning him, I now felt I could have done with another minute. I pretty much understood what had happened to the Logans' hostages; why they chose them continued to elude me. In the grand scheme of things it didn't really matter. All that was important was that I'd managed to free the girls, they were safe and their tormentors were now all dead. Nevertheless, a part of me wanted to understand the motivation of the beasts. If it had been about sex, then why had they discarded a beauty like Jay Walker, stuffed her in a hole in the ground to rot? Nicole said the men had each taken turns on her, but had spared Ellie the same treatment. Ellie was little more than a child, but if that meant anything to the Logans then they wouldn't have stripped her naked in the first place. No, there was more to their motivations than the base need for sex, yet I could only cast conjecture now, because there was no one around to straighten things out for me.

Not unless there was still a spark of life left in Samuel.

I walked quickly for the front door, holding both my and Carson's guns ready, because if Samuel had survived his wounds he might take a second try at me.

That eventuality didn't come about. Even as I approached the exit door, I could hear the roar of a vehicle powering across the desert towards the ranch. Stepping outside, I watched gumball lights strobe across the desert, blue, red and white, causing the rocks they touched to appear like they flickered and jumped.

Good, I thought. Jay managed to get safely to the police.

25

Officer Lewin was no calculating murderer, and Jay understood now that his actions were driven by panic after his sergeant had challenged him on his part in the Logans' schemes. He hadn't thought through the shooting of Espinoza, had merely reacted with violence the second he thought that the game was up. She didn't believe he'd taken part in the kidnapping of any of the women who'd ended up at the ranch, but he was stuck between the proverbial rock and hard place. Like he'd said to the sergeant, blood is thicker than water. He likely suspected that his kin were involved, but had swayed any investigation away from them out of familial loyalty. One thing she was positive of was that he hadn't taken as much as a look at their ranch when Helena Blackstock's husband had reported her missing. The chains in the barn, the holes in the ground: all would have been dead giveaways that the Logan men were keeping prisoners there.

The sergeant had also intimated that Lewin had given false alibis for the men, and had put him off searching the ranch. How could a man who'd sworn to protect and defend the people under his care do such a thing? It was obvious: he cared more for the Logans than he did anyone else. In some dim recess of her mind, Jay could understand why. Family loyalty was important to her too, but if she suspected her father of committing something as heinous as what the Logans were up to, she could never hold her peace. Or could she? No. It was an alien notion to her, protecting monsters. She would have to tell someone.

Lewin had snapped his cuffs on to her wrists, thrown her in the back seat of his radio car. The seat was hard and flat with little give and she bounced with each jolt of the vehicle as Lewin powered it across the desert. She tried to sit upright, but, having her hands clasped between her knees, her balance was off, so instead she'd turned in order to brace her back against one door. Lewin was a hazy figure beyond the thick perspex screen that separated the compartments. The plastic was almost opaque with scratches and graffiti etched by previous prisoners, yet she could still see that he was sitting tense in the driver's position, and she could hear him muttering to himself. She'd already tried to reason with him, but her pleading had gone ignored, and in the end she knew that he was beyond sense and had given up. The closer they got to the ranch, the more agitated he grew and on a couple of occasions she'd heard him snap out a curse that she thought was aimed at himself, or maybe at his kin for forcing him into this position.

He'd murdered his sergeant, for God's sake! Bundling Espinoza into Joe's Yukon, he'd rammed a cloth into the gas tank and set it ablaze. He'd watched as the tank erupted and the SUV went up like a torch. He'd crowed that he'd frame Hunter for murdering the sergeant, but that was ridiculous: the ballistics report would prove otherwise. Then there was the fact that she would tell what really happened, but she understood what that meant. He was returning her to the beasts who'd tortured her. If he were to get away with this she couldn't be allowed to live, and this time the Logans wouldn't waste time with torture. He wasn't acting rationally; every action he performed was only making things worse for him – and far worse for her.

Night had descended as if a blanket had been draped over the sun, but she could still make out the landscape and recognised the mushroom-shaped mountain Hunter had led her past earlier. Travelling at this speed, her life could be counted in minutes. Before long the ranch would come into view and soon after she'd be thrown down at the feet of the murderous family. She couldn't just sit there and allow Lewin to deliver her to her prospective murderers. But what could she do?

'Officer, please! You must know how insane this is?'

'Shut up!' Lewin slapped a palm against the Perspex.

'You're a police officer, for God's sake!'

'I was. But that's over now, isn't it? God damn it! Shut the hell up and let me think.'

'Yes. Think. Think about what you are doing. You can't go through with this. Can't you see?'

'I said *shut the hell up*!'

'It's not too late to save yourself.'

'You're not concerned for me. All you're thinking of

is saving your own worthless life. Now, for the last time, shut up, or I'll stop the car right now and shoot you myself.'

'Please!'

Jay's plea was drowned out by a string of curses, the force of which was savage enough to push her down in her seat. Lewin was so frightened that she was sure he was on the verge of going through with his threat. She clamped down on her next words, turned her face so that he wouldn't be able to view her in his mirrors. She didn't want him to see her weeping. Ridiculous as it was, she didn't want to be perceived as pitiful: if she was going to die it would be with a challenge in her stance. She'd tried reasoning with him, so it was time for something else. She must fight back. But what was she going to do when her hands were linked by steel cuffs? She couldn't think like that. When she'd been imprisoned in the box she'd been in a far more precarious position than she was now. She'd managed to escape then, and though Hunter had later helped, she was sure that she would have done all right relying solely on her own wits.

When Officer Lewin had thrown her inside the radio car, he had been thinking like a criminal, not an officer of the law. That very fact had served her well, because there was something about her that the man did not know. It was her only chance for escaping his clutches and launching a counterattack against his kinsmen. If she was to die in the process, then so be it. She'd grown the balls her dad advocated, and she sure as hell was going to use them rather than let the men have their own way. With her head dipped for another reason now, she slipped her chained wrists around her side, concealing her movements with her body. Occasionally she glanced up, but Lewin was heedless of her, still lost in the panic in his own mind. Good, she thought, keep on panicking and let me prepare myself. Suddenly he demanded her attention: he flicked on the bar lights on the roof of the car and, if anything, sped up as he neared the ranch buildings. The light play of different hues danced across the desert floor, giving the landscape a surreal cast. He was announcing his arrival to his family, maybe via a prearranged signal. She was loath to look, but she twisted her head so she could press her cheek to one of the windows. Within a couple of hundred yards of the ranch the buildings were reflecting the gumball lights and it took a moment for her to differentiate one flickering shadow from the next.

Lewin grunted something she failed to catch, though it was definitely an oath. He began to slow down, but at the last second span the car to the left, and the movement flung her across the seat. Jay was struggling back up when he braked, dust clouds whirling and conspiring with the lights to block her view. Still, she saw the figure come out of the door of the main house, holding a revolver over his head. The gun was upside down, hanging by one finger through the trigger guard. He showed the gun to Lewin, and then bent slowly to place it on the floor of the porch. The dust and the strobe-like effect of the lights made the figure judder in her vision, but she was certain it wasn't one of the Logans. It was Joe Hunter.

Her benefactor was stepping out, trusting that it was safe to relinquish his weapon now that the police had arrived on the scene. Officer Lewin was already getting out of the car, and Jay saw him snap his service pistol out of its holster. Lewin twisted so that he was leaning over the top of his door, his gun aimed directly at Hunter's chest. 'Police!' he yelled. 'Stand still and show me both hands.'

Hunter lifted his open palms. He took a step away from the revolver and then set his hands on the top of his head. He stood stock still, returning Lewin's gaze. 'Everything's OK now, Officer. It's over with.'

'Not yet it isn't.'

Jay heard Lewin's whisper, but no way could Hunter have. Lewin leaned into the door further, and Jay knew what was coming next.

She'd never doubted Hunter's word. He promised her he'd return to the ranch and free Nicole and Ellie. It looked like he'd done exactly that, but to what effect when he was now stuck there like a sitting duck while Lewin was lining him up for a killing shot? She could see it now, a bullet punching into his chest, knocking him down on the stoop of the house, never to rise again. With Hunter dead, what hope would the three women have then? She could not let that happen. Her screech was wordless and high-pitched, but it was all the warning she could summon.

Before the scream had tailed off she heard the bang of Lewin's pistol. She jerked her head, as if she'd the supersonic power to follow the trajectory of the bullet, but she had no hope of that. Before her head was even halfway to the target she saw in her peripheral vision Hunter falling to the ground, and the timbre of her scream changed from one of defiance to one of despair. Her head continued to track, her eyes widening, expecting to see the splash of blood as Hunter rebounded off the deck.

But that wasn't how it happened.

Hunter wasn't falling. He was in a controlled drop, both knees spreading wide as he squatted low and to one side. His hands had dropped from his head: one out to the side to steady him, the other thrusting under the tail of his shirt. In a blur his hand came out from under his shirt, swung up and she saw the flash of his return shot a second before the sound wave hit the car. Again she could not follow the play of gunfire, but she heard the corresponding whack of Hunter's bullet strike Lewin. Lewin gasped, cursed and then staggered back to place the car firmly between him and Hunter. His body was jammed up against the window next to her face, and she saw where Hunter's bullet had struck his Kevlar vest. Lewin fired back, yelling something animalistic, even as he reached for the handle of her door. She guessed what he was thinking, and this time she was right. He tore the door open and reached for her, intent on using her as a shield against Hunter's bullets.

No way was she going to let that happen. Jay threw herself across the back seat, kicking at his arms as he reached for her. Lewin was too distracted, trying to watch where Hunter was, and her heel painfully struck his forearm. He swore, yanking his arm out of the way. The respite was momentary, because he then swung his gun hand inside to take its place. 'I don't need you out the fucking car to kill you,' he yelled.

His words were meant for the two of them, and if they didn't work on Hunter she would never know if she didn't do something *now*.

Jay lunged across the seat, pulling out of concealment the knife that Hunter had given her hours earlier. She had it clasped between both fists, the blade spearing towards Lewin's arm. Lewin couldn't watch them both at the same time, and she was certain that he'd be more intent on a gunman than a seemingly helpless woman. But then, she wasn't always right.

The boom of Lewin's pistol sounded like an atomic detonation within the confines of the car.

26

Something had been troubling me for some time and it seemed that my suspicions were correct. I recalled the first occasion I'd met Officer Lewin at the burned-out husk of Peachy's gas station. Then I'd thought him a good man, someone who could help, but in his words there'd been a note of warning, and also one of suspicion. When he'd allowed Helena Blackstock's name to slip into our conversation a flicker of unease had passed across his features. At the time I'd decided he was inwardly berating himself for admitting that there was a problem with missing women within his jurisdiction, but I knew otherwise now and it went deeper than that. Scott Blackstock said the police had visited the Logan ranch and their search had come up empty. Well, the cop responsible must have been blind, because the chains in the barn weren't a new addition and it was clear what they were used for. More likely the cop knew about the Logans and their unhealthy fascination with certain women and had turned a blind eye.

On first arrival at the ranch I'd conducted the shortest of searches and discovered the barn, the lean-to where Jameson Walker's SUV was hidden, and the pit where Jay had been chained. The SUV wouldn't have been a factor when Helena went missing, but there sure as hell hadn't been a search conducted here since the gas station robbery. Considering that the Logans were known as the local hellraisers any cop worth his salt would have paid them a visit; and seeing as this was Lewin's neighbourhood, it stood to reason that it should have been within his remit.

I'd no idea what hold the Logans had over him, but I could make a good guess. Recalling that ninety-five per cent of the local population was Navajo, it made sense that of the remainder a proportion would have family ties. Was it a stretch to think that the Lewin and Logan clans were not far removed? Made me wonder about Carson's wife, and what her maiden name had been.

It was a pity that I hadn't formed this opinion until after I'd sent Jay to fetch the police, and it had only firmed in my mind once I saw the reaction from Nicole when I told her what I'd done. I had intended asking Nicole about that reaction but too many things had taken precedence and it had slipped my mind; now I wondered if she'd overheard the Logans discussing their law enforcement ally.

Everything I'd considered could have been bullshit, but over the years I'd learned to trust my senses. As I saw the cruiser speeding towards me I made a snap decision: I shoved the semi-automatic I'd liberated from Carson into my waistband. The Smith and Wesson I dangled from my finger, offering the approaching cop no threat. Then I'd placed it on the porch and stood away from it, assuming the position with my hands laced on my head. For all I knew, I was totally off track, and couldn't even be sure that it was Lewin who'd responded.

Next second, the young fair-haired cop threw open his door, and, using the cruiser as a shield, he targeted me. That wasn't unusual and wasn't what told me that he intended shooting first and asking questions later. It was the rage in his face. My presence on the doorstep could mean only one thing, especially considering the gun I'd just put down: the Logans were no longer a threat to me. Ergo, I'd killed them. And he was now the only one left to resolve the terrible situation.

I couldn't see Jay, but I heard her scream. I was already moving by then, dropping out of Lewin's line of fire and going for the semi-auto at the small of my back. Lewin's shot went over my left shoulder and through the open door, striking something metallic inside the house. The *spang*! of the spent bullet was echoed by my return shot. At this distance I'd no option but to aim for his centre of mass, most of which was concealed by the cruiser. Nevertheless I watched Lewin respond by rearing away and twisting his body so that he could check where my bullet had struck his anti-ballistic vest. Like many US cops, he wore his vest beneath his uniform shirt, but I'd been under no illusions that it was there. My shot hadn't been designed to kill, merely to stop him killing me while I was out in the open.

He snapped his gaze my way, just as I vaulted off the porch and ran at an angle towards the cover of the

Dodge pick-up. 'Bastard! I'll kill you!' His yell came out as an hysterical scream, and he fired at me. Again his shot went wide and I threw myself down at the far side of the pick-up, placing the wheel hubs and engine block between us.

For a couple of seconds I had no line of sight, but it was a fair trade considering the cover it offered. I took the respite to eject the magazine and check the load. Carson had been shooting wildly, and judging by the weight there weren't that many shells left in the gun. In fact, only two bullets remained, one of them already in the breech. I'd .357s in my pockets, but this mag wasn't chambered for them. Crap. Never mind, I'd just have to make them count. One thing I was sure of: I wouldn't be aiming for his bulletproof vest next time.

'I don't need you out the fucking car to kill you.'

Lewin's shout wasn't only for Jay's ears. He'd yelled loud enough that I knew what he intended, and it wasn't to warn me that he was about to kill her. He was trying to draw me into the open again. If he shot Jay there and then, what leverage would he have against me?

I didn't concern myself with his bullshit at first, because I didn't think it was an immediate threat. But then I heard Jay screaming again and I dodged around the back of the pick-up. Lewin was so incensed with rage – or fear – that he wasn't acting in a rational way. He was grappling with her, leaning inside the car and, for a long enough time, his attention wasn't on me. I kept low, running towards the rear of the cruiser.

Bang!

Lewin's gun went off and the rear of the car lit up like a match had been struck. Then all was dark again and I could no longer hear Jay. Not necessarily because she couldn't speak, but for the fact Lewin's scream was deafening. He reared up and away from the back compartment, and his left hand was busy trying to pluck a knife out from between the biceps and triceps muscles of his right arm.

I went over the back of the car in a hurdle and slide, landing on my feet beside him. Lewin's face was a picture of shock, both at the stabbing and at my sudden appearance. His reaction was far from considered, and maybe if he'd acted differently he'd have found a way out of this alive. But he swung his gun on me. I wanted answers, yes, but not at the expense of my life, or that of any of the girls. I shot him, point blank between the eyes.

The impact didn't knock him flying like you see in the movies; his body merely dropped directly in front of me, collapsing like a house of cards. He ended up propped within the open door and the sill, his knees one way, his arms the other. There wasn't much left of his head to talk about.

Cop Killer.

The notion struck me, a cold sliver of steel that drove right through my guts.

There was going to be a shit storm over this. No doubt about it.

I looked down at the corpse and thought, No. This piece of crap was no police officer. A uniform didn't make him a good man. It's what was in his brain and his

heart that defined him, and he was no cop. He was
almost as sick-headed as the Logans, allowing this to go
on as long as he had.

I hadn't killed a policeman, but a beast, and I could
live with that.

A moan drew my attention and I leaned down to peer
into the prisoner compartment. Jay was looking back at
me, her eyes wild with fear, but also a touch of triumph.
Her face was streaked with dust, blackened with tears,
and her hair was matted to her skull. Her clothing was
in disarray, equally smeared with dust and God knows
what else and one of her shoes had fallen off and was in
the well between the seat and Perspex screen. Other
than lumps and scrapes from her earlier beatings and
incarceration, she looked well.

'I did it, Joe,' she said very softly. 'I did it.'

I took it she was referring to fighting back: jamming
the knife I'd given her through Lewin's arm. If she
hadn't brought herself to do so, I fear there'd have been
a different resolution to my fight with Officer Lewin.
She'd done it all right. Her distraction had allowed me
to get close enough to kill the bastard. Her counterattack had quite possibly saved both our lives.

How Lewin missed shooting her in such a confined
space I couldn't fathom. It was too dark to see where his
shot had gone, but I knew from the way Jay looked back
at me that she hadn't been hit. I wondered if an ounce
of compassion had remained in Lewin's soul and at the
last moment he'd redirected his aim. Maybe he only
intended panicking me by making it seem like he'd killed

the woman. Then again, maybe Jay had stabbed him forcefully enough to knock his gun aside at just the right moment. I would never know now, and it wasn't something I was about to take up with Jay. She'd been through enough. There would be plenty of opportunities to learn the story in the coming weeks, to a point where we'd both be sick of repeating it.

Jay made to clamber out of the cruiser, but then had second thoughts as her gaze alighted on the ruin of Lewin's head. She cringed.

'Wait there.' I took hold of the corpse by the ankles and dragged it away from the car. Lewin's service pistol had fallen to the ground. It was best that I didn't touch it: the forensics would prove everything that had happened and I didn't want to confuse things by handling the cop's gun now.

Returning to the cruiser, I looked back at the house. Brent, Carson, Samuel and now, Officer Lewin: all of them were dead. It was over but for one thing.

'C'mon, Jay,' I said. 'I'll take you to Nicole and Ellie.'

To use the police cruiser would cause us too many problems in the long run, and not only because of the impact it could have on any subsequent forensic examination. I was concerned that – on seeing the police car approaching – Nicole might panic and open up with the shotgun I'd left her. Jay watched dispassionately as I went through Carson's effects. The keys to Jameson Walker's SUV were in his trouser pocket. I remembered that she'd called him the Tin Man because he'd been so heartless. Now it was Jay who looked like she possessed not an ounce of compassion, but who could blame her?

She also looked across at where Brent Logan was laid out and her only reaction was to blink like a bullfrog, slow and languid.

I took her by the arm and led her towards the back door. She followed but then came to a halt and stared back into the living space.

'The other one? Samuel? What about him?'

I felt a tremor of fear course through her body, and I put a comforting arm around her. 'As dead as the rest of them. He's outside.'

'Thank God,' she sighed. She rested her head against my shoulder, then moved with me for the exit door.

I thought about checking on Samuel, but decided enough was enough. Jay didn't want to be parted from me for even a second and I didn't wish to subject her to more corpses than she'd already seen. I guided her across the yard towards the lean-to shed. With no need for stealth now, I gripped the plyboard covering and tore it aside. Jay gave a sob as she recognised her father's car. Not that he'd berate her for the damage it had sustained, but it obviously brought back everything about her original kidnapping. For a second or two I thought she'd refuse to get inside. I fired up the engine and edged it out from under the tin shed. Jay had no qualms about climbing in, and I'd to warn her off while I swept the crystals of broken window glass from the front seat. Once in, she tucked the seat belt round her, snapping it secure. After all that she'd endured, the action brought a smile to my lips. She didn't notice; she had her head in both hands and was now openly crying.

I allowed her a few minutes as I drove back out and across the yard. A rickety fence made things awkward for driving around the right-hand corner of the ranch, so I was forced to go left. I glanced across at Jay as we passed where Samuel had fallen but her hands were still obscuring her face. Good. She was spared what I saw.

Giving the SUV its head, I swung us past the watering hole and beelined for the distant cliffs where I'd left Nicole and Ellie. With the headlights on they'd see us coming, but I hoped Nicole would have the good sense to ensure they kept their heads down until I could reassure her that it was safe to show themselves.

There was no trail to follow, as we were reminded by the jouncing of the wheels over the same ruts I'd recently used for concealment. Jay braced one hand on the dash, while using the other to wipe the tears from her face. Between watching the desert for hidden dangers, I checked her out and saw that she'd managed to rein in her emotions for now. Or, more accurately, she'd cried for herself, but now she was more concerned about her friends' well-being.

I hadn't told her what Nicole had suffered, but it was apparent that she had figured it out for herself. I bet she believed her own ill-treatment was nothing in comparison, and guilt was setting in once more.

'She's a strong young woman,' I said. 'Stronger, I think, than many people give her credit for.'

'I promised I wouldn't let anything happen to her.' Jay's voice was small.

'And you followed through with your promise, Jay. Look at what you've had to do to save us all.'

She frowned at my choice of words. 'It was you that saved *us*, Joe.'

Shaking my head, I said, 'If you hadn't got Samuel off me that first time, I don't know what might've happened. He could quite easily have killed me, and I dread to think what would've happened to you all if he had. Then, when that dirty cop almost killed me, you saved me again. That's twice I owe you my life.'

She went silent for a while, working through what I'd said, but she wasn't entirely convinced. She told me what had happened between the two cops, and how Lewin had murdered his sergeant when he'd realised the gig was up. And how helpless she'd felt when Lewin had taken her prisoner a second time.

'I should have thought about his connection to the Logans sooner. I'm sorry I put you through that again.'

'Everything turned out well in the end,' she said. 'And we now know everyone responsible. At least it's over with.'

A couple of outstanding issues still remained, but I wasn't about to bring them up. Not yet. Notwithstanding the whereabouts of Helena Blackstock and Carla Logan, the reason for the Logans selecting specific lookalikes continued to elude me.

'Let's collect the others and get the hell out of here,' I said.

Jay perked up, anticipating the longed-for reunion with her friends.

The cliffs were etched under the glare of the SUV's headlights, the yawning caves like the open mouths of a choir. Flicking the headlights to announce our arrival, I guided the vehicle to the foot of the cliff where I'd left Nicole and Ellie. We were a good distance from the ranch, but I didn't doubt that they had heard the recent gunfire. They couldn't know who had triumphed, of course, and would still be wary of whoever was arriving so soon after. I'd have preferred a more low-key approach, but Jay had unbuckled her seat belt and was out of the door before I could caution her.

'Nicole! Nicole!'

Jay had no clue which of the caves held her friend, but it didn't stop her running for the foot of the cliff. From inside the SUV, I searched for the cave mouth I'd tagged in my memory and saw two figures emerge from it. There were corresponding shouts of joy as Nicole and Ellie began clambering down the rock face. I didn't want to interrupt their reunion, so busied myself with another task. I climbed out of the cab and turned to survey the nightscape, holding my reclaimed S&W in one hand and Carson's semi-auto in the other. The girls were safe for now, but I wondered how long that status quo could be maintained, because there was yet another outstanding issue I'd neglected to mention.

As we'd driven past where Samuel had fallen, his body was no longer there.

27

I'd expected a shit storm and that's what happened. Investigative teams descended on the area en masse: cops, crime scene investigators, dignitaries from the Navajo Nation, the mayor of Holbrook, camera crews and newspaper reporters. Crime scenes were marked at various locations on a large triangle that included Peachy's gas station to the Logan ranch and back to the road where my rental and the body of the dead police sergeant were located. Even a troop of National Guardsmen was press-ganged into helping cover the extensive search area. The only ones missing were the FBI; I wondered how long that would last.

Thankfully we were spared much of the circus that erupted, but the compromise was that we were all held in separate rooms at the police office in Holbrook. For hours, we were each interviewed over and over again about our respective involvement in the case. I'd briefed all the girls during our drive to the town, stressing one point: I told them to hide nothing, tell everything else as they remembered it and everything would be OK. The truth was the best policy and attempting to cover up the fact I'd killed three men wouldn't help in the long run.

The men I'd killed were monsters and deserved what they got, and I didn't think there'd be too many recriminations when the full story came out. Yet there was a major complication.

Because two Navajo County police officers were involved in fatal shootings, their case was farmed out to the State Police Office ensuring 'transparency' was maintained during the ongoing investigation. Jay's testimony, she told me, was at first met with disbelief, but I suspected that the forensics would prove everything and Lewin would be confirmed as Sergeant Espinoza's murderer.

Two state police detectives took over from the local cops, who'd been hammering me with cross-examinations since our arrival at Holbrook, and they loaded me into an unmarked Lincoln sedan to transport me to an office in downtown Phoenix, apparently the one where the infamous Miranda versus Arizona investigation took place. Funnily enough, as in that landmark case, I wasn't offered my rights either. Though I took that as a good sign.

Detective Andrew Chambers was the younger of the two, a man indisposed to smiling. He had straight black hair, finger-combed back from his high forehead, and pointy ears. Maybe he was conscious that he looked like a Vulcan from *Star Trek* when he allowed his bangs to fall forward. He was wearing a navy blue suit, a pale yellow shirt and no tie. His shoes were scuffed at the toe, a sure sign that he did most of the driving. His partner, a fifty-something guy called Michael Witherspoon, with a florid face and a gut that overhung his belt buckle, was the more amiable of the two. I guessed he was supposed to be the good cop.

I was parked on an uncomfortable bench in the busy waiting area while the detectives organised their next move. When they returned to collect me, Chambers just grunted and jerked his head at me to follow him. The cubicle they took me to was your standard interview room, with a video camera, audio recording equipment, and bolted-down table and chairs. If not for the flickering overhead strip light I'd have thought there was a power outage, because all the electronic equipment was dead. Isolated more like, because our conversation was the type they refer to as 'off the record' in police circles.

I chose the seat reserved for the bad guy: the one nearest to the recorder and opposite the lens of the CCTV camera. My chaperones sat across from me. Chambers had a ring folder with him that he placed on the table top. He opened it to reveal a single acetate pouch containing a number of papers. Through the semi-opaque plastic, Chambers made a perusal of the details on the uppermost sheet. It was a printout from my military file. There wasn't much on it that hadn't been blacked out under the Official Secrets Act, other than a ten-years-out-of-date mugshot, my birth date and service number. He glanced up at me, then across at his partner. I waited for the inevitable.

'You're a bit of a mystery man, ain't you?' Chambers said.

'What you see is what you get. There's no mystery.'

Chambers tapped the acetate, as if confirming something, then closed the file. He frowned, exhaling loudly. Witherspoon only offered me a twinkling eye.

'Care to tell me a little more about yourself?' Chambers asked.

'I've already gone over everything with your buddies at Holbrook.' I leaned forward and mimicked his action of tapping the file. 'It's all in there and I know you've already read and absorbed it. I don't know anything extra I can add.'

Chambers scowled now, his intimidating look, but it had no effect on me. 'See, the way I see it, when we get hold of a military file that has more lines scored through it than my school report, it tells me we've got a problem on our hands.'

'You were academically challenged? I'm surprised you made it to detective.'

Chambers sat back, his face frozen, more at Witherspoon's chuckle than at my sarcasm.

Now it was Witherspoon's turn to tap the file, but his action was dismissive. 'I think we can stop blowing smoke up each others' asses. What do you say, Hunter?'

'I'm all for a clean air policy,' I said. 'I gave up smoking years ago. Have a real bad habit with caffeine, though. I get cranky when I haven't had a coffee. Any chance of a brew?'

'You don't seem to have a problem when it comes to killing,' Chambers said. 'Is that another of your bad habits?'

'Self-defence,' I pointed out, 'and in defence of life. What

would you rather have me do, Detective, allow the Logans
to continue raping and murdering innocent women?'

'You could have come to us.'

'You saw what happened when the police were
involved.'

'That son of a bitch Lewin isn't indicative of the
entire force.'

I shrugged. I didn't intend having a pissing competition with Chambers, but my flippancy was allowing
him to get his way. I changed tack. 'I've already covered
everything in my previous statements. I've nothing to
answer for and you both know it. I haven't been arrested,
and I don't expect to be. So what's the real reason for
bringing me here?'

'The real reason?' Chambers gave me a look of
disbelief.

'I have no idea.'

Chambers snapped a glance at Witherspoon. 'Can
you believe this asshole?'

The older cop just lifted his shoulders noncommittally.

Frustrated, Chambers slapped his palms down on
the table. The sound ricocheted round the small room.
It engendered a blink of annoyance from Witherspoon,
the first time he'd looked anything but a genial guy.

Witherspoon turned to his partner and said, 'Go get
our guest a cup of coffee, Andy. I'll handle this.'

Chambers stood up quickly, maybe aiming for
dramatic effect, but the action was thwarted by the
bolted-down seat and he swayed in place to check his
balance. 'Don't see why we're pandering to him. Jesus

H. Christ! It's a bloodbath out there and all we've got is his word that he's one of the good guys. That goddamn file says otherwise, you ask me.'

Chambers wasn't playing bad cop, he really was pissed.

He stabbed a finger at me. 'There's still the issue of the gun you were carrying. I could push for charges over that, don't forget.'

He had a point. I wasn't licensed to carry a firearm here in Arizona. If he wanted to be a bureaucratic arsehole he could indeed have me brought up on charges – if I admitted to having taken the gun to the ranch. 'I told you already . . . I took the gun off Samuel Logan when he tried to kill me and Joan Walker.'

I could see he didn't buy the lie, but what else could he do? I'd told Jay to say the same thing, the one concession to self-preservation we'd agreed on during the drive to Holbrook. 'I have a problem with your type,' he said. Then without another word he yanked open the door, slamming it behind him.

'You think he'll spit in my coffee?'

Witherspoon chuckled, but all pretence of humour had been put aside now. He rolled his neck, then leaned forward on his elbows and clasped his hands together. He stared at me for a moment. 'I were you, I'd wait until you were outta here before drinking anything that isn't from a sealed container.'

'What's his problem with me? I just helped save the lives of three innocent women. You'd think he would be pleased.'

'He doesn't like vigilantes.'

'I'm not too fond of the term myself.'

'See, a guy once decided to take the law into his own hands. He used a shotgun and killed the man accused of raping his daughter. Shot him in the balls.'

I shrugged. 'Just deserts.'

'That's why Chambers doesn't like you. Your attitude. See, the way things turned out, the accused guy was innocent and was proven so when the real rapist was arrested later the same day. The guy who died . . . that was Chambers' older brother.'

'He has my sympathy, but what has that got to do with me?'

'We've heard you've made a habit of taking the law into *your* hands.'

'So you've likely heard about the type of men I've gone up against.'

'Some cops would applaud you. Chambers though, he thinks that you're a loose cannon. He thinks that you went to the Logans with only one thought in mind.'

I had no lie for him. Instead I asked, 'What about you, Detective?'

He slowly unfolded his hands so that he could tap his fingers together. It wasn't exactly applause, but he got his message across. 'Doesn't make a difference what I think. I've a warning to give you and you'd best pay attention.'

'I'm listening.'

'Samuel Logan escaped.'

'I know. I heard. He took Officer Lewin's cruiser after I left with the girls. He hasn't been found yet?'

'You know he hasn't.'

'And you're concerned I'm going to go after him?'

'Kinda sounds like something you'd do.' He smiled but it was a hard look now. He placed his hands on the ring binder for emphasis. 'And we don't want history repeating itself. You get my drift?'

'Loud and clear.'

'It would be a shame if we had to lock you up . . . after all the *good things* you've done.'

'Yeah. But it's not something you need fret over.'

'So you're gonna do as I say? Forget about Samuel?'

'I'm not interested in him. Soon as I'm out of here, I'm taking Jay and Nicole home. You're welcome to Samuel Logan as far as I'm concerned.'

'You said you shot him twice.'

I hadn't mentioned that I'd put the second round into him when he was already on the floor and wasn't about to now. 'I did.'

'So we don't expect him to get far.'

'That's good,' I said. 'The sooner you get him the better. Like I said . . . he's all yours.'

'Keep thinking like that and you'll be outta here in no time.'

'No argument from me.' I started to stand up, but Witherspoon waved me down again.

'I thought we'd put things straight.'

'We have. But I just sent for coffee. You don't really think that Chambers will spit in your cup?'

'It's not spit I'm worried about. I've a bad feeling that it'll taste distinctively salty after that jerk-off's finished with it.'

Witherspoon chuckled, and the twinkle had returned to his gaze.

'Go on. Get outta here, before I change my mind and lock you up until Samuel Logan's safely behind bars.'

I looked down on him and the file. I gave him a none-too-subtle sly grin. 'Samuel Logan's safe from me.'

I meant what I said, but with one caveat: so long as he stayed away from the women.

28

A few minutes later I was standing out under the desert sun, squinting at the reflections of light bouncing off the edifices of glass and steel opposite me. In downtown Phoenix the air was full of exhaust fumes from the traffic stalled at the lights. There was a steady thrum of engines, a babble of voices, the swish of tyres from the cross street to my left. For a second or two I wished I was back in the solitude offered by the desert. I looked for a cab, but there wasn't one in the queue on this side.

I didn't take that coffee from Detective Chambers, and I was definitely ready for one. I looked for a Starbucks. The street here was dominated by official-looking high rises, but I thought there must be a coffee shop nearby. I checked my pockets for cash. Then I turned and walked to the right. It was a random decision and as good a direction as any. The detectives had been keen to bring me here but hadn't offered to return me to Holbrook and I didn't push them for a ride. I was happy enough to be out of their way because I'd much to plan and didn't want them listening in.

I meant what I'd told Witherspoon. I did intend taking the women home, and if Samuel Logan ventured no further than the Arizona state border, then fine. But I didn't believe he'd let things rest at that. I'd shot him twice – as far as I knew – but obviously not as badly as I'd hoped. Samuel struck me as the type who wouldn't let things lie. Chances were he had a couple of priorities to see to, namely surviving his wounds and evading the manhunt that had been launched to find him, but then he'd want to get revenge on me for slaying his kin. Let him come for me: I didn't fear him, and if the truth be told, I welcomed a second shot at the title. However there was one thing I was certain of: he wouldn't demand a stand-up man-to-man encounter; he'd try to get to me by what he'd see as my weakness. He'd target the women first.

From what I'd learned from Jay and Nicole, he'd delighted in hurting them, but he hadn't shown any sexual predilection for them the way Brent and Carson had. He hadn't paid Ellie any attention, so I thought she was safe now. Back with her parents, Ellie would be out of sight and mind, but I took it that he'd enjoy hurting the older girls if he thought it would hurt me. I'd have to prepare for that eventuality. My weapons had been seized as evidence, I hadn't retrieved my cellphone from Jay and it too had been placed into an evidence bag. Luckily I had my wallet and a roll of dollars left over from the advance on expenses that Jameson Walker had given to me, so I wasn't stuck. As soon as I got round to feeding my need for coffee and food, I'd hire a cab or rental to get me back to Holbrook. But before that, the first thing on my mind was ringing my friend, Rink.

I found a coffee shop and took a booth at the back where I could watch the door and everyone who entered. Not that I expected Samuel Logan to come charging in but I had a feeling Chambers and Witherspoon might keep an eye on me for the next few days. I wasn't worried about Witherspoon: he was old school, and in his time he'd probably slapped the heads of many recalcitrant criminals, but Chambers was a different story. I could understand how his image of me might be clouded by what had happened to his brother, but I couldn't allow him to get in my way.

After I'd downed one mug of coffee and ordered another, I went to a payphone at the end of the serving counter, inserted coins.

'I was just planning on how I was gonna bust you outta prison,' Rink said, after I told him where I was. 'What the hell did they take you to Phoenix for?'

'To keep me out of trouble, I guess.'

'Like I haven't been trying the same thing for years, and you know how successful I've been.'

'You know me, Rink. I'm a trouble magnet.'

'You can say that again. That text message I got? It kinda ruined a nice evening with Rene.'

'What text message? Oh, never mind, I get you now.' When I'd spoken to Jay earlier, she'd told me she couldn't contact anyone on the cellphone during her flight from the desert, but had written a text and set it to retry. Somewhere along the way the signal must have been strong enough for the cell to send it.

'Is Rene mad at me?'

'Nah. She knows what you're like. Plus, I forewarned her that you'd gone on a solo job and would likely need me to haul your ass out of the fire. I'll get the first flight out, OK?'

'Everything's cool, Rink. There's no need for you to come here.'

'You sure? I could be there in no time.'

'Everything's fine now at this end. You concentrate on entertaining the good lady vet.'

'Heard there was still one bad guy outstanding.'

'Guy called Samuel Logan. Don't worry about him. I shot the bastard twice. I expect the search parties to find him soon, dead from blood loss or the heat.'

'I should come down then . . .'

'No, Rink. You should stay there. I'll be back soon.'

'Why not immediately?'

'Couple of loose ends to tie up first.'

'You're gonna go look for this punk, ain't ya?'

'Nah.'

'Bullshit. I'm coming.'

'No. It isn't necessary. But you can do something for me.'

I asked him to Fed-Ex my spare weapons from Florida to Holbrook.

'And you're tellin' me you ain't planning on going after this punk?'

'Who knows, Rink? Maybe he'll come looking for me first.'

'Jesus,' he moaned. 'I'd best get back to formulating a plan for a jail break.'

29

The following morning, Ellie Mansfield's parents both hugged me. They had tears of gratitude on their cheeks, and alternated between weeping and laughing and then hugging me again. I felt a little uncomfortable, but persevered. Gratitude wasn't something I expected or demanded, and it was thanks enough for me when Ellie waved goodbye from the back seat of their minivan. I waved back and watched as they drove away from the Great Western motel in Holbrook where I had returned from Phoenix the evening before.

I hoped the kid would get over the nightmare soon.

Thankfully the Logans hadn't touched her the way they had Nicole, but she had been a witness to their depravity. Not only that but she was there when the bastards slaughtered the Corbin family: her best friends and their parents. I shook my head, thinking about the poor family I'd been too late to help. Out there at the ranch, and later in the cave, Ellie was suffering from shock and was withdrawn, but I'd just seen a spark of life back in her eyes. I thought she'd do OK if her parents showed her the same amount of love they just had to me.

It had made a difference to me: trading hugs for

punches. Don't know about hugs, I thought wryly. Aiming for pathos, instead I coughed out a laugh. But I knew how to handle punches.

Across the parking lot a pick-up truck was pulling in. Three guys were staring through the windscreen at me. What was that I just said?

After returning to the motel last night I'd telephoned Rink again, and I'd another call to make but had put it off. I'd showered, shaved, eaten and drunk more coffee. Then I'd hit the sack and slept soundly for almost eight hours. Now I felt a tad guilty that I hadn't made the call. I owed it to Scott Blackstock. Not that it mattered, because he'd turned up in person, bringing his buddies, Burt and Robert, along for the ride. They parked up then clambered out of the truck, Scott hailing me like I hadn't already noticed them.

Scott approached ahead of his friends, extending his hand. I took it and we shook.

'I wanted to thank you for everything,' he said.

'There's nothing to thank me for. I'm sorry I didn't find Helena for you.'

He looked down, scuffed a toe on the ground. 'It was always too late for Helena. I'm glad that you killed those fuckers though. You saved me the job.'

'It hasn't been proved that they took Helena yet,' I cautioned him.

'You ain't heard?' At my bemused look, he continued. 'The cops called me this morning. Tests on Carson Logan's pick-up found blood on the wing next to where the mirror used to be. DNA profiling ain't in yet, but preliminary tests showed it was most likely Helena's blood.'

'They ran her over?'

'Looks that way. But I don't think she was dead. Other tests found traces of her hair and blood at their ranch. I think those bastards saw her walking to Indian Wells, sideswiped her with their truck and then took her back to their place. Jesus, man, part of me hopes that she did die when she was knocked down.'

I thought of what Nicole had suffered. 'Yeah, maybe that would have been for the best.'

'The cops tell me you found another hostage who'd been buried in the desert. They're bringing in cadaver dogs and experts with ground-piercing radar to search the rest of the property. Maybe I'll get to give my wife a decent burial after all.'

I didn't think that Helena would be found on the Logan ranch. The fact that they'd suddenly gone out and snatched three new hostages told me that something had forced their hand. I now believed that after four months of incarceration, Helena had found a way to escape them and had unwisely headed off into the desert. Sadly she hadn't made it home and had probably succumbed to the heat and dehydration. In my opinion the search radius should be extended. I spared Scott those thoughts.

'You heard that Samuel escaped?'

'Yeah,' he said, with a nod to his friends. 'We're on the lookout for that piece of crap.'

'Best you do watch out for him. He might figure out

that it was you who sent me out to the ranch and look for some kind of payback.'

'We'll be waiting.'

Robert and Burt shared a glance. Burt even folded his arms on his chest, flexing his muscles like a tough guy, but it didn't work for him. Neither of those men would last more than a few seconds against Samuel, and Scott would quickly follow them to the grave. 'You see any sign of him, call the cops immediately.'

'The cops didn't do a lot of good the last time. That fuckin' Lewin . . . I can't believe that asshole was involved.'

'You didn't know that he was related to the Logans?'

'No, I'd no idea.'

'What was Carson Logan's wife called before she was married?'

'Don't know.'

I hadn't confirmed it yet, but I'd a good idea. She was most probably an aunt of Officer Lewin.

'Did you know Carla Logan?'

'Not personally. She didn't leave the ranch that often, and only when she was chaperoned by one of her kin.'

'But you've seen her?'

'Yeah, she was a good-lookin' gal. Looked a bit like my Hel—oh, shit . . .'

Scott looked like he was about to vomit, and it went some way to confirming my theory. Once Arlene passed away, Carla had been the only woman in residence at that remote ranch. Had those sick monsters treated their own flesh and blood the same way they had Helena and Nicole? The thought was abhorrent and alien to me, but I'd heard much worse. In recent years a number of stories had come to light where men driven by unhealthy sexual appetites had kept women prisoners, some their own daughters, using them for years as their personal playthings. Was it too much to assume that the Logans had been seeking women to replace the one they'd fixated upon for so long? My hope was that Carla had indeed managed to run away to the West Coast, but another part of me believed the cadaver dogs or ground-piercing radar crew might turn up a corpse after all.

'The son of a bitch. His own sister? If I ever . . .'

I held up a palm to stop him.

'Samuel Logan's a dangerous man,' I said. 'Don't try to take him on. Do as I said. Go straight to the police.'

Scott wiped his mouth with the back of a wrist. Maybe he was recalling the last time they'd met and Samuel had almost crippled him with a single blow to the solar plexus. 'Yeah, you're probably right. Not that he'll show up around here. He knows that the cops are hunting for him. He'll be miles away from here by now. I don't think we'll have to worry about him again.'

His final words had sounded hopeful. I too was hopeful because despite Burt and Rob being a pair of hapless goons, I'd grown to like Scott Blackstock. I didn't want to see him or his buddies dead.

'So what happens now?' Scott asked.

'I'm heading to Florida and back to work. You know us private dicks, always looking to make a buck off someone else's misery.'

Scott laughed with embarrassment, reminded of how

he'd first greeted me on the telephone. 'Well, if you're ever out this way again, look me up. I owe you a beer.'

'You've got a deal.'

We shook hands, then I accepted the hands of Burt and Rob. Seems I was forgiven for smacking them around. I felt bad about having done so, but, at the time, it had been necessary. They wandered back to their pick-up and bunched inside. Scott hit the horn and then peeled out of the parking lot.

I was uneasy at having just lied to them about going back to Florida.

But that had been necessary too.

Scott I could trust to keep his mouth shut. The other two I wasn't so sure of. Robert didn't have much to say, but I suspected the first time Burt got drunk his lips would start flapping. One thing I'd learned was that family connections ran deep in this part of the desert. Who knew who might carry tales back to Samuel?

If that was the case I wanted him to think I was well out of the way, so that if he went for the women again he wouldn't be expecting me.

A lot of good my lie would do if Samuel chose a different course of action. I was counting on the fact that he cared enough for his family to try for a second go at the women. Maybe the sick-headed freak couldn't give a damn and was already heading for the Mexican border.

It would be preferable for Nicole and Jay if he was; but not for me. I wouldn't be happy until Samuel Logan was dead and gone, for choice by my hand. The first time we fought I'd been more concerned with the fate of the girls, and had kept things as low key as possible. Samuel had latched on to that weakness and had taken a liberty. I was still in pain from the clubbing that he'd given me and wanted nothing more than to pay him back. Of course that was selfish of me, but I was looking for revenge for Helena, Carla, and who knew which other women fallen victim to his demented family.

I'd checked out of the motel and had already slung my belongings into a rented Chrysler, so was ready to go. I only had a short drive to another hotel further along the strip. There Jay Walker and Nicole Challinor were waiting for me. They'd been given lodgings at the state's expense: five-star luxury at the Tipi Hotel. The only concession was that they had to put up with a uniformed guard at their door for fear that Samuel might make a try for them sooner than anyone expected. I was glad that the guards were there, but couldn't see how Samuel would be ready yet. I was positive that my first bullet had struck him, but the second?

I have this ability. I can snapshoot a scene for recalling later. Usually I can recollect the most minute of details. The only problem with my skill is that I must make a conscious decision to do so otherwise my memory is as woolly as anyone else's. As I drove, I thought back to the incident at the ranch and how I'd surprised Samuel on his return to the house. I was down on one knee when he'd shambled out of the darkness and on seeing me he'd given a start, before leaping for his life as I'd fired. And that's what was bothering me most. I recalled him spinning with the impact of the bullet, his arms flailing. But was that a true memory, or was I conjuring what I wanted to see? Had the spinning to the floor been his instinct to escape the bullet and had it even hit? When he struck the ground I'd fired again and saw him jolt as my bullet impacted his body. Then again, it had been dark and I'd heard no corresponding shout of pain. At the time I believed I'd mortally wounded him, but I'd also wanted to be sure and had lined up a third shot only for Carson to thwart me when he launched his attack. I ransacked my memories, trying to find something to assure me that I'd seriously injured him, but wasn't confident. No, I had to accept that Samuel wasn't hurt bad and that he could be ready much sooner than any of us thought.

As unlikely as it sounds, there was the possibility that both of my bullets missed their mark, but for one thing. If I hadn't hurt Samuel, he'd have launched a counterattack while I'd been engaged in my duel with Carson or minutes later with Officer Lewin. So he was injured. He had to be. Then again there had been times in the past where I'd been shot, stabbed, hit by shrapnel, but had managed to survive my wounds. Back when I was with Arrowsake, and deep in the middle of combat, I'd witnessed men with their entrails pooling out of their eviscerated bodies still laying down covering fire for their comrades. Once I heard of a woman who was stabbed more than forty times by her abusive husband, only to turn the knife on him and end the torture with one thrust. The woman lived. The human body can sustain terrible injuries and survive, or something totally inane can kill it. It's all about the luck of the draw, and Samuel could have been very lucky that day.

30

When he was a boy it had become apparent to Samuel that he was unlike other children. When he took a tumble, or banged his head, or scuffed his knee it didn't move him to tears like it did the others. His resistance to pain hadn't concerned his parents, and if anything his father was proud that his boy was as tough as the rugged desert around them. He was seven years old before he'd become fascinated with his 'condition', and in the intervening years it had never been far from his thoughts. At school there was much pinching of flesh, slapping of ears, kicking of shins, and he had wondered why it elicited howls from his schoolmates when to him it was nothing. He felt the force of a punch, or a kick to the guts, but there was nothing immediate or lasting about the way it affected his body or mind.

His fascination with his inability to feel pain had morphed into something else, something that he now understood as sadism, but in the early days he looked upon the agony he doled out as an exercise in self-knowledge. Countless times he'd nipped and dug at the nerve clusters lying beneath his skin, feeling little more than a tickle, yet when he did the same to another child they'd howl in torment. As he'd grown older, his experiments had progressed to punching, kicking, head-butting and biting, and he'd learned much about causing pain to other human beings. He'd discovered books on ancient Chinese systems of martial arts; he thought that the talk of meridians conducting the life force throughout the body was a pile of bull crap, but the corresponding Chi points equated to those same places on the body he'd found elicited most pain. There had to be something in it, and he'd delved deeper.

He learned of another Chinese art: Dim Mak. Supposedly there were masters of the art who could touch certain points on the body and induce death. He thought that was a load of crap as well, but couldn't deny that by striking or pinching certain nerve clusters he could momentarily paralyse someone, or even make them succumb to an unconscious state through the intense agony he inflicted. He didn't have any truck with the reputedly magical skills of the old masters, and knew that it was rooted purely in the physiology and neurology of the human body. So too was his inability to feel pain. There was something loose inside him. That was it. Some juncture that should carry the nerve impulses to his brain simply wasn't working right, as if a circuit breaker had flipped to the off position. He didn't find it an encumbrance, seeing as it had made him fearless, but it had made him careful. Many times he had injured himself without realising. He recalled a time when he'd leaned his weight on a cooking range and had only become aware that his flesh was sizzling when a smell like frying pork had reached his nostrils. He'd suffered serious burns to his backside and never felt a damn thing.

It taught him he wasn't invulnerable. He could be cut or burned like any man, his bones could be broken, and even if he didn't feel the debilitating agony, he could still perish from his wounds. Shot twice, he'd have died as quickly as any man if he hadn't sought medical assistance. Now, with his wounds cleaned and dressed, his body swathed in compression bandages, he felt OK. He couldn't be irresponsible about his injuries though. If he opened his wounds again, or they grew infected, he'd be in real trouble. He had a slight temperature, and though he didn't feel the corresponding pain, his body was stiff and less agile than normal. He couldn't immediately go after that bastard Englishman – not for a couple days at least. Frustration was building inside him, causing his innards to flutter wildly, and he supposed the weird feelings must equate somewhat to the pain ordinary people felt. It was a strange sensation and an alien one.

All of this had come about due to sensation. But not his.

His cousin Carson had an unhealthy appetite for sex, and it was something that Brent had inherited from his father. He didn't comprehend their need for forcing themselves on women. Pleasure he believed was very close to pain, and someone whose neurological system was impaired could experience neither the way others did. The only time he derived any satisfaction was when a woman – or man for that matter – was squirming in

agony beneath his fingers. But it seemed that his kinsmen were slaves to their desires. He'd known all along
that it would bring them trouble of the worst kind. His
sadism came hand in hand with another condition: that
of apathy. He couldn't care less for those that Carson
and Brent kept as their playthings, but even in that
uncaring state he could see that it was *wrong*, particularly when they'd started in on his younger sister. Not
that he cared what they did to Carla, for he felt no
attachment to her in any way. It was *wrong* because he
knew it would lead to their downfall.

When Carla had finally snapped, and had gone for
Carson with a knife, he had responded in the first way
he could think of. He'd struck his sister hard in the side
of the jaw, knocking her down. He hadn't meant for the
base of her skull to slam the corner of the stone hearth,
but what was done was done. Carson and Brent were
both distraught as they'd buried her out in the desert,
not because of what had happened but because they
had lost the object of their fixation. It had been his idea
to get another one.

He had seen Helena Blackstock and thought she
bore a passing resemblance to Carla. He took his kin to
the bar where he'd learned that she was drinking with
her husband, Scott, to show her to them. Maybe it was
a good job that the police walked in when they did, or
Carson and Brent might have tried to snatch her there
and then and this trouble could very well have come
on them much sooner. They'd had to be patient; they'd
waited things out, and allowed enough time to pass

that they wouldn't be immediate suspects in Helena's abduction. When they did finally take her, Carson had pulled favours with the police department. He wasn't surprised that Lewin had agreed to cover for them, in exchange for favours of his own. Whoever had dropped the gene that controlled the sexual urge, he must have been on Carson's side of the family. Lewin was the illegitimate child of Arlene and Carson before they were wed, and a half-brother to Brent. No one knew the full story of how the boy was raised by a distant cousin in Holbrook, but there was no denying that he was a Logan.

Because familial ties didn't affect Helena the way they had Carla, they'd had to keep the woman a virtual prisoner, chaining her in the barn, and at night locking her in the box they'd constructed in the desert. They only released her when Carson and Brent required appeasement, and that was when they'd taken to making her parade naked before their eyes.

If she hadn't slipped her bonds that time, sneaked away into the desert, he wondered if his kin would still be alive. While searching for Helena they'd come across the others at Peachy's gas station. Again it was he who'd had the idea to take the women. Christ, you couldn't look a gift horse like that in the mouth. Two for the price of one: a woman to replace Helena and a girl to keep and nurture for when the first was worn out. The third bitch was all his to do with as he pleased. He'd had big plans for Jay Walker. He *still* had big plans.

But he had to get well first, and that wasn't something

he could do while he was so frustrated. He *needed* to hurt someone, and he'd just thought of the very person.

He was in the back office of Doug Stodghill's auto shop, the owner sitting on the chair opposite him. The man had been that way since finishing dressing his wounds.

'How bad are my injuries?'

'The one in your shoulder is superficial. It didn't hit any major arteries or bones and should heal OK.'

'What about the other?' Samuel touched the bandage that was wound tightly around his ribs. Blood was leaking through the crêpe, pink rather than red.

'It could cause problems if you aren't careful. The bullet went through your latissimus dorsi muscle, but ricocheted off your ribcage. It broke one rib, cracked the two either side of it. The greatest threat to your health is if the wound becomes infected. Even if that doesn't happen, it will impede movement, particularly on your left side.'

'So I should be able to use my right arm OK?'

'Uh, yeah.'

'Good.'

'Wounds like yours,' Stodghill went on, 'they'd put anyone else in a hospital bed. I can't believe you're even on your feet, never mind using your arms.'

'I'm a man on a mission, Doug. I won't stop for nothing 'til I'm done.'

'You should, Samuel. Give it up now. Get away from here as fast as you can.' Stodghill's face was moist with perspiration, and it wasn't through hard labour. After stealing the abandoned police cruiser, Samuel had realised that he must ditch the vehicle at the first opportunity and had called Stodghill to meet him at the wrecking yard he had part shares in. The cop car had gone through the crusher and was then buried beneath a mound of other squashed cars bound for smelting. Then Samuel had demanded that Stodghill put his previous trade to use. The man had done a tour in Vietnam, and had trained as a medic. It was decades since he'd treated gunshot wounds, but it appeared he hadn't lost his touch. Samuel didn't think of him as a loyal friend: he had helped Samuel out of fear. Now all he wanted was for Samuel to be gone, out of his life for good. Samuel wasn't leaving. He knew that the first opportunity Stodghill had he'd run to the police and give him up.

Samuel tested his right arm. It seemed to be fully functioning, and though he could feel a pulling in his opposite side, it didn't impede him. He smiled at Stodghill.

Stodghill smiled nervously in return.

His mouth stuck like that as Samuel's hand shot forward and clamped tightly round his windpipe.

'Sorry about this, Doug, but you gotta go.'

Stodghill could barely inhale let alone argue for his life.

Samuel pulled the mechanic out of the chair, then propelled him backwards so that his spine cracked painfully against a workbench. There were tools scattered on it, plus sheaths of oil-smeared documents, an old manual typewriter, and a chipped mug. The man grimaced in pain, and Samuel took a moment to study his features, watching blotchy pink patches grow on his cheeks. Samuel squeezed tightly, feeling cartilage popping under his powerful grip.

'You know something, Doug? I think you're correct. My right arm seems to be working fine.'

'Pleeeaaasssseee,' Stodghill wheezed.

Samuel ignored him, as he lifted his left hand and formed a fist. 'But look at *this.* This you got wrong. My left works just fine too.'

Since his days as a medic, Doug Stodghill's outlook on life had changed. Back then he was concerned about his patients and it was his only desire to patch them up; never would he have dreamed of hurting them. But that was then, and none of them were trying to kill him at the time. He was almost blacking out from lack of oxygen, but his natural instinct was to fight for his life. His hand scrabbled along the workbench until he found the coffee mug. He snatched it and, with all the power he could muster, slammed it against the side of Samuel's skull.

Samuel blinked. Blood trickled from a gash in his hairline, following the contours of his ear and neck to pool in the trough formed by his clavicle.

Yet he hadn't felt a thing.

'OK, Doug. I'll allow you that one.' He bared his teeth in an exaggeration of a smile as he continued to exert pressure on Stodghill's windpipe. 'But you don't get to hit me again. From now on, only I get to do the hitting.'

31

'You think he might try to take Nic back again?'

The women had returned to their hotel rooms to freshen up, and it was left to me to deal with their parents who had arrived in Holbrook only a short time earlier. Their reunion had been an emotional affair, at first dominated by tears, then mild recrimination, followed by more tears, but within minutes it had segued into laughter all round. While their mothers accompanied Jay and Nicole inside, Jameson Walker, and Nicole's dad, Herb, had cornered me in an alcove adjacent to the exit door of the Tipi Hotel. Jameson looked like the burly landowner from a John Wayne Western; in contrast, Herb Challinor was a small balding man who shared the same bone structure as his daughter. We made an odd-looking grouping. Nearby, hotel guests sucked on cigarettes that had been denied them inside, but none of them was in earshot. Both men wanted to show their gratitude to me for bringing home their babies. There was more hugging. I didn't grow up in a family where men hugged, and it was something I'd had to grow used to after meeting Rink. Lately though, I'd kind of had my hug quota and was a little embarrassed.

My get-out was to mellow the proceedings by

informing them of my fears that Samuel had survived and still represented a threat to the girls.

'Yes, Mr Challinor. That may very well be the case.'

'Herb,' he said. 'Please call me Herb.'

Nodding, I went on, 'I'm not going to run out on you, so don't worry. If you want me to, I'll stay until Samuel has been captured.'

'How long must the girls stay here?' Herb asked.

'The police may need to speak to them again, but I'm sure they'll be allowed to return home soon.'

Jameson surveyed the hotel, and it seemed to his satisfaction. 'I'll arrange rooms for us all here, as well as one for you, Hunter. If there's anything else that you need, just tell me, and it's yours.'

When I'd set off on this search it had been as a paid employee; now the cash was secondary. Ordinarily I'd have refused his kind offer, but this five star joint was beyond my usual expense bill and it was important that I stay close to the women. I nodded my thanks.

Then I touched on a subject that I would rather have avoided like the plague, but it was necessary. To Herb I said, 'You're taking Nicole to a clinic?'

My words engendered a typical response from a loving father. Tears sprang from the corners of Herb's eyes, and he chewed down on his bottom lip. The blood drained from his face. His hands curled into half-formed fists and I knew if Samuel chose to show his face now, the little man would likely rip it off.

Nicole had endured rape. She had undergone examinations by doctors engaged by the Navajo County police department, but that had been for forensic evidence. Now she must tolerate a second round of tests. As horrific as the notion might sound, any of those beasts could have been carrying a sexually transmitted disease, but, worse still, Nicole could be pregnant. I haven't given the subject of abortion much thought in the past, but here was a firm argument for termination. With luck that wouldn't be an issue and Nicole would be given the all-clear.

'Do you think that this . . . this *man* could make a try for her at the clinic?'

'I can't see how that's possible, Herb. I've no doubt that he'll find out Nicole's identity, the story has been in all the papers and on the TV networks, but he'll be too busy avoiding the police at present. I think it'll be a day or two until he's ready for his next move. That's if it ever comes. I shot him twice. Best-case scenario is that he's out there in the desert somewhere, his corpse being picked at by the buzzards.'

'You don't believe that though, do you?' Jameson had jammed his thumbs into his belt. I could imagine a pair of six guns holstered on his hips.

He was right. I'd just been trying to allay some of Herb's fears. 'If he has survived, I'm going to be waiting for him.'

It was apparent that Jameson and Herb had spent some time together in the last few days, and the subject of my legend had come up during their discussions. Jameson must have spoken well of me because Herb looked reassured by my promise. Still, I was only one man and couldn't be there twenty-four hours a day.

'If necessary I can call in more help.'

'Hopefully things won't come to that,' Jameson said.

After our telephone discussion yesterday, I had caught a bus back to Holbrook, but on my return to my room at the motel I'd called Rink again to organise where I should collect my weapons. He'd already had one of his employees send them overnight to a nearby Fed-Ex depot.

'You're expecting trouble, don't deny it. Just give the word and I'll be there,' Rink had offered.

'We've fought psychos before. But this one's different: I don't think that Samuel will come here.'

'I think it's a given. You attract the frog-giggers like you're some kinda magnet to nut-jobs.'

'That doesn't say much for you.'

'Opposites attract, brother.'

If there was a sliding scale for measuring this kind of thing, then Samuel Logan and I would be at opposite ends.

Jameson and Herb went inside to check on their daughters. There would be more hugging and tears, so I elected to keep out of the way. I bought vending-machine coffee from the lobby and again stood outside with the smokers, craving something as acutely as they did nicotine. I spied to the north, fading out the nearby structures as though I could see through them all the way back to the Logans' ranch.

Jameson Walker was a very wealthy man now, but things hadn't always been that way. It was only in the past few years that his business had boomed, and that the dollars began rolling in. It explained why Jay hadn't attended any of the Ivy League universities but the state-run Pennsylvania State University. Due to her enrolment at Penn State the family had found an affinity with Pennsylvania, but since their wealth had grown, Jameson had purchased further properties down the Eastern seaboard, and amongst others he owned a penthouse on Park Avenue with a view of the Empire State Building. The apartment in the heart of Manhattan could be easily defended but there was too big a risk of collateral damage in the heart of the city. Once the police were finished with us and the women free to leave I'd requested that the family go to one of their other properties and Jameson had suggested a beach house at Ellisville on Cape Cod. For the purpose of protecting both the women, Herb had agreed that Nicole could stay over with Jay for as long as she liked.

It was a dilemma. The remote house had its obvious problems, notwithstanding the fact that if Samuel took me out first, then help for the girls could be long in coming. But I was thinking more of the advantages. If I chose to fight Samuel in New York City, or any of the other major conurbations where Jameson had property, then I'd be on a timeline of minutes before the police came down on us like a ton of bricks. Out on that wooded coastline, where the nearest neighbour was over a half-mile away, I'd have the time needed to put Logan down without any outside interference.

When I was with the Special Forces the message had been drummed into me over and over: preparation is the key. Some of the lads called it the Six Ps. Proper planning prevents a piss-poor performance. Although plans are something I often frown at, because speed and the ability to think on the move beat anything static, it does make sense to plan some things in advance. When thinking of the situation: protecting the girls at all costs – and the objective: killing Samuel – and achieving both within a short time frame, then it was imperative to choose your battleground wisely. The house at Cape Cod was surrounded by woodland and shallow inlets of salt water, with only one road in and out. Ordinarily it would be a trap, but this time it would provide the ideal location in which to ambush a killer.

Yet I wondered now if this was another wasted plan.

I had a hunch that our final battle would not play out in Massachusetts, but here in this desert where it had begun.

Still staring into the distance, I hoped that I was right and the bastard was coming. Like my nearby smoking friends who were dragging hard on their cigarettes, it was the only way I could feed my addiction.

'Where are you Samuel, you sick son of a bitch?'

I wasn't conscious of having spoken out loud, but I received a dirty look from an elderly woman tugging a wheeled suitcase behind her.

'Uh, excuse me, ma'am,' I said.

She pursed her lips, shaking her head, like she was sucking on a sour grape. Then she flagged a cab pulling into the hotel's forecourt. She looked back at me as the cab pulled away, shook her head again. I don't know if her disapproval was for my bad language or the look of murder on my face.

32

After beating Doug Stodghill to death and jamming him inside a locker in the office at the rear of his auto shop, Samuel had taken the keys to a vehicle that the mechanic had just finished fixing. The car he stole gave him a head start, but he knew that would only last for so long. Soon, the car would be on the police BOLO system – an all points bulletin otherwise known as 'be on the look out'. Samuel had driven the car via desert roads that he was familiar with, going beyond the border and into New Mexico. He'd dumped the car in a weed-choked lot behind a taco stall and hot-wired another car a little further up the road. It was an ancient Oldsmobile and the suspension creaked ominously but it carried him to Gallup. There he spent a night in a 'no questions asked' flophouse where he used some peroxide purchased from a drugstore to both lighten his dark hair and clean out his injuries. Most people would have screamed as the chemical invaded the raw wounds; Samuel barely felt an itch. The wound in his shoulder was knitting together nicely, but the one in his side was more troublesome. It felt mushy where the bullet had struck his ribs, and he guessed that the bone would take much longer to heal than did his flesh. The thought was troubling.

He didn't feel pain but that meant nothing if his body failed him without warning. He had a mission to fulfil, and it couldn't be put off for fear that his wounds had become infected. He'd just have to speed up the process and find Jay Walker as quickly as possible. This wasn't about gaining revenge for his slain kin, because he felt as little for them as he had for his younger sister. The only reason he tolerated them was because both Carson and Brent had shared his sadistic tendencies. They'd been a good team but he wasn't going to grow sentimental over them – even if he could. No, the reason he wanted his time with Jay Walker was solely for his own gratification. The bitch had given him the slip, thwarted him when he was about to beat her saviour to death and had spoiled the good times he had planned for her. It was only just that he balanced everything in his favour again.

He would have liked to finish what he'd started with the Englishman. From what he'd heard on the street, Stodghill had told him that the man was a private dick called Joe Hunter, and that he'd returned to Florida. Maybe another occasion would present itself; right now he desired quality time with Jay Walker. He'd wondered about Carson and Brent, and their fixation on women who resembled Carla. Women were simply women to him. Now though he understood his kin in a way he hadn't before, because there was only one woman who was going to satisfy him.

Now it was time to go get her.

But to achieve that, there were things he had to do first.

Primarily he had to complete what he'd started when bleaching his hair. There was no way he'd get within grabbing distance of Jay Walker dressed the way he was now.

He'd stolen money from Stodghill, but it was down to less than thirty dollars, nowhere near enough to buy the clothing he required.

Early that morning, he left the flophouse – a dingy hotel advertising 'clean linen' – and walked towards the more opulent centre of town, if Gallup contained such a thing. The kind of people in this poor neighbourhood weren't what he was seeking. His walk took him along West Hill Avenue, and he followed it downtown until the McKinley County Courthouse dominated the skyline. There, he thought, he'd find people more fitting. Before reaching the court buildings he looked for someone to his liking. Buildings here were decorated with murals depicting the Native American cultures prevalent in the city: Navajo, Hopi and Zuni. He had no interest in them. He found a park that looked alien when compared to the dusty streets, like it had been ripped from somewhere semi-tropical and dropped at random in the heart of the desert city. The gardens weren't huge, yet to someone who'd grown up in the middle of an arid waste it was about the most greenery he'd seen in his life. There were people out strolling, others sitting in the shade beneath the trees, but Samuel was looking for someone of a specific type.

He spotted the person he'd been searching for. Samuel was short and squat, wide around the shoulders and arms. He needed someone of a similar build if the man's clothing were going to fit him. The man he spotted was nowhere near as muscular, but was rotund with fat. He was wearing a grey suit, shirt and tie, more suited to a fancy hotel than the workshirt and jeans Samuel was currently dressed in. Samuel leaned against the bole of a tree and watched the man. He was reading a newspaper and drinking coffee from a waxed cup: probably on his way to the office. Samuel wondered if he could take him here, but there were too many people around. So he waited.

Finally the man stood up, heaving his bulky body away from the bench as he aimed his empty cup at a trash can. He folded his newspaper and tucked it under his arm. Samuel thought he'd head for the nearby courthouse, but the man surprised him by turning north and wending his way through the garden towards the next road over. Samuel fell into step behind him.

The traffic was already building up as the rush hour began, but over the grumble of engines Samuel could hear something else that reminded him of the thunderstorms that occasionally cut a swathe across his homelands. He couldn't quite define the sound until the fat man led him out of the park and on to a road on the other side of which was a building site that dominated an entire block. The rumble he'd heard was the movement of large construction vehicles, cranes and a workforce of dozens of men. The fat man crossed the road and walked on the sidewalk adjacent to the site.

Samuel glanced around and saw that most pedestrians

were on the park side, keeping away from the noise and the dust. It suited him. He jogged across the road, feeling his ribs grinding. He continued jogging, and, as he approached he tugged from his jeans pocket his battered wallet and held it in his left hand.

'Sir! Excuse me sir!'

At first the fat man couldn't hear him, or chose to ignore him. Samuel picked up his pace, caught up with the man and finally swerved in front of him. The man reared back, bringing up both palms as if to push Samuel away.

Samuel knew he looked sinister, with his bruised eyes and nose, and his grin didn't do much to allay the man's fears. Samuel held out the wallet.

'Sir, you were sitting in the garden over there and as you walked away I noticed you'd dropped this.'

The man did what anyone would do, his eyes went to the proffered wallet, and Samuel knew that he was contemplating whether or not to take it. Those of an avaricious nature would wonder if the wallet contained cash and if they were on to a good thing by lying and agreeing that it was theirs. An honest person would deny it belonged to them. The man, it seemed, was honest.

'Thanks, but it isn't mine.'

While the man was still studying the wallet, Samuel took a discreet look around. Nobody was paying them any attention.

'Are you sure, sir?' Samuel asked.

'I'm positive.' The man dropped his guard, and his

right hand sneaked round to touch the wallet in his back pocket. 'Mine is right here.'

Samuel shrugged. 'Oh. Then I wonder whose it is?'

'Sorry, but I can't help you.'

'OK, sir. I guess I should take it to the police.'

'Maybe you should.' The fat man stepped past and Samuel twisted his torso as if to allow him passage. Samuel's left hand blocked the man's pudgy left wrist. It was an innocent enough collision and the man didn't immediately respond. Then Samuel snaked his strong hand back through the gap between the man's arm and rotund body. Because he was still blocking the man's wrist he helped rotate it so that he could place his right palm over the back of the man's hand and clamp on to the flesh nearest his pinky finger. Samuel immediately reversed the movement, twisting the man's trapped hand with him. The action locked both the wrist and elbow and brought the man up on his toes. He began to yelp in pain, but already Samuel had nudged his shoulder into the man's elbow and he both turned him and propelled him over a small wire fence towards an embankment sloping into the construction site. At the last second he released his grip, but there was nowhere for the fat man to go but down.

The embankment extended a good few yards into the site, and was pitched at a forty-five-degree angle. Even an agile person would find it hard to check their fall. The fat man didn't stop until he'd rolled all the way to the bottom. Samuel took the time to check no one had noticed, then stepped over the small fence and followed him into the pit. By the time he'd reached the bottom, the man had just lifted his face from the dirt. He was plastered in damp clay. Samuel had intended stealing his suit, but that wasn't a consideration now. Samuel forced the man back down into the muck, pressing him down with a heel on the back of his neck. The man struggled and he was stronger than his unhealthy weight would suggest, so Samuel decided for a quick dispatch. He raised his foot then stamped down at the base of the man's skull. The struggling stopped. Samuel stamped twice again for good measure.

He rifled through the pockets of the suit and found what he required: a wallet and keys. A quick check inside the wallet identified the man as Roger Hawkins, and his address was nearby. Samuel thought there was no way this man had walked a great distance to work each day.

Samuel checked all around him but the racket from the site, the billowing dust, had all concealed the mugging from the workers. He grabbed Hawkins by his ankles, and, though it was a struggle dragging him and likely played havoc with his injured ribs, he placed him at the edge of the embankment. There were sheets of board stacked nearby, as well as other random pieces of junk that Samuel piled over the corpse. Hawkins wouldn't remain undiscovered for long, but Samuel trusted it would be enough time to visit the man's apartment. He bounced Hawkins's house keys in his good hand, then went back up the embankment.

All being well he could be back in Holbrook and ready to take Jay Walker by the end of the day.

33

'You think your idea will work?' Rink asked.

I was sitting on the balcony outside my room at the Tipi Hotel, strategically placed so that it was adjacent to the one Jay and Nicole now shared. Earlier I'd called at the Fed-Ex depot and collected the items that McTeer had shipped there. Sealed in boxes was a SIG Sauer P228, as well as a Ka-bar combat knife. I'd taken them out on the balcony while cleaning and prepping them, and now had a recently purchased 'pay as you go' cell-phone to my ear. I kept my voice lowered so I didn't wake the women. Exhaustion had finally caught up with them and while their parents were taking dinner in the hotel's restaurant they'd both retired early. I'd followed them back up, because the police guards had been recalled to other duties now that Samuel Logan had fallen off the face of the earth.

'He isn't like the others we've fought in the past,' I said. 'Tubal Cain, Dantalion, Rickard, they were all pros in their own right. You ask me, Samuel Logan's a few sandwiches short of a picnic. I don't think he'd have the capacity to find us if we didn't hang around and wait for him.'

'He's maybe dumb, but it doesn't make him any less dangerous.'

I thought of the pain in my body, a dull ache by now, and had to agree. 'I'm not going to underestimate him, Rink. In fact, if anything, I have to be extra careful. Cain, Luke Rickard, they had similar backgrounds and training to us and because of that we could sometimes predict their movements. It's different here. Samuel Logan, I don't know what motivates him, and it's difficult to second-guess him.'

'What if he doesn't go there?'

'Then I find some other way to bring him to us.'

'You lookin' for another stand-up drag-'em-out brawl?'

'It's a case of heart versus mind. I'd love to go at him man to man, but no. Soon as I get the opportunity I'll put a couple of rounds in his head.'

'Make sure you don't miss this time.'

'That's the thing, Rink. I'm sure I didn't miss last time.'

'So you're fighting Superman?'

'No, not Superman. But there's something unnatural about him.' I told Rink how I'd repeatedly smashed Samuel's face with my fists and forehead and he'd barely reacted.

'You know the deal,' Rink said. 'When the blood's up, you sometimes don't feel the pain until after. I can guarantee he was swallowing Tylenol like they were M&Ms later on.'

'Maybe.'

'There's no maybe. When I was fighting in those knockdown karate tournaments, I saw guys breaking their shins against each other, but they carried on to the end of the fight. Broke my wrist once, but I still won. Tell you what, though . . . later on I was moaning like a bitch in heat. It'll have been the same with that nut-job. Guarantee it, brother.' Rink paused and I knew he was considering taking the next flight out here. 'An' if I'm wrong, let's see how he gets on with a load of shot up his ass.'

'You'd have thought a couple of three-five-sevens would have put him down for good.'

'So maybe you missed.'

The conversation was going round in circles.

'Won't next time,' I said, trying my best to put a lid on it.

'Don't,' he said. 'There's too much at stake there.'

He was right, this wasn't just about me. Because I was leading their tormentor directly towards them, my crazy plan was a sure way of causing Jay and Nicole further nightmares. Not that I intended placing either of them within his grasp, but what if Rink was wrong and there was more to this man than met the eye? OK, he was no Tubal Cain or Luke Rickard, but he was a determined and violent antagonist. In fact, his unconventional style might prove to be more dangerous than any of the professional killers I'd faced in the past.

I experienced a slight fluttering in my guts, the first trickle of adrenalin as I responded to the challenge. Rink has often accused me of getting off on the thrill of battle; maybe he had something. I was looking forward to meeting Samuel Logan and the sooner the better.

The silence at the other end of the phone had grown palpable.

'What?'

'Take it easy, bro.'

'What do you mean?'

'Don't let this frog-giggin' sumbitch draw you into his world.'

'I don't get you.'

'I don't need to be looking at you to know you're wearing your war face. Shit, man, you ask me you're fixating as hard on Samuel as the Logans did on the girls.'

'I think that my kind of fixation's a lot different from theirs.'

He breathed heavily into the mouthpiece. 'Whatever. But it's still unhealthy . . . whichever way you look at it.'

'You turning into a shrink these days, spouting all this psychobabble?'

'Ain't spouting nothin'. Just offering the voice of reason, you understand?'

'As long as you don't start feeling my bumps, Rink.'

'I might give you a couple bumps when I see you. It's the only way to knock some sense into your fat head.'

We both laughed, and it was a good point to ring off. I was looking forward to personally finishing things with Samuel, but, truth be told, it would make sense if Rink was there to watch my back. If I had my way that wasn't going to happen though, not this time.

34

Samuel Logan was barely recognisable now and he felt the disguise would get him all the way to Jay's room without alerting anyone to his true identity.

Earlier, he'd used Roger Hawkins's keys to gain access to the man's apartment. Though palatial in comparison to the shack he'd shared with his family, it was a soulless place at basement level, steps leading down from the street to the front entrance. On opening the door he'd found an open-plan area with hardwood floors, heavy leather furniture, a large plasma screen TV and entertainment centre, and, thankfully, no sign of a family. He wondered if Hawkins had a wife and kids who lived elsewhere and if the businessman kept this place for when he was in the city. Off the main living room was an en suite bathroom and a kitchen with appliances that he was unfamiliar with, as well as a large bedroom with a walk-in dressing closet. That was what he was most interested in and he'd found a two-piece suit not unlike the one Hawkins was wearing earlier. Shirts on hangers hung in colour-coordinated ranks and below them shoes and boots for every occasion. Samuel stripped down to his boxers, studying himself in a full-length mirror. He looked like a beer keg on legs, but unlike Hawkins his sturdy frame wasn't formed of pulpy fat. Like his face, his body was a network of fine white scars from past injuries, whereas a couple of others – burns primarily – were lumpy with pink scar tissue. His bandages were soiled. The pink had become red, and was fast changing hue again to an ugly brown. He stank. He didn't have time to waste on showering, so looked instead for toiletries and sprayed his body liberally with cologne from a glass bottle. Then, at random, he chose a shirt and pulled it on. It almost fit. It was tight across his shoulders and upper arms, whereas there was plenty of loose material at his waist. He then dressed in the suit. He had to add a belt to keep the trousers up, but again the jacket was snug up top. He studied himself in the mirror again, and saw that his greasy hair and roughly shaved face belied the expensive clothing, but didn't care too much about it. There were razors and scissors in the bathroom. Hawkins's shoes were too small for him, so he'd no option but to pull on his own boots again. He didn't think that anyone would be astute enough to notice such detail as his work boots anyway.

He sheared away the longest hair and combed it into a side parting, used Hawkins's razor to scrape his beard off. The man who stared back at him from the mirror was a stranger. With his hair bleached and cut short he barely recognised himself, and he leaned towards the glass to check that it was indeed his own eyes staring back at him. He even went so far as to reach out and jab a fingertip against the glass, just to make sure. He left an oily smear on the surface. Samuel couldn't give a damn for forensic evidence. The cops were already after him, and it wouldn't matter if they tied him to the death of Roger Hawkins or anyone else: they'd have to catch him first, and when they did he didn't expect to walk away from the confrontation alive.

He bundled some spare shirts into a leather attaché case he discovered in the living room, as well as the bottle of cologne. He expected that he would stink more as the hours progressed and the cologne would help disguise the odour.

He left the apartment and headed back past the courthouse he'd noted earlier, following signs to the Amtrak station. As he walked he checked out the other pedestrians and was glad to note that his bruised features didn't attract as much as a glance, so was confident his disguise was working.

There were more murals decorating the walls as he'd approached the train station. One of them depicted a buffalo draped in the Stars and Stripes, and Samuel paused to study it. He thought that, should the mural become animated and the animal rear up on its hind legs, they'd share a similar body shape. He liked the analogy he conjured from the notion: that he was akin to a wild beast that symbolised power to so many people. He'd offered the buffalo a nod of respect then went on.

After everything he'd done to effect a new persona, he felt a sense of anticlimax when he wasn't given as much as a cursory glance by the bored teller who sold him tickets for the next train west.

He found a bench where he could wait for his train.

Other passengers avoided him. It was as though an invisible bubble surrounded him, with an impenetrable wall that no one would attempt to pierce. He didn't know if this was an effect of the cologne he'd doused his body in, or if they sensed some imperceptible warning he must radiate. He was happy with either, because he had no desire for company other than that of Jay Walker.

Soon his train arrived and he found a seat at the rear of the lattermost carriage. No one sat next to him, or in those chairs adjacent, and he hoped things would stay like that all the way to Holbrook.

35

Jay was back in the box.

Her hands were free and she scrabbled at the metal sheets entombing her, fingernails ripping down to the cuticle and leaving red slashes on the tin. Though she was in shadow, the smears of blood were vivid, lit by an internal light. They mocked her, flashing like the fiery eyes of demons. Jay screamed but nothing issued from her constricted throat. She was too thirsty to make a sound.

Last time she was able to hook her fingers around the top end of the corrugated sheet and slide it but now it resisted her efforts. There was no way she could budge it, and the knowledge made her more frantic.

Though her world had been silent, she thought she could hear the steady tread of boots approaching her prison. She stopped struggling. Her stomach felt like it had lifted into the hollow at the back of her mouth. She did not dare guess who was out there. She didn't have to. The wizard from behind the curtain was there waiting for her; ready to reveal his true face, and his true intent.

A keening noise filtered from above.

A scream?

Was Nicole being attacked again?

The sound of boots in thick sand retreated.

Jay began tearing at the metal again, and when she next looked she'd rubbed her fingertips down to the bone.

The red was more livid than ever, gouts of blood splashed from one end of her coffin to the other, dripping from the tin sheeting to splatter on her face. She shook her head side to side, blinking it off her lashes. She looked again. Two particular smears were in her line of vision.

They blinked.

She recognised those demonic eyes peering back at her.

Samuel Logan wasn't outside, he was right there with her, watching from within her nightmare.

Jay screamed, and this time there was a hoarse, tearing sound that ripped painfully from her throat.

She kicked and writhed, then fell sideways into a chasm that had opened without warning . . .

She sat up, the scream from her nightmare caught in her throat. For a long heartbeat afterwards she sat blinking in the dark as tendrils of the dream refused to relax their grip and tried to tug her back into their embrace. A mild panic caught her and she struggled to extricate herself from the sheets, finding them damp with perspiration and wound tightly around her legs. She yanked them free and then swung her feet off the bed and dug her toes into the rug on the hardwood floor, seeking contact with something firm and in the real world. She lowered her head into her hands and pushed the matted hair back from her brow.

There was faint light leaking from around the shutters, enough for her to make out the unfamiliar shape of furniture, and she heard the rush of a breeze through treetops outside. She was a long way from the box in the Arizona desert, yet its hold on her still sent a tremor through her body. She lowered her hands, expecting to find the glistening nubs of bones protruding from her fingertips, but they were whole and undamaged. They trembled, though.

She stood up quickly and moved for the door, pulling her nightdress down to cover her slick thighs. She snatched a robe off a hook. Not that she was cold, but she remembered now where she was and couldn't wander about in a state of undress. She pulled it on as she went out of the bedroom, tying the belt loosely around her hips. Immediately to the left of her room was the one where Nicole slept. She stood alongside the jamb, bent to lay an ear against the door. There was nothing to hint that Nicole shared the dream that she'd just experienced, but then, she realised, Nicole's must be much worse. She crept away without disturbing her friend, to retrieve her clothing from where she'd laid it on a chair. Dressed appropriately, she left her room and closed the door behind her.

Her recent terror was subsiding now, but not her intense thirst. She wondered if there would ever be a time when she would feel sated. The floorboards creaked softly under her feet, and self-consciously she glanced at the room further along where her mother and father slept. No one stirred, but she was careful to regulate her footing and avoid the boards most likely to squeak underfoot: it was bad enough that her sleep had been disturbed without her waking the entire hotel.

She turned, seeking a way down.

Like most structures here in Holbrook, the Tipi Hotel was built primarily of wood and cladding, albeit in a different fashion from its neighbours. Whereas most of the other hotels here were the familiar split level type, serviced by external stairs and walkways, the Tipi reminded her more of a Gothic mansion. In keeping with its style it had internal stairways so she had no fear of being seen by anyone lurking in the grounds. Around her she could hear the subtle movement of the timber joists contracting as the hotel settled for the night, and from a room on her left drifted the muted strains of music from a TV. From further away came the sound of vehicles on the highway. The hotel was built on land set back from the road, concealed by tall fir trees that had been imported from some distant corner of the US to offer insulation, but always the background noise of the highway was there. Sometimes it was just a hum, a lullaby to help send you to sleep, but tonight the traffic noise was carried on a stiff breeze, tumultuous and noisy.

She heard all those things but she did not hear the man who was suddenly standing beside her.

Jay's hand went to her throat, and she caught the yelp of surprise before it escaped.

She recognised the form standing there and relaxed: he was too tall to be the man from her nightmare.

'Is everything OK, Jay?'

She nodded up at Joe Hunter. She realised now that he had been sitting in a chair in the hallway in order to have a view of her room, as well as being positioned to guard access up the stairs. He was holding a matt black pistol down by his thigh.

'I couldn't sleep,' she said. 'I'm thirsty and thought I'd get a drink.'

'You didn't call room service?'

'I wanted to stretch my legs a bit,' she nodded back at her room, 'get out of that . . . that box for a while. Is it OK?'

'You can do whatever you like. So long as you tell me first.'

Jay appreciated Hunter being there to guard them, understanding that for him to do so there were rules to be followed, and she didn't want to compromise them in any way. She had listened to his ground rules for remaining safe, and one of them was that neither she nor Nicole left the hotel without him. She supposed that creeping from her room in the middle of the night wasn't a contravention because she'd no intention of going outside.

'I'll get us coffee if you'd like one,' she offered.

'That'd be good.'

'What about Nic?'

'I'm sure she'd prefer to sleep.'

'Uh, I meant . . .'

'I know.' He offered her a smile. 'She'll be fine, so long as I can watch who comes in or out of the hotel. There's a vending machine in the lobby.'

'You don't think he'll come tonight?'

'Samuel Logan? No, I don't. But . . . you never can tell.'

'Surely the police will catch him before too long?'

'Yeah,' Hunter said, but she wasn't easily fooled.

She smiled at his attempt at allaying her fears and he returned a flicker of a grin. His teeth glistened in the pale glow from a night light at the end of the hall.

Jay said, 'Well, if he is coming, I wish he'd hurry up and get here because the waiting is the worst part.'

The calm Hunter radiated told her he was the type who could wait out the melting of a glacier, but he nodded anyway.

He followed her down to the lobby. The doors to the restaurant were locked tight, the room beyond in darkness. There was a clerk manning the desk, but as he began to rise up out of his seat, Hunter waved him back down.

'Over here,' Hunter said, leading her towards an alcove where machinery purred. 'Let me buy you one instead.'

Still conscious that they might rouse everyone in the hotel, she moved through the lobby on the balls of her feet, her clothing swishing with the sway of her hips. Hunter watched her, but there was nothing lascivious in his observation, and she felt he was at ease in her presence. The same couldn't be said for her. When she was under his gaze she felt like a schoolgirl experiencing her first crush and knew that she'd no right. Joe was in a relationship, he was happy with his girlfriend Imogen Ballard, and she should get him out of her head. It wasn't easy, and some of the dreams she'd had tonight hadn't been as horrifying as being back in Samuel Logan's box.

She surprised herself by asking, 'What's your story, Joe?'

Hunter's mouth turned down at the corners, but it wasn't because he was unhappy at her question. He just appeared uncomfortable speaking about himself.

He laughed self-deprecatingly. 'I'm a good guy, despite what some people might think.'

'You're more than that. Despite how you made it sound to me that time, *you* saved our lives: mine, Nicole's and Ellie's.'

'That's Joe Hunter for you.'

'You were a soldier, right?'

'Yeah. Special Forces.' Hunter adjusted the gun in his belt so that it wasn't apparent should another guest enter the alcove. Beyond him the vending machine hissed and plopped. Hunter winced and it wasn't at the intrusive noises.

'It's an honourable profession,' Jay said. 'You should be proud.'

'I am. I'm damn proud.' The way he lowered his head told the lie.

'I just bet you've seen some terrible things.'

'Ycah.' Hunter grunted as he returned his attention to the vending machine. 'I had to do some terrible things too.'

'Is that what's so difficult to let go of?'

He handed her a waxed cup full of steaming coffee. Jay studied the man opposite her. From her time with him in the desert she recalled that his gaze was intense, and even in the half light of the alcove she could tell that his eyes were more guarded than usual. He seemed to find the floor interesting. Once before she had wondered if Joe found it difficult coming to terms with his past, and the thought struck her again. It was as if he read her mind and he shifted, bringing his head up to meet her stare. 'What I did out there in the desert? I didn't do that because your father paid me to find you, I did that because I *needed* to. Do you understand?'

'You mean you needed to kill those men?'

Hunter shook his head 'No, not exactly. I needed to find you and the others and punish the men responsible for hurting you.'

Jay did understand. Hunter thought that by helping victims now it would help him come to terms with those *terrible things* he'd done in the past.

'You're seeking absolution?'

'Not from any god,' Hunter said.

'Isn't it a little self-destructive? I mean, trying to find peace from a violent past by continuing to be violent?'

'I don't see things like that.'

'You think that if you save someone it counterbalances the bad that you've done?'

Hunter retrieved his cup of coffee. He lifted it to his lips but paused. 'I'm not explaining myself very well. It goes much deeper. Maybe I shouldn't even be sharing this with you.'

Jay followed Hunter out into the lobby, thinking that maybe she shouldn't have broached the subject. Hunter was obviously uncomfortable. The pain was evident in the set of his shoulders. She reached out and touched his arm.

'It's good to talk to a friend sometimes . . .'

He shook his head.

'Talking doesn't help. I've tried. It's as simple as this, Jay: the Logans were monsters who deserved to die. One of them's still alive, but, if he shows up here, I'll kill him. That or I'll die trying.'

'That's the only thing that will make you happy?' Jay asked. 'When you kill Samuel Logan . . . or he kills you?'

Hunter didn't reply.

36

The police would expect Samuel to flee Arizona so he was not concerned when the train pulled into the station at Holbrook and he alighted on to the platform alongside other passengers. If anything they'd be watching for him trying to board a train, not getting off one. His disguise was working fine, especially with the bonus of the attaché case: it reinforced the image of a businessman in town for a meeting, even at this late hour.

He wandered outside and stood in a dusty swirl of cars circling outside the station as they picked up and dropped off passengers, watching for a cab. The cabs were being snapped up as soon as they arrived, and there were still a half dozen people waiting before him. He had considered stealing another car but thought that the third time would be the charm, an unlucky one at that. He had a raging thirst and walked to a nearby booth hawking cigarettes and soft drinks. He purchased neither but pulled a newspaper from the stand. On the cover was an update of the story that had rocked his homeland. The latest headline carried the shocking discovery of Doug Stodghill's body at his auto shop. Samuel tossed the vendor a couple of rumpled dollars and walked away, perusing the story. The journalist had taken liberties with his report, much of it speculation, but Samuel was interested in a quote stating that the female victims had remained in Holbrook to help police with their ongoing inquiries.

Never one to worry about consequences, he joined the much-dwindled queue for a cab and told the driver to take him directly to the hotel where Doug Stodghill had told him the girls had been holed up since Friday.

On the journey over he caught the cabbie glancing in his rear-view mirror, paying him too much attention for his liking. On the second occasion he stared back and the driver's eyes returned to the road.

Ahead of them Samuel caught sight of the Tipi Hotel, though much of his view was obscured by tall swaying trees. 'No, I've changed my mind. Don't stop here. Go another couple of blocks.'

Further along the strip Samuel indicated a less luxurious place. This motel looked like it had only recently been saved from demolition, but its new owners hadn't progressed that far with the renovations yet. It was a place he was familiar with, but the new staff would not know him – he vaguely recalled that they were out-of-towners. 'Pull in here.'

He gave the driver a handful of notes taken from Roger Hawkins's wallet and got out of the cab on to the high sidewalk. The driver lowered his window and leaned out. 'Hey, mister!'

Samuel felt a bubble of anticipation pop in his chest. Had the man recognised him? Surely he wouldn't be calling after a wanted killer? He wondered if he could drag the driver out of his window and silence him before he attracted too much attention. No, there were a couple of guys hanging around on the opposite corner.

'What is it?'

'Your bag,' the driver said with a nod over his shoulder. 'You've left it on the seat back there.'

Samuel relaxed. He retrieved the attaché case, then peeled a couple more dollars from his roll and handed them to the driver. 'Thanks, buddy. Important meeting coming up. I'd have been lost without my notes.'

The driver wasn't interested in his bogus story, and Samuel realised that his concern had been unfounded. He hadn't been recognised: the guy was probably in the habit of checking out his passengers, making sure they weren't the type to run off without paying for the trip. Or the type to mug him.

From where he stood, Samuel could see down Central Avenue to the Tipi Hotel, marked by the swaying trees. He pinpointed the landmark and as soon as the taxi was out of sight began walking towards it. He maintained a steady pace, but he was wheezing slightly by the time he stopped on the sidewalk. Usually fit and strong, he knew the laboured breathing was a result of his injuries. Had his wounds become infected? Did it matter now? He shook off the prickle of concern. Through the trees he peered across to where Jay was staying, trying to decide which of the rooms might be hers. He had no way of knowing. He gave up on the idea, and concentrated instead on peeking around, wondering if this was some sort of a trap and if, in the next few seconds, NCPD uniforms would flood the area to take him down. It didn't happen, and he walked across the road and stood at the base of the steps leading into a brownstone building decked out with hanging baskets at every window. He lifted the newspaper, as if reading it, but was in reality staring back across the way at the hotel he could now see beyond the trees.

A couple strolled by; a thickset man with a brush cut and smoking a cigarette and his wife who appeared unsteady on her feet. The man offered her his arm. They were locals judging by their accents but he didn't recognise them. They didn't give Samuel as much as a glance. He took that as a good sign, and didn't believe anyone else would pay a man in a suit any undue attention. The way in which the man had lent a supportive arm to his wife made him think of Joe Hunter – Jay's protector – and he wondered if the Englishman had indeed retreated to Florida, or if he was inside awaiting his arrival. Samuel hoped so. He was going to enjoy killing the fucker this time. But what were the chances? Like he'd already thought, three times was the charm. Twice Hunter had beaten him to date, but that was as lucky as he'd get. If the saying held true, then next time they met it would be Samuel who walked away the victor.

He watched a little longer, considering heading directly for the hotel, knocking hell out of the lobby staff and checking the records for Jay's location. After that it would be a case of smashing into her room and doing to her what he'd planned all along. But something held him back, and it took him a moment or two to recognise the alien sensation of fear. What if Hunter was inside? He knew the term for his physical condition: *congenital insensitivity to pain*. Although he was incapable of feeling the neurological effects of pain it didn't make him superhuman. It gave him greater staying power in a fight, but the truth had never escaped him: a bullet to his heart or brain would kill him as easily as anyone else.

Recently he'd considered that he could be walking into a trap. The same feeling was with him now. Going into that hotel was tantamount to suicide, because he'd be heading directly into the sights of a gun, but this trap wouldn't involve the police. If the cops had genuinely expected him to turn up at the Tipi Hotel he'd be in handcuffs by now. Somebody else was waiting in there for him and he knew who.

Did Joe Hunter think he was dealing with some ignorant hick?

He thought back to his conversation with Doug Stodghill and how the mechanic had told him that the private investigator had supposedly returned home. Stodghill had obviously been misinformed, and likely on purpose. He realised now that Joe Hunter had been laying plans for a rematch. Well, if that's what the asshole wanted then that was what he was going to get. The difference being, Samuel wasn't about to go charging in like some mad bull. It was time to change his approach and show Hunter just who he was dealing with.

37

That's the only thing that will make you happy? When you kill Samuel Logan ... or he kills you?

I was in the lobby of the hotel, observing the comings and goings of guests and workers, watching for one man in particular. I'd been there since dawn, and was beginning to attract the attention of the lobby staff. They knew why I was there, but still they persisted in giving me funny looks: maybe my presence had them on edge, thinking that I would attract danger rather than deter it. They weren't wrong. I didn't want to cause them worry, but thought I'd give it a little while longer, because on a stake-out you have plenty of time for thinking.

I was mulling over what Jay had asked me last night, and admit that it was a troubling notion. I can't pinpoint why, but I did feel a need to redress things with her. Now that I thought about it, I hadn't offered the best argument. In fact, my words cheapened me somewhat, made me sound like a manic depressive bent on self-destruction.

Or worse . . .

Jay had left without comment, retiring to her room

again. I liked her, and the last thing I wanted was for her to think I was some sort of demented thug with a death wish. That couldn't be further from the truth.

When I was with Arrowsake I did see and do some terrible things but at the time they had been a necessary evil. I'd hunted and killed men who were mass murderers, torturers, sadists and thieves working under the guise of freedom fighters and soldiers. They were neither; they were terrorists who made the lives of others unbearable. I'd had no qualms then about killing them, and the same remains true to this day. I feel justified in saying they deserved what they got.

Maybe I'd tell Jay so.

It wasn't those bastards who haunted me; it was the innocent people I'd failed to help soon enough to make a difference. The military designated them as *collateral damage*; but that didn't change a thing. It was the brutal murder of innocent people whatever euphemism they attached to it. Those were the deaths that preyed heaviest on my mind, and those I now worked so hard to avenge. I know I was juxtaposing one problem with another, and that facing Samuel Logan wouldn't help any of those who had already died. Yet the point persisted: if I could stop even one bad man from hurting others then it went some way to redressing the balance. There was no room for animals like Samuel Logan, not when good people had perished to allow him his place on earth.

I would only be happy when the bastard was dead and buried, and if that also meant my death then so be it. But that was what was troubling me now. When Jay asked her question I hadn't answered because I couldn't: I'd have been speaking for the both of us, and I didn't have the right to map out her fate as casually as I did my own.

It made me think about what the hell I was setting up here. I was inviting a brutal man to come after the women for my own selfish reasons. However well meaning, I was actually putting Nicole and Jay at risk, their parents as well. I almost left the lobby to call the group together and move them out before Samuel Logan showed up. But I didn't. I wondered how remorseless an enemy Samuel was. Would he ever stop hunting the women?

It was better to wait here and finish things as soon as possible, I decided, rather than subject them to constant fear while he was still on the loose.

I only wished the madman would get a move on.

38

There were three of them, Native American boys though you wouldn't think it to look at them. They didn't embrace their heritage the way others of their generation did, but rather the Goth scene that had boomed in the past decade. Even in the sultry heat of the evening they were dressed in leather coats, heavy boots and eyeliner. One of them had a shaved head and enough metal piercings in his face to make him top heavy. The other two had long black hair, worn so that it concealed one each of their eyes. One had his hair parted to the left, the other the right. When they stood shoulder to shoulder they looked like mirror reflections.

Samuel had been watching them for some time as they haunted the doorway of an abandoned shack in the back streets of Holbrook. Other kids came and went, their visits to meet with the Goths short and sweet. Cash changed hands for small bags of white powder. Samuel had tried cocaine on more than one occasion and had liked the effects but that wasn't why he was interested in the small group.

Arizona has a relaxed gun law: so long as a firearm isn't loaded you can carry one without recrimination or fear of prosecution. That made Samuel's task so much simpler than if he'd been in a more liberally minded state. He could possibly have picked up a weapon without much problem, but he wanted something that was ready to go, and chances were that the young hoods trading drugs in this shanty area were prepared to defend themselves from others who might have the idea to move in on their business. Once, as he'd watched them from the shadows of an alley opposite, he'd seen the bald one delve in his trouser pocket for a pack of cigarettes; his heavy leather coat was an encumbrance that he swept back out of his way and Samuel had recognised the semi-automatic pistol jammed in his belt. In all likelihood the other two would be similarly tooled up.

Could he take three armed men?

Damn right.

These young punks had no idea. They were so open about their trade that they had grown sloppy. Customers regularly arrived without any of the gang checking them out first.

A pale blue sedan car pulled up at the kerbside and a young white girl leaned out of the window. She waved a handful of dollars at the group, and Samuel watched as one of the mirror men went to her to deal through the open window. He could hear laughter. The car pulled away and the youth went back to join his buddies in the doorway. Samuel moved from the shadows of the alley and walked across the street towards them. Only the baldy saw him approaching as the other two were sharing a joke, probably at their recent female customer's expense. The Goth didn't seem perturbed by his sudden appearance, and his study of Samuel was cursory. He would see a middle-aged man in a suit and think he was some businessman suffering executive stress and seeking release for the evening.

Maybe the bald one was more aware than Samuel initially gave him credit for because he suddenly hissed something to his friends and they turned quickly to face him. Of course, Samuel realised, another reason that a guy in a suit would approach them would be if that guy was a detective.

'Relax, guys,' Samuel said showing them his open hands. 'I'm no cop.'

The three eyed him up and down. They seemed interested in the bruises on his face. Maybe they thought he was an easy target for a mugging. That suited Samuel because it would make them underestimate him. They were tall guys, although enhanced by their thick-soled boots. Nevertheless Samuel barely stood as high as the shortest one's eyeliner.

'What do you want?' The bald one was the elected leader.

Samuel raised his brows, opened his palms by his sides. 'I think that should be obvious.'

'Show us the money,' Baldy said.

'I don't have any money.'

'Say what?' The three shared incredulous glances. Then the baldy stuck out his hand and shoved Samuel's shoulder. 'Get the fuck outta here man, wasting our time.'

Samuel glanced down at where the hand had touched. He dusted himself off. The three Goths made a loose semi-circle around him, puffing out their chests. Baldy had felt how solid he was under the suit, but the others hadn't yet. Samuel peered directly at the bald one. 'I don't have money, but I still want to deal. Give me what I want and when I walk away you'll all still be alive.'

The mirror men laughed, their long hair swinging. The baldy pushed Samuel's shoulder more forcefully this time. 'Are you fucking insane?'

Samuel grunted. 'Yeah.'

The laughter suddenly went brittle. His forthright answer was the last they expected.

Baldy rolled his neck. 'You need to walk away now, crazy man. You're scaring off valuable *paying* customers.'

Samuel took a look around. At a far intersection traffic flashed by, but there was no one else currently on the street.

'I am?'

'Yes. Now get outta here.'

Samuel didn't move.

'Look, last chance. You go or we move you on,' the baldy said.

One of the mirror men said, 'Don't know why we're giving this asshole any of our time. Kick his ass, Duane.'

'Duane?' Samuel twisted his lips into a sneer. 'That doesn't sound like the name of a tough guy.'

'The fuck?'

Samuel pointed at Duane's right ear. The lobe was

elongated, a thick steel circlet embedded in it. 'Does something like that hurt?'

Duane leaned in, shoving his chin directly in Samuel's face. 'Not as much as my fist in your face will, asshole. Now, last chance, get away from us.'

'I thought the last time was my last chance. You should make yourself clear if you want people to understand.' Samuel shot out his left hand and made a fist around Duane's earlobe. He twisted counter-clockwise, and the baldy had no option but to go with it to avoid his ear ripping off. He let out a startled shriek. 'See, that's how you get someone's attention,' Samuel added.

'Get your hands off him!'

Samuel wasn't sure which of the mirror men yelled at him. He didn't care. He continued to twist Duane's ear and the Goth reared up on his augmented boots, his spine arching backwards to alleviate the agony. His coat fell open and with his right hand Samuel tugged out the gun. Samuel wasn't an aficionado of firearms but he thought the gun was a Glock. The butt felt heavy where he gripped it, indicating a full load. He lifted the gun so that it was aiming loosely at the mirror men.

'I'm not an unreasonable man,' he said. 'Seeing as you gave me a chance, I'll offer you the same terms. Leave now.'

The mirror men didn't know what to do. They looked at each other, then at their friend who was still writhing in Samuel's grasp.

Right Parting said, 'Let him go, man.'

Samuel exhaled. Then he shot the youth in the face.

Left Parting let out a girlish scream as he watched his friend collapse to the ground. Samuel turned the gun on him. 'See, last chance means last chance with me.'

He shot the second youth. The bullet took him through the throat, cutting off his squeal of terror.

But now Duane's screams had grown louder.

His howling was magnified threefold: he'd just watched his friends brutally gunned down, he thought he was next, and Samuel had just ripped the steel ring off – and the lobe it was attached to.

The Goth fell to the ground, his hands trying to stem the flow of blood. His eyes were hollows of disbelief. He couldn't get his legs to move, no matter how much he wanted to flee the scene.

Samuel studied the ring between his fingers, the gun momentarily forgotten and hanging at his side. He used his thumb to rub off some of the adhering flesh then held the steel ring up to see it more clearly. It was a quarter-inch thick with a deep groove around its entire circumference. Samuel jiggled it round and allowed it to slip on to his pinky finger. He showed it to Duane. 'Does this mean we're going steady?'

Duane let out another howl, then tried to propel himself away. His boot heels caught in the hem of his leather coat and he sprawled on his back. He rolled over, tried to get his feet under him, but Samuel stepped on his lower back, forcing him down in the dirt. 'What, you're breaking up with me already?' Samuel asked. 'Well, sorry Duane, but that just doesn't work for me.'

He leaned down and placed the muzzle of the gun to

the nape of the youth's neck. Duane squealed, but it was cut short. Pressed deep in the flesh of the youth's neck, the retort of the Glock was muffled.

He allowed the earring to slip from his finger. 'We're finished, Du-ane,' he said.

Somewhere a dog was barking. Samuel could hear startled voices rising in alarm. He surveyed the three dead boys scattered around him. Then he looked at the gun dispassionately. Not much fun to be had with a gun in your hand, he thought. But he could see its value.

He went quickly to the mirror men. He could tell them apart now that they had different wounds. Neither had a firearm, but one of them had a bone-handled knife, the other a regular lock-knife. He pocketed both items, then went back to Duane and checked his coat pockets for extra ammunition. He didn't find any, just a handful of small baggies with white powder. Samuel took them.

The dog was barking louder now, or more correctly closer to him. The voices were also approaching.

Samuel walked away quickly, escaping through the alley towards the main strip. He could hear the wailing of approaching sirens. He wasn't too worried that he'd be identified as the shooter. In this neighbourhood, a middle-aged man in a suit would be the last person anyone would suspect.

Back on the main strip he watched as two police cruisers swept by. He pursed his lips, deciding that this was as good a diversion as any. He began walking towards the hotel where Jay waited for him.

39

There were further questions to be answered by both Nicole and Jay, and I chaperoned them to the police station. Jameson Walker and Herb Challinor had come along as well, but they were currently consulting with legal representatives hired by Jameson. While they were all led into offices behind the scenes and offered refreshments by a chirpy policewoman, I got a hard plastic chair in the public area at the front. The SIG Sauer nestled in the hollow of my back felt exceedingly heavy, but even at the police station I didn't want to relinquish it. I felt very conspicuous, as if every uniform in the place was aware of my concealed weapon, but while I sat there quietly there was no reason for a cop to come and shake me down.

I had a long wait, but it was time well spent for the family groups when finally they came out. They were all exhibiting varying degrees of relief, sharing smiles all round and shaking hands with the detectives and attorneys. It looked like they had fulfilled their duty to the investigative team and were finally allowed to go home. I stood up, ensuring my shirt concealed my gun. I watched the families hugging again as they made their way towards me. I was happy for them, but there was a needle of annoyance jabbing at me. If they all headed for home, that would mean I wouldn't get the opportunity to finish things with Samuel Logan. I'd be leaving with them, before returning to Florida.

Jameson came over, extending his hand to me. I took it, though I didn't feel like congratulations were in order.

'We're done here at last,' Jameson said.

'So what happens now?'

'I'm taking everyone to Cape Cod for a holiday; to help the girls get over this.'

'The threat's still out there, Jameson.'

'The police say not. After he murdered Doug Stodghill, he stole a car from his garage. They think Samuel Logan has run away.'

'I don't think so.'

'You're welcome to come if you like. Up to Cape Cod, I mean.'

'It'll take more than one man to offer round-the-clock protection.'

'I didn't mean you should come as a bodyguard.'

'The girls still need protecting.'

'So bring in Jared and whoever else you need.'

'It would be much better if I'd ended things here.'

'Well, that's not going to happen now. We'll be leaving first thing in the morning, and like I said, you're welcome to come with us if you want to.'

I looked up and saw Jay staring at me. What was that expression on her face? Hopeful? I stared back, thinking.

She lowered her head, breaking the connection. Nicole stood alongside her and they entwined their fingers, lifting their hands up and down as if repeating a pact. Then Nicole released her grip and walked towards me. I wasn't expecting what happened next. She took hold of my hand and led me to the door.

We exited the station house and stood on the sidewalk outside. The evening had grown still after yesterday's high winds. The heat was still oppressive, and beads of perspiration broke along my hairline. I glanced back and saw Jameson, Herb and Jay in conversation with their attorneys once more. Nods and smiles were reciprocated on both sides. Nicole hadn't said a word yet, but I could hear her breathing shallowly.

'What is it, Nicole?'

She wouldn't let go of my hand, only rotated her grip so that she could stand facing me. She had to tilt her head to meet my gaze. 'Jay told me that she talked with you last night.'

It wasn't a question, so I didn't offer an answer.

'I understand you,' she said.

'You do?'

'Yes. After what Samuel and his family did to us, to those other women, he deserves to die.'

Hearing those words from such a delicate girl made me reconsider. Maybe when I'd said much the same to Jay she'd had a similar reaction to mine now. I should have said something, encouraged Nicole to forget about Samuel and get on with her life. But she surprised me again.

'But you shouldn't suffer, Joe. You should walk away from this. This isn't your battle any more.'

Whose words were those? Were they Nicole's alone or had Jay put her up to them? I knew that Jay felt an attraction to me, though it wasn't something I wished to take advantage of: I was still in a relationship, and I loved my girlfriend. Jay knew that too, but maybe she couldn't help feeling protective of me, the way I did her. Perhaps she was trying to offer affection in an attempt to heal me.

'If I don't stop Samuel, then who will?'

'The police,' she said, but she didn't sound convinced.

'The police will arrest him. They'll put him in prison. After everything that he's done, he doesn't deserve such an easy way out.'

She closed her eyes for a long heartbeat before looking at me once more.

'The Logans raped me. They beat me. They tortured my best friend. I want them all dead . . .'

'Then we're on the same wavelength.'

'But not at the expense of your life, Joe,' she finished.

'I don't intend dying.'

'That's not what you told Jay last night.'

I frowned. That wasn't what I'd meant. I offered her a short laugh. 'She picked me up wrong.'

'Promise.'

'Who would want to die?'

'I did. Back at that ranch. But now that it's all behind me . . . I'm happy to be alive.'

She stood on tiptoe and kissed me on my cheek. Her lips were warmer than the night.

'Come on,' I said. 'Let's go and fetch the others. We need to get ready if we're heading off for Cape Cod in the morning.'

A vehicle pulled up at the front of the station, an unmarked Lincoln but definitely a cop car. There were two figures in the front, and I wasn't really surprised when the two detectives who'd taken me to Phoenix climbed out. Their attention was fixed on me, and I nodded at Nicole to go back inside.

Chambers was the sprightlier of the two, and approached me three steps ahead of Witherspoon.

'You still here, Hunter?' His pointy ears were almost twitching with anger. 'I hoped we'd seen the last of you.'

'You'll be happy to hear I'm leaving, then?'

'Not soon enough.'

Witherspoon came puffing up alongside us. 'How long have you been here, Hunter?'

'In Holbrook? Since I made my way back from our little day trip.'

'No. Here.' He indicated the police station.

'Couple of hours.'

'Hope you have witnesses,' Chambers snapped.

'Will a roomful of cops do?'

Witherspoon clucked his tongue, but it was for his partner's sake. 'Let it go, willya,' he said. 'I told you Hunter had nothing to do with this.' He swung to gaze back at Chambers. He lifted his head, nodded his subordinate inside. Chambers swore under his breath but strode inside the police station, stiff-backed.

'What's up with Mr Spock this time?'

Witherspoon got the joke, but his features soon flattened out and he was all seriousness again. 'There's been a shooting. Three dead. He thought that you'd been up to your old tricks.'

I felt a lump in my chest expand. 'Who are the victims?'

Witherspoon waved me down. 'No one for you to be concerned about; all indications are that it was a drug-related shooting. The vics are known to us. Small-time coke dealers.'

'And your buddy thought I was responsible?'

Witherspoon squinted. 'After you left Phoenix he did a little more digging into your background. Seems you've been in the frame for similar shootings in the past. The latest being an incident in Callaway, Florida, a week ago.'

'I didn't shoot anyone in Callaway.'

'You discharged your weapon.'

'My finger slipped.'

'You dislocated some kid's knee.'

'He fell off his skateboard.'

Witherspoon shook his head.

'Don't worry, Hunter. I knew the shootings here weren't your style.'

'I bet Chambers was pissed when you pulled up and saw me standing here, though?'

'I told you. He doesn't like people taking the law into their own hands.'

'Then he's got nothing to worry about. Ask your buddies inside: I've been sitting here the past two hours admiring their stellar work.' I thought about what

Witherspoon was intimating. 'The three that were killed: it was a revenge shooting?'

'No, looks like a plain old robbery to me. Whoever it was took their dope and their weapons. Probably rival drug dealers.'

'Does that happen a lot in Holbrook?'

'Nah,' Witherspoon said. 'We don't normally have any problems.'

I thought about the last time a cop told me something similar. Officer Lewin had been lying through his teeth, but I believed that Witherspoon was a straight-up kind of guy.

'No witnesses?' I asked.

'None that are coming forward.'

'So you've no suspects?'

'Not yet. But I have uniforms canvassing the neighbourhood, checking CCTV and the rest. I'm sure they'll turn up something soon.'

'What about Samuel Logan?'

'From what I hear he prefers to use his fists.'

'He did, that was for sure.' My body still bore testament to the truth of that statement. But what about now that he was injured and growing desperate? A strange feeling rode the length of my spine. 'What are the uniform resources like in a town this small?'

'Why? You planning on robbing a bank while they're all tied up on inquiries?'

'No. But someone else might get ideas.'

40

I took the rented Chrysler back to our hotel ahead of the families, with instructions to Jameson Walker to give me an hour before they returned. He ushered them away in search of a restaurant where they could continue their celebrations. That suited me because if my suspicions were founded then I didn't want the women near that hotel.

Holbrook isn't exactly a large town, and I was back within minutes, but didn't drive directly into the hotel's car park. I left the Chrysler on the main strip outside, then went forward on foot. The trees that had been planted to form a break between the hotel and highway offered cover for me until I reached the entrance drive. I thought they'd also be a good location for someone to hide if they were watching who was coming or going. Taking a quick glance around, I checked that no one was observing me. Happy, I drew my SIG then stepped over the small wire fence and into the trees. It was little more than a copse, and the landscapers had done a sterling job in keeping the undergrowth at bay. Sprinklers hidden in the grass fed the lawns while a more elaborate irrigation system kept the trees from succumbing to the desert heat. The trunks of the trees weren't thick enough to conceal a man, but in the darkness they looked to have all bunched together so it wasn't easy defining where one ended and the next began. If Samuel was out here, I could stumble over him before I was aware.

Placing my back to a gnarly tree-bole, I stood quietly and allowed my other senses to seek danger. There was too much noise from the nearby highway for my liking, and all that I could smell was the mixed aromas of wet grass, exhaust fumes and frying chicken from a nearby fast food outlet. I have the same inherent instinct as everyone else – the one that warns of hidden danger – but tonight it seemed that it was on hiatus. I'd no sense of Samuel Logan or anyone else hiding in the woods.

I went on, wending my way between the trunks until I reached a point where the lights from the hotel began to brighten my way. I paused there, hunkering down so that I could study the swathe of concrete and brick that formed the car park and retaining walls of flower beds adjacent to the hotel itself. There were a few vehicles parked on the lot, but no sign of their drivers. A valet stood outside the main entrance, waiting for the moment his services might be required. He was a Hopi guy I'd nodded to a couple of times in passing. Bored, his hands clasped behind him, he rocked on his heels while he waited for guests to arrive. He looked unperturbed, so I guessed there'd been nothing unusual that had recently caught his eye. He'd probably spent many hours stand-ing in that very spot and anything different would immediately draw his attention.

It didn't mean that Samuel wasn't around, only that he was well hidden.

Could he even be inside the building?

He would stand out like a whore in a convent in there, but that was supposing he looked the way he had last time I saw him. He could dress well, change his hair, but anyone with even the slightest sense would see him for what he was. Surely?

I knew all this was purely speculation, that Samuel could be thousands of miles away by now, and that I was raising my expectation based upon a random shooting. Nevertheless I'd learned to trust my hunches and, though they were occasionally misinformed, more times than not I'd guessed right. I wondered if Samuel had thought things through and had killed those men as a diversion, or if that was simply a by-product of the act. I didn't think he had any need of cocaine, but he'd gone for other items: their weapons. Witherspoon couldn't confirm what had been taken from their bodies, but two of the men had empty sheaths on their belts that indicated they'd been carrying — most likely knives.

I looked down at my SIG, considered putting it away and transferring my Ka-bar to my hand. It was a stupid idea. I held on to my gun. First chance I had I was placing a round between Samuel's eyes.

Watching the valet, I saw him come to attention.

I pricked to attention too, but when I saw a taxi pull in front of the hotel and discharge an elderly couple carting hand luggage I settled down again. The valet carried their belongings into the hotel, returned and took up position. He surreptitiously counted the dollars tipped to him but didn't look over-impressed at the couple's generosity. The valet soon went back to gently rocking to and fro, and his movement served to lull me. I remained hunkered down, watching, waiting.

The window for a diversionary tactic was rapidly closing. I had to assume that – if he had been responsible – Samuel hadn't tried to draw the police away and the killings had been purely to steal weapons. So what was the asshole waiting for? The obvious answer was that he knew Nicole and Jay were absent. Had I made a mistake sending them off to eat at a restaurant in town where he could find them? No. He wouldn't scour the eateries on the off-chance he'd locate them. If he was coming for the women I believed it would be here. But, more and more, it looked like Samuel Logan was a no-show.

I couldn't just walk out of the woods. That would raise the eyebrows of the valet, and perhaps get tongues wagging. I decided to retreat the way I'd come, collect my car and drive in like a normal hotel guest. I was in the process of backing away when I again noticed the valet stand to attention. I followed his gaze, and though my vantage cut off some of the view of the front gate I saw the minivan nosing in.

Glancing at my wristwatch, I thought: What the hell are they doing back so soon? It was barely more than an hour since I'd left the police station. They couldn't have had very big appetites, that was all.

The minivan swung into the turning space before

the hotel. I could see Jameson in the front alongside the driver, and a sea of heads clustered in the back. Their faces made pale ovals as they scanned the grounds. The valet came forward to meet the taxi, opening a sliding door from which spilled first Herb Challinor, followed by his wife and daughter. Jameson came out next, before leaning back inside to pay the driver. Jay climbed out, then loaned a hand to help her mother step down. I paid them little more than cursory attention: if Samuel was out there waiting for them, now was the time for him to show.

While the group bunched at the entrance, Jay looking around, possibly wondering why my car wasn't in the parking area, I centred myself, allowing my gaze to fade out so that I wasn't looking at anything in particular. In a throwback to ancient days when our forebears were prey to more savage beasts, they relied on their peripheral vision much more than we do now in the modern age. But the fact persists, subtle movement is easier to identify in the extremes of the vision than when looked at directly. Thankfully the windless night helped, because if it had been breezy like yesterday I'd never have distinguished one moving shadow from another.

As it was I caught a flash of grey off to my left.

I didn't immediately swing my head to seek out the source of the movement, just opened my mouth and listened. The traffic noise from the highway was still a hindrance, but this way I could at least hear more than the blood rushing through my inner ears now that my pulse was up. It allowed me to hear the metallic scuff of a foot slipping off a sprinkler head and thudding into the grass. Conscious that the clumsy stalker's senses would be heightened following his slip, I didn't move. I waited, and heard a low curse that would carry no further than the copse of trees.

Slowly I came out of my crouch. Having been in a static position for so long, I allowed the blood to course through pinched veins before attempting to move. The soles of my feet tingled, but at least my legs hadn't fallen asleep. Then, using a tree trunk as a shield, I went towards the man hiding in the trees. I wondered how long he'd been there, waiting exactly as I had, and was confident I would have been alerted to him sooner if he'd arrived while I was there. He had to have been in place before my arrival, and it was only sheer bad luck on his part that he hadn't noticed me first. Or, more accurately, good luck on mine. I couldn't make out any details yet; he remained a vague shadow in the darkness, but where his hand was extended I made out the unmistakable shape of a handgun.

Glancing towards the hotel front, I saw the families still grouped on the pavement, watching as the minivan pulled away from the kerb, offering waves of thanks to the driver. Shit, get inside, I thought.

I stalked towards the lurker, seeing him move behind the bole of a tree. I caught another flash of grey, possibly a snatch of clothing.

I was only twenty feet away from the man.

The stalker was moving forward, but with trees between us. I wasn't sure if it was Samuel Logan. But who else would be out there in the dark with a gun? I swung my gaze back to the cluster of people outside the hotel. From this distance I could drop any of them, but I was a highly trained gunman: could Samuel do the same? I saw his gun rise, and couldn't take the chance.

I didn't have a clear shot, so instead I rushed him.

The man heard me coming, twisting round to face me, and as I raced towards him, my gun extended to shoot, his mouth opened in a startled 'O'.

Stumbling to a halt, I looked down at him.

I allowed my gun to drop.

'For God's sake,' I said in a harsh whisper. 'Do you realise how close I came to killing you?'

Scott Blackstock was too shaken to answer.

41

'What the hell are you doing hiding out here in the dark?'

'I think that should be obvious. Considering you were supposed to have gone back to Florida, who else was going to get Samuel when he turned up?'

'Jesus Christ,' I said. 'How long have you been here?'

'Couple of hours,' he said. He was over the initial shock of my appearance now, his voice a little steadier.

'I was that close to killing you.' I held my index finger and thumb close to his nose: you'd have been hard put to push a piece of paper between them.

'Good job you recognised me, then.'

'Wasn't it just?'

Scott was wearing a grey hooded top and faded jeans. The hood was pulled over his head and it was a damn good job he'd looked up at me when he had because I'd been a hair's breadth from pulling the trigger.

'Where are the other two, your buddies?'

'Back at Indian Wells. They'll be drunk by now, I guess.'

'Smells like you've had a couple yourself.'

'Dutch courage,' he said.

'And a sure way to get yourself killed, you idiot.'

Scott's shoulders rose and fell. 'Those bastard Logans murdered Helena. What did you expect me to do?'

Who was I to preach?

I rested a hand on his shoulder, while I checked back over mine. The Walkers and Challinors were still gathered outside the hotel. They were chatting animatedly. They were exposed. But it looked like I'd misread everything. Standing there in the shadows with Scott, I felt as much of an amateur as he was.

'Go home, Scott. Have another drink with Robert and Burt. Raise a glass to your wife's memory for me.'

'I'm not going.'

'You are. Leave this to me.'

'What gives you the sole right? Helena was *my* wife.'

'Yeah, and she wouldn't want you risking your life like this.'

'I'm not leaving.'

'Lower your voice at least. I don't want anyone hearing us.'

'If Samuel's around, I think it would be a little too late for that. Don't you?'

'I'm not talking about Samuel.' I indicated the group at the hotel entrance.

Scott followed my gesture, and I saw that his mouth had hollowed again. I knew who'd caught his attention. Nicole was the obvious one. He leaned forward, and even in the darkness I could see tears welling.

'It isn't her, Scott,' I said gently.

He slowly blinked, and was unaware – or careless – of

the tears that streamed down his cheeks. 'Is she one of the girls that the Logans snatched?'

'Yes. Her name is Nicole.'

'I remember now. From those photos you showed me. God, I didn't realise how much she looked like Helena till now.'

I didn't think that was true, because I'd raised the issue of their similarity with him. But seeing Nicole standing there must have opened the floodgates to memories of his wife. He was looking at Nicole but seeing Helena, and ignoring any of the superficial differences that existed. For a second I expected him to walk out of the trees and rush towards her. To prevent this, I gripped him by the elbow.

'I don't want them to know I'm out here,' I warned.

'Why not? You're here to protect them, aren't you?'

'It would panic them if they knew. They've suffered enough. Let's just keep an eye on them until they're safely inside.'

'Then what? You expect me to go back to my fucking trailer and get drunk with my buddies. No way. I'm staying.'

'What are you going to do . . . sit out here in the woods all night?'

'I might ask you the same thing.'

'I don't need to. I've got a room.'

Scott stared at me.

'I'm not leaving,' he reiterated.

'Jesus . . .'

'We could take turns,' he offered. 'You can't stay

awake all night, and neither can I. C'mon, Hunter. Let me help.'

I didn't know what to say. Scott was a liability. He'd be someone else I'd have to protect, and the odds would rise in Samuel Logan's favour. But he did have a point. Once the families were back inside, my place would be beside them, not out here. From within I couldn't keep an eye on all the approaches to the hotel, so maybe an extra pair of eyes would help. If it had been Rink or Harvey Lucas offering assistance, I'd have snapped their hands off, but it was neither. I wasn't about to change my mind.

'Go home, Scott.'

The Walkers and Challinors had exhausted whatever conversation had held them outside and were now heading for the entrance to the hotel. Jameson paused to hand notes to the valet. By the look of things Jameson was a more generous tipper than the elderly couple earlier. The valet was positively beaming. They shared a joke, and the others joined in with the laughter. While I was distracted, Scott crouched down once more and held his pistol out before him. 'You'd best get yourself inside,' he said.

'Scott,' I warned.

'I'm not leaving.'

I didn't have time for this.

'Have it your way.'

Using the butt of my SIG I struck him hard behind his right ear. His eyes rolled up at me, but already they were unfocused, unseeing. I held him and lowered him to the ground silently.

Then I moved forward, heading for the edge of the treeline, homing in on the movement I'd noticed on the opposite side of the parking lot.

From behind a large sign that welcomed guests to the hotel and offered instructions for parking their vehicles, I'd seen a man bob out for a closer look.

He was a middle-aged businessman in a suit, his short white hair combed neatly to one side. But I wasn't fooled.

It was the monster I'd been waiting for.

Samuel had finally arrived for our showdown.

42

Jay had come to re-evaluate her relationship with Nicole over the past few days. When they had set off on their cross-country adventure, it had been she who had offered promises to their parents that she would look after Nicole, and keep her safe from harm. It had been an arrogant attitude, now that she thought about it, because Nicole was no weakling in need of her protection. If anything Nicole had proven the stronger of the two and Jay had witnessed a change in the dynamics of their friendship. Jay couldn't help being afraid. She was frightened for herself, but more than that she was terrified for the welfare of all those who had come here to support her. It was different with Nicole, though; it was almost as if she'd built a solid fortification around herself, impervious to any threat. Jay remembered her timid friend and wondered where she'd gone. She barely recognised this calm young woman, who greeted all of Jay's concerns with steady reassurance.

She thought back to when she'd been locked in that foul prison in the desert, and how she'd apportioned the Logans fanciful names gleaned from a fantasy she'd read as a child. In Oz anything could happen, sometimes with only the clicking of heels; had Nicole sought safety in a similar fantastical world? Was she still in there, locked within the dream, because she no longer knew the woman standing beside her?

Jay wished that she could join Nicole wherever she was now hiding, instead of suffering the constant fear that she did. Her own illusory world had been ripped apart when Officer Lewin had come on the scene. Everything had changed then. She tried to tell herself that it had been for the best, that by fighting back against the twisted lawman, the Cowardly Lion had found courage, but she knew that was bull crap. She hadn't fought the police officer. Hell! She couldn't even bring herself to open her eyes and had only struck out in panic; it was pure luck that had guided the knife into the man's arm and thrown off his aim. Where was the bravery in that?

Since then she had constantly been on edge for the moment when the curtain would be thrown back to reveal the true face of the Wizard. Unlike the trickster from the story, this man wouldn't show her the way, but would prevent her return home, the same as all of the other women he and his kin had taken. She knew she was thinking in childlike metaphors, but she couldn't avoid them: when she looked down at the ground she half expected to find a yellow brick road beneath her feet.

The ground was concrete.

She scuffed her heel against it, heard grit scraping underfoot. It jarred her back into reality.

She looked around, searching for the car that Joe had rented earlier. She'd expected him to be here, waiting, but the Chrysler wasn't in the car park. She experienced another tremor of fear. Had Joe gone already? She remembered their conversation from last night and how she'd tried to talk him out of his misguided war with Samuel Logan, and now wished she'd kept her fat mouth shut. It was ironic, since all of this had come about because she couldn't keep quiet. She'd even asked Nicole to talk with Joe and persuade him to walk away from the fight. If it had been the old Nic then perhaps she'd have had more success, but Jay suspected that the new Nicole had actually encouraged Joe to kill. Jay only had to look at her friend's unwavering gaze to know what Nicole planned should she ever see Samuel Logan again. But if that was the case where was Joe Hunter now? Why wasn't he here to offer the protection *she* needed?

Her father was busy chatting and laughing with the bellhop. The others joined in. Jay did too but knew neither what she was laughing at nor why. She had nothing to laugh about, except when her dad finally waved them all towards the entrance. One more night and they would be out of here; she couldn't wait to leave. There's no place like home, she told herself.

Yet it looked like she would never make it there alive.

She saw the man come out from behind a sign on the grounds and start towards them.

He looked different, the trickster, the Wizard, but it was him. His face wore the same malicious anger as it had that time he'd visited agony on her in the barn, and then again as he stared down at her before entombing her under the tin sheets in the desert. How she wished that she'd had the fortitude to shoot the monster that time she'd broken up his fight with Joe in the ravine.

She could barely tear her gaze away as he advanced on her, and it was like time had slowed so that she watched him as if he was wading through treacle. Jay could hear the panic swelling in her breast, but as yet it had not voiced itself in a scream. Her family and friends were unaware of the monster's approach. She tore free from the hold his appearance had on her, lunging to place herself between him and the others. He was coming for Nicole, she realised. He would not get her: not if Jay stopped him. But she was afraid.

She screamed.

Chaos erupted around her, the screams of her and Nicole's mothers, the throatier voices of her dad and Herb, lifting in panic as they recognised the danger.

Jay felt hands tugging on her clothing. In her frenzy she misunderstood and pulled free of her father's protective arms. She looked around wildly, from Nicole, to her father, back to Samuel Logan. He was so close now she could smell a wave of something sickly sweet with an undertone of rot wafting off him. There was white powder all around his nostrils and on the front of his suit jacket. His mouth was wide in a shout she couldn't hear as he brought up a gun and aimed it directly at her.

Oh my God, he's going to shoot me!

Her eyelids began to droop. She was back in the rear of Officer Lewin's police cruiser again and this time there was nothing she could do to stop the bullet shattering her skull.

There was a blur of movement and someone was between them. In reflex her lids bolted open. For a briefest moment she expected to see Nicole leaping at Samuel, her teeth bared, her nails poised to rip and gouge. But it wasn't Nicole, it was her dad.

Jameson was roaring in denial but Jay's hearing was stuttering, coming in fits and starts.

'. . . get away from my daughter!'

'Daddy, no,' Jay croaked.

Jameson Walker was a big man. Once he'd have been a force to be reckoned with, but that was decades ago. Now he was an old man trying to stand against an unstoppable monster.

Samuel slapped the butt of the gun into the side of Jameson's head and her father went down like a felled tree.

Now Jay could hear everything. Above all rang the scream loosed by her mom. Jay felt a jolt go through her frame, as though her mother's horror had empowered her. Samuel loomed over her fallen father, staring down at him, a look of glee on his lumpy face. He began to lift a knee, and Jay knew he was about to crush her dad like an insect underfoot.

Despite the gun in his hand, Jay sprang at Samuel, all her fear forgotten. With her open hand she struck him, not in a slap, but with the heel of her thumb driven forward and her arm locked behind it.

The force of the blow ricocheted back up her arm, almost dislocating her shoulder in the process. But it had the desired effect: it slammed Samuel's head backwards, throwing him off balance. He had to settle his feet to avoid falling, and missed stamping down on her father's throat as he'd planned. Samuel shook his head, his eyes screwed tight. But then he slowly opened them once more and it was as if he'd locked on to hers with heat-seeking lasers. There was a trickle of blood leaking from his nose, and he paused to wipe it away with the sleeve of his jacket. He grinned at her, blood-flecked saliva stitching his teeth together. His pupils looked like dark pits.

Jameson was moaning, coming round, and Samuel looked down at him. His inspection was brief, because the man was of no interest to him now. He stepped over him and lunged for Jay.

Jay didn't care. She'd saved her dad and that was all that mattered.

Samuel grabbed her head in his left hand and pulled her close. The stench off him was unbearable. It grew worse when he opened his mouth to speak. Hot spittle showered her cheek, corrosive and foul.

'Do you have any idea what I'm going to do to you?'

Jay couldn't conjure such depravity.

All she could do was peer into the eyes of her nemesis, and in that instant she felt pride that she could do so.

She stared at him, her eyes blazing in challenge.

And this time she saw death descending.

43

I had to count on the probability that Samuel Logan's natural instincts were to strike out with his fists as he was used to doing and not fire the gun. It was the only thing that would save lives because there was no way I could get to him quickly enough. I trusted my aim, could drop him at this distance, but what if he proved as impervious to my bullets as before? The group were bunched directly in front of him and his gun was up. If I fired then so might he and I didn't want to see one of them fall. Instead I ran, swerving around parked cars to come at him from behind his right shoulder.

The Walkers and Challinors were milling around in a panic. Why weren't they seeking shelter inside the hotel? Samuel didn't look prepared to shoot any of them yet and was only using his gun to gain control of them; if they could get beyond the door then I'd have no qualms about taking him down.

I saw the problem.

Jay was rooted to the spot.

Shock could do that to the bravest of souls.

Even when her father tried to pull her away she

yanked free of him in order that she didn't lose sight of the man striding towards her.

I wanted to shout at her, but that would alert Samuel to my presence. Instead I ran harder.

Jameson Walker threw himself between his child and the man threatening her then went down in the next second. Samuel raised his heel to stamp the man to death, which was when Jay surprised us both: she drove her palm into Samuel's chin with sickening force. It was a strike driven by desperation but it staggered the killer, if only for the briefest of seconds. He lunged after her, snared her head in his thick fingers and pulled her close.

Shit!

I still had no clear target.

I got a snapshot of the tableau.

Nicole was trying to go to her friend's aid but was being held back by her parents. Mrs Walker had gone to her knees at her husband's side, one hand on his face, the other reaching out to her daughter. The valet was the only one with the sense to run for the entrance door. From within the hotel voices were raised at the commotion outside.

Then that moment was broken as I finally reached a vantage point.

I still didn't shoot Samuel, but used my gun in a wholly different fashion. The SIG isn't the favoured weapon of some people because of the disproportionate weight of the butt when fully loaded, but to me, in my line of work, it was an asset. At a run, I launched myself through the air, raised my gun past my shoulder, and brought down the butt against Samuel's right temple.

The blow was enough to shatter the skull of any man.

Even Samuel, whom Rink had sarcastically called Superman, couldn't withstand it.

He collapsed over on his side, but to my disgust Jay went down with him.

Her mother grabbed at Jay's ankles, trying desperately to heave her daughter from the killer's clutches. Nicole broke free from her parents and came to help.

'Get out of the way!'

My yell fell on deaf ears.

Now I had Samuel at my feet it should have been a matter of seconds to end it all, but not with the three women entangled with him. Looking for a clean target, I couldn't find one: not without one of the desperately scrambling women falling across my line of sight. I waded in, trying to clear a way through.

Samuel was hurt. Not in the sense that he was in pain, but the percussive effect of my blow was still ringing in his skull, and his eyes were out of focus as he peered through the tangle of limbs at me. He shook his head like an enraged bull, then rolled away from me, his arm was still looped around Jay. The bastard was using her as a shield while bringing round his own gun. I couldn't kill him.

Not yet.

But for a split second I saw his left leg disentangle itself from behind Jay's writhing form and it was all the time I required.

I fired.

The bullet struck the meat of his thigh, holing his suit trousers as though a pencil had been jammed through them. The hole where the bullet exited at the back would be ragged and gaping, as the blood and tissue that sprayed across the concrete bore testament.

Samuel wasn't impervious to bullets after all.

He had an extremely high tolerance of pain, but that made no difference to what excessive trauma did to a body.

The shock of the bullet ripping through him was enough to change the course of everything. His arms opened wide as he let out a hoarse scream. The gun he held was always secondary, and in the mind-numbing aftershock of having his thigh shattered he loosed his grip on it and it clattered away across the floor. Quickly I drove in, looped an arm under Jay's waist and yanked her to safety.

My back was turned for a few seconds as I shoved Jay towards the waiting arms of Nicole and Mrs Walker.

I turned back to Samuel and my features were set in stone.

The man surprised me.

I had thought to find him writhing on the floor, trying to staunch the flow of blood from his leg.

The son of a bitch was already coming back to his feet.

He was unsteady and his right leg wouldn't bear weight, but he looked ready to continue our battle. Maybe it had something to do with the cocaine that was smeared around his bloody nostrils and down his front, but he still thought he was indestructible. He opened his mouth in silent challenge, beckoned me forward with his deformed hands.

That suited me fine.

I so wanted to take the bastard on man to man but I'd already made myself a promise.

I lifted my SIG, aiming between his teeth.

Let me see you brush this one off, I thought savagely.

'Put down your weapon!'

The command came straight out of left field.

Despite my desire to finish Samuel once and for all I skated a glance past his shoulder to the man aiming his firearm at me.

Detective Chambers.

'I said put down your weapon, goddamnit!' Chambers yelled again.

There was more movement, and I saw Detective Witherspoon moving in from across the parking lot, his gun extended. I was grateful that the older cop's aim was trained on Samuel's head.

I didn't lower my gun.

'Hunter, I swear to God. Shoot that man and I'll make sure you burn for it.'

I snapped my gaze on Chambers. He was unwavering as he aimed his Glock at me.

I was in the zone, where the red mist descends and all that you're aware of is the threat before you. Chambers was a good man with – in my eyes – a misguided outlook. I firmed my finger on the trigger.

'Don't do it. *I will fire.*'

I looked from Chambers back to Samuel and the pig was gloating.

Witherspoon advanced a few steps and he was adjacent

to Samuel now, his gun threatening, but his eyes were on me. 'Hunter,' he whispered harshly. 'Drop your weapon, for Christ's sake.'

'*Now!*' Chambers screeched.

I lowered my weapon.

But it wasn't because of the plea of one cop or the demand of the other, but because Jay had laid her hand on my wrist.

'It's over,' she said softly. 'Don't ruin your life because of this monster.'

I nodded.

Gumball lights flooded the scene as police cruisers came screaming into the lot. Uniformed officers piled out of their cars, weapons trained on Samuel. When I squinted at the flickering lights, I adjusted so that I was again looking at Chambers. He was sneering, but not at me: he was moving in on Samuel now.

A snort of disdain left me, or maybe it was pure disgust.

Samuel was forced down on the ground, his fingers laced at the back of his head as uniforms swarmed over him, frisking him for weapons. I saw two knives come out of his pockets and dropped into plastic evidence bags. Another cop retrieved his dropped gun, holding it by the trigger guard.

As I moved back, both Jay and Nicole wrapped their arms around me, laying their heads against mine. They were both uttering reassurances and thanks but I couldn't make sense of them. I was still bubbling with anger. I wanted to see Samuel Logan dead, but, now that the cops had cuffed him and rolled him on to his backside, his eyes had shaken off the effects of trauma and narcotics alike and were brimming with insane humour. If he'd vocalised it, I swear I'd have shot the fucker there and then and Chambers could go and fuck himself.

Perhaps she felt the tremor of rage that flooded through my frame, because Jay said, 'He's not worth it, Joe.'

She was right. If I shot him in cold blood, where was the satisfaction in that?

'How is your father doing?' I said.

Jay stiffened, then ran to where her mother was tending Jameson Walker. Jay threw herself at him, kissing him repeatedly on the cheeks and forehead. I caught the man's eyes and though he was still a little stunned he had shaken off most of the knock he'd taken. Now he appeared bemused by the hero worship his daughter lavished on him. It was a priceless moment and the only bright spot that I could find.

Nicole was still holding on to me.

'What about you, Nicole? Are you happy with the way things have ended?'

'I told you what I thought earlier,' she said. 'I haven't changed my mind.'

Looking down at her I saw something reflected in her eyes. It was my face, but it was definitely her will.

'Lend me your gun,' she said.

'No. No way.'

'Please,' she said.

'No.'

Samuel was hauled up to his feet and was partly supported, partly dragged towards one of the police cruisers. I was glad he was being taken away, because I was tempted to accede to Nicole's demands.

The thought passed, and did so from Nicole's mind too. She collapsed against me, weeping in relief.

Chambers and Witherspoon approached.

Though Chambers' face was rigid, his eyebrows arched, it wasn't his look that perturbed me but that of his partner. Witherspoon looked embarrassed. Worse than that, he looked ashamed.

'Please, Miss Challinor,' Chambers said. 'I need you to stand aside.'

'What's going on?' she asked.

'Just do as he says, Nicole,' I said and gently pressed her away.

'What are you doing?' Nicole demanded of the detective.

Chambers ignored her. 'I'm going to need your weapon, Hunter. Please place it on the ground and take a step back.'

Nicole moved towards me again, but she addressed Chambers. 'You can't *do* this.'

'Nicole,' I said gently. 'Just let him do his job.'

I placed my SIG down and Chambers offered me a sour smile.

This time he did read me my rights.

'Is there any chance I get to share a cell with Samuel Logan?'

44

Samuel watched from where he was seated in the back of a police cruiser. The cop the vehicle was assigned to scowled down at him, eyeing with distaste the blood that was pooling on the scuffed vinyl seat. Samuel understood that was the only reason he hadn't been taken away to lock-up before now. A duty of care existed even when a prisoner was a wanted murderer: the cops were awaiting the arrival of an ambulance so that his wounds could be tended to. Samuel wasn't bothered about that; he was too engrossed in what was happening across the lot.

Joe Hunter was being frisked for other weapons. His handgun had already been taken away by the young cop who had also arrested him. Now Samuel saw a wicked-looking knife disgorged from Hunter's right boot. The man was a fucking walking arsenal, but it looked like the police had now seized everything. He recalled that the man could fight, so wasn't totally without means of defending himself, but even carrying the dramatic wounds he did, Samuel was confident he could take him.

Maybe they'll put us in the same holding cell, and we'll see.

Samuel scanned the faces around him. There were cops everywhere now. Also guests had come out of the hotel and were standing in the forecourt watching the proceedings with ghoulish fascination. Some cops were speaking with them, identifying witnesses. He could see no sign of Jay Walker or Nicole Challinor. He was disgruntled that they weren't around to witness what he planned next, but it was only a mild sensation. His fixation had jumped to another more worthy recipient.

He stared at Joe Hunter.

Hunter stared back.

Samuel laughed.

'Keep it down in there.' The cop standing guard banged his hand on the roof of the cruiser.

Samuel spat bloody saliva on the Perspex partition.

The cop leaned close to the window, which was cracked open a quarter-inch. 'Do us all a favour, asshole. Hurry up and bleed to death.'

Exsanguination was a very real possibility. Blood pulsed from his wounds. Also, Samuel wasn't sure that his skull was in one piece after the crack he'd taken from Hunter's gun butt, and his previously broken rib felt more malformed than it had before rolling about on the floor. He was in bad shape. Anyone else, he assumed, would be unconscious due to the intense agony. Most would already be dead.

He knew that he was short of time and if he didn't kill Hunter soon he likely would never get the opportunity.

His jailer had turned away, watching as an ambulance entered the hotel grounds, negotiating its way slowly between the other parked vehicles. Samuel's hands were cuffed behind him, but that was good, because his body would block him should the cop turn around too soon. Samuel strained, yanking savagely. He couldn't care less if he peeled the very skin from his hand like a glove. He continued to exert pressure, and the flesh began to tear. The blood helped make his wrists slick, except he still couldn't free his hands.

He didn't feel pain, but he was sickened by the thought of what was necessary, and only the unreal buzz of cocaine in his mind gave him the fortitude to go ahead with it.

He took his left thumb in the palm of his right hand.

The car must have rocked, because the cop spun around.

'What the hell are you doing in there?' he demanded.

Samuel was cringing and thick beads of cold sweat were streaming down his brow. He must have looked like he was suffering heart failure.

'Holy Christ! Medics! Get over here. *Now!*'

The cop yanked the door open and leaned in, his fingers probing at the carotid pulse in Samuel's neck. Samuel's flesh was slimy with sweat and the cop couldn't pinpoint a pulse, not helped by the shuddering of the body beneath his fingers. He made the mistake of turning to look for support from the approaching medics. It was what Samuel had been waiting for. He pulled free his right hand. The bracelet was still snapped tightly to it, but the other loop was empty save for adhering shreds of skin. The cop's gun was on his right hip and out of reach, so Samuel grabbed at the next available weapon. He pulled the canister off the cop's utility belt, flipped open the lid and depressed the button. The contents of the pepper spray were disgorged directly into the cop's face. He reacted by attempting to rear back out of the car, his eyelids screwed tight, mouth hanging open as saliva flooded from it. Samuel held on to the cop, used his motion to tug him up and out of the car. He dropped the pepper spray and grabbed at the cop's belt again, this time on his right side. The cop, bewildered, senses in disarray, still had the presence of mind to protect his sidearm. He grappled to retain it. Samuel butted his forehead into the man's face. The cop was tough, but he was in a no-win position: Samuel head-butted him again. The cop now tried to flee, but Samuel wouldn't relinquish his hold on the gun and it was torn from its holster.

Samuel turned the gun on the fleeing cop.

Pulled the trigger.

It dry-fired.

Cop protocol, he realised. They didn't carry a pistol charged with one in the spout. He was unfamiliar with the gun, but it was easy to work out. He racked the slide, using his left hand, and even he frowned at the mess of it. By the time he was ready to fire the cop had thrown himself down behind another cruiser, out of sight.

Samuel didn't care: the cop was never the primary target.

He swung around to where he'd last seen Joe Hunter.

The commotion had already spread a wave of panic through the crowd, but it was still early enough that no one was ready to halt him yet. The other cops on the scene were too busy taking up positions of cover or exhorting the civilians to get down and out of the line of fire.

He had a direct line of fire on Hunter and the two detectives who'd initially arrested him. Hunter was unarmed and the cops might as well throw down their weapons, given the lack of action they were taking.

Through the mêlée Samuel marched, his right leg unsteady beneath him and trailing droplets of blood.

He grinned feverishly as he lifted the gun and aimed it at Hunter's face.

45

I thought that Detective Chambers was an insufferable asshole, but he was a good cop really. He was doing the right thing however lopsided you looked at his actions. I'd been captured red-handed, had discharged an illegally owned handgun, so he was duty bound to take me in. It didn't matter that I'd just saved the lives of innocent people because the letter of the law states that two wrongs don't make a right. I knew things would be cleared up; in fact, after a trip to the station and having my version of events backed up by all the witnesses at the scene, I'd probably be kicked out without charge. Chambers was happy that he'd arrested Samuel Logan and that outweighed his dislike for people he deemed vigilantes.

Witherspoon was totally embarrassed by it all, but what could he do? He knew that his partner was doing things by the book and he could only go along with the decision to take me in. He offered me shakes of his head and a pursed mouth in condolence.

'Like I told Nicole, Chambers is only doing his job. I don't hold it against him.'

'Shit, we wouldn't have got him if it weren't for you,' Witherspoon said.

'I got you thinking back there, did I?'

'It's why I grabbed my partner and followed you here.' Witherspoon leaned in conspiratorially. 'Pity I didn't come alone. I'd've waited a few seconds longer before asking you to put down your weapon.'

Chambers had been signing chain of evidence dockets to be attached to evidence bags, but now he was done and turned from the uniformed officer carting away my weapons. Those pointy ears of his weren't just for show.

'Then I saved us all a whole bundle of shit,' he said. 'You do know I've just spared you a murder charge, Hunter?'

'You're all heart, Detective.'

He snorted, but then he shook his head. 'Look. We got off to a bad start yesterday; let me see what I can do about getting you back on the street soon. Of course, to do that you'll have to fully cooperate.'

'Hey,' I said. 'I'm one of the good guys. What else do you expect?'

I couldn't exactly feel the love in the air, but Chambers and I had just crossed the boundary. He grinned. It was an odd look on a Vulcan. I smiled back, then my smile froze in place.

Distracted by our peace-making we'd taken our eyes off Samuel for less than a minute, but it had been long enough for everything to go sour.

I caught movement near the cruiser and recognised it as a uniformed cop on his hands and knees. He was spitting and streams of mucus hung from his nostrils.

I'd only to turn my head a fraction to see the white-haired businessman shambling towards me. He dragged one leg like the old Universal Studios' Mummy, one arm extended in front of him. The other hand was a floppy mess knocking against his left thigh, and even in that instant I could see that Samuel had broken his own thumb and torn the skin from the back of his hand in his efforts to free his cuffs.

What a demented bastard.

But he was also relentless. If it wasn't for the fact he was coming to kill me I could respect his determination.

'Look out!'

It was Witherspoon who shouted. All around us uniformed cops were seeking refuge behind their cars, while others attempted to steer the hotel guests out of harm's way. They should have been shooting at the goddamn killer.

Witherspoon dropped to one knee, going for his gun. It was clipped on his trouser belt, and awkward to get at under his jacket. Chambers on the other hand slapped down and came away with his gun all in one movement. He wasn't fast enough though and Samuel fired first. The bullet knocked Chambers against me. He wheezed, making an agonised sound deep in his chest. Samuel turned the gun on Witherspoon and the older cop rolled aside with all the grace of a hippopotamus. Bullets struck the ground, sending up chips of concrete. Thankfully Witherspoon avoided the rounds but he was on his side, his gun trapped beneath him. He was in no position to return fire.

Samuel kept coming, and I was encumbered by Chambers.

'Shit.'

'Care to join me in hell?' Samuel said.

I'd always expected that I'd go out with a pithy remark, but right then I'd nothing to say. Why waste my final breath on that arsehole?

'I'd love to do this the old-fashioned way,' Samuel said, lifting his torn hand, 'but as you can see I'm not in my best shape at the moment.'

He aimed the pistol at me, even as other cops began shouting at him to lay down his weapon. He was beyond that now: Samuel knew that as soon as he dropped me he'd be fired upon but I could see that he no longer cared. He told me once that he wasn't afraid to die. He wasn't. And he was set on taking me with him.

Suddenly there was another figure standing alongside him.

I recognised the grey hooded top at much the same time as Scott Blackstock fired a round into Samuel's side. The force of the round knocked Samuel sideways and the bullet he fired at me missed and struck the wall of the hotel.

Samuel went down on his injured leg, but he wasn't dead yet.

Shoot him again, I wanted to yell at Scott, but Scott was too busy screaming.

'What did you do with my wife? You bastard, tell me! *What did you do with Helena?*'

Blood was pulsing out of the wound in Samuel's right

side, and whatever damage had occurred inside made his right arm weak. But he still retained enough strength to bring his gun round and aim it at Scott. Scott seemed oblivious to the threat and continued to demand answers. I'd tried to keep him out of harm's way by knocking him out, but I hadn't hit him hard enough. I owed him my life but it looked like he was going to die and there was nothing I could do to repay him.

'Here.'

I looked down at Chambers. He was still bent in pain, but he offered me his gun.

'Take it,' he said.

'Willingly,' I said, and then emptied the entire mag into Samuel Logan's body.

As the killer collapsed over on his back, Scott threw an incredulous look my way.

'No! No, I need him to tell me where Helena is.'

Scott leaned in close to Samuel.

With Chambers on one side and Witherspoon offering cover from the other, we advanced on the prone man. I looked down and even after his body had been torn apart by gunfire there was still a spark of lucidity in Samuel's gaze. He blinked at me.

'Tell him what happened, Samuel. If there's any pity left in your heart, tell the man what happened to his wife.'

Samuel began laughing, frothy blood popping on his lips. His voice was paper-thin, but still pitiless.

'We'll never know,' he said.

46

Jay didn't get to go home the following morning, or the day after that. In fact it was the third day following the horrific incident at the hotel before the investigation was at a point where the witnesses were free to leave. The extra time spent there didn't jar on her the way it had previously because now she knew there was no Samuel Logan lurking in the wings. As he had passed, so had her fear. In fact it had fled before that, the moment she'd fought the monster to save her father's life. Jay didn't feel Nicole's sense of satisfaction at seeing Samuel gunned down, but had to admit she was glad he was gone. She understood now that part of Nicole's relief was due to the fact that she hadn't succumbed to temptation and murdered the man. After they'd wept together and the old Nic was back, the two young women had laughed themselves giddy.

'Do you still want to live dangerously?' Nicole had asked.

'No, thanks, I've had quite enough of the wild life.'

'So we won't be taking that two-centre holiday we were planning in Iraq and Afghanistan?'

They'd roared with laughter then, tears streaming down their faces and they'd made so much noise rolling about on their beds that her dad had knocked on their hotel-room door to check on them. It was like they were kids again, and it was a wonderful feeling.

The sight of her dad's face had sobered Jay somewhat. Where Samuel had struck him with the gun his cheek was swollen and a dark bruise the colour of liver had spread all the way down to his jaw. Otherwise he was OK and Jay had hugged him until he was laughing with them. When her mum arrived, along with Nicole's parents, the other guests in the hotel must have thought they'd booked into a lunatic asylum.

Jay wasn't laughing now, though. In truth she was hard put to hold back the tears as she went to say goodbye to Joe Hunter. She owed that man more than just her thanks, but she knew that was all he'd take. Maybe in another life things could have worked out diffcrently. No, she then thought. She'd had enough of alternate worlds. Oz – and all other fantasy worlds – were banished from her mind from now on.

Joe had spent more time at the police station than she had. Some of his time there had been as a prisoner, but apparently he'd known better service than many others in his position. He had saved the lives of more than one person, and the two investigators in charge were indebted to him for saving their lives too. Detective Chambers had been spared when his anti-ballistic vest had taken Samuel's bullet, but without Joe Hunter's selfless act – *his civic duty* – in taking out the gunman, who knew what might have happened? All charges against him had finally been dropped.

Leaving the police station, he hadn't returned to the same hotel as the rest of them, but to the less salubrious surroundings of a motel at the western end of town. Her dad had offered to extend his hospitality to five stars but Hunter had graciously refused. He was a private man, she guessed, who needed time to himself, the only way he could heal. She remembered their discussion the night before Samuel's attack and how she'd thought to change him. There was no changing a man so set in his ways, she understood that now. It would be wrong to try. Hunter had his demons, his ghosts that followed him, but that was what defined him as a person and a good man.

She had walked the length of Central Avenue, past the landmark Wigwam Village, a motel where guests stay in rooms designed to resemble Native American tents. She didn't give it much of her attention; she was too involved with ordering her thoughts as she made the journey, but now that she approached Hunter's motel she wasn't sure what she should say. She paused outside, studying the stucco walls that were grimy with exhaust fumes from the highway, trying to determine which of the rooms belonged to Hunter. The sun was behind her and reflecting from the windows so she'd no hope of seeing him. He could be inside now, watching her approach.

Entering the foyer, she was surprised to find it was neater than she'd expected. The air conditioning was on high and the air pleasantly chilled after her walk in the sun. The walls were whitewashed with garlands of flowers painted at the ceiling line. Soft seating upholstered in Native American blanket designs dominated the alcoves each side of a polished counter that glowed warmly under overhead spotlights. Jay preferred the atmosphere here to that of the stuffy, soulless place where she was staying. The motel was an ideal fit for Joe Hunter, she thought: the rugged exterior belied the caring heart that beat within. It was a better analogy than the wolf she'd thought of when they'd first met.

A young woman popped her head out of an office behind the counter, a beaming smile on her face. She was dark-skinned, and her teeth flashed in greeting, accentuating the highlights in her raven hair.

Jay smiled back but shook her head at the woman's offer of assistance and pointed a finger towards the room she'd noticed to her left. She should have known where to find Hunter. He had a taste for coffee and she could smell the beans roasting from here. She walked into the small dining area and took the seat opposite him. He was nursing a large cup of coffee so black she thought of the dark side of the moon.

'How do you ever sleep?' she asked.

'Would you like one?'

'I'm good,' she said.

'Are you?'

She missed a beat, but then she nodded slowly. 'Yes. I think I am.'

He lifted the mug, watching her over the rim as he took a long gulp. His irises reflected the dark liquid and the usual blue flashed chocolate-brown. As he placed the mug down she noted that it took a moment for the colour to recede, but maybe that was just her imagination. She suddenly became conscious that she'd been staring a tad too long and lowered her face in embarrassment. She could feel a flush creeping into her cheeks.

'You look beautiful this morning,' Hunter said.

Whoa! She placed her elbows on the table and her palms over her cheeks, then looked up at him from under her lashes. 'I bet you say that to all the girls,' she said, trying to sound funny.

'Only the beautiful ones.'

She laughed in self-deprecation, but could swear that her ears were glowing furnace-hot by now. Hunter reached across and took her right hand in his. He held it across the table top. 'I'm sorry, Jay. I didn't mean to embarrass you.'

'I'm not embarrassed.'

His eyebrows rose and fell.

'OK. I am. Just a little. But there's nothing for you to be sorry for. Joe . . . I, uh . . .'

'There's no need.'

'No need?'

'To thank me.'

'Oh, God! How wrong can you be?'

Hunter released her hand, took up his coffee again.

'The pleasure was all mine,' he said.

'Nothing that happened could be defined as pleasurable,' she said.

'Not even making a lifelong friend?'

OK, she had to acquiesce. There was that.

He stood up and she mirrored the movement.

'I mean it, Jay. If you ever need me, all you have to do is call.'

She moved round to stand beside him, one hand trailing on the table. She peered up at him. All the heat had gone out of her features now. Her shyness with him, like her fear, was a thing of the past. She went up on tiptoes to place a kiss on his lips, slow in drawing her mouth away, and as she did so, whispered, 'And if you ever need *me*, just call.'

47

After waving the Walkers and Challinors off at Gallup Municipal Airport with a promise to join them in a few days at Jameson's Cape Cod retreat, I drove back over the borderline into Arizona and picked up the road to Indian Wells. I didn't like breaking promises, but this was one that I'd maybe bend to fit. Jameson had asked me to bring my girlfriend, Imogen, with me. Maybe that wouldn't be a good idea with Jay being gripped in the throes of a crush on me. I'd beg out of the trip, say that business was taking up too much of my time and put the visit off for a couple of weeks or three. By then Jay's romantic flush should have passed, and there'd be fewer complications. Jesus, never mind Jay's crush, when she'd whispered in my ear I'd almost succumbed and taken her in my arms. I dread to think what would have happened if I'd given in to the weakness. Crazy redneck kidnappers and murderers I could handle, but two jealous women? No way.

I didn't make it all the way to Indian Wells. I'd already phoned ahead and had arranged to meet with Scott Blackstock. The guy didn't want to go to the Logan ranch alone, so we'd set up a rendezvous at the truck stop where I'd first learned of the frequency of women going missing. The old Navajo cleaner and his broom were conspicuous by their absence. I was sorry to have missed him, but when I asked other workers about him they only looked at me blankly. Not one of them knew who I was talking about.

While I waited for Scott to arrive I nursed a mug of strong coffee and mulled over the old man's identity. I wondered if all the Logans' victims had been female, and who else was buried out there in the desert. I recalled they had no love for their Native American neighbours. Plenty of ghosts troubled my dreams, but they were figments of my imagination, weren't they? No, it was a totally ridiculous thought, but one I had trouble shaking. I was pleased when Scott finally arrived and I could turn my mind to something more tangible.

He had travelled down from the trailer park in his pick-up truck. It was battered and could do with a lick of paint, but it was still better suited to the terrain than my rental. I climbed inside the cab and Scott took the road out to the ranch.

'My head still hurts,' he said as we rattled along the uneven trail.

'I didn't hit you hard enough,' I said.

He chuckled. 'I don't hold it against you.'

'Glad to hear it. I did it for your own good.'

'I know that now. You were trying to protect me.'

'Nah, I just didn't want you getting in my way.'

'But you're pleased I did?'

'You saved my life, Scott. I'm indebted to you.'

'You owe me nothin',' he said. 'You avenged Helena for me.'

'So you're not mad I stole your thunder at the last second?'

He laughed again, but it was a melancholy sound. 'Whatever I threatened to do to him, Samuel wasn't going to come clean. He was just laughing in my face.'

'Doesn't matter now, Scott. You got the last laugh.'

'Yeah,' he agreed. 'I did.'

We completed the remainder of the journey in companionable silence. The mushroom-shaped mountain that had set the stage for many of the frantic events in the desert loomed out of the dust clouds. It was a landmark I'd never forget, and, once I left this place, one I wished never to see again. We passed along the trail on the far side, unfamiliar ground for me, then entered the basin-shaped valley beyond which waited the scene of so much depravity. As we approached I first saw the sparkle of sunlight reflected from water, then the decrepit house and sheds grew out of the haze. Much of the activity here over the last few days had been in the shape of police officers, but now most of them had left. There was still one police cruiser on the scene as well as an unmarked sedan. Other vehicles belonged to the county coroner's office, and to National Guard troopers who were still helping with the massive search area. White tents had been set up alongside the ranch, and I'd no wish to go inside any of them. I knew that each one marked a separate grave and that forensic technicians laboured at bringing the victims home in their entirety.

Some of the graves were years old, one of them more recent, and the corpse within it had been preliminarily identified as Carla Logan. Her skull had been fractured. Blunt-force trauma, the coroner had said. It didn't take too much deducing who had been responsible for murdering his sister. I put the poor woman's death out of my head.

We hadn't come here out of ghoulish fascination.

As Scott drew up alongside the police cars he let slip a ragged breath.

I reached across and patted him on the shoulder.

'You want me to take the wheel from here?' I asked.

'Please.' He could barely see for the tears welling in his eyes.

As he slid over into the passenger seat, I got out and walked around to the driver's side. Chambers and Witherspoon were standing by their car; both men nodded silently and got in. They drove past the watering hole and I followed. We went at a respectful speed across the desert towards the ridgeline where I'd so recently hidden Nicole and Ellie Mansfield.

I pulled up alongside the Lincoln, looking up towards the caves as I'd done when bringing Jay to her reunion with her friends. One of the small hollows bore a ribbon marker at its entrance. Two National Guardsmen stood sentry at the foot of the cliff. Jesus, I thought, the cave was barely fifty feet from where I'd been. The body of a naked woman had been discovered inside it. Either before she'd crawled here across the desert, or as a result of a fall while trying to reach her hiding hole, the poor thing had broken a leg. She had escaped the monsters torturing her, fled to safety, but then fate had dealt her a sorry hand. The coroner approximated her date of death, and I could only hope she hadn't suffered in torment as long as he thought she had. He couldn't be sure, but from his estimate it looked like she'd succumbed the same night that Nicole and Ellie had hidden in the neighbouring cave. If only I'd known it then . . .

I couldn't think like that.

'Are you ready, Scott?'

He sniffed, rubbed his sleeves over his face. When he sat up there was a hint of steel in his jaw.

'I'm ready,' he said.

'Then let's go and bring Helena home.'

AFTERWORD

I have taken certain liberties in the writing of this book – known to us writer types as 'artistic licence' – where a modicum of suspension of disbelief is expected of the reader.

For the purposes of the story I've grown Holbrook, Arizona, into a much larger city than it actually is, introducing motels, hotels and truck stops that do not genuinely exist there, although entities like the Wigwam Village do. I set much of the latter third of the book in and around Holbrook as it is the nearest major conurbation to the desert lands featured in the earlier segments, and it would be logical for the city to be the base for any police investigation into the fictional crimes conducted by the equally fictional Logan clan. I hope that the residents of Holbrook and their law enforcement community take the story in the spirit of thrilling adventure that I set out to write, and allow me this latitude with their fine home town.

Congenital Insensitivity to Pain (CIP) is real but very rare, with approximately thirty individuals in the USA diagnosed with the condition. Persons with CIP cannot feel, and have never felt, physical pain, although

cognition and sensation – though not always temperature – are otherwise normal. Usually there are no
physical abnormalities associated with CIP, though
some people with the condition suffer fractures to
their bones, wounds and infections due to their lack of
recognition of the severity of their injuries. CIP does
not make anyone super-human; they can be injured as
easily as anyone else, and in many cases are more
prone to injury. Again I have allowed myself a certain
latitude with the condition when assigning it to the
chief villain, Samuel Logan. There is no suggestion
that persons with CIP have sadistic tendencies: Samuel
Logan's need to hurt others is purely a fictional adap-
tation and a product of the family environment in
which he was raised, and I hope that this is evident
from the story.

Matt Hilton

THANKS AND ACKNOWLEDGEMENTS

When I sit down to list the recipients of my grateful thanks, certain individuals immediately spring to mind: my agent, Luigi Bonomi, Alison Bonomi, my editor at Hodder, Sue Fletcher, Swati Gamble, Eleni Fostiropoulos, and Alice Wood. It is these individuals who work tirelessly and passionately to ensure my excitable ramblings come up to a publishable standard. Without their input I feel that Joe Hunter's adventures just would not be the same. I thank you all.

I would also like to thank the following authors for their friendship and support: Adrian Magson, Sheila Quigley, Col Bury, Lee Hughes, and Jim Hilton. Then there is the wider pool of authors, friends and supporters who have helped with my writing in ways they might not realise: Richard Gnosill, Stuart Hall, Ann Magson, Pete Nicholson, Val Steventon, George Steventon, Sean Black, and Chris Ryan. And of course my family: thanks to every last one of you.

May I also extend my thanks to you, the reader, for taking the time to read this book? I hope it was time spent in enjoyment.

Last but not least: my undying gratitude and love go

to my wife, Denise, whose efforts equal mine in bringing the latest Joe Hunter thriller to the page. Someone has to crack the whip, I suppose.

JOE HUNTER
BRITAIN'S BEST VIGILANTE V AMERICA'S WORST CRIMINALS

'Without my sense of decency, I'd be nothing more than a big thug amid all the little thugs'

'I'm a firm believer in Rapid Intuitive Experience, the soldier's very own ESP'

'SIG Sauer P226: my weapon of choice'

'My training wasn't simply geared towards weaponry but the use of the body to achieve the desired results'

'Military issue Ka-Bar knife. I don't do surprises'

CURRICULUM VITAE – JOE HUNTER

NAME: Joe Hunter.

DATE OF BIRTH: 8th August.

PLACE OF BIRTH: Manchester, England.

HOME: Mexico Beach, Florida, USA.

MARITAL STATUS: Divorced from Diane, who has now remarried.

CHILDREN: None.

OTHER DEPENDENTS: Two German shepherd dogs, Hector and Paris (currently residing with Diane).

PARENTS: Joe's father died when he was a child and his mother remarried. Both his mother and stepfather reside in Manchester.

SIBLINGS: Half-brother, John Telfer. Deceased.

KNOWN ASSOCIATES: Jared 'Rink' Rington, Walter Hayes Conrad, Harvey Lucas.

EDUCATION: Secondary school education to 'O' level standard. Joe received further education and underwent self-teaching while in the British Army and Special Forces.

EMPLOYMENT HISTORY: Joined British Army at age 16. Transferred to the Parachute Regiment at age 19 and was drafted into an experimental coalition counterterrorism team code named 'ARROWSAKE' at age 20. As a sergeant, Joe headed his own unit comprising members from various Special Forces teams. Joe retired from 'ARROWSAKE' in 2004 when the unit was disbanded and has since then supported himself by working as a freelance security consultant.

HEIGHT: 5' 11".

WEIGHT: 13 stone.

BUILD: Athletic.

HAIR COLOUR/STYLE: Short brown hair with slight greying.

EYE COLOUR: Blue/brown.

APPEARANCE: Muscular but more lean than bulky, he has the appearance of a competitive athlete. His demeanour is generally calm and unhurried. Due to his background, Joe has the ability to blend with the general public when necessary, but when relaxed he tends to dress casually. He doesn't consider himself handsome, but women find him attractive. His eyes are his most striking feature and the colour appears to change dependent on his mood.

BLOOD TYPE: AB

MEDICAL HISTORY: Childhood complaints include measles and chicken pox. As an adult Joe has had no major medical conditions, but has been wounded on several occasions. Joe carries numerous scars including a bullet wound in his chest and various scars from knife and shrapnel wounds on his arms and legs. He has had various bone breakages, but none that have proven a continued disability.

RELIGION: Joe was raised in a Church of England environment, but is currently non-practising.

POLITICS: Joe has no political preferences and prefers morals and ethics.

CHARACTER: Joe can come over as a little aloof at times. He is a deep thinker who prefers only to speak when he has something important to say. He is very loyal to his family and friends. He dislikes injustice, hates bullies and will stand up to defend others in need of help.

MUSIC: Wide choice of music, but particularly enjoys vintage rhythm and blues.

MOVIES: Joe's favourite movie is 'It's a Wonderful Life'. It is a morality tale that resonates with his belief that a person's actions – good or bad – continually affect those around them.

BOOKS: When he was younger he enjoyed classic fiction by HP Lovecraft, RE Howard and Edgar Allan Poe, but currently reads a wide range of crime and suspense novels.

CIGARETTES: Smoked various brands but gave up.

ALCOHOL: Drinks only moderately and infrequently. Prefers beer to liquor.

DRUGS: Has been subjected to drugs during his military career, but has never personally taken any illegal drugs. Joe hates the influence that drugs have on the world and stands against those producing and supplying them.

HOBBIES: Fitness. Joe works out whenever he can with a combination of running, circuit training and martial arts.

SPECIAL SKILLS: As a soldier Joe gained many skills pertinent to his job, but also specialised in CQB (Close Quarter Battle), Point Shooting, Defensive Driving and in Urban Warfare Tactics. He is particularly adept with the handgun (usually a SIG Sauer P226) and with the knife (usually a military issue Ka-Bar).

CURRENT OCCUPATION: Joe describes himself as a security consultant and sometimes PI, but some people call him a vigilante.

CURRENT WHEREABOUTS: USA.

Want to find out what Joe Hunter does next?

Here's a taster from Matt Hilton's
Rules of Honour

I

'Stay in bed, I'm going to take a look.'

''I'll phone the police.'

'No. Just wait until I check things out. Could be just the wind.'

'That wasn't the wind, Andrew.'

'Maybe not, but it's too early to call the police. Just wait and I'll go see. If I'm not back in two minutes, call then.'

The woman watched her husband pull a robe over his bulky shoulders, then move for the closet in their bedroom. He opened the door and reached for the top shelf, from which he retrieved a locked box. Inside the box was a relic of her husband's past. He glanced at her briefly, an apologetic look, but then withdrew the gun that winked dully in the lamplight. Inside the box was a rapid loader, and Andrew fed the six bullets into the gun with precision. Done, he looked at his wife again.

'It's only a precaution,' he whispered, closing the cylinder and latching it tight.

'Be careful . . .'

His wife had switched on the bedside lamp, but the rest of the house was in darkness. As he eased open the door and peered into the upstairs hall he pressed his body close to the opening to stop light spill. He paused there a moment, allowing his eyes to adjust to the dark. Then he slipped out into the hall, surprisingly agile for a man of his advanced years. Andrew was a septuagenarian but looking at him most would guess he was at least ten years younger. His height had barely been touched by the years, and he still had the broad shoulders and heavy arms of his youth. His knees bothered him these days, but not now while a bubble of adrenalin coursed through his frame. He went along the hall with the gun held close to his side. He didn't concern himself with the guest bedrooms or the bathroom because the sound that had woken them had definitely come from below in the living room.

Recently there had been a spate of burglaries in the neighbourhood, the cops putting down the breaking and entries to drug addicts looking for cash, credit cards and items easily pawned. Andrew and his wife, though they weren't rich, were wealthy enough to attract the attention of a sneak thief. That angered Andrew; he'd worked hard all of his life, even put his safety on the line, to make an easy retirement for him and his wife. No sneak thief was going to take anything from them.

A lifetime ago he'd fought in Korea, had survived the worst that war could throw at him, and for decades afterwards had striven to be the same soldier. He had failed to protect his girl child, who'd succumbed through illness, and one boy following suit with a military career had been killed in the line of duty. So now he was more determined than ever that he would not fail his wife and allow some punk to invade their home and take their lives' worth. He was old but he'd lost none of his military acumen and thought himself more than equal to a drug-addled thief.

From the head of the landing he peered down the stairs.

Moonlight flooded the vestibule at the bottom, a skewed oblong cast from the window in the front door stretching across the floor. Within the light grey shadows danced, but Andrew recognised them as those of the trees in his garden dancing to the breeze. He took the stairs one at a time, avoiding the third step down that was prone to squeak under his weight. As he descended the stairs he looked for the blinking red light on the alarm box on the hall wall, but it was steady. Whoever had found a way inside was clever enough to dismantle the alarm. Or they knew the code and had turned it off. There was only one other person who knew the code, but he wasn't prone to dropping in uninvited like this in the dead of night. Alone, the sound they'd heard wasn't proof that an invader was in their house, but the dead alarm now clinched it. Andrew considered going back upstairs and telling his wife to telephone the police immediately, but something halted him. Pride. Foolish pride perhaps, but he wasn't the type to run from danger.

Some would have been tempted to call out a challenge, but Andrew knew that it would be a mistake. A desperate drug addict might run for it, but if Andrew had managed to corner him then his desperation might turn violent. Better that he initiated any beating than the other way around. He went down the stairs, paused to check the alarm box and saw that the guts of it had been teased open and a wire clipped on to the exposed workings to form a loop in the system. The alarm had been neutralised, but the automatic signal to his service provider would not have kicked in, as it would if the wires had been merely torn out. If he'd stopped to think for a moment he'd have realised that it was too sophisticated a method for an addict only intent on his next fix. But he wasn't thinking, he was reacting. Threat demanded action.

He glanced once towards the kitchen but discarded it: a thief would go for the living room where the possibility of rich pickings was greater. He moved along the short hallway and saw that the door to the sitting room was ajar. Always conscious about home safety, fire and smoke being the worst threats to sleeping inhabitants, he was careful to turn off electrical appliances and to close doors tight. He had got it down to a bedtime routine and knew he'd closed that door tightly, as he did every night. He paused there listening. He thought he heard a soft footfall, but it came from above, probably his wife. Placing a fingertip to the door, he teased it inward, the revolver held steady against his hip. Then without warning he shoved the door hard and stepped quickly into the room, sweeping the familiar space for anything alien.

There was nobody to be seen.

If not for the jerry-rigged alarm he'd have thought he'd been mistaken, that the noise that woke him was nothing but wind throwing the garden furniture around the yard. He wondered if the burglar had heard him as he'd risen and had made himself scarce. But in the next instant he knew that he was wrong.

A cold metallic tickle behind his right ear made him halt.

'You know what that is, don't you, old man?'

Andrew nodded slightly, a minute movement because he didn't know how hair-triggered the gun pressed to his skull was.

'Mine's bigger than yours,' whispered the voice over his shoulder. 'I suggest you drop that old revolver and kick it back to me.'

'OK, son, take it easy now.' Andrew lifted the revolver and flicked the latch to open the swing-out cylinder. He rattled the gun and allowed the shells to tumble out and clatter on the hardwood floor.

'Not good enough.' A fist was jabbed into Andrew's back, directly above his left kidney. Pain flared through the old man, sending a white flash across his vision. 'Now, as I said first time, put down the gun and kick it back to me.'

'It's useless,' Andrew said, desperate not to relinquish the weapon having placed some spare rounds in his robe pocket.

'Is it?' The man clubbed Andrew across the back of his head and sent him sprawling into the living room.

As he fell, the revolver was knocked from Andrew's hand. In the seconds afterwards it didn't matter because he used both hands to cover the split in his scalp. 'Son of a bitch.'

'You see,' the man said. 'Even an empty gun can be a

good weapon.' He levelled his semi-automatic handgun on Andrew's chest. 'Not that mine's empty.'

Andrew struggled up to a seated position, grabbing at a settee for support. He could feel blood trickling through his hair. He looked up at the man, squinting to try to make sense of the face.

'Who the hell are you? What do you want?'

One thing Andrew was sure about: this was no addict looking for a quick payday. The man was large and solidly built, dressed in black jeans, black jacket and a black baseball cap. Backlit by the meagre moonlight in the hall he looked like a living silhouette.

'If I answered your first question, you'd probably guess the second.'

'If you're after money, you've come to the wrong place. You'd be better off . . .'

'I'm not here for money.'

'That's good, son, because I'm old and haven't worked in years, I don't have much to get by on.'

'Save it,' said the man. 'You're wasting your time trying to make conversation. I know what you're trying to do: humanise yourself in my eyes, making me think twice about doing you harm. You're wasting the few breaths you have left.'

Andrew was thinking clearer now and studied his surroundings for a way out of this. He didn't like what the man had just said, it sounded like he had only one agenda. No way was Andrew going to sit on his ass and offer his would-be killer an easy ride. He thought of his wife upstairs and knew that she'd be next, but not if he did enough to alert her to the danger, and slowed the bastard down. He looked for something to use as a weapon.

'Don't even think about it.'

Andrew returned his gaze to the man. He'd stepped inside the room and was looming over Andrew. The gun was held steadily, the barrel aimed directly at Andrew's face. 'I want you to know why I'm here, why I'm about to kill you. It'd be a shame if I had to put a bullet through your skull before I showed you this.'

From his jacket pocket the man took out a cellphone. He'd readied it beforehand, and he held out the glowing screen so that Andrew could see the photograph on it. Andrew screwed up his eyes to help focus the picture and saw that in fact it was a photograph taken from one much older. The image was of a man in uniform, sepia in colour. It was many decades since Andrew had seen that face but he recognised it and knew who this man might be.

'Who is it?' Andrew tried, but he knew the man saw through the lie. 'You don't remember? Well that's a shame, because he's waiting to greet you in hell.'

The man's voice had risen in pitch and volume, and Andrew knew that the rest of his life could be counted in seconds. He coiled himself, ready to call out, to fight back, to do *something*.

Andrew squirmed round so that he was partly side-on to the man. To anyone uninitiated into violence it might seem that the old man was frightened and trying to make himself a smaller target. 'You do know what he did?'

'Oh, so you're admitting that you know him now?' The man put the phone away and from his pocket took out a long tubular object. Andrew recognised it as a sound suppressor. It was both a bad and good sign. It meant that the man was not a first-time killer and had come prepared, but also that he did not want to raise an alarm by firing indiscriminately.

'He deserved everything he got,' Andrew said.

'No one deserved *that!*' The man screwed the suppressor onto the barrel of his gun with a few practised twists. He did it blindly, but couldn't resist the natural reaction to glance at it once, to make sure he'd secured it correctly. It was only a brief second of inattention, but Andrew took advantage of it.

From his side-on position he could chamber his left leg, and he shot it out, aiming with his bare heel at the man's shin. Better that he aim for the knee, but he didn't have the range. His heel struck bone, at the same time as he swung his other foot to hook behind the man's ankle. Andrew scissored his legs. An untrained man would have been upended, giving Andrew time to swarm on top of him and to snatch away the gun. Unfortunately this man had come with violence in mind, and though he was briefly off balance, he was agile enough that he was able to disengage his trapped leg and to hop aside . . . bringing round the gun.

'No!'

Andrew's yell wasn't out of fear of the bullet destined for him.

A slight figure had appeared as a shadow behind the

man, one arm raised in the air. With all of her strength his wife brought down a plant pot she'd lifted off a hall-way dresser. The man had somehow felt her presence behind him and was already turning. The plant pot struck him on the shoulder, but it was nothing to the man. He continued his turn and swung with the barrel of the gun, striking the woman across the side of her skull. She hit the floor quicker than the falling plant pot, which shattered in a way that Andrew feared her skull had. The man gave one disdainful look at the woman before turning his attention back to Andrew.

He took a step back. Andrew had come up from the floor much faster than a man of his age should have been able to.

'Bastard!' Andrew came at him with animal ferocity, throwing two solid punches at the man's chest, but both fell short. 'If you've killed her I'll—'

The man shot him: three rapid bullets to the chest.

Andrew staggered at each impact.

'*This time* you'll do nothing,' the man sneered.

Andrew collapsed to the floor, jammed in the door-way. He didn't look at the man now, but at his wife. She lay on her side, her head cradled under one arm. He could barely see the rise and fall of her shoulder as it rode each breath.

'Please,' he moaned. 'Take me, but don't harm my wife.'

The man snorted.

'Why not? It's your lying wife's fault it came to this.'

He shot Andrew again, this time in the head.